*David Burnell was born and b
matics at Cambridge, taught
then spent his professional career applying the logic to
management problems in the Health Service, coal mining
and latterly the water industry. On "retiring" he completed a
PhD on the deeper meaning of data from London's water
meters.*

   *He and his wife live in Berkshire but own a holiday cottage
in North Cornwall. They have four grown-up children.*

   *David is now hard at work on further "Cornish conun-
drums".*

*"Slate Expectations combines an interesting view of an often
overlooked side of Cornish history with an engaging pair of
sleuths who follow the trail from past misdeeds to present
murder."*

   *Carola Dunn, author of the popular Daisy Dalrymple and
Cornish mysteries.*

*"This book has an original atmospheric setting, which is sure
to put Delabole on the map. A many-stranded story keeps
the reader guessing, with intriguing local history colouring
events up to the present day."*

   Rebecca Tope, author of the popular Cotswold and West

A Cornish Conundrum

Country Mysteries.

"Cornwall and its richly storied coast has a new writer to celebrate in David Burnell. His crafty plotting and engaging characters are sure to please crime fiction fans."

Peter Lovesey, author of the Peter Diamond crime stories and winner of the CWA Cartier Diamond Dagger, gave this review of Doom Watch, the first "Cornish Conundrum".

Happy readings!
David Burnell
Dec 2014

SLATE
EXPECTATIONS

A Cornish Conundrum

David Burnell

A Cornish Conundrum

First published May 2014.

This book, although set in a real location, is entirely a work of fiction. No present-day character is based on any real person, living or dead. Any resemblance is purely coincidental.

ISBN-13: 978-1497519954
ISBN-10: 1497519950

The cover shows an old slate quarry between Tintagel and Trebarwith Strand. Port Isaac Bay, Pentire Head and the Rumps are in the background.

NORTH CORNWALL

JANUARY 2009

SPLITS AND SCHISMS

A History of the Delabole Slate Quarry
Dramatised by Arno James

Act 1 1843-1869

Humble Beginnings
Winning ownership
Railway to Rock?
The Quarry and the village
1860s: Ups and downs
The Quarry Disaster

Act 2 1870-1899

Welsh Management
Battles with recession
Packhorse and sail
Strikes and consequences
Emigration challenges
The Railway finally arrives
Slow but steady growth

There will an interval of 20 minutes
Hot refreshments are on sale

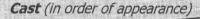

Cast *(in order of appearance)*

Job Hockaday: Narrator   Joe Stacey

Tom Avery: Last Owner   Quintin Hocking
Dr James Yong: Chairman   Harry Rowe
Dr Edmund Rendle: Director Martin Thorne
William Evens: Chairman   John Jasper
Robert Coad: Surveyor   Jim Melhuish
James Bampton: Track buyer Simon Hill
Emily Hockaday   Martha Avery
Dr Charles Rendle: Director   Martin Thorne
James Kellow: Quarryman   Jim Melhuish
Greg Wallis: Quarryman   Paul Wood
Robert Cowling: Quarryman R Penhaligon
Bessie Cowling   Beth Howell
Fannie Wallis   Freya Wood
Edward Jago: Chairman   Quintin Hocking
Robert Roberts: Manager   Evan Williams
Henry Penfound: Quarryman Geoff Martyn
Philip Richards: Quarryman Jim Melhuish
Francis Cowling: Quarryman R Penhaligon
Rev Kinsman: Magistrate   John Jasper
Edward Allen: Director   Daniel Nute
William Chapman: emigrant Steven Bate
Hugo Higgins: Director   Harry Rowe
Sir Douglas Fox: Surveyor   Quintin Hocking

Lighting and special effects   Laurie Lane
Director : Arno James

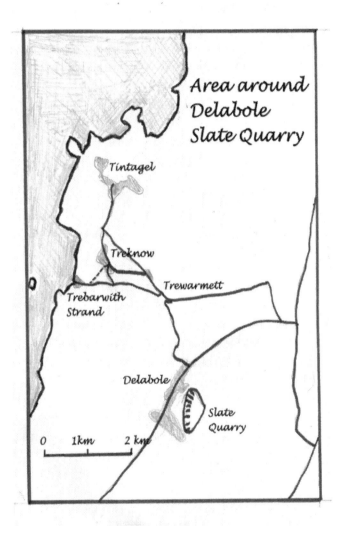

Area around
Delabole
Slate Quarry

Tintagel

Treknow

Trewarmett

Trebarwith
Strand

Delabole

Slate
Quarry

0   1km   2 km

CHAPTER 1

The first intimation that something was wrong was a sharp crack, like the sound of a starting gun.

Greg Wallis looked up from his toil, shifting pieces of rough slate into a large pannier, near the top of the steepest face in Delabole Quarry. 'Did you hear that? Sounded intense. I didn't like that noise one bit. It reminded me...'

'Never mind the memoirs. Shouldn't we should tell the captain?' said his fellow-worker, James Kellow. 'Thomas likes to pretend he's in charge. He's paid more than us: should know what to do. Where's he likely to be, this late in the day?'

Greg shielded his eyes against the bright late-afternoon sun and peered across the vast pit that stretched out below them. For a moment he could see no detail among the shadows. Then, in the distance, he saw some figures, in dispute, beside a waterwheel. He pointed: 'That's him over there. With the bloke in a top hat - that Director we were introduced to this morning. What was his name?'

It was late in the day and they'd been toiling away for hours. The lads who were helping them saw the opportunity for a break.

'Pendle?'
'Sandall?'

'Jingle?'

'Bongle?'

'No, don't muck about lads. It was Rendle. I bet he's trying to explain to Dr Rendle, yet again, why they don't pump the water away by some shorter route. I'll go and have a word.'

'You do that. But hurry.'

As Greg trudged off down the incline, to the side of the face, which led into the pit bottom, James stepped across. He bent down to take a closer look at the point in the ground, further away from the edge, from where he judged the noise had come.

He inspected the stony soil then pursed his lips.

'Never mind the sound, I don't like the look of the thing. The line runs right along here. I'd say it's a long quartz seam that's starting to break up.'

'Does that matter?' asked one of the lads who were helping him load the slates. He stamped his foot then flinched as his heel took the impact. 'Ouch! The rock here seems solid enough.'

The lad looked across to the gantry on the edge of the Quarry, further along. The machine was hard at work, hauling up a bundle of slates hewn by the workers on a terrace below them. 'That new poppet head's built of solid iron. Metal won't break up easily.'

'Could keel over, though – down into the pit. It's poised right on the edge.'

'No it couldn't. Look at those guy ropes, running back to

those posts in the ground. They won't give way in a hurry.'

'Well, I don't know about you lads, but I'm worried,' said James. 'From now on we're going to load the panniers on the village side of that crack – well away from the edge. I've never seen a vein of quartz crushing like that before, but I've heard stories...'

The lads didn't understand James' anxiety, couldn't make sense of it, but even without being spoken the fear seemed to spread to the youngsters. The banter fell away. With some effort they dragged their piles of loose slate, piece by piece, further from the edge and past the suspect fault-line of quartz.

Slowly they resumed their work, filling the baskets. There was tension in the air. Something was going to happen - but they couldn't imagine what it might be.

On the terrace below, Robert Cowling was just being given his afternoon tea by daughter Bessie. Bessie was a plump nine year old. She had been sent with the scones and flagon of tea by her mother from their terraced house in Delabole, just behind the Quarry. Her friend, Fannie Wallis, stood beside her.

In the 1850s, less than twenty years before, women and older girls had been routinely employed in the Quarry. When the pressure had come to cut the workforce, as orders fell, there was no chance they'd be retained in preference to the men. Now a few women toiled down in Port Gaverne, helping to stow slate into boats, ready to ship to other parts of Cornwall. Inside the Quarry there would still be seen young girls, visiting fathers, grandfathers or older brothers, but none were on the Slate Company's books.

'It's a fine afternoon, Father,' said Bessie as she handed over his scones. 'Mother says it will rain later in the week. "April showers", she said they were. She sends you her love.'

'Thank you, m'dear,' said Robert. 'As I've said before, no-one makes scones like your mother.' He glanced at his second visitor. 'Don't go too near the edge, Fannie. I'm sure your father wouldn't want to lose you. It's a long way down. Have you got his cakes?'

'I went to the top to find him – that's where he normally is. They said he'd gone to find the Quarry Captain. He'd heard some vein of quartz crumbling or something. As Father wasn't there, I've come down with Bessie. I've still got his cakes.'

'Oh, I saw your father not long ago. He was making his way to the bottom.' Robert turned, shielded his eyes and looked across the pit below. 'Yes, there he is – right down in the bottom.'

Fannie followed the line of his arm. 'Oh, yes, I see. Thanks, Mr Cowling, I'll go and catch him now.' She disappeared onto one of the short-cuts running down the steep cliff face. It was far from safe but the youngsters were used to it.

'M'm. Greg heard a vein of quartz being crushed, did he?' Robert looked up. 'That must be right above us. Let's shift along a bit, shall we, Bessie. It might be nothing, but on the other hand...'

They had just reached the terrace end when a sharp, warning shout came from above. At almost the same second they heard a rumbling noise which rapidly grew louder. Bessie wondered for a second if it was the start of a thunder-storm – though she could see no rain-clouds in the sky.

'Get right over to the side, lass,' urged Bessie's father, bellowing to be heard over the roar. 'You first; you're more nimble than me.'

As they both inched their way to the side, the whole of the rock face behind them seemed to start to slide. Pieces of soil, small pebbles and then loose boulders started to ricochet down the hillside.

Looking below, Bessie saw to her horror her friend Fannie being struck by one of the rocks and sinking to her knees. Then a second, larger boulder seemed to bounce right on top of her. 'Fannie,' she screamed, 'Father, she's been hit.'

Fannie was not the only one in trouble. Looking across, it appeared that the whole rock face was on the move – and she knew there were many men working on the terraces below. The movement was almost imperceptible at first but was accelerating even as they watched. The noise was terrifying – and deafening.

As she tried to take in the dreadful cacophony of images, another movement above them caught her eye. 'Look Father, the poppet head's coming adrift.' It was true; the guy posts had been shaken out of the ground and the huge iron structure was now teetering on the edge. Slowly, irresistibly, it started to lean further and further; then it keeled right over and crashed, remorselessly, down the rock face.

'Aagh.'

Bessie turned back to her father and saw that he was clutching his head. His hands were covered in some dark liquid that, to her horror, she realised could only be blood. One of the flying blocks must have hit him. 'Keep in as far as you can, Father; I'll go for help.'

By some miracle the young girl managed to scramble onto one of the inclines at the side, which for a moment was free of falling rocks. The choking dust made it hard to see clearly but she'd been on the Quarry many times and knew that this route led to the top – if the top was still there. Throwing away the flagon of tea, she took the canvas belt and tied it round her face – the clouds of dust were making it increasingly hard to breathe or to see. Then, her skirt tucked into her knickers, she started, slowly, to inch her way up the incline.

Afterwards, in her fear, she had no idea how long the ascent had taken. Probably it was no more than ten minutes – though it seemed like hours. There were loose rocks everywhere and she had to jump to dodge flying boulders as they careered down the incline. In one respect she was lucky: the incline was to the side of the main rock fall and was protected from the worst of the damage.

'Bessie! Bessie!' In all the chaos it was James Kellow who spotted the dust-encrusted girl through the debris and turmoil as she reached the top of the incline. For a few moments, as the avalanche grew in intensity, there had been nothing he could do - except to make sure his lads kept as far back as possible. He was overjoyed to see evidence of life amongst the chaos.

Quickly he rushed forward and bent down to give her a hug. 'Where's your father, Bessie?'

The girl gave a sob. 'Oh Mr Kellow, I left him down there. He'd been working on the top terrace - almost made it to the incline. He was hit on the head by one of those rocks. I told him I'd go for help.'

'Right. I want you to keep safe. See those lads over there. Go on this path here and stay with them till I come back. I'll go down and see what I can do.'

Bessie had heard her father talking occasionally with other quarrymen about rock falls, but she had never seen one – even after the event, surveying the aftermath, let alone as it happened. She could not know that this was the worst incident of its kind ever to hit the Slate Quarry at Delabole.

In the end sixteen people – twelve workmen, three boys and one girl - would be killed that day in April 1869. Her father, shielded by James Kellow from further falls by planks placed above him, would survive.

It would take hundreds of workers at the Quarry nearly three years before they had cleared the thousands of tons of rock and slate from the bottom of the pit – three years before the company could once more make any profit.

No-one who worked at that Quarry would ever see it in the same way again. The Great Disaster would cast long shadows in the decades ahead.

CHAPTER 2

'So we're off to refurbish an old cottage that's been abandoned for months – and remind me, what did the last owner die of?'

The speaker was Sophie Collins, a tall, thin and fashionably minimalist Kilburn artist, who was dressed as if for a photo-shoot. Her long, golden hair cascaded over her shoulders, adding sparkle to her silk, deep purple blouse. She didn't look ready for heavy labour.

'Yes, it'll be dirty work. I hope you've got some working clothes,' replied her female companion, George Gilbert, who was driving her heavily-laden Mini Cooper down towards Cornwall. Her jeans and sweater looked better suited to the task. 'And no, I've no idea what happened to Ivy Cottage's previous owner. Don't worry; I don't suppose it was particularly infectious.'

Sophie's offer of help had come just after Christmas, in response to the news in George's Christmas circular. It would be good to have company, George had thought, in setting up her newly-acquired Cornish cottage. It wasn't as if she knew a lot of people in North Cornwall. Already it was clear there would be some differences for the women to work through.

A Cornish Conundrum

The two had last shared a house sixteen years ago, George's first year after university. A mathematician, embarking on a career in management science, she'd been glad of a room in the household of three sturdily non-scientific women. Though thinking back, she recalled many arguments about how the place should be run: logical science versus artistic freedom. She hoped Sophie had matured since then.

'So how did you land on this place then?'

'I have a friend in Delabole: Brian Southgate, the local doctor. He knew I was wanting to buy a cottage nearby; he alerted me when one of his patients died. "If a holiday cottage in Cornwall is worth buying," he said, "it's best to be ahead of the queue".'

'So what's special about this cottage?'

George smiled. 'Guess.'

Sophie mused for a moment. 'Is it a listed building?'

'Not as far as I know – although it's quite old.'

'Was the previous owner a composer – or an author, maybe?'

George looked embarrassed; in truth the place had little artistic celebrity. 'I'll tell you. It was the location, actually.'

'George! You can't have chosen a cottage because it was in Delabole?'

'Oh, no, it's not in Delabole. It's near the coast - overlooking the local beach.'

'Hm.' Sophie hesitated. 'Does that mean it's in Treknow?'

'Sophie, how on earth did you work that out?'

'Didn't you know? I was brought up in North Cornwall;

14

went to school in Camelford. My family moved north when I was a teenager. I haven't been back for years, but I still remember the places around there. I had several boyfriends I explored it with.'

Such inside knowledge might be useful, George thought, even if out of date. She recalled that Sophie had several more boyfriends during the year when the two shared a house. In this dimension she was no minimalist. On balance, though, she was glad Sophie was with her.

'I wouldn't mind hearing the news,' asked George. What she really meant was that her companion's Heavy Metal CD was giving her a blinding headache.

'It'll still be about that plane crash.'

Sophie fiddled with the radio. The news was dominated by the story of the airliner which had been brought down, both engines stalled, onto the Hudson River. Despite the bitter night cold it appeared, miraculously, that there were no casualties: all hundred and fifty passengers had been rescued. The pilot – who used to fly fighter jets - was being fêted to the skies.

'That'd make a dramatic painting,' commented Sophie. It was her passion. George had been secretly dismayed to see her loading artist's equipment into the heavily-packed boot, when she'd picked her up earlier that morning after dropping off her daughter Polly. Whenever did she hope to find time to use that?

'It'd be better with a video camera,' retorted George. She

15

had just bought a new camera and was keen to use it. Even in January she might catch some dramatic shots of waves crashing into cliffs.

'Provided you had it with you as the plane came down - with a tripod. I use a camera regularly. It needs to be steady when the lighting's poor.'

The conversation gave Sophie an idea. 'Hey - have you any pictures of your cottage?'

'I'm afraid not. To be honest, I've only seen it a couple of times. Once when Brian called me down to Cornwall to have a first look; then at the old lady's funeral service, when I met the relative who agreed to sell. He went back to Australia a week later. I haven't had chance to see it since.'

'This isn't just buying a pig in a poke: it's buying the whole poke.'

'I've had a survey done,' protested George. 'They say it'll need a lot of work – the old lady hadn't decorated for years - but it's structurally sound. What sold it for me was the position: on top of the hillside, with a view down the valley to the sea. When all's said and done, you can change the décor but you can never alter the location.'

'I assume you've had the place cleared?'

George looked embarrassed. 'Well, I thought about it. Remember, this is a second home. I've got no spare furniture to take down there.'

'You could have ordered stuff online and had it delivered.'

'I haven't measured anything yet. I don't know what I want – or what will fit. I thought I'd start with what's there, throw out most of it and buy new. I've got a skip on order. Our first task is to create a minimalist cottage.'

Sophie was silent for a moment. George wondered if she, too, was having second thoughts.

'Is there any form of heating?'

'The survey said the old lady – she was called Lily Taylor - had night storage heaters. I was thinking of installing a wood burning stove as well.'

'That's your best idea so far. We'll make Wadebridge top priority, first thing tomorrow morning. They're bound to sell stoves there. It's an emergency – we can plead for urgent delivery. I can live with old-fashioned décor but I do need to be warm.'

There was a pause then another fear surfaced. 'I assume this woman – Lily - did have proper beds?'

'There was a double bed in each bedroom when I had my tour but I don't remember any duvets. You did remember your sleeping bag?'

A howl of frustration told George that the answer was no.

'Don't worry, when we're in Wadebridge we'll hit Tesco's and buy some bedding. You can have my bag tonight and I'll find some blankets.'

'This isn't a minimalist cottage, George, it's a Boot Camp.'

'Think of it as character building.'

'My character is well-built already, thank you very much.'

Silence reigned as they travelled west. George realised that she had not sold Ivy Cottage well. Sophie, for her part, was wondering what other horrors were in store; and how soon she could respectably return to London.

'So Lily's son met you at his mother's funeral and agreed a price on the spot – didn't even bother with an estate agent?'

'It wasn't as simple as that. The funeral was delayed because of the inquest. That gave her son Dan time to travel over from Australia – he'd emigrated in 1977 and hadn't been back since. It also gave me time to convince myself that buying a cottage in Cornwall was what I wanted to do; and that my finances could stand it. In October 2008 taking money out of a bank and putting it into property looked a good idea.'

'Dan didn't want to keep the cottage as a UK retreat?'

'Well, he'd be letting himself in for a mountain of modernisation. He didn't have happy memories of Delabole. He'd been laid off from the Quarry in 1975; his dad died a year later. He didn't want to come back. The Quarry had bad associations. He was settled in Australia, had no relatives in the UK; just wanted to claim his inheritance and be off.'

'Why such a rush?'

'He'd talked to Lily's solicitor - and to my doctor friend Brian. He'd discovered that his inheritance would be bigger if he didn't have to pay for an estate agent. Somehow or other he'd got a valuation for Ivy Cottage that he and I both thought was fair.'

'Huh. You mean it was lower than you'd expected?'

'Well, it recognised that a lot of money would still need to be spent. So we shook hands on the deal and set the lawyers to work.'

There was another silence. At least it wasn't pounding Heavy Metal. George wondered about loading her latest Vivaldi CD but decided that might provoke another disagreement. She had no idea if Sophie liked classical music.

'You mentioned that Lily's death had prompted an inquest.' Sophie was obviously still brooding on how the previous owner had died. 'So her death – whatever caused it - must have been unusual. You don't need an inquest if someone has died of old age.'

'I suppose so. It wasn't my place to worry. I'll introduce you to Brian once we're settled and you can ask him for yourself. As her doctor he's bound to know the inside story. I'm sure you can wheedle it out of him.'

'The inquest probably means she died inside Ivy Cottage. You've not mentioned anyone else, so I take it she lived – and died - on her own?'

'That's right; as far as I know. As I say, her husband died ages ago.'

'Do you believe in ghosts, George?'

'Certainly not. I'm a scientist. Do you?'

'I'm open to the possibility. We don't understand everything in life and death. I hope we're going to sleep alright in Ivy Cottage.'

CHAPTER 3

'I'm fed up with excuses. You promised me a stage - here - two weeks ago - and it's still not arrived. As you can see.' The speaker, Arno James, pointed to the empty car park on the far side of the road.

His companion in the car, Della Howell, could see he was angry. Shoulders arched, arms stiff, beard bristling, the man was hunched impatiently over the steering wheel. No doubt this was the notorious artistic temperament. It was something that she would just have to deal with.

'I talked to the scaffolding people again this morning, Arno. It's top of their schedule. Absolutely. Trouble is, they said, they've been overrun with work for people wanting to install chimneys for new wood-burning stoves. It's a very cold winter.'

'Della, you don't need to tell me it's cold here. I've observed it at close quarters. We've been rehearsing, on this car park, for two weeks. Two hours or more, every evening, whatever the weather; and sometimes the weather's been bloody awful.'

'Go on - everyone's been dressed up in coats and scarves. Even my daughter. They've not had to suffer too much.'

Arno thought it was rather easy for a woman dressed in a

smart, thick coat and living in a well-heated house to under-estimate the miseries of others. It might be best, though, to keep this observation to himself.

'All the cast knew what they'd agreed to do. I reminded them of the traditions of outdoor theatre, from Porthcurno and elsewhere. "The show must go on." I made sure they all signed those contracts before they were given their parts. They'll perform in a blizzard if they have to.'

He turned toward her. 'You told me you wanted an outdoor production and that's what you'll get. Let's hope there's a decent audience and they're up for it. They'll find it cold, just like the players. In fact colder, as they won't be moving about.'

'I talked to the marquee people yesterday.' Della was glad she could prove her competence in one area. 'No problem there. They're coming tomorrow morning to put them up. The audience will be dry and sheltered at least.'

'Though not too warm, I suspect.'

'Oh, and I've got fish and chips from Camelford booked to provide hot refreshments at the interval.'

'Huh. The men'll be off to warm themselves down the road in the Port William.' He gestured down the road. 'Maybe won't be keen to come back for the second half.'

'That's your challenge, isn't it? To make the drama so compelling the audience is desperate to know what happens next.'

'I'm sure my script would do that in normal conditions.'

'Arno, when you and I agreed terms for this last autumn,

we thought we'd be performing the thing in the spring – the hundred and fortieth anniversary of the Quarry Disaster. Not January.'

'Since then I've had a commission that requires me to go north by February. The anniversary of the 1909 Colliery disaster at West Stanley, County Durham. That killed a hundred and sixty five – ten times the Disaster here. Even the BBC will be covering it - on BBC4. So our drama had to be advanced to January.'

There was a pause while both speakers took stock. Some disagreements between patron and leading artist were inevitable; but they had to be kept under control. Arno took a deep breath.

'Della, from now on we really do need that stage. Especially for the scene which depicts the Quarry Disaster. I had to work very hard on that part of the script. We need at least two levels to show what happened – one on the top and the other down below. Come on, woman, it's only six days to the dress rehearsal.'

'I know Arno, I know. Don't worry, the publicity's all in hand.'

'Oh yes, that part of the whole thing has been done well. Thanks to Jenny in the Tourist Office. I've seen the posters out across the area, advertising a "Dramatic Re-enactment of the History of Delabole Quarry", to take place in Trebarwith Strand car park. They look very striking. It was a masterstroke to feature your daughter halfway up the cliff face. The trouble is, if anyone comes down to see what's going on, there's no sign of anything. I'm all for live performance but life on the stage still needs to be rehearsed; it can't all be spontaneous. Not for a historical reconstruction, any-way.'

Della thought for a moment.

'You say you've been rehearsing on the car park. Wouldn't that do for the performance itself?'

Arno took a deep breath and counted to ten. Della Howell was a wealthy woman and the financial powerhouse of the production. It wouldn't do to throttle her – whatever his feelings. She had guaranteed the cast would each be paid a small fee and that the production expenses would all be covered (as well as a generous commission for himself).

It was Della that had first imagined the possibilities of reconstructing nineteenth century quarry life: had seen an upmarket alternative to the village pantomime. 'We've had Jack and the Beanstalk or Puss in Boots here, Arno, for years. It's a prime cause of dementia. My daughter refuses to play Puss ever again.'

For his part he, Arno, had been desperate to win the commission to write and then direct the production. "Splits and Schisms", he'd called it, after "Disaster at Delabole" had been deemed open to parody. He'd learned that "splitting" was a key part of breaking raw slate blocks into usable slabs.

It was a chance to bring to light nineteenth century capi-talism, warts and all. There were plenty of warts in the script he had written. He'd been amazed, as he'd looked at the background material, how downtrodden the quarry workers

23

had been. The financial collapse of autumn 2008, which unfurled as he was writing, had made the nineteenth century reconstruction seem almost topical.

'Della, even if we did perform on the car park, rather than the edge of the cliff, we'd need a stage so the players would be seen. We'd need to raise up all but the front rows of seats - which still involves scaffolding. But it wouldn't be nearly as dramatic. Whereas where I want to perform it is a few feet above the height of the car park – the seats themselves are all on the level. Come outside, I'll show you.'

The two got out of the car, hastily buttoning their coats. Even at two o'clock it was bitterly cold: the wind seemed to howl up the valley. Arno led his companion to the far edge of the car park. 'We really must have a stage.'

He pointed to the space down below, between the car park and the cliff. 'You can see it's just rough ground down there – bracken and boulders. You couldn't possibly use it for acting without levelling it out; and unless you've got access to bulldozers, a stage on scaffolding is the only way to achieve it.'

Della looked like she was about to intervene, so he ploughed on. 'I've talked to the scaffolding people myself. They can't see any problem in erecting it. It's just the concept of deadlines that... that they struggle with.'

He had been going to say "was beyond them" but managed to tone it down. There was no point in insulting his sponsor. After all, it was her husband's business that was supposed to be supplying the scaffolding.

'OK, Arno, you've convinced me. Stop talking and I'll ring Bill.' She wandered up the road to improve reception and pulled her mobile from her coat pocket. She was not bothered if Arno overheard her conversation; in fact it would be good for him to know how hard she was trying to support him.

An hour later, just as Arno returned from a late lunch at the Port William, the scaffolding team arrived. Della had long since gone home.

Arno expected they would look shame-faced at the time it had taken to fulfil the order, but that was a vain hope. Somehow they'd managed to avoid the knock-on effects of Della's rollicking – her blistering words over the phone had made Arno wince, glad he was not married.

Sometimes, as he reached his mid-forties, Arno regretted not having settled on a life partner. There had been plenty of candidates for the flamboyant theatre-man to consider. Several had been actively evaluated. The episode he had just witnessed, though, had made his lack of long-term commitment seem almost sensible.

Whatever had happened back at the office, and whichever households were left hoping in vain for their new stoves, the scaffolding men were now here. Arno got out of his car, put on his most optimistic face (he was an actor, so could look cheerful when required) and set out to show them exactly where the stage was to go.

There was no problem with materials: their lorry carried

25

huge numbers of poles, clamps and planks. He was pleased to see the men working well together. They seemed to relish the challenge of the steep slope. No doubt it was a contrast with the routine work they'd been doing on cottage chimneys.

Arno had feared that the soggy ground in the bottom of the gully might be a problem but the workers took that in their stride. First a series of huge pillars were hammered into the ground. Then scaffolding was erected above them, linking them together. Decking was laid down to cover the swamp below. Then more pillars were inserted and a second set of scaffolding attached.

'We need long poles to hold the top level stage,' Arno observed. 'As high as you can make it. With fixed ladders on both sides, so the players have got access.'

'Don't you worry, mate. I see what you're after. You can clear off now if you want: you look cold. We'll have the whole thing up in a couple of hours. We'll need to work fast, mind – our lads don't much like working in the dark. It could be dangerous.'

CHAPTER 4

It was already dark before George and Sophie reached North Cornwall, parked in the Camelford car park and strode down the road to Lily Taylor's solicitor.

In the absence of an estate agent, George and the solicitor had agreed that this was the easiest way to hand over the keys. They were only just in time: a young, honey blond – presumably the firm's receptionist – looked like she would soon be off home.

'Welcome to Cornwall. I'm Rachel,' she said, once George had introduced herself. 'Yes, Mr Gifford did mention he was expecting you. I'll take you in straight away.'

The solicitor had cleared his desk; he, too, looked like he was about to go. 'You're lucky to catch me. I don't normally work beyond five on a Friday.' This was a different lifestyle to London, thought George.

He rummaged in a drawer. 'Yes, these are the Ivy Cottage keys. I'm afraid I've no idea which one's which.'

They were in and out inside five minutes. Back in reception, Sophie was about to ask Rachel if she had plans for the evening when she saw George had already started to move away. Having got her keys the analyst wanted to be into her cottage.

'That's a respectable-looking fish and chip shop over the road,' said George, as the pair settled into her car. 'Early evening and there's already a queue. It'll do as a last resort if we can't get the oven to work.'

'If there's no heating we'll be eating out just to stay warm – at least till you get your stove. But there are pubs much closer to Treknow. Do you want me to navigate?'

Now they were away from the main road and onto country lanes their pace slowed. A couple of miles further on, they reached Trewarmett and passed one of the pubs Sophie had mentioned. George remembered that this village had been the starting point for the vicious crime she had helped solve the year before. Probably best not to worry Sophie about this until her anxieties about Ivy Cottage's last owner had been resolved.

'We'll soon be at the turn off to Treknow. Crumbs, they don't waste much money on street lights around here.'

'There's no point in wanting Cornwall to look like London.'

A few minutes later they turned into Treknow and pulled up outside a pair of unlit cottages, arranged around a small courtyard.

'Ivy Cottage is the one on the right.'

'Not that you'd know it. There's no name-sign.'

'Lily lived here all her life. Maybe she didn't need one – or it fell off.'

Sophie pointed at the cottage on the other side. This had a sign: Holly Cottage. 'Do you know who your next door neighbour is?'

'I met him once, briefly, in the dark. He was quite prickly. I'll tell you about it later.'

George got out after reaching under the dashboard for a torch. 'In case the electricity's not on.'

'Great. So we could be in the dark as well as the cold.'

George frowned. 'It should be OK. I rang South West Power a few days ago to ask them to reconnect us. It's been off, of course, since Lily died.'

The new owner wrestled with the keys she had been given and after a moment's panic worked out which key was intended for which keyhole. 'Welcome to Ivy Cottage, Sophie,' she said as she opened the door and stepped inside. 'Be careful here, there's a step down.'

The sound of the trip, the muffled curse and the feeling of Sophie thumping into her back made it clear that George's warning had been a split-second too late.

'As you've now discovered,' she continued. 'For goodness sake just stay still till I've got the lights on.'

George tried the hall light but it had no effect.

'First you'll have to turn the electricity on at the mains. I presume the last time you came here was in the daylight?'

'I'm afraid so. Hold on.' George shone the torch slowly around the hallway, looking for the master switch. The meter must be here somewhere. Then she saw the shiny black box, out of her reach on a ledge over the door.

She wouldn't be thwarted. Her torch had picked out a chair at the far end of the hall; she pulled it over.

29

'You're not going to stand on that are you? It looks very rickety.'

This was the second slightly-too-late warning to be uttered since they'd arrived. George had just clambered onto the chair and was about to reach the switch when both her legs disappeared through the seat. Unable to move her legs, she thrashed about – which in turn caused her to keel over and crash onto the floor. As she went over her torch fell out her hand, smashed on the slate floor and went out.

There was a few seconds of pitch-black, agonised silence.

'The old lady's having her revenge, I see,' stated Sophie, with what George suspected was a malicious grin. 'Maybe she resents anyone else being in her cottage. Are you ok?'

There was a noise of George muttering as she extracted herself out of the chair and scrambled back to her feet. 'Mercifully nothing's broken, as far as I can tell. Just a few knocks and bruises. Erm... I don't suppose you have another torch?'

Before Sophie could answer George heard her mobile ringing in her fleece pocket. 'Hold on a minute... hi?'

Sophie could make out that it was a male voice on the other end but not what he was saying. She had no idea who the caller was. She could sense though that, despite the timing, George was pleased to hear from him.

'Yes, we've just arrived. I haven't managed to get the lights on yet.'

A few seconds later: 'No, I'm not alone. I've come with a friend - Sophie. She's going to help me with the makeover –

once we can see what we're doing.'

Another pause then 'Of course we'd like a meal if you're offering. Tonight? Great; what time shall we come?'

'Well if you're sure. Then maybe, afterwards, you could lend us a torch for the evening? I brought one but I've just fallen over and dropped it.'

Sophie guessed that the response to this was open laughter.

'OK, it wasn't my finest hour. Anyway, to find you, we should drive into Delabole, turn right and then left – and you're at number 15. Great. We'll be with you in twenty minutes.'

George switched off her phone and turned to where she sensed Sophie was still standing. 'You know I told you about my friend Brian Southgate?'

'That was Lily's doctor – the man who recommended this pitch-black cottage?'

'That's right. He knew when I was coming down and realised I'd probably be in a mess for a day or two. He's just invited us to supper. So all we need to do now is to find our way back to the front door.'

After the pitch darkness of Ivy Cottage the streetlights were welcome and not so feeble. Both women were bucked up by the unexpected invitation.

Sophie had been half-expecting to struggle to cook pasta – or something equally simple - on an antique oven. As they drove back through Treknow, she tried to learn what she could about their prospective host.

'How long have you known Brian, George?'

'I don't know him all that well, to be honest. He was Mark's friend more than mine.'

Sophie reminded herself that George had been widowed less than a year before. She didn't know all the details but it must have been a dreadful shock. She hadn't, though, shown any need to talk about it on their journey down to Cornwall. It was good that her friend seemed to be coping with her loss – so far, anyway.

'So how did you and Brian meet up?'

'I came to Padstow last September to do a project – the town was drawing up development options and wanted some help. That's the kind of work I do. I ran into Brian and we've kept in touch ever since.'

'He's about our age then. Is he married or anything?'

George recalled Sophie's amorous appetite. She didn't know if this had faded over the years but thought it best to avoid confusion. 'He's happily married, as far as I know. I haven't met the wife yet - though I've talked to her on the phone; she's called Alice. By the way, you're not vegetarian or anything?'

'It's been a long journey, George. I'd eat practically any-thing. It's bound to be healthy – he's a doctor. What's his wife do?'

'No idea. Oh, I remember, she's a primary school teacher in Delabole.'

'So the meal will be really healthy – whoever cooks it.

Even if it only comes up minuscule portions.'

'Sophie, Brian's a generous man: we won't starve. What's the best way to Delabole?'

Ten minutes later they found the doctor's house in Delabole and rang the doorbell.

'George, it's good to see you,' said Brian, as he opened the door and gave her a warm hug.

George uncoiled herself and indicated her companion. 'Brian, this is my friend Sophie Collins. We shared a house in London before I was married.'

Brian inspected her, noted her flamboyant clothes, then shook her warmly by the hand. 'You're welcome too. Come in, it's cold tonight. Give me your coats. Now, can I get you a drink?'

Sophie asked for a glass of Merlot and George settled for lime and lemonade. 'I'll be the one driving back later.'

The women were shown into a smartly-furnished lounge and took positions at either end of a long settee. Brian disappeared then returned a minute later with their drinks, plus some red wine for himself. 'I'm not on call this weekend.' He flopped into the chair opposite.

'George, have you ever met Alice?' asked Brian as he took his first sip. 'It's her turn to cook tonight. The main course is beef wellington, I believe. She knows you're here; she'll be with us shortly.'

He turned to Sophie. 'So you're going to be the first to stay in Ivy Cottage after Lily Taylor; what did you make of it?'

33

'To be honest we haven't got very far yet. We had trouble getting the electricity on so we've not actually seen anything.'

'I presume George explained how she came by her cottage?'

'She told me some of it on the way down. It sounded quite mysterious.'

'The lady who owned it, Lily, was my patient for many years. Not that she was ill very much. I knew where she lived: Ivy Cottage is in an idyllic holiday location. Off the main road, with a view right down to the sea. As you'll see tomorrow.'

'Sophie was worried that something dreadful might have happened to Lily,' added George. 'I told her you'd be the one who could reassure her. Did she die in the cottage?'

'I'm afraid she did. Very suddenly. It was a neighbour that found her.'

'Was it a heart attack?' asked Sophie.

'We're not absolutely sure.'

'Sounds mysterious.'

'There was some reason for doubt. She was dead for a day or two before anyone discovered her.'

'She might just have died in her sleep?'

'Well...'

'At least she was found in her bed?'

'You're pushing me to reveal medical facts about one of my patients.'

George thought it best to intervene. 'What Sophie really

wants to know, Brian, is, which bed did she die in? It'll affect where she sleeps. Surely you can tell us that?'

Brian pondered for a moment. 'I suppose as the next occupants of her cottage you're entitled to a few details. Her only relative's back in Australia, anyway, so I don't think he'll mind.'

'He won't know, will he?'

'The truth is,' the doctor went on, 'she wasn't in any of the beds in Ivy Cottage when they found her.' He glanced at his guests in turn. 'So you don't need to worry which one each of you sleeps in.'

'So go on then: where was she found?' asked George. 'We'll worry ourselves sick until we know.'

Brian paused again. His medical conscience troubled him; but he could see that he couldn't stop at this point - not with this audience, anyway.

'Sadly, I'm afraid that Lily Taylor died in the bath. The most likely scenario is that she fell asleep there, slid under the water and drowned.'

There was silence as both women contemplated this awful end-of-life.

'How terrible,' said George. 'Is that sort of death common?'

'It happens quite a lot with small children, but very rarely with adults. By the time we've grown up we develop survival mechanisms that come into play.'

'You mean, some instinct would make her wake up as soon as she was under the water?'

35

'Exactly.'

'So why didn't that happen in this case?'

Brian wished he could wind back the clock by a few minutes. He should never have got into this conversation. 'I really don't want to talk any more about my patient; and in any case I can't be sure. Speaking generally, the most common reason why adults die like this is that they've been drinking before they take their bath.'

'So she was an alcoholic!' gasped George.

'Drowned her sorrows and then her sorrows drowned her,' added Sophie poetically, taking a large swig of her red wine.

Brian was thankful that at that moment Alice Southgate joined them. He hastened to make introductions; and to move the conversation on to more general topics.

CHAPTER 5

As George and Sophie travelled to their meal in Delabole, a rehearsal was about to begin on the new stage at Trebarwith Strand car park.

The choice of location had been contentious. But Della Howell, the drama's patron, was a friend of Annabel, the woman who owned the house at the top of the village, close to the car park. Annabel had been signed up as a Friend of the Production. (The only Friend, one of the cast had muttered.)

It had been agreed that Annabel's next electricity bill would be covered by the project. In return she would let electricity cables be run from her house, powering the lights for the production. Next week she would also provide space for the cast to change. The event would take over her property, but Della knew Annabel had been a drama queen in her younger days.

In the last week a large van had arrived: the control van for lights and sounds. A second van, a mobile fish and chip shop to feed the audience during the drama, would come on the first night of performance.

In December many rehearsals had taken place in the Community Hall; but now, in the final weeks, the company had to grit their teeth and perform in the open air. They now understood why the director had insisted that they signed an agreement before they were offered roles, that they would perform the drama whatever the weather.

Although the site was convenient for power, its disadvantages would now emerge. The steep-sided Trebarwith valley seemed to act as a wind-tunnel, amplifying the local weather. For now they rehearsed in multiple layers of fleeces, scarves and coats. They would soon reach the final rehearsals, when they would lose most of their protection.

'Now the stage is up and Laurie's finally got somewhere to aim his lights we can walk through the outdoor scenes.' Arno James was director of the forthcoming drama. Laurie Lane was a local electrician, who had volunteered to help before he realised the seriousness of the undertaking – or at least, how seriously it was being taken by Arno.

'The clamps have been on order for weeks, Arno,' retorted Laurie. 'Don't blame me that theatrical suppliers are so slow. I mentioned your name, like you said, but it didn't seem to have much impact.'

'I 'spect they're busy with pantomimes.' Paul Wood was local plumber and odd job man. 'My wife says that's what we should be doing – like last year.'

Arno tried with difficulty to suppress his irritation. Bloody pantomime. Della had mentioned it to him. If he'd known how popular it was with everyone else in the area, he'd never have taken the commission. 'Look, you can do pantomimes every year in the future. This year - 2009 - I was invited to write a historical re-enactment of the life of the Quarry. "Make Delabole the cultural centre of North Cornwall." I like a challenge. So whatever it takes, that's what we're going to do.'

He looked around him. Most of the cast were there, but one key person was missing. 'Where's Beth?'

Her friend Freya responded: 'She helps in the Spar on Friday evenings. Maybe they had a late rush of customers.'

'Not in January. Bond Street, maybe, but not Delabole. Someone give her a ring.'

'Arno, we found out – after you'd chosen the site - that for some reason mobiles don't work here. We're at the bottom of the valley.'

Further discussion was curtailed by the arrival of Beth. An attractive, blond-haired sixteen-year old, her petite figure allowed her to be cast as a ten year old. Arno had been offered a nine year old to play the part but he had found an excuse to overlook her. Beth, on the other hand, was a budding actress with plenty of talent – in all sorts of directions.

'OK folks, let's get started. If we keep our minds on the job we can be down to the Port William in an hour.'

'And if we're more than two hours the place'll be shut. They don't stay open late this time of year.' Richard Penhaligon could speak with authority: he was the Port William landlord.

'Right. This is the most difficult scene in the whole

39

drama.' Arno was in his element now, his beard bristling, dark eyes gleaming, voice authoritative. 'We're going to play the great Disaster at the Quarry, which happened in April 1869. It's quite a challenge.'

'This is where several of us get killed,' offered Paul. He didn't sound too sorry: it was bitterly cold. At least once dead you could get off the set. 'How are we going to do that exactly?'

'You've all seen the account of the Disaster which I pulled together from the various sources?' This was one of the background documents he had prepared to educate the cast.

There were nods. 'It was very moving,' offered Laurie. 'The Disaster doesn't get much talked about these days.'

'Hey, couldn't Job Hockaday tell the whole story from his lectern?' asked Joe Stacey. He had been pleased to be assigned the part of Hockaday, one of the strong characters of Delabole in the nineteenth century. As rehearsals progressed he had found himself growing steadily into the role.

'That was my first idea,' admitted Arno. 'I thought it would be beyond a company like ours to simulate a Quarry Disaster. Then I looked at what other dramatists had done when facing similar challenges and I thought it must be possible. One drama company – Riding Lights - even managed to replicate the fire which destroyed York Minster. This is a doddle in comparison.'

Arno had won grudging respect from his players for his ideas; they had no doubt that he was an accomplished playwright. Maybe being dictatorial was a necessary part of directing the performance.

'So what did you come up with?' asked Martin Thorne.

'Well remember, the performances take place in the evening. There's no matinee. The audience will only see the things we want them to – i.e. those which Laurie's lights illuminate. My plan is that we'll create the feeling of the great slide in the Quarry, as the rock face thunders down, mainly by a horrendous noise in the darkness.'

'So we'll need a large-scale amplifier and sound deck?' asked Laurie, in a forlorn voice. Was he being asked to produce more kit to use in the real performance? That was now less than a week away.

'Yes. Don't worry. Harry Cobbledick has the kit in his Caravan Park. He'll bring it down tomorrow. Tonight we'll manage without it. It means you'll be able to hear my instructions more clearly.'

The cast had learned that the best way to handle Arno was not to argue but to follow his commands. It meant less time in the cold. The sooner this was over, the sooner they could warm up at the Port William.

'The first part of the scene takes place on the upper ledge. So can we have James Kellow and Greg Wallis – that's Jim and Paul - up there, please.'

This scene had been rehearsed many times in the comfort of the Delabole Community Hall. Both men knew their lines. What they hadn't experienced was the exhilaration (or fear) of performing their lines on the top stage, high up on the hillside.

Quickly the men scaled the ladder and took up their positions.

'You'll need to be up there beforehand,' shouted the director. 'The spotlight won't come on you till the scene begins.'

'I'm in a preceding scene,' protested Jim. 'I'll need to climb up in the dark. Can't we have some light? It's high up here – and this stage isn't very deep.'

'Trouble is, I don't want the audience to know it exists until this scene starts. You'll just have to stay as far back as you can. Once your lights are on, the edge is obvious. We agreed we wouldn't muck about with safety ropes, so keep to the back. Now, let's try it.'

Arno turned to Laurie. 'Top-stage lights, please.'

Laurie walked over to the control van. A short delay. Then a spotlight, located next to the road behind them, shone onto the top stage.

'Let's go,' shouted the director.

There was a few seconds pause.

'Did you hear that!' exclaimed the actor playing Greg Wallis, looking behind him. 'That sounded ominous. I didn't like that noise one bit. It reminded me –'

'Never mind the memoirs, Greg,' responded the man playing James Kellow. 'We'd best tell the Quarry Captain. Where's he likely to be, this late in the day?'

Greg shielded his eyes and looked out beyond the stage, across the car park. 'That's him over there. With that Director bloke we met this morning.'

'You mean Rendle. Look, they're arguing about drainage again, I bet. '

'I'd better go and have a word.'

So saying, Greg started to clamber down the ladder.

The spotlight faded. A second light shone, illuminating the lower stage. Here Beth and Freya – playing Bessie and Fannie - were approaching Richard Penhaligon - Robert Cowling - as he heaved away with his pick.

'Here you are Father,' said Bessie, offering him a flagon of tea. 'It's tea time. Mother sends her love.'

'Thank you, m'dear.' He stopped work then looked across to her friend, standing close to the front of the stage. 'Mind yourself, Fannie. Don't get too near that edge. Shouldn't you be with your father?'

'I expected to find him on the top, Mr Cowling, but he's gone off somewhere. Mr Kellow said he heard some vein of quartz on the top crumbling and wanted to be the one to tell the Quarry Captain.'

'Oh, that explains why he went past a few minutes ago.' Cowling turned and looked around. 'Look - he's over there.' The actor pointed off beyond the Treknow end of the stage.

'Thank you Mr Cowling. I'll go and catch him.' The girl slipped to the far side of the stage and started to scramble down into the gully.

On the stage Robert pulled Bessie towards him then looked up. 'Heard a vein of quartz shattering, did he? That must be right above us. I don't like the sound of that. It might be nothing but … why don't we move over to the side?'

'This is where the noise of collapsing hillside will first be heard,' yelled the director. 'Keep going.'

Cowling led his daughter over towards the other side of the stage, pointing to the ladder.

As they reached it, the girl ahead of him, he gave a cry and clutched his head. Copious red liquid covered his hands.

'Father,' screamed Bessie, as she turned back to him. 'Are you all right?'

'I think so. I can't see very well.'

'Stay as far back into the hillside as you can. I'll go for help.'

'Fine so far,' shouted Arno. 'This'll be when the low rumbling in the background turns into an awesome noise. Freya, pretend to fall and to lie on the bracken at the bottom.'

Grimacing as she felt the cold, soggy ground beneath her, Freya did as she was told.

The director turned to two other men who were watching the scene beside him in working clothes. 'Start from under the stage then slip out to lie there as well. Preferably not on top of Freya.'

As the men arranged themselves, Arno shouted to Laurie. 'Spotlight on the ladder now. I want the audience to see Beth struggling up it, to fetch help for her dad.'

He turned to the rest of the cast. 'I've ordered a couple of smoke machines; we'll use them to simulate dust and add to the confusion. They're coming on Monday. One'll be in the gully where the bodies are found. The other one will be down below Beth.'

He called to the girl, 'Start climbing now, m'dear.'

Beth started to climb, but only slowly, hanging on tightly to each rung. It might have been lack of makeup but her face was deathly white. Rehearsing on the level had been fine; climbing a ladder in the dark was different. It was clear she was terrified.

'Poor kid, she's scared to death,' muttered Joe. 'It's a long way down.'

'It'd be worse if there was a gale.'

'It'll be worse once that smoke machine's operating.'

'She'll be ok as long as it's just smoke. Let's hope Arno doesn't order tear gas to pep us all up.'

It was an odd comment; but they all knew Arno would do anything to maximise impact and demanded total commitment from his cast.

The whole project had almost come to a grinding halt on New Year's Day, when he had tried to force the entire cast to go for a swim in the sea at Trebarwith Strand. 'We don't know what the weather's going to be like when we perform,' he had insisted. 'You need to prepare yourselves for performing in freezing wind and rain. A cold dip – maybe every week - will thicken your blood.'

Fortunately Joe Stacey had taken courage on their behalf. 'We'll all go in, Arno,' he'd said. 'Only you'll need to lead the way.' It was a master stroke; Arno was no keener to be frozen than the rest of them and had quickly backed down. Even so, fear of his ruthlessness remained.

It was an edgy production; and the edge on the drama would only get sharper.

CHAPTER 6

'This is delicious - delightful, even - but we must leave by ten,' George warned, as she helped herself to another profiterole. That meant she'd had only one more than the figure-conscious Sophie. 'We've still got to get into Ivy Cottage, remember, make those blasted lights work, unpack the car and sort out our bedding.'

'Of course,' responded Brian, his eyes twinkling, 'but you do realise it's already five to eleven?'

'What? It can't be. Look at that clock.'

'Yes, it is rather confusing,' admitted Alice. 'It's like some of his patients – its face has slipped. I'm always telling Brian we should treat ourselves to a new one - but this one was inherited from his grandfather.'

'Half my patients have a squint. That's what it's corrected for,' protested her husband.

Now realising how late it was, George attacked her last profiterole with gusto. 'We really must be off,' she affirmed. 'Thank you so much, Alice; that was a wonderful meal. So very welcome after all our teething problems.'

'You told me you needed to borrow a torch,' remembered the doctor. 'Excuse me, I'll go and get one from the garage. Then I'll drive down with you – just to make sure everything's OK.'

Though she wouldn't admit it, even to herself, George had no qualms about the cottage now she had sturdy male reinforcements. Soon the three were inside the hall; Brian was tall enough to reach the electricity master switch without the need of a chair. Seen with all its lights on, the cottage looked peaceful and welcoming, even if the furniture and downstairs curtains were dreadfully old fashioned.

Brian led the way upstairs, turning on lights as he went. The surveyor had been right, George thought: the place is fundamentally in good repair – even if very old-fashioned. The walls were white and covered with pictures - including a batch of what George took to be Delabole Slate Quarry. Lily must have had connections with the Quarry in her earlier life. Had her late husband worked there? George wondered what had caused his death.

There were two reasonable-sized bedrooms, each with a firm-mattressed double bed; also a box room that was completely empty.

'I bet this was the one used by Lily,' said George. It was the bedroom nearest the bathroom. It contained a large old-fashioned wardrobe and a matching set of drawers. Round the walls were more photographs.

George oriented herself. 'That window probably looks down the Trebarwith valley.'

'It's too dark to be sure.'

The curtains were a gloomy green – but at least they had

no holes. 'I'll have this room,' George announced.

The second bedroom was comfortable but with less furniture; George guessed Lily had used it for visitors. 'I'm happy to have this,' said Sophie, 'especially as we know Lily didn't die here.'

So far both women had been holding back from the bathroom. Brian sensed their wariness and led the way back along the corridor.

'This is probably the room you'll want to refurbish first,' he said, as they gazed in from the doorway. The bathroom was tidy – clear of any evidence of a fatality - but its colours were dowdy and the paint was starting to peel.

'Pink baths were once the rage,' recalled Sophie. 'My parents had one when I was a child. I remember asking my Dad if my Mum had gone colour-blind. This one looks like something out of the ark.'

'Noah wouldn't have coped with this,' conceded George. 'Can you recommend a bathroom fixer, Brian? One that'll do a rush job. I'm not sure we'll want to use that bath at all. In any case I'll certainly need a shower.'

'I'll find someone. In the meantime you're both welcome to come to Delabole for a shower,' offered the doctor. 'Or maybe your neighbour can help you out for a day or two?'

'We'll go and introduce ourselves in the morning,' replied George. 'Exercise our charms and see what happens.'

'Fine. Anyway, I'll leave you to settle yourselves; but would you like to come for another meal tomorrow? That'll give you breathing space till you get your kitchen working.'

'We can't impose ourselves on you two days in a row.'

'It's my turn to cook tomorrow. Honestly, it's no burden. We love having company – especially making contact with the wider world. It'll be a simpler meal though: do you both like chilli con carne?'

Two nods: the answer was yes.

'We normally eat around seven. Come earlier if you want a shower.'

It was after nine next morning before either woman stirred. George was the first to wake. In the distance she heard what sounded like the clatter of horses' hooves: where on earth was she? Then she remembered.

Slipping on her dressing gown she crept quietly down the stairs with a feeling of pleasurable excitement: this was her very own cottage, to enjoy as she wanted. A retreat from the pressures of working life in London; a place for holidays; somewhere she could lend to friends - maybe somewhere to let out to paying guests? She hadn't yet firmed up her plans.

Whatever its eventual use, the cottage needed to be modernised, so it no longer looked like the home of an old lady. That was their challenge.

First she needed breakfast. She found the kitchen, tucked away at the rear, surprisingly modern. Lily must have had this revamped: all the equipment was up to date. The notice board held a 2008 calendar. Glancing, she saw that Lily had had an active social life, two or three visitors a week. In October alone she was seeing Martha, Mary, Will, Simon and Gerald. There was no microwave but the Diplomat oven was 'state of the art'. Obviously the old lady had much enjoyed her cooking.

A few minutes later Sophie joined her. She had thrown a turquoise jumper over her pyjamas and was wearing matching slippers. Somehow, even in sleeping gear, she looked stylish. 'My, isn't it peaceful - though not warm. What's for breakfast?'

'All we've got is toast and honey. I didn't have much room for food; we'll go shopping later. Tintagel, d'you think, or Delabole?'

'Neither - today we're in Wadebridge, ordering your new stove. There's a big Tesco's there.'

'Big enough to sell bedding and duvets?'

'I 'spect so - I haven't lived here for twenty five years. Is there no heating at all?' asked Sophie, as she huddled into her jumper.

'There are night-storage heaters but they're not working.'

'You need an electrician. But ordering a wood burning stove comes first. I'll look up a suitable store. We'll need to look pitiful and desperate to get to the top of the queue. Are you any good at acting?'

'I don't need to act. We really are pitiful and desperate - and both very cold indeed.'

CHAPTER 7

George decided making the cottage warmer trumped the need to meet their neighbour – "Mr Holly" as Sophie had dubbed him. What they presumed was his vehicle – a red sports car – was parked outside, but there was no sign of life.

'Not an early riser,' said Sophie, as they headed for George's Mini Cooper.

'Be fair: it's Saturday morning. We don't know what he does for a living.'

'He was late home, though – that car wasn't there last night.'

As they watched, a pretty, teenage girl came out of Holly Cottage and started walking down the road.

'Wonder what she's been doing?'

'No wonder Mr Holly hasn't stirred.'

'Don't judge everyone by your standards, Sophie. She might live there - she might be Mr Holly's daughter. Hey, do you reckon she wants a lift?'

'George. Yes, you want to get to know locals - but not at this very minute. Isn't our top priority to make the cottage less like a fridge?'

'Hm, I guess so.' The two slipped into the car and set off

down the road.

From her laptop Sophie had identified a stove seller in Wadebridge, fifteen miles away. They were open on Saturdays – at least until lunch time.

Sophie drove; George sensed she was a good driver. That was fine - as long as all the other drivers they met were equally alert. She was thankful it wasn't the tourist season.

Half an hour later they were parking in the yard of Wadebridge Stoves. 'Remember, we're pitiful females, struggling with a freezing cottage.'

George had not realised how many stoves were on offer; or how much they cost, to buy or to install. There was no doubt, though, of her need. It was one claim on her contingency fund she couldn't avoid.

George browsed around. When she approached the counter Sophie had already caught the attention of the storekeeper.

'I've just taken ownership of a cottage near Tintagel,' George began, 'but I'm only down for a couple of weeks. Can you recommend a stove? It needs to be easy to control. And might you install it in the next week? My cottage is ever so cold.' She looked at him with pleading eyes.

'I've already told your friend our normal delivery time is a month. But we've just had to cancel an order due on Tuesday - so you might be in luck. Now, what's the size of your cottage?'

'I knew there was something we should have done beforehand,' said Sophie sadly.

'Hold on a minute.' George took out her notebook and flipped to some hand-drawn plans. 'I paced these while you were getting dressed.'

George turned to the storekeeper. 'I've got the room measurements here.'

'OK, I'll work out the volume – hence the size of stove you'll need.'

Half an hour later the women walked out with a stove on order, due in three days time. The scaffolding, to allow top level access to the chimney, would arrive the day before.

'Wasn't that Barry a lovely man,' simpered Sophie.

'I've just spent three thousand pounds in his store. He ought to be pleased,' retorted George.

The visit to Tesco's was equally productive. At least, George thought, I don't have to worry about Sophie throwing herself at the till girls. They emerged with trolleys filled with duvets, pillows and coverings, modern crockery, a microwave and some food – and a pair of hot water bottles.

'We should sleep better from now on,' observed George.

'I'm not eating in Ivy Cottage until it's got some heating.'

'We'd better find somewhere nearby then.'

'I reckon the nearest is the Port William Inn. That's in Trebarwith Strand, overlooking the beach - easy walking from Ivy Cottage.'

'We'll try as soon as we're home: we might still be in time for lunch.'

The walk down the hill was the first time George had the chance to enjoy the setting of her new cottage and its proximity to the sea. They set out as soon as they could; Sophie feared the pub would soon stop serving.

The route was obviously much-used by Treknow locals. It led across a slope, down a narrow path enclosed by trees, over a couple of slate stiles then out onto a grassy slope. This, they deduced from the picnic tables, was the top end of the car park for Trebarwith Strand.

'What's going on there?' asked George. In the main park men were erecting three large, white marquees, all in a long line.

'It's an odd place for a wedding reception.'

'Or maybe it's a barn dance? We'll ask at the Inn.'

All the life of Trebarwith Strand was around the beach. On one side, closed for the winter, was a teashop and a shop selling surf boards. Opposite, another one offered shells and trinkets. The beach itself had plenty of rock-pools.

The Port William overlooked the beach and a sign proclaimed the Inn was open. Their first impression on entering was of warmth – even heat. A log fire blazed at one end and most customers occupied tables near it.

'Are you still serving food?' asked Sophie.

'Of course, m'dear – till three. What would you like?'

They were just in time. Both women ordered jacket potatoes, filled with cheese.

'I love the Cornish accent,' said Sophie dreamily. 'That

landlord sounds like he's lived here forever.'

'You behave like you've not seen a man for a decade. Where shall we sit?'

The bar was spacious but the empty tables at the far end looked uninviting. All the tables nearer the fire were occupied.

One woman, sitting with her partner at a table near the bar, saw her predicament. 'Come and join us if you like. There's no point in being cold.'

'Thank you.' The two took the remaining chairs at the table, hung up their cagoules and sat down.

'I've just moved down here actually. I'm George; this is my friend Sophie.'

'You're both welcome to Cornwall. I'm Morwenna - my husband is Joe.'

'We live in Delabole,' her husband explained. 'I'm down here for the rehearsal so we decided to come out for lunch.'

Light dawned for George. 'Is this something to do with the marquees up the road? We saw them as we walked down.'

Morwenna spoke again. She was obviously the main talker. 'That's right. They're to keep the audience dry.'

'I'm sorry. We only got here yesterday. What are you rehearsing for?'

'My Joe's the star. He narrates the whole story – he's playing Job Hockaday and he'll have a long white beard.'

For a second George was tempted to respond with a nonsense remark of her own. If they were waiting for Joe to grow a long beard they'd have a long wait: he didn't even sport a moustache. And who was Hockaday?

Fortunately Sophie could see she had a problem.

'We haven't been here long enough to see any posters, I'm afraid. It sounds exciting. What's the show all about?'

'Normally we have a pantomime. This year, though, is the one hundred and fortieth anniversary of the Quarry Disaster of 1869. So the head of our Women's Institute, Della Howell, decided we should do something to mark it.'

Their food arrived at this moment, giving George and Sophie some breathing space; but it didn't disrupt Morwenna.

'So Della found someone who could turn the story of the Quarry into – how can I describe it? – a sort of pageant, would you say?'

'It's more than that, m'dear. A "Dramatic Re-enactment" is what Arno calls it. Based on the history of Delabole - as assembled by yours truly.'

This was information overload. Sophie tried to disentangle it. 'We want to hear more. It sounds fascinating. Could we start our lunch first, though?'

'I'll get another drink,' said Joe, seizing the opportunity. 'D'you want another glass, m'dear?'

'Better not, Joe, I'll be driving. But if you ladies wouldn't mind guarding my place, I'll nip to the loo.'

For a few minutes the women attacked their potatoes in silence. Fortunately, for different reasons, their two companions were stuck in queues.

57

By the time both had returned, Joe clutching a pint of Doom Bar bitter, the jacket potatoes had been largely dealt with.

'If you can tell us what's going on we'd love to hear,' invited George. 'Just remember we're not local - so we'll need lots of explanation.'

Slowly, over the next hour, with many detours, the tale of the Delabole Dramatisation emerged. Joe was one of the churchwardens in Delabole. He had set out years ago, with the vicar's encouragement, to assemble a history of the church, the village and the Quarry.

'I started off talking to folk in the congregation. Then I learned about the Cornwall Record Office. I have to go to Truro from time to time anyway —'

'We run the Photo Gallery in Delabole. We go to Truro most months for updates -'

'Yes. On one of these trips I came across the Record Office and found they'd information about the Quarry — the minutes of all Board meetings, for example, since 1841. They even gave me copies of photographs of the key characters.'

'Is that where you learned about — what did you say his name was - Hobday?'

'Hockaday. Job Hockaday. Yes, that's how I know he had a long beard. He worked at the Delabole Slate Quarry from 1851 to 1899. He started as a clerk, rose to be Commercial Manager and ended up as Secretary to the Board — who met, by the way, in Plymouth. In his spare time Job was a pillar of the Methodist Church.'

They learned how Arno James, a well-known author and director, had been invited to stay for six months so he could turn Joe's raw material into a series of dramatic episodes.

'I handed over all my material. To be fair, he's stuck to the main facts – elaborated, of course, to make it watchable. He had other sources too.'

'Delabole Community Hall, which was fine for panto-mimes, was judged unfit to stage this,' explained Morwenna, '- it had to be put on outdoors.' Then the date was moved from April to January.

'April would have been fine. January is cold,' complained Joe. 'But we'd all signed contracts saying we'd perform come what may. That director's a real tyrant: drives us like slaves.'

'When does it go live?' asked George. 'It would be great to come along.'

'First night's next Friday,' said Morwenna. 'Our family are coming home for it. Joe's never been in a play before. They all want to see him in action.'

'Yes, it's rehearsals every evening from now on.' Joe glanced at his watch. 'In fact the next one starts in twenty minutes. Morwenna, we need to go.'

'We need to be going too, Sophie,' said George. 'We ought at least to think about the makeover before our next meal with Brian.'

She turned to explain to Morwenna. 'My cottage is in Treknow. We walked down. I'd rather not walk back up in the dark if I can help it.'

59

'You'll probably hear Arno bellowing as you go past the marquees,' said Joe. 'I wouldn't stop to watch. Otherwise you might end up in the cast. Believe me, you wouldn't want that.'

CHAPTER 8

'Right,' bellowed Arno, 'It's Saturday. In less than a week we'll be performing *Splits and Schisms* for real. With a live audience in those seats.' He turned and pointed to the newly-erected marquees behind him. The fact that the seats had not yet been installed was taken as artistic licence.

'They'll probably include your friends and neighbours. Jenny's done a fantastic job with publicity, with her posters and the local radio. I was told today that all the seats for both nights have been sold. They're coming to see you perform. They want to know the real story of Delabole. It's a gripping tale: the whole area needs to hear. So let's give it our very best shot.'

There were some mutterings amongst the cast. Most were surprised that the drama had sold so well. One or two had hoped, secretly, that ticket sales might be so bad that the whole performance would be cancelled. A few were still hankering after the traditional, indoor pantomime – though there was no chance of that this winter.

Arno continued, 'This evening will be the first run through using the real stage for Act Two. The life of Delabole from 1870 to 1900. We'll do each scene without a break. That'll help Laurie practise the lighting. We need to watch for any

61

mismatches in the positions where the actors are supposed to appear. Is everyone here?'

The cast looked around, checking faces. No-one appeared to be missing. Even Beth was in place. 'We're all here, Arno,' yelled Joe.

'This weekend will be the final time we'll rehearse in casual clothes and extra layers. I've agreed with Annabel that from tomorrow we can use her spare bedrooms as dressing rooms. I don't control the weather but the forecast for the next few days is not too bad. From tomorrow you can all get used to performing in the cold.'

'Let's hope the milder weather lasts for the whole week,' said Martin Thorne to Joe Stacey. Both men had parts that recurred. Martin played Dr Rendle, one of the more innovative Board Directors; Joe was the ever-present narrator, Job Hockaday. Nerves in their stomachs tightening, the two proceeded to their starting positions, ready for Act Two.

Job Hockaday stood on a covered podium at the side of the stage with a lectern in front of him, ready to begin.

Arno had agreed there was no real harm in him reading his narrative. Joe had pleaded, and the whole cast had backed him up, that it would be a terrific strain to have to learn the commentary off by heart. He only spoke at the start or end of most scenes; but he was expected to shout his lines.

Arno had wrestled with the idea of equipping the whole cast with radio mikes. To do so for everyone would be complicated – and expensive. How could radio mikes be protected from rain? And just one player forgetting to turn their mike off, when back in the dressing room, could lead to mayhem.

In the end he had settled on three well-protected microphones fixed to different parts of the stage. These would be coordinated by Laurie Lane.

Since the car park had never been used to perform anything, its acoustics were unknown. An open space was always difficult. No-one knew how audible the microphones would make the performance. All he could do now was to hope for the best.

'OK, we're all ready: let's go,' shouted the director.

'Fellow-citizens of Delabole, let me continue my tale,' bellowed Job.

'We ended Act One with the Great Quarry Disaster of 1869. There was terrible loss of life: in all sixteen people died – each one a Delabole local. I have to tell you that one of those bodies – that of young Fannie Wallis, who we saw talking to Robert Cowling – was not found for four long years.'

Job paused, imagining the shudder going round the audience.

'Imagine the grief, and the guilt, of her father, Greg Wallis. He had been so keen to earn the honour of telling the Quarry Captain about the collapsing quartz vein, so eager to trail across the Quarry to find him, that he wasn't where his daughter expected when she brought his afternoon tea. Which led directly to that young girl's death, beneath thousands of tons of rock and rubble. We can only hope her death happened quickly.'

Another pause.

'There were other consequences for the Quarry – consequences that even the Board of Directors, far away in Plymouth, making but a token contribution to the Disaster Fund, could appreciate. For it took three whole years for the workers at the Quarry to shift the rubble that had fallen; three years till they could start once more to produce slate; three years before I, Job Hockaday - the newly appointed Commercial Manager - had any slate to sell; three long years before the Quarry could make any sort of profit.'

'Even after that the road was not smooth. For in the 1870s the whole country was in recession - more "stop" than "go". Now growth means new factories with new workers. They in turn require new homes and slate for their roofs. Conversely, when growth is absent, so is the market for slate. In those days no one bought slate for decoration. So recession meant a slump in demand.'

Job stopped and shook his head. 'There were simply no funds to develop the Quarry further.'

Then he looked up, his face happier. 'Even so, all was not hopeless. Amongst the Directors was one with a spark of imagination: Dr Charles Rendle. The son of an earlier Director, he could see new ways of working needed to be found; and he was prepared to fight to achieve them.'

The spotlight on Job faded and Arno launched into a

critique. Inch by inch the amateurs of Delabole were being cajoled into a plausible looking outfit.

Darkness was closing in as George and Sophie puffed back up the path from Trebarwith Strand. They had crept past the rehearsal preparations, helped to maintain a low profile by the marquees across the car park.

'There's one thing I want to do before it's completely dark,' said George. 'It's Saturday evening. I've had the keys to Ivy Cottage for twenty four hours, yet I've not set foot in the garden. Ever, in fact. When I came with Dan Taylor last October it was raining so much we didn't even open the back door. Where did we put Brian's torch?'

Sophie was not much of a gardener but she was interested to see whatever her friend had acquired. Buying a cottage plus all its contents was like winning a free ticket to a giant boot sale.

'I wonder how Lily managed her garden? She probably had someone to help her; but did it end up a rubbish heap or a masterpiece?'

'I guess it'll be something in between.'

'If there are any fruit trees you'll be glad of them next summer. The trouble is, they might be a bit hard to make out.'

'We won't see much, Sophie, but I'd like to make sense of the location. Do you reckon we'll see the lights from the drama?'

After a short search they found a back door key in a

kitchen drawer and stepped outside.

'It's tidy,' observed Sophie, as George shone her torch around.

The garden was a sensible size - ideal for an absentee owner. Half was lawn and the rest assigned to vegetables. It would not be hard to maintain.

'I reckon the fruit bushes are round the side, George. Probably blackcurrants. I love blackcurrants: I hope you'll invite me down in the summer.'

They were about to go back in – it really was too dark to see much – when George spotted a glint of light on glass at the end of the garden.

'Bless her, Lily even had a greenhouse. That answers the question about whether she was a serious gardener.'

'She might just have used it for afternoon naps. On sunny days it's probably warmer than her cottage.'

'Let's see.' George stepped cautiously down the path – they'd both had enough of surprises the evening before – and opened the greenhouse door. Sophie followed close behind.

'Look, here's her chair. She did use it for naps.'

George shone her torch around. 'You know, Sophie, this hasn't been visited since Lily died. Here's her newspaper.'

Sophie took it, glanced at it, was unimpressed. 'Come on Watson, you can do better than that.'

'Alright Holmes, what am I missing?'

'The date on the newspaper. It's mid-April - but not 2008.'

George took it from her. 'Wow. Why on earth was she looking at the North Cornwall Chronicle for 1925?'

'For that matter, how did she find it? I mean, it's the original paper, not just a recent copy. They can't be that easy to get hold of.'

It was another question for the Lily Taylor portfolio – but not one that was easy to answer. George picked up the newspaper and they returned indoors.

Now night had fallen, after several months with no heating, the cottage felt cold and damp.

'Remind me to push Brian for an electrician,' said George. 'I can't believe Lily could cope with this much cold. There must be a trick to get the storage heaters working. Without them it's like Siberia.'

'It's too cold to sort cupboards now. Why don't we take our shopping upstairs and make up the beds? Then we could arrive at Brian's early and have nice hot showers.'

'Good idea.'

Alice Southgate didn't seem surprised to see them arrive early.

'Brian's out. He had an emergency call. I don't want to sound rude, but he warned me you might want the bathroom?' Both women nodded.

'Have you brought towels? Which of you'll go first?'

Brian returned as George emerged from the bathroom in her best jeans and jumper and Sophie took her place.

'Welcome. Come into the kitchen: watch the master chef

67

at work.'

'Fine. By the way, where's Alice?'

'When I'm cooking she normally retreats to her study. She's head teacher here in Delabole so there are always reports to read or write. She enjoys the meal more if she doesn't know how I've cooked it.'

Although these words suggested an idiosyncratic chef, Brian was obviously competent at cooking basic meals such as chilli con carne.

'Has your first day in Treknow gone ok?' he asked George, as he diced an onion and started to heat the oil.

'We haven't spent much of it in Treknow. I was in Wade-bridge, ordering a wood burning stove.'

'Good idea. It felt bitterly cold there last night. It'll take a while to arrive, mind.'

'It won't, as it happens. Sophie and I persuaded them we were special. The stove will be delivered on Tuesday.'

'Well done. I won't enquire how you pressed your case. They're normally very busy.'

'All above board, I assure you. No bribes – not financial ones, anyway. Talking of heating, my night storage heaters aren't working. Could you recommend an electrician?'

'Sure. It's probably the way the electricity was turned off. There's a chap called Laurie Lane who lives in Tintagel. He does most of the electrical work around here. I'll get his number once this lot's simmering. Mention my name and you can probably persuade him to come at short notice.'

'Great. While you're at it, do you have the name of a

plumber that could refit our bathroom? Save us trekking up here every day. I know it's silly but I really don't fancy using Lily's bath.'

'The best one, I think, would be Paul Wood. He's local too – based in Delabole. Alice and I had him upgrade our bathroom last year – did you like it, by the way? He would understand you're a special case too.'

Brian's chilli con carne, when he had dished it out, proved delicious.

'It's a good job we didn't have much lunch,' said Sophie complacently, as she eyed her substantial portion.

'We just had a bite at the Port William,' explained George. 'Mind you, we met an interesting couple, didn't we?'

'Yes. Joe and Morwenna. They were telling us about some outdoor drama that's taking place next week. It sounded really exciting. Do you know anything about it?'

'You're talking about *Splits and Schisms*,' said Brian. 'The dramatised history of Delabole. Alice knows all about that, don't you dear?'

'It's the only event being talked about in Delabole – has been for months. I get all the memos from Arno as I'm the makeup lady. I said yes as I'm only needed for the final stages. I haven't time to be there night after night - I've a school to run and governors to manage.'

Alice looked across to her husband. 'Brian will be in the audience on both nights. I've a feeling, mind, they've sold all

69

the tickets – astonishing, really. The pantomime never sells out even though they've only seats for a hundred. You'd best ask Jenny: she's the Tourist Officer in Camelford. She's the one handling publicity and ticket sales.'

'If you can't get tickets for the main performance, try the dress rehearsal,' suggested Brian. 'That way you'd at least see a near-final production. It'd be a good way of starting to learn the history of Delabole.'

'As seen by a left-wing writer,' added Alice.

George wasn't clear whether this was a damning condemnation or an accolade.

Even so, the dress rehearsal would be well worth seeing. There wouldn't be much else going on around Delabole in this coming week.

CHAPTER 9

George woke up pleasantly warm in her thick duvet on Sunday morning and saw it was already half past nine. She luxuriated in the silence for a moment before forcing herself to get up and face the cold. Brr... how early dare she ring the electrician?

She put on as many layers as she could fit over her slim body, including her thick fleece, and stepped downstairs. She was surprised to find Sophie already in the kitchen, cooking porridge. 'We might as well start off the day warm: my mum always said this was the best start-up food in winter.'

'I'll ring the electrician after breakfast. Those night storage heaters must still work. With a bit of luck we'll be warmer by tomorrow.'

'We could go and introduce ourselves to our neighbour. His cottage might be warmer than ours.'

'It'd be nice to think so. What I'd like to do first, though, is to go through the cupboards. I got some empty boxes in the supermarket. We'll make a pile in the hall of things for the skip. If we keep moving we'll stay less cold.'

'The old lady didn't keep much rubbish.'

'No, but there's no doubt her tastes were old fashioned.

71

We need to chuck everything unless we really like it.'

'Or it's a valuable antique.'

'I doubt we'll find many of those.'

Two hours later the women were emptying cupboards in a cheerful mood.

Laurie Lane had agreed to come at three – 'On my way to rehearsal at Trebarwith,' he'd said. George had gleaned that he was the effects man on *Splits and Schisms*. She hoped he could have some effect on her cottage.

The cupboards had been tackled at speed. George was relieved that Sophie had not started to wax sentimental – or arty - about the old items, as they were transferred to the boxes in the hall.

The living room and kitchen/diner had been cleared. They were now going up and down stairs with each load of discards. If she got much warmer, George thought, she'd have to take off her outer fleece.

It was as she finished emptying Lily's clothes from the chest of drawers in her bedroom that George made her discovery.

'Hey, Sophie, I've solved one riddle about Lily Taylor.'

'What's that?' asked Sophie, coming through from the second bedroom.

'I've found out where she got her old newspaper. Look.' She pulled out the newspaper which was lining the bottom dressing-table drawer.

'The North Cornwall Chronicle, April 1925. Maybe that's

when her parents moved in here?'

'She must have spotted it and decided to catch up on local news.'

It was progress but not the whole story; and George didn't like to leave a problem half-solved. 'To take an edition of the paper outside, there must have been something that caught her attention. Come on, we're due a coffee break - let's work it out.'

As the kettle boiled, they spread out the eighty four year old newspaper from the greenhouse across the table. Most of the events recorded seemed irreducibly trivial. Then, on page five, Sophie found a news article about Delabole. 'This might be the one.'

The article described the arrival of the new curate in Delabole, the Rev Jack Bucknall. A photograph showed a dark, handsome man in a black cassock. His eyes seemed to gleam with enthusiasm, presumably at his new posting. In his right hand he held an unlit pipe.

'He looks like a man to charm the ladies,' suggested Sophie. 'They'd be fainting in the aisles at his sermons.'

'Lily wouldn't – she'd only be five when he got there - too young to need a sweetheart. He might have been her Sunday school teacher. I wonder how long he stayed?'

Sophie was reading the article. 'He was a controversial choice. Not just a polite-but-harmless minister, trying to please everyone. You can't tell from the picture, but he was well over six foot tall.'

George looked further down the page. 'His previous post

73

was with a vicar renowned as a Christian Marxist. When you think about it, 1925 was only eight years after the Russian revolution.'

'So young Jack was a militant socialist. I wonder how he got on with the owners of Delabole Quarry?'

'Perhaps that was what intrigued Lily. Were there any later newspapers?'

Five minutes searching showed that all the downstairs drawers contained modern newspapers. There were a few other last-century newspapers in the upstairs wardrobes, but they were even older than the one in the greenhouse – so did not mention the curate.

'We need to find out how long Bucknall stayed in De-labole,' said Sophie. He and Lily might have had a relation-ship. If he was, say, twenty five when she was ten, he'd still be only thirty five when she was twenty.'

'It should be possible to tell if he was married. We're talking Anglican priests here, remember, not celibate Catho-lics.'

George had decided mid-day was a good time to catch their neighbour.

'Even if he's still in bed he can hardly complain at being roused.'

'If he's had another live-in hot water bottle she'll be gone.'

George thought Sophie was being harsh. The two women banged their front door noisily to give their neighbour some warning, walked to the road and then back up the path to Holly Cottage. There was no bell so George knocked as hard as she could.

For a few seconds there was no response. Sophie was about to suggest their neighbour was sleeping off a hang-over and they should try again later when they heard a shuffling sound from inside. Then they heard the door being unlocked; finally it opened.

A bleary-eyed, stocky man with a dark beard, dressed in a silk dressing gown but with bare feet, stared at them. He looked surprised to see visitors.

'Hello, I thought it was time we introduced ourselves,' began George. 'We're your new neighbours.'

'Ah, yes. I'd heard someone had completed the purchase recently.' He had a fine, melodic voice. 'Please come in. My cottage isn't very warm, I'm afraid – that's why I was still in bed. I was fine-tuning the script. You've arrived just in time.'

'To help with the script?' This wasn't the start she'd expected.

'No, George, idiot.' Sophie turned to face the neighbour. 'You're Arno James, aren't you? The famous author and director – creator of outdoor dramas. I'm very pleased to meet you, my name's Sophie – Sophie Collins.'

'And I'm George Gilbert,' added George quickly. She didn't want to be left out. 'I own Ivy Cottage and Sophie's an old friend; she's come down to help me get it operational. We only got here on Friday.'

'Come right in, ladies, come in. I'm afraid I can offer only a limited range of drinks. Would you prefer coffee, brandy or both?'

'Coffee would be fine,' replied George hastily.

'If this isn't a good time we can come back later,' added Sophie.

'No, it's fine. I'm due for a break anyway.' Arno disappeared through the open doorway into his kitchen.

The women sat on the settee and glanced around. The cottage was a mirror-image of Ivy – the two must have been built at the same time but Holly had been furnished to attract long-term lets. It looked pleasantly modern but a little bland.

'Your cottage is warmer than ours. Is that the night storage heaters?' shouted George, as she heard Arno filling the kettle and clattering mugs.

'I suppose so,' he shouted back. 'They're hot in the mornings and cool down over the day. I'm out every evening with rehearsals so that doesn't bother me; I don't eat in very often. It takes a lot of time writing and producing a new drama. I generally eat at one of the local pubs – with some of the cast, if I can contrive it. You'd be welcome to join us.'

He reappeared, carrying a tray of mugs.

'Tell me about yourselves. As a writer I'm always interested to meet new people – especially if they can be worked into future material.'

George wasn't sure she wanted to feature in Arno's portfolio but she was happy to sketch out her situation.

'I'm an industrial mathematician. I do work for all sorts of companies, helping them with technical problems – especially when they have to handle uncertainty. I came into some money last year and decided to invest it in a little cottage in Cornwall. I happen to know the doctor in Delabole – he was a friend of my late husband - and he alerted me when his patient, Lily Taylor, died. I came down to have a look, fell in love with the cottage and its location, put in an offer – and here I am.'

'Hm. Sounds like the basis of a short play on its own. What about you, Sophie?'

'I'm the complete opposite. I'm an artist, designer, photographer. I live in London too, though I was brought up in this part of the world. George told me about her new cottage at Christmas. I managed to arrange things so I could be here to help her settle in. So here I am, too.'

'Please help yourselves to coffee. Sugar? No, both far too slim.' Arno took a spoonful to illustrate the converse.

'I presume you're on a long-term let?' asked George. 'How long have you been the tenant?'

'I came at the start of October. I was invited down by Della Howell – she's the chairwoman of the local Women's Institute. Della had the idea of a drama based around the Quarry. It's 140 years since the Quarry Disaster and they wanted to mark it in some way. I saw lots of potential. The Quarry's been in operation for seven hundred years and is the hub of life in the village. The nineteenth century is a particularly interesting time. As you'll see if you come to the production next weekend.'

'We'd love to; but we heard you'd sold all the tickets.'

'What my doctor friend suggested,' added George, sensing an opportunity, 'was to ask if there was any chance of coming to the dress rehearsal? We'd keep very quiet.'

'You're not the first ones to ask about the dress rehearsal. The trouble is, if you have any audience at all it becomes another performance. That makes it harder for me – as director - to challenge faults and make improvements. Which, to be honest, I still need to do. The whole drama is an ambitious venture, carried out by a pretty inexperienced cast.'

There was a silence for a moment. The women concentrated on their coffees. How could they deploy their charms? Arno was obviously wrestling with competing ambitions.

'You said you did photography, Sophie? Have you any experience of outdoor video recordings?'

George saw the way his mind was working.

'Had you thought of recording the production, Arno? We could do the filming. We've both got high definition video cameras. Then, assuming the videos came out OK, you could hire an editor to collate them.'

Sophie saw the need to fan his enthusiasm. 'I'm sure all the villagers would buy copies. They'd sell for years afterwards in the local Tourist Office. You might even make some money.'

Arno started to look for the snags. 'The trouble is, you couldn't stand in front of the audience. All you could get would be long distant footage or pictures from the side.'

'That wouldn't be true at the dress rehearsal. You say you're not allowing any audience. So we could stand right in front of the stage and take close-ups.'

'Then put the cameras at the back, up by the road or something, for the performances themselves.'

'Unless we're unlucky with the weather, the perform-ances will look much the same. With six tries at recordings, an editor could have a field day.'

Arno gave a sigh. 'All right, girls, you've convinced me. If it doesn't work we've not lost anything. You're hired – meta-phorically, at least.'

The director glanced at the wall clock. 'Hell, is that the time? I'll have to throw you out. I've got a Sunday lunch date down the road at the Mill House. We'll have to carry on this conversation later.'

CHAPTER 10

George and Sophie returned from their lunch, roast beef with multiple vegetables including creamed celeriac, at the Trewarmett Inn, shortly before three. George had been tempted by the chocolate fudge dessert which she'd spied on a neighbouring table, but they didn't dare to risk being late for Laurie Lane.

Ivy Cottage, when they got back, was as cold as ever. Neither woman removed her fleece. They had just made themselves a pot of tea, to enjoy in their striking new mugs, when they saw a white van pulling up outside.

Laurie Lane, when he entered, was tall and cheerful, with a strong Cornish accent.

'Yes, I'd be glad of a mug of tea, m'dear, but let's see if I can sort your problem first. None of them night storage heaters working, you say? No heat at all? Maybe a master fuse has blown.'

It took the electrician only a few seconds to locate the electricity meters and master switches over the front door; to find a stool in the kitchen to give him extra height; and to inspect the equipment.

He muttered as he worked. 'Dear old Lily Taylor would have known something was wrong and got it sorted if she was still here. She wouldn't have left other people a problem; it won't be anything too drastic.'

Two chilly women watched with hope in their hearts.

'I think that'll do the trick,' the electrician announced a minute later. 'Mind, you won't be able to tell for sure till tomorrow morning. Those heaters only charge up in the dead of night, see.'

Gratefully he took the proffered mug of tea. 'I can see why you wanted me so urgent. Hell, it's cold in here, ain't it? It's almost warmer outside.'

'We've been here less than forty eight hours,' explained George. 'We've hardly had time to notice the cold.'

Something of an overstatement, thought Sophie, but she didn't say anything out loud.

'While I'm here, shall I check if you've got any loft insulation?' asked their knight in shining armour. 'Old people like Lily Taylor don't always realise they need it; they just suffer the cold.'

'If you wouldn't mind,' responded George. 'Once I've got some heat I don't mind spending money to retain it. We haven't even found the loft yet.'

Laurie led the way upstairs and wandered from room to room, his eyes searching for the entrance hatch. Finally he spotted a wooden square in the corner of Sophie's bedroom ceiling.

'All I need now is a pole to open it.'

'Would this do?' asked Sophie, offering him a three foot wooden stick with a hook at one end. 'I didn't know what it

81

was; almost threw it away.'

'That's the one.' Laurie gave the hatch a poke and it swung down. In the darkness behind something was glinting. The electrician reached up once more with the pole and gave a pull; a metal ladder appeared and swung down.

'Just as I'd hoped.' Laurie pulled the ladder down. 'That's very smooth: like it's been recently oiled. Someone's been up here in the last few months.'

'I don't think so,' replied George. 'The cottage has been empty since Lily died.'

'Maybe the old lady used to go up there herself then? She was quite fit for an eighty eight year old. Anyway, let's see the state of her insulation. Do you have a torch?'

George handed over the torch she had borrowed from Brian. 'D'you mind if I follow you? I'd like to know what's up there but it's a bit daunting to go on my own.'

'You're dressed too smartly to go crawling round an attic,' she whispered to Sophie, who looked like she wanted to add herself to the party.

Laurie had already disappeared. Swiftly George climbed after him and stuck her head into the loft. She spotted a switch half-hidden under the nearest rafter. She tried it: a split-second later the loft was plunged into light from a bulb hanging from the main beam.

'Well done, I missed that. My, this is a well-organised loft,' commented Laurie as he peered around. 'This end has got a set of boards and there's not much rubbish. Lofts normally collect all sorts of clutter over the years. Even so, I find it hard to believe Lily came up here on her own.'

'How does it score on insulation?'

Laurie gestured towards the far end. There were no boards there but a thick layer of fibreglass lay between each cross beam.

'You can see - there's plenty. With that depth of fibreglass it's probably been put in recently, on the latest government scheme. Maybe that's why the loft's so empty – they'd chuck everything out before they started.'

George cut to the chase. The important thing was that there was insulation. 'So once the night storage heating's working, it should stay warm?'

'Not too cold, anyway,' said Laurie cautiously.

They were about to climb back down when George spotted a shelf rack, set against the end wall. 'Can I borrow the torch a minute, please?'

She peered at the contents, which were a series of books. 'It looks like Lily's diaries. One for every year. They go right back to 1940, when she'd be...'

'Nineteen or twenty,' said Laurie, now beside her.

'They're her private diaries. We ought to burn them.'

'I don't suppose they contain much scandal; just local history. You never know – they might be worth publishing. I mean, if Arno James can breeze in from nowhere and write a sell-out drama about Delabole, what might someone who was actually here have to say? Could be a best seller.'

'Are you two alright?' Sophie's distant voice reached them up the ladder.

'We've been here long enough, Laurie. I'll take one down to have a look.'

Which one? In the end George picked the first in the series. She noticed that the following year -1941 - was missing. All the other years as far as 1970 seemed to be in place.

'I made you some more tea,' called Sophie, as the two explorers descended and Laurie shut the loft.

'Bless you,' responded Laurie. 'I can't stay much longer though. The tyrant will want me before long.'

'You make him out to be an ogre. Is that fair?'

'He's very driven. I suppose you need to be to make a production happen. It's not the way things usually work. Promising to do a job "directly" round here normally means you'll get around to it within a month.'

'Is he hard on everyone?'

'I cop it the worst. Maybe that's 'cos I've no one to share my responsibilities. There's no-one else he can yell at when the lighting's not spot on or the sound effects are late. He behaves ... well, he behaves as though it's a West End pro-duction. I've never seen half the equipment he wants, never even heard of one or two items. It's a very ambitious pro-duction. Much bigger than anything this area's ever seen.'

'We met Arno this morning, actually. He lives next door. We might have joined your technical team. We volunteered to make a video of the event.'

Laurie seemed at first surprised; then reassured. 'I can see why that happened. Two smart women – both much

84

closer to his own age than the girls in the cast. I wish you well. Though, if my experience is anything to go by, you should prepare yourselves for a few explosions along the way.'

CHAPTER 11

'Did that Morwenna say something about a gallery in Delabole?' asked George.

It was Monday morning – and, thanks to Laurie, the cottage was warm. The night storage heaters were once more working. Getting their breakfast was no longer like being a chef in the Antarctic.

'You're thinking of buying some modern pictures? Good idea. Now you've ditched so many of Lily's photographs, the walls look rather bare.'

'We'd better go this morning. The scaffolding men are here this afternoon.'

'We don't need to be here for them?'

'Strictly speaking, no. All their work's outside. I'd still like to meet them - and I'm sure they'll be glad to have mugs of tea once the scaffolding's up.'

'It's going to be another busy day, then. Tonight we'll be attending a rehearsal of *Splits and Schisms*, taking our cameras – we must make sure the batteries are fully charged. I gather from Laurie that the cast are in costume this week. It'll be a rehearsal for us too.'

An hour later they were driving to Delabole: Sophie at the

wheel, George glad of the chance to be driven. The artist took them up a narrow road which started with a sharp hairpin bend, but got to Delabole quicker. George was thankful they didn't meet anyone coming the other way.

George spotted Stacey's Gallery halfway down the main street. Parking anywhere near it was another matter. Eventually Sophie found a gap between two parked cars and they walked back a quarter of a mile.

The Gallery was based around large-scale photographs of North Cornwall, either framed or printed on canvas. Practically every one had been taken in bright sunshine. 'You'd think it never rains here,' commented George.

The two were the only customers. Morwenna recognised them but sensibly left them to browse.

'Sophie, do you reckon we want one or two really big pictures; or more small ones?

'You need a long thin one over the fireplace, anyway. How about this one of Padstow harbour?'

George remembered the source of her legacy. 'That's very appropriate. What striking colours.'

'The photographer must have taken that very early one June - probably standing on the outer jetty, looking across to the town. There's not a soul in view - just hundreds of boats.

'Yes, I'll definitely have that.'

After discussion two more substantial photographs were chosen. One was Trebarwith Strand beach, with the waves pounding in onto the rocks and a storm-lashed Gull Rock further out to sea. The other, Sophie declared, was a view

across Bossiney Bay, taken from the cliffs above Rocky Valley
– 'that's the far side of Tintagel.'

'That's one for the landing and one for the main bedroom. I'll need two or three more, but it's not far to come, is
it?'

'Is Joe practising his lines somewhere?' asked Sophie, as
George started to pay for her purchases.

'I doubt it. We only need one of us here on a Monday,'
replied Morwenna. 'He's probably doing more research on
Delabole.'

Her reply reminded George of one of her puzzles.

'Does his research cover the Rev Jack Bucknall? We found
an old newspaper about him at Ivy Cottage. Lily Taylor had
been reading it just before she died. He seemed an interesting character.'

Morwenna smiled. 'Jack was a character alright: though
very divisive. He split the Anglican church here. After a while
the churchwardens and established flock left and met over
the Co-op. At the same time Jack built up a much larger
congregation to replace them with his left-leaning preaching. It was very charismatic.'

'Presumably he was on the side of the workers and
against the management? Had there been much industrial
strife at the Quarry?'

'You'll see if you come to *Splits and Schisms* – you are
coming, aren't you? One scene is about a strike in 1888. It
only lasted ten days. They didn't have Trades Unions in
those days so the management could do more or less what

they wanted. The workers had no alternative employment.'

'Couldn't they go somewhere else?' asked Sophie.

'Cars hadn't been invented - they couldn't commute to jobs in Wadebridge. The men just couldn't afford a long strike.'

Morwenna paused. 'Joe tells me the management could be really vicious. That probably built up a lot of resentment over the years. Which was why Jack had such an impact.'

'What happened in the end?'

'There was a long-running battle: it lasted several years. The leaders of the church community kept lobbying to have him moved but he had support from the Bishop of Truro. In the end the church's sponsors took against him. Once the funding had run out the Bishop had no choice but to let him go.'

'It sounds a dramatic tale - more exciting than most curacies. It'd make a good book; but it doesn't explain why Lily Taylor was interested in 2008,' commented George.

'Was Jack married?' asked Sophie. 'Lily can't have been that much younger than him.'

'He was married when he came to Delabole. To a Cornish girl, I think. You'd need to ask Joe.'

'What are your husband's best sources?'

'The old folk in the village. The Methodist Church puts on a Community Lunch every Tuesday. They're always glad to chat. They've given Joe memories as far back as the 1920s.'

'Are they reliable?'

'There are a few tangles. Sometimes Joe had to bring

conflicting sources together – occasionally over a pint. Mind you, that wouldn't have worked for Lily. She was a strict Methodist. The process has taken Joe a long time.'

'What about events before anyone here was alive? Isn't *Splits and Schisms* mainly about life in the nineteenth century?'

'The old folk Joe's talked to - his primary sources - have an interest in their own pasts. Most recall being told key events in the lives of their parents and grandparents. They lived all their lives here as well.'

'I thought you were digging in for the morning,' complained Sophie, as the two women returned to their car, clutching three large parcels. 'It's one thing to show a polite interest in her husband's hobby; you sounded like you wanted to take it over.'

'No. Morwenna didn't mind – she was glad someone was interested. As a new homeowner I want to know what the inhabitants of Delabole do with their spare time. We did learn something about Lily, though.'

'Well, that she was teetotal. So what?'

'Brian wanted us to believe that the old lady had been found drunk in her bath. How could that happen if she never drank alcohol?'

'Could she have drunk it unawares? Say... if a friend had given her a sherry trifle which she'd overloaded in sherry. If Lily never usually drank, even a small amount might have made her tipsy.'

'It's a question for Brian when we next see him. Right now we'd better get back for the scaffold-builders.'

Going back to a warm Ivy Cottage was not the trial it had been. The large skip George had ordered the week before was parked outside. A large amount of bric-a-brac was soon removed from the hallway.

'Just as well we're rid of that,' said George. 'It'll make it easier for the stove men.' She was looking forward to having a wood-burning stove; the night storage heaters might be lukewarm by the evening.

The scaffolding lorry arrived as the women were having lunch. Once assured they were in the right place, the two men eyed up the cottage for a few moments. Then they set to work.

George and Sophie kept out of the way; there was plenty of tidying needed inside. By now George had got hold of the plumber. The man had promised to be with them the following afternoon – he, too, was in *Splits and Schisms* so could drop in en route to rehearsal.

With their resolve to attend the final rehearsals, the women knew they would have to work hard at the cottage in the daytime. At least that was no longer a Siberian nightmare.

Two hours later there was a knock at the door. 'D'you want to see what we've done, m'dear?'

George was glad of an excuse to stop cleaning. Slipping on her fleece, she followed him outside.

A series of platforms had been erected: planks side by side, resting on the scaffolding, linked together by ladders. The first spanned the kitchen, the second ran past George's bedroom, the third was on the roof, surrounding the chimney.

'Would you like to climb up?'

George was daunted but unwilling to let it show. Steadily she climbed over the kitchen roof, the constructor close behind. She was pleased to see a hand-rail.

Telling herself not to look down, she climbed once more, this time to the planks stretching past her bedroom window.

'You get a good view down the valley.'

George gripped the hand-rail before looking down. The car park at Trebarwith Strand could be seen round the edge of the hillside, with the slate-grey village and the sea beyond.

'D'you want to go right to the top?'

The honest answer was no, but this might be her only opportunity. The analyst wished she'd thought to put on gloves.

George seized the next ladder. The wind was much stronger out of the shelter of the cottage.

Rung by rung she pulled herself up, her hands very cold. Finally, she eased herself onto the highest platform. Thank goodness there was a hand-rail; she gripped it tightly.

'We're really high now,' the man told her. George couldn't think of a sensible response.

'You can see the stage for the drama. We helped build

that.'

George turned from the chimney to look down the Trebarwith valley. It was four o'clock and starting to get dark. Even so the structures needed for the drama – the two-level stage and the line of marquees – were clear.

'You'd get a good view from here.'

'You wouldn't hear much, though. That's enough for today, I'm very impressed. Can we go down now, please?'

Back in the cottage, Sophie had already made the men a pot of tea. 'I assume you both want sugar?'

'How did you know? Hey, do you have biscuits?'

'There's an amazing view across the valley, Sophie,' enthused George. 'You can see right down to the stage.'

'Do you think, if we mounted a camera up there, we'd get any worthwhile pictures?'

'It'd be worth a try.'

The man who had accompanied George wanted to be helpful. 'We're in no hurry to take the scaffolding down, m'dear. People often want it left up so they can paint their cottages. If you don't mind me saying, that chimney of yours could do with a fresh coat.'

As the men prepared to leave, Sophie whispered to George, 'Will you take me up tomorrow?'

'Course; but you'll need to make sure you're wearing suitable clothing. It's not the place for a short skirt.'

93

CHAPTER 12

Early that Monday evening the two women prepared themselves for the rehearsal. George had a suitcase full of warm clothes to choose from. Sophie, it turned out, had just one pair of designer jeans amongst her myriad dresses and skirts. She was too tall and slim to borrow any trousers from George, but at least the cottage owner could provide her with a couple of extra jumpers. Cagoules and woolly hats completed their garb. It wasn't raining but that wasn't guaranteed to continue.

'Hey - what'll we do with the cameras if it does start to rain?' asked Sophie, as they set off down the hillside, finding their way with the aid of Brian's torch.

'Mine certainly wasn't sold as waterproof. We can keep them dry, I suppose, under our cagoules – though we're not the BBC. If Arno wanted to film the event whatever the weather, he should have hired professionals. We'll do our best, but it can't possibly be as good.'

'Probably not – though we're not novices.' Even in rural Cornwall Sophie was mindful of her artistic reputation. 'That's one thing we need to watch out for – undercover locations that we could film from in the rain.'

'We need to take footage while it's fine. They're going to

be in costume from now on, Laurie said, so one enactment will look much like another.'

'They may not do everything in the correct order, though. If Arno thinks one scene's weak he may give it extra attention. I suspect he's a brutal perfectionist – probably far too good for this level of production.'

'It'd be as well to have a programme, wouldn't it,' said George. 'When d'you reckon those will be available?'

'We'll ask Arno at a break in rehearsal. Even a rough draft would be useful. Hey – do you reckon we could get hold of the script?'

'Arno said yesterday that he was still refining it – that was his excuse for being in bed when we arrived.'

'He's a script-writer – used to making up stories. You can't believe everything he says. It must be finalised by now.'

Down in the car-park there was a hum of excitement. They would be performing before a live, paying audience in just four days time. Reality was starting to hit home.

To be fair to Arno, his methods, whatever they were, seemed to have inspired his cast. Most seemed confident of their roles. Preparations had been going on for so long that it was a relief the end was in sight. Most were excited rather than daunted.

The cast were unknown to George or Sophie. Then they spotted someone they knew. Laurie Lane was flitting between his control van and various pieces of equipment, making sure all the connections were working. He gave the women a wave. George walked over to tell him her cottage heating was now working. Now, though, his mind was on other problems.

'The smoke generators only arrived this morning,' he explained, 'from the Alhambra in Plymouth. I've hardly had time yet to find out how they work. I don't know how long to allow between them being turned on and the smoke starting to billow out. There's a dial on each machine to control the volume; goodness only knows what setting we need. So you might have nothing but smoke to film in the Disaster Scene. That's the mid-point of the whole production, by the way.'

George wanted to ask him if he had a full list of the scenes, but before she could do so he'd rushed off to check his loudspeakers.

Sophie had spotted that Arno was standing alone and went over to greet him. For a second he looked unsure who she was – she'd been wearing a flamboyant emerald green dress the day before, not jeans; her distinctive golden hair was now tucked away under her balaclava – then he spotted her camera, remembered, and shook her hand. 'It should be a good night for a first run through – not much wind, anyway. Could you bring the results around tomorrow morning to let me have a first viewing?'

There was no time for Sophie to ask more. The rehearsal was about to begin. Arno bellowed a few more instructions then there was total silence.

'Let's take one side of the stage each,' whispered George. They scurried to matching positions on the edge of the car-park, mounted video cameras onto their tripods and awaited the action.

In the darkness there was the sound of a Cornish folk song. The melody came from speakers in front of the stage; but the stereophonic effect made it appear to come from up the hillside towards Treknow; and to grow louder as it got nearer - as if a wandering band of minstrels were heading down from Treknow. As the song ended a spotlight shone onto one side of the stage.

Two cameras, on either side of the stage, were trained on whatever would happen next.

'Ladies and gentlemen, fellow citizens of Delabole,' shouted Joe Stacey in a Cornish lilt, from his podium off to the side of the stage, 'welcome to this re-enactment of the history of Delabole and its famous Slate Quarry. I could begin this story seven hundred years ago – for that is how long this Quarry has been operating. I know, though, that some of you are busy people, so we'll restrict ourselves to the abridged version. Tonight we will present key events for the Old Delabole Slate Company, from 1843 up to 1899.'

'Excellent,' thought George to herself. 'How many other Cornish villages could provide such a starting point? Yet I knew nothing at all about it until two days ago.' She glanced across to the silhouette of Sophie, peering carefully down onto her camera screen, hoping she was feeling the same.

Joe went on to introduce himself as Job Hockaday - a

97

manager at the Quarry for almost the whole period presented. The opening scene began a few moments later.

This showed the first Board Meeting of the Company in 1843. George found herself torn between wanting to listen to the dialogue – which was sparky, and suggested a great deal of conflict with the preceding owner, Thomas Avery – and trying to take close-ups shots of the various Board members as they spoke.

The trouble was that it was a rapid dialogue; and as soon as someone else began to speak, it took several seconds before she could work out who that was, and then refocus the camera.

It was very frustrating - made her realise how much work must go on behind the scenes in professional filming or live television.

In the end the analyst decided that tonight she would settle for a wide-angle record of the scene taking place on stage; and hope to add closer pictures of key players later. Armed with a full script an editor should be able to interlace the two. An additional record was being made by her friend. A lot of talking would be needed to make sure their videos were complementary.

George also tried to follow the story. It was ludicrous to be filming a drama about which she knew nothing. There was scope for personal improvement here as well. If Arno wouldn't help her maybe Joe could.

So hard was George concentrating, as scene followed scene,

that it was a surprise to realise that they were almost at the half-way point - the Quarry Disaster, mentioned earlier by Laurie Lane.

By now the analyst had refined her approach. She ignored Joe Stacey, not because his words were unimportant, but she found she was missing the start of each stage scene as she swung back her camera.

So although it was a surprise to hear voices above the main stage – she hadn't even realised there was a higher level stage - George was swiftly able to pan upwards and to catch the start of the drama, in which the faulty quartz seam cracked and Greg Wallis set off down the ladder and out across the valley to find the Quarry Captain.

The action moved to the lower stage. A man was pounding away at a block of slate with his pickaxe. Two girls came towards him, one his daughter. They wore short, white cotton dresses and socks up to their knees; and looked extremely cold. George felt sorry for them and was glad she wasn't playing either of their parts.

The men were in costume, too, but theirs were thick, warm jackets with jumpers underneath. She assumed the scene must be short and the girls would soon be back to a warm dressing room. Where was this located? She and Sophie had had no time to explore behind the scenes beforehand.

The scene ran on. A thundering, rumbling noise began then the lights which illuminated the hillside behind the stage started to glow and fade. The noise grew deafening as cascades of smoke erupted. One of the girls had dropped off the end of the stage. She disappeared from sight. The other had just started to climb to the "safety" of the top stage when the smoke appeared below her. She was lost to sight but her whimpers could be heard. George didn't know if these were part of the drama or had been induced by the smoke.

A few moments later the girl could be seen again, being helped off the top. If she had more lines to deliver they were not spoken. The youngster was choking and shivering, incapable of anything beyond an inaudible whisper.

Her rescuer gave her a hug and then ad-libbed to cover her. 'You stay here, m'dear. I'll go and help your dad. Don't worry, you'll be safe now.'

The spotlight went off the upper stage and the wretched girl was left in total darkness. George hoped there was a thick coat for her to put on.

The noise became intense. Then, on the other side of the stage, a party of men appeared offstage from the grassy valley, heading for the place where the second girl had last been seen. 'This is the last place I saw movement,' one of them muttered. 'Don't worry Greg, we'll find her – and the rest.'

Slowly the noise faded away and the lights on the hillside dimmed. A spotlight reappeared. Joe Stacey was once more illuminated in his pulpit.

'Ladies and gentlemen, as you can imagine, it will take us a while to sort out the after-effects of this Disaster. We therefore invite you to take a twenty-minute interval to warm yourselves up. Fish and chips, beef burgers, tea and coffee are all on sale from the van behind you. Twenty minutes. Be sure to be back here, though, if you want to discover what happened next.'

CHAPTER 13

It was late by the time George and Sophie returned to Ivy Cottage, exhausted but exhilarated. It wasn't that the rehearsal had overrun; it had been over before nine. After this the whole cast had decamped to the Port William Inn – this, seemingly, part of their nightly ritual. The 'camera girls' – as they found themselves dubbed - had been welcomed to join them and had been glad to do so.

'It's really clever of Arno to think of videoing the production,' said one of the cast to another, as they walked down the road through Trebarwith Strand. 'My missus'll be glad of copies for Christmas presents next year.'

'What's really clever of Arno is to claim the credit for every good thing that happens,' muttered George to Sophie, as she picked up this gem from the men in front.

'Maybe that's all genius ever is,' replied her colleague.

There was no doubt that one side-effect of being camera-girls had been to bring them closer together. Though they had shared a house, it was the first time they had ever combined on a project. The roles gave them a direct line into the whole production. It helped that both were attractive women, younger – but not much younger – than most of the men in the drama.

Both teenage girls had been taken home by their parents as soon as the rehearsal ended. They might not have had much appetite for socialising after their cold and smoke-sodden evenings but they weren't given the choice. Laurie confessed to George that he would need to reduce the volume control on the smoke machines before the next rehearsal. He was glad he hadn't been bawled out for the error by Arno.

The women had found themselves separated when they got to the Inn, but each was well capable of holding her own. They were glad to learn about the players – and how they interacted off-stage.

The only downside was the plod back to Treknow. This was now George's home village so she needed to own it. She judged it safer to walk than to accept a lift from one of the cast's drivers. Sophie would have been glad to seek a lift for them both from Arno - then realised his sports car was only a two-seater.

Tuesday was the day when Ivy Cottage's new stove was to be installed. The night storage heaters were gradually taking the edge off the cold, but George was looking forward to adding some direct heat.

The analyst had got dressed and had a large helping of porridge cooked and ready to eat before Sophie appeared, dressing gown thrown over pyjamas and long hair in a mess, looking half asleep. It wouldn't be worth initiating a discussion of the videos - or anything else - until breakfast was

103

over.

It was only when George had brewed coffee that a stuttering conversation began.

'Arno was interested in our videos, George. Said he'd like to take a first look this morning.'

'Well, sorry, I'm busy today. It's Tuesday – the day the comely Barry is to deliver our new stove. That's why the scaffolding came yesterday.'

Sophie put her hand over her mouth. 'George, I'm sorry – I forgot. You don't really need me, though, with the stove men. It'll be much better if I'm out of the way. Then you can make sure the stove goes exactly where you want it. Make sure you find out how to light the thing, mind.'

She paused. 'It'd be good to get some early feedback on the videos.'

George would have liked to have feedback too, but she could see Sophie was right. The Wadebridge stove men had said they would come at ten thirty; she didn't have long to make sure the cottage was ready.

Sophie came downstairs as the owner was on her knees, cleaning out the inglenook. She was once more wearing her emerald green dress.

'You're dressed to impress. It's the video the man wants to see.'

'Always best to give them a choice though.' Sophie smiled roguishly; George hoped she was only play-acting.

'Take your time: learn as much as you can. No doubt Arno has experience of making videos as well as all his other skills.

Do your best to keep his expectations modest - and see if you can get hold of a script.'

'Do I need to take a front door key?'

'Don't bother. The plumbing man's coming after lunch for the bathroom. I won't be going far.'

Sophie disappeared. George had just finished her cleaning when she glimpsed a van with the words 'Fire Up with Wadebridge Stoves' splashed across it, parking in the road outside. Ivy Cottage's refurbishment was about to begin.

'There's no doubt, when this beast goes in, it'll make you warm, m'dear,' assured Barry who, to George's surprise, had jumped out of the van after the fitters. Did he often help with installations?

She hoped Sophie would not return too soon. Her absence might speed up their work-rate.

'Our longest-serving fitters: Eric and Fred.' The two men used a trolley to manoeuvre the stove into the cottage. The hall, with its step inside the doorway, was a challenge. George hadn't realised how heavy wood-burning stoves were. 'It's all cast iron, see,' explained Fred, 'and ready assembled. Once they're fired up, it makes 'em good at radiating heat. And the heat'll be in the room, not up the chimney.'

Once the stove was in position, the fitters split up. Fred remained in the living room while Eric went on the roof. This was a problem, she saw, that could only be solved by being attacked from different angles.

Fred's task was to fashion a metal plate to fit above the stove and under the inglenook. He made a pattern out of card then started to cut the metal plate to match it.

The whine of the power saw was hideous; he saw George flinch. 'Sorry, love, but we can only do this on site.'

It might be less painful, George decided, to be with his colleague.

'Could I go up to see what Eric's doing?'

'Sure - as long as you're OK with the height?'

George zipped her fleece; and also – this time - found scarf and gloves. Then she climbed up until she reached the man beside the smokestack.

Eric gave her a smile. 'We don't get many women up here.'

'I've a good head for heights. I wanted to see what you were doing.'

'Fair enough. See, here's the aluminium flue.' He showed her a long flexible tube, a foot in diameter.

'Your chimney goes straight up and down.' He took a piece of cord with a metal weight attached and started lowering it down the chimney.

A shout from below showed contact had been established. George hoped it hadn't hit Fred on the head. Eric pulled back the cord, counted turns on the flue then used giant pliers to cut it. 'The key thing now is not to drop it.'

He mixed some mortar then lowered the tube down the chimney and fastened it at the top. Finally he mounted the new pot.

'Right, m'dear. That's all we need to do up here. We both deserve a hot cup of tea. I'll go first and wait at each level.'

Great words as far as George was concerned. A large mug of tea was desperately needed.

Sophie had still not returned from her session with Arno by the time Wadebridge Stoves had demonstrated how to light the stove and driven away.

George thought about going round to join her but decided to have lunch first. By this time it was quite likely Sophie was having lunch – somewhere or other - with the director.

In any case George wanted to make sure her stove stayed alight. The men had made lighting it look easy but she wasn't completely convinced. She wouldn't light it every day, but Ivy Cottage was still in remission from several months of zero heating. It was delicious to feel really warm for the first time since she'd come to Cornwall.

Sophie and the plumber arrived almost together. Sophie had a sparkle in her eyes and George, sniffing, smelled alcohol. Whether this had been provided from Holly Cottage or from a local hostelry was not clear. George couldn't cross-examine her friend with the plumber standing behind her.

'Good afternoon, m'dear, Paul Wood, plumber.' George was delighted by his strong Cornish accent. 'You said on the phone yesterday you wuz wantin' someone to refurbish your bathroom?'

George decided she would leave Sophie to sober up and

concentrate her energies on the plumber. 'Thank you for coming so quickly. It wouldn't have been a problem but I only found out, when I got the keys to the cottage a couple of days ago, that...' She gulped.

The plumber saw her distress and plunged in. 'Lily Taylor drowned in the bath here. Yes: very sad. To battle through all life can throw at you, lose a husband to silicosis and a son to Australia then finally snooze away in a deep bath. She must have had a good lunch. Those Methodists feed 'em well.' He paused. 'But I can see it might give you an odd feeling to bathe in the same cottage and the very same bath.'

'Come upstairs, please, and take a look. Lily's death's not the only problem. The bath's an outlandish salmon colour – that on its own makes me want to replace it. While I'm at it I'd like to put in a shower. Baths are fine for people with plenty of time – like Lily - but personally I'm more of a shower person.'

Their voices faded away. Sophie sat down in the corner of the armchair nearest the stove and within a minute was fast asleep.

'I see what you mean.' The plumber stared at the bright pink bath and shook his head. 'Poor woman. Wuz she colour blind?'

'Not as far as I know. She might have worn sunglasses in the bath?'

'Or maybe bathed in the dark?'

It was a mystery, but not one they were ever likely to solve. The plumber continued, 'So you've not even checked that all the plumbing works?'

'No. We've used the sink, of course, but we haven't touched anything on the far side. You'd better try it out. You'll need to know if you're replacing all the pipe work as well.'

She thought for a moment. 'I guess the outflow pipe might have been blocked when they emptied out the water after...'

'I'm a plumber not a mortician, m'dear. Dead bodies weren't covered on my course. I gather it wuz several days before she wuz found.'

No doubt the delay had added to the villagers' distress. The consequences for the pipes were obscure.

'Anyway, m'dear, it'd be worth checking the bath fills at a decent rate – and then empties easily.' So saying, the plumber leaned forward, inserted the plug and turned on both taps.

As the water gushed in – at a decent enough rate, George thought - Paul turned his attention to the shower.

'It's not a big bathroom. There's not enough room for a shower cubicle. You'd need to fasten a shower to that end wall then add a shower curtain round the bath.' The plumber started to take measurements.

'Now, how high should we position the shower?' He turned to her. 'You're not tall, Mrs Gilbert, but there might be a six foot man needing a shower, I suppose?' It wasn't clear if this was a personal question about George's love life or a hydraulic conundrum.

It turned out it was simply rhetorical. 'Anyway, I'll put it as high as I can. Once the bath's empty would you mind standing in it so I can check that'll work?'

For a horrible moment George thought he was asking her to strip naked and then stand in the bath. Then she realised he was simply wanting to mark her height on the wall.

Before she could reply, a horrendous noise erupted around them - a steady vibration behind a deafening roar. There was a dissonant clash of frequencies; George put her hands to her ears. It felt as if the whole cottage was shaking. What was this - this some form of earthquake?

Uncertain what was happening, unable to communicate with the plumber over the noise, George retreated from the bathroom and raced down the stairs. The noise gradually diminished; it was just about bearable by the time she'd stepped outside.

It didn't seem to be an earthquake. At least, there was no sign that the cottage was falling down; and when she looked the other way the neighbourhood wasn't moving at all.

Feeling embarrassed, George stepped back inside the hall, just as Sophie emerged from the living room, her face white with shock. 'What the hell is that?'

'I don't know. It's something the plumber started.'

'Well, now he's proved we're not deaf, tell him to stop.' Sophie stomped back into the living room.

George smiled, shrugged her shoulders and made her

way slowly back upstairs.

Then, just as suddenly as it had started, the noise stopped - as if a celestial switch had been turned off by a guardian angel. George turned to the plumber, still trying things out in the bathroom.

'What on earth was that?'

'It was coming from the loft - caused by me filling the bath too quickly. Perhaps I shouldn't have used both taps at the same time. At any rate, now I've turned them off and waited a few minutes, it's stopped. Pretty raucous, eh?'

'Are you saying poor Lily Taylor had to put up with that noise every time she had a bath?'

'Probably. Maybe I should have filled the bath more gently – or one tap at a time. It might depend on the water pressure. That'll vary over the day and be highest at night. So it might depend on when she had her bath.'

'Poor woman - but... how on earth could she go to sleep in the bath with a racket like that going on over her head?'

'Perhaps she wuz deaf as well as colour blind? Don't worry, I'm sure it's fixable. I can get rid of the vibration as part of the refit. Let's see. A new ball valve on the cold water tank; extra stays on the water pipe. It wuz the pipe going up there that wuz vibrating: I could feel it shaking. Here, can I show you?'

'Not if it means listening to that racket again. I've had quite enough for one afternoon, thank you very much.'

'OK, Mrs Gilbert, I get the message. Trial over. Let's see if the outlet pipe's working.' Paul pulled out the plug; the

111

water started to run away without any problem.

'Nothing wrong there. So I can offer you a choice. Either I simply replace the bath with a new white one and add a new shower on the wall; leave everything else alone. Or I can give you a complete refit - new tiles, new lino, new paint, everything.'

'Hm. What sort of timescales are we talking?'

'The simple job I could make a priority. Fit it in next week, once the drama's out of the way – maybe Wednesday? If you wanted the full refit, though, that would take a whole week. I'd need to schedule it in between other jobs. It'd best be done once you were back to London. Of course it would be a lot more expensive.'

George looked around. The bathroom sink was already white, as were the tiles around it. Replacing the ghastly, ghostly bath was by far the most urgent task needed.

'Thank you. Your first option sounds all I need for now. If you could do it next Wednesday that would be wonderful.'

CHAPTER 14

Sophie was still asleep from "lunch" as George gave Paul a mug of tea then quizzed him about his role in *Splits and Schisms*.

She'd gathered that he had no intention of doing any more jobs before the early evening rehearsal, so he had a few minutes in hand. On her side, she'd made a good dent in the jobs needed in Ivy Cottage. She could relax and enjoy the warmth from the newly-installed stove. She gave it no more fuel, though: the cottage would be empty for most of the evening.

As they talked she remembered the scaffolding on the roof above; and the view offered of the drama down the valley. 'I've got an idea, Paul, for an alternative video angle for tonight's rehearsal. Would you mind helping me fix it?'

A few minutes later the two were climbing successive scaffolding ladders up on to the roof of Ivy Cottage. It was already starting to get dark and there was a biting wind.

Paul had found a special clamp in his tool bag. 'It'll fasten to the scaffolding – hold your camera firmly in place.'

'It should be a fine evening,' he remarked. As he spoke George was twisting her body to see the distant stage then amplifying the image. The zoom was too fuzzy unless the

113

camera was held rigid.

She could see the end of the stage and the point below it where the victims of the Quarry Disaster would be found. Once the stage lights were on, she hoped, the picture should be distinctive.

'I haven't yet had to act in heavy rain,' Paul went on, as he took a turn to look at the picture. 'I doubt our luck will last all week. You don't want to leave your camera up here in Cornish rain.'

'I'll try it this evening. We're experimenting with different angles each night. Arno's said he's happy to hire an editor to pull them all together.'

Sophie was awake when they returned inside the cottage, puzzling over their disappearance. She looked a lot better for her sleep.

'We need to get a move on if we're walking down,' urged George, after she'd seen off Paul. 'I assume you're still up for it?'

'Oh yes. Arno was very impressed with our first attempt. He hadn't got a spare copy of the script, but said I could come round and borrow his master tomorrow morning. Is that OK?'

'It'll have to do. Anyway, this evening you can do the filming. Take account of all the advice you've been given. You've had plenty of mentoring.'

Had her dig provoked Sophie? When nothing came she continued. 'Tonight I want to watch the overall perform-

114

ance, make sense of the key message; and scout around for places we could film from in the rain.'

George was itching for an account of Arno's critique - but perhaps this wasn't the time. She was also curious to know what else Sophie had been doing. Once more the women wrapped themselves up warmly and set off down the hill. The narrow path didn't make for easy conversation so George was left baffled as to what – if anything - had happened.

She hoped whatever it was wouldn't complicate her stay in Treknow.

'This evening, ladies and gentlemen, will be our last ordinary rehearsal. It's been a long slog for all of us and I thank you for sticking with it.' The director was in "inspire the troops" mode.

'Tomorrow night will be the technical rehearsal,' he went on. 'You're all needed but we won't be running right through every scene. The aim will be to get the lights and sound effects as slick as possible. You'll need to be ready, though, for a long rehearsal: Laurie needs all the help he can get. Then Thursday's the dress rehearsal; after that it's the performances themselves. So if you want to try anything out – any new expressions or reactions - tonight is your last chance.'

As the rehearsal got under way, George left Sophie to pick an angle for her videoing and wandered off to work out how they would cope with wet weather. Where was a sheltered position from which the drama might be filmed?

What about a car, parked above the car park? She walked up to have a look. There were one or two folk wandering past in thick coats, including one she faintly recognised. The amplified sound was fine; but unless she was on a double decker bus the marquees would block off half the stage. The road wasn't quite high enough above the performance area.

Next she tried inside a marquee. The view of the stage was excellent; but here George was worried about sound. Tonight, with the tents all empty, it was fine. During live performances, though, with an excited audience, the camera would be bound to pick up background chatter.

After all, this wasn't an audience steeped in the conventions of watching an opera – silent until the last note faded away. This lot would have come to watch their friends in action and no doubt to comment on what they were seeing. The marquee wasn't the right place either.

George continued to wander about as the performance battled on. Occasionally Arno's acerbic comments could be heard between scenes – even at this late stage he was seeking perfection. Would one possibility be a car, parked alongside one end of the marquees? The perspective would be off-centre - but the camera would be shielded from the crowd.

Then, as Job Hockaday launched into another narrative, George spotted a solution. Job's pulpit was off to the side with a tarpaulin roof overhead. It also had a good view of the stage. A camera mounted beforehand, focused on the stage, switched on by the narrator at the start of each Act, would capture all the action. It surely wasn't too much to ask Job to press a button.

The only doubt was Arno. He had made it clear that the videoing must not disrupt the performance. He might not want a key player burdened with an extra duty this late in the day.

Joe Stacey himself wouldn't mind. The best thing to do might be to ask him discreetly; and, if he was willing, then to set the camera inside the pulpit just before the start of the performance.

Now she had solved one problem, George settled down to watch the rehearsal. She was particularly interested in one or two scenes that had so far made no sense at all.

The darkness was broken by a spotlight on the pulpit. Job Hockaday began to paint the background for another scene.

'The 1870s was not a good time for the Slate Quarry in Delabole. Wages in this part of the world were frozen – there was no pressure of strikes, nowhere else for the men to go. After the Quarry Disaster a new manager had been brought in from Wales – Robert Roberts. The Board of Directors in Plymouth thought that a man from North Wales must know more about slate quarrying than anyone from Delabole – or even a man like me, born up the coast at Crackington Haven.

'It turned out that wasn't true. Of course, the best Welsh quarrymen were good. The trouble was, ones prepared to

117

leave their families and their beloved homeland and settle in faraway Delabole weren't the best. Mr Roberts knew how to do things in Bethesda; that might not work here in Delabole. Eventually a campaign started in the newspapers, anonymous letters from men at the Quarry, criticising the way things were being managed. From there things got steadily worse.'

The spotlight faded. Another lit up the stage, where a Board meeting was in progress, Dr Edward Jago in the chair.

'Gentlemen, let me read you a letter published recently in the Cornish and Devon Post.' He rustled among his papers, brought out a newspaper, turned to an inside page and began to read.

'"*How can poor mice act like men when they are continually under the eye and claws of a large pussy*" – by which they mean Roberts - "*who prowls about the quarry and boasts that he has not a rat in the place – mice only. The poor little mice dare not peep round the corner, or squeak to each other, but this vicious cat pounces upon them and tears them all to pieces.*" The manager of our Quarry is being turned into a laughing stock.'

'Who is the author?' asked Higgins. 'Surely we can have him sacked?'

Dr Jago looked down at his newspaper, 'He's not stupid enough to give his name, Mr Higgins. Goes by the name of "Fair Play". I fear the newspaper won't tell us who he is, even if we asked them.'

'In these hard times the men are lucky to have jobs at all.

We must find out who he is: make an example of him. Crush the rest into submission.'

Subdued murmurs of agreement from round the table.

The spotlight faded - switched to Hockaday. 'The Directors would never have taken this bravado any further. Except that the next month a strike began.'

Lights back to the stage, a group of quarrymen in discussion.

'Now Harry Penfound here gets six shillings per hundred tons of slate tipped. Whereas Philip Richards, working further along the quarry, only gets five shillings. It's not fair.'

Another man joined in. 'It's that manager, see – bloody Welshman, Roberts. He makes us compete one with another – like rats in a sack. He doesn't know us or our families. All he cares about is driving down costs.'

Harry Penfound, for one, had been pushed beyond endurance. 'Well, I've had enough. I'm going to see Mr Roberts at the end of my shift. Demand an increase in pay – for all of us.'

'Oh yeah. And what'll you do when he turns you down?'

'I'll tell him... I'll tell him I'm not working any more – and neither will the rest of us. If we don't arrange those slate blocks ready for the splitters, production here will grind to a halt.'

The lights turned back to Hockaday. 'For twenty four hours it looked as if Harry Penfound's courage had been rewarded. Roberts was weak; an increase in wages was being talked about.

119

A second light came onto the stage, where events were mimed as Hockaday continued the narrative.

'Then one of the tippers – Francis Cowling - decided to ignore the strike and start work. At once he found himself surrounded by other workers, led by Penfound, who told him in no uncertain terms that the strike was still on.

'Manager Roberts had seen the confrontation and saw his chance. Penfound and Richards found themselves dragged off to a magistrate in Tintagel, accused of violent behaviour towards Cowling.

'Cowling wasn't having any of that. Hadn't been afraid at all, he claimed; it was just a misunderstanding. For several hours the argument went back and forth; at the end the baffled magistrate said the charge was dismissed.

'Matters couldn't end there. Roberts dare not lose this battle or he would have lost all authority. His resolve was strengthened by the monthly visit of Directors. Dr Jago spoke to the men and urged them back to work. "If you have any grievance, bring them forward and they will be heard."

'Then Penfound was summoned. "You have brought the Quarry into disgrace."

'In vain did Penfound protest that he had been found innocent in court. He had committed the far more grievous crime of challenging the Quarry Manager; and maybe – though it couldn't be proved - of writing protest letters to the newspaper.

'Penfound found himself summarily dismissed. Then of being evicted from his workman's cottage, which he leased from the Quarry. Now he understood what the Board made of Fair Play.

'And when, a few months later, he found employment of a sort with a local farmer, whose land neighboured the Quarry, the farmer too was warned: "Never again offer employment to someone who has been sacked by the Quarry".

'No grievances were ever brought forward by the workers to the Board. I wonder, ladies and gentlemen, why that should be?'

CHAPTER 15

George and Sophie had found themselves separated in the Port William, George with Laurie and Sophie with the group around Arno, beside the open fire. 'I'll get a lift back with Arno,' she'd muttered, as George passed her en route to the toilet.

It was slightly unnerving, thought George half an hour later, to walk up the path alone - though not nearly as frightening as crossing a London park by night. She still missed Mark but couldn't imagine anything horrible happening in this quiet and peaceful village – it was now, after all, her home.

As she arrived back at Ivy Cottage she remembered the video camera. It had to be brought down: there was no guarantee it would stay fine. She turned on all the cottage lights then went out the back door, up the ladders and onto the platform at the top. She disciplined herself not to think about how far it was down.

The camera was still there. She wouldn't leave it up here again: rescuing it was too stressful. Carefully, the camera round her neck, she retraced her steps back to ground level and into her cottage.

It had been a long day and she couldn't be bothered to

wait for Sophie; her friend had the spare key. Before long she was fast asleep.

On Wednesday morning George was woken once again by the sound of horses outside. They too had a schedule. Opening her curtains, she saw it was another fine day; one she had to make the most of.

The analyst ranked her priorities as she prepared porridge. Her timetable was set by her daughter Polly's student exchange to Germany. That gave her just two weeks in Cornwall. There was certainly a need for new furniture. That meant a trip to Truro or Plymouth. If painting and decorating was needed, that would best be done before it was delivered.

Come to that, wasn't a fine day, with scaffolding in place, the best chance to paint her chimney? Once she would have been daunted - but she had climbed up the night before. There was no reason not to try it.

It would be a moral statement, asserting her ownership. Even Lily Taylor, whatever she'd managed to do inside the loft, didn't shin up ladders outside – at least not in recent years.

Sophie still hadn't appeared as George started her porridge. She wondered whether to give her a call but reflected that it was barely nine o'clock – maybe too early for an artist.

The analyst wanted to get on: time here was precious. The first thing was to buy paint. She scribbled a note for

Sophie then set off for Delabole. Half an hour later, paint obtained, she was back in Treknow.

There was still no sign of Sophie. But now George had the bit between her teeth. She'd do this, if necessary, on her own. She had to tackle that chimney before it rained. Adding another line to the note, she stepped outside.

The view over the grey Atlantic to Port Isaac was spectacular; but fiddling with her brush, thirty foot up in the air, above a Cornish hillside in January, was cold work. She was glad when she could come down.

Still no Sophie. She had moved on to sugar-soaping the living-room walls when her phone rang. It was Brian Southgate.

'I called earlier but there was no answer. How's it all going?'

'Hi Brian. I'm fine. I've just painted the chimney.'

'I'm impressed. Please don't take this the wrong way but Alice was wondering whether you needed a bath? She asked me to see if you'd both like to come for a meal this evening?'

'Well, I'll certainly need a bath by the end of today – I don't want my hair left permanently white. About seven? Thank you very much indeed.'

The women set off at quarter to seven. Sophie had appeared at lunch time; 'I was next door, discussing the latest video.' George was too polite to press her on how long she had been there, though she noticed that the spare porridge had not been consumed.

Alice had prepared a haddock fish pie and soon the conversation was rolling along merrily. After they'd explained how they were getting to see the re-enactment, George thought this was a chance to discuss the death of Lily Taylor. Brian was, after all, the doctor who had certified her dead.

'We've picked up one or two odd things about Lily Taylor that I wouldn't mind running past you.'

'Go on.'

'First of all, we found an old newspaper she'd been reading in her greenhouse – she obviously used it as a conservatory.'

'Guess how old it was?' added Sophie.

Brian was bemused. 'I'd say greenhouses are all post war so...'

'I meant the newspaper.'

'Oh, I dunno. Twenty five years?'

Two heads shook.

'Fifty years?' hazarded Alice. Another no.

'Eighty years?'

'Just over. It was dated April 1925. One article in the newspaper – the one she was reading - covered the recent arrival of the new curate, the Rev Jack Bucknall. Have you any idea why that should be of interest to Lily?'

'No idea.' The doctor was trained on facts, not conjecture.

'The only thing I can think of,' said Alice, 'is that a lot of interest in local history has been stirred up by *Splits and*

125

Schisms. Lily had been here a long time; maybe she wanted to add an item of her own. After all, as you've discovered, she was living next to the author.'

'OK,' said Brian. 'So what's the next observation?'

'We had Laurie Lane round to fix the night storage heating. While he was with us he offered to have a look in the loft – make sure we'd got proper insulation.'

'I wasn't allowed up there,' moaned Sophie, 'they said my clothes were too smart.'

'Designer dresses have a downside. I could go; we found Lily's old diaries – back as far as 1940, when she'd be a young girl of nineteen.'

'Another offering for the local history brigade?'

'I brought one down to have a look. She had beautiful handwriting. Laurie suggested I should check to see if it contained anything useful.'

'How intriguing. And did it?'

'It was dealing with life in wartime. It covered the year Lily left school and found herself a caring job - looking after some old lady in Tintagel.'

'Who was that?'

'The diary was very carefully written: it didn't say. Maybe Lily had been told not to? I went back for another one. The 1941 diary was missing; and by 1942 Lily was away, working in a munitions factory in Plymouth.'

'The old folk of Delabole certainly saw life. Anything else?'

'Was she deaf at all?'

'She had excellent hearing. Why?'

'We had the plumber to discuss the bathroom. He tried filling the bath and it made a horrendous racket.'

Sophie concurred. 'Yes, I was asleep downstairs and it woke me up. How could Lily have gone to sleep with that racket going on?'

'I hinted at one possibility the other day,' said Brian coyly.

'Yes, but she was a Methodist; had just been to the Community Lunch. She hadn't had any alcohol.'

'M'm.' Brian pondered for a moment. 'I suppose it's just possible something had happened to make her commit suicide.'

'When we got here, the calendar for 2008 was still hanging up in her kitchen. She'd got meetings planned with her friends for weeks after the date she died. There was no sign at all she wanted to end it.'

'It's slightly odd, I agree. I doubt we'll ever know.'

Brian was probably correct but George hoped something else might be found. She didn't like unsolved riddles around her cottage.

CHAPTER 16

It was a relief to reach Friday, the day of the performance. By some quirk the weather, though cold, was still fine; and likely to remain so until Sunday.

George and Sophie had given themselves two hard days, working amicably, to paint the interior of Ivy Cottage. They had completed all the main rooms; the hall and the box room could wait. Next week, all being well, they would choose new furniture and curtains in Truro. Alice had told them a new Department Store had opened there recently with a good reputation.

The dress rehearsal, the evening before, had been stressful. One or two players had forgotten key lines or missed vital prompts. Some sound effects had faltered. Arno, though, had insisted that was a good omen for the real performance. 'It's better to make your mistakes now, rather than in front of paying customers.'

George and Sophie had made the most of the unoccupied marquees. Sophie's camera was placed on a tripod in front of centre stage. George's focused unblinkingly on the narrative from the pulpit. They wouldn't admit it, least of all to Arno, but they were too tired from all their painting to be bothered following the action in detail.

Tonight the "camera girls" could reap the benefit of their earlier diligence. If all else failed, they already had the whole drama captured from several angles.

Sophie was keen to capture the atmosphere of the live performance. She wanted footage of the crowd arriving and their sense of expectation. She placed her camera on a tripod beside the car park entrance, where she could ask questions of the audience as they arrived. She knew hardly any of them but was pleased to see Brian Southgate. The doctor waved his Red Cross armband. 'Arno asked me to be the medical backup,' he confided, 'I'm hoping I won't be needed.'

George meantime had crept into the pulpit, fastened her camera on one side and focused it on the stage.

Sophie had used the script they had wrestled from Arno to pick out the key moments of the drama. She had noted the scenes when these appeared, where a close-up would be invaluable, and was looking forward to filming them. Now she'd finished filming the crowd she was keeping warm in the control van with Laurie Lane. He was very busy, checking all his switches and controls were working.

Eventually the crowd were seated, whispering among themselves, waiting for the show to begin. Then, gradually, the lights inside the marquees dimmed and the audience fell silent.

The stage was in darkness. Then in the distance a haunting Cornish folk song could be heard. It seemed to be coming down the hillside from Treknow. As the sound faded away a spotlight came on, pointing to a figure huddled in a thick coat with a long white beard, standing in a pulpit on the other side of the stage.

'Ladies and gentlemen, friends,' he began. 'Thank you for your company this evening.' The show was underway.

The audience clapped enthusiastically at the end of each scene, picking out most punch lines as they went along. Even performed by amateurs it was an excellent script. George couldn't see Arno – he'd disappeared somewhere behind the stage – but no doubt he was lapping up the appreciation.

The whole production proceeded more slowly than in rehearsal; the actors sensed that the audience was with them and played up accordingly. In the pulpit, Job had more gravitas; spoke his lines more slowly; and enticed a sympathetic response from his listeners.

The first sign of anything amiss came with the Quarry Disaster. The debate between James Kellow and Greg Wallis on the top stage, as they spotted the quartz seam starting to fracture, achieved a striking shock amongst the audience.

Hardly anyone had been aware there was a higher stage until the scene began. Those sitting on the back row couldn't see where the sound was coming from - it was obscured by the roof of the marquees. They had to lean fully forward to see the two fellows talking so high above them. That only added to the atmosphere.

The scene moved on. Two teenage girls in white dresses

appeared on the main stage, one with a snack for Cowling, the other seeking Wallis. His daughter was despatched off to the side and started to climb down into the rough area below the stage. The other headed for the ladder up to the top.

A rumbling noise began. It grew louder and louder as the lights played on the hillside behind the auditorium. Then smoke began to appear below the stage; but something had gone wrong with the settings. The machines were generating far more smoke than had ever come before – even the first time it had been used, when Laurie was learning how the equipment worked.

'It's a fire,' screamed someone in the audience. 'Help!'

The panic was infectious. The audience had had no warning of what to expect. They had sat for an hour in the cold, watching their own local history re-enacted in a new way; they were well outside their comfort zone. The spotlights were waxing and waning on the hillside and the din from the sound effects was deafening.

Rational discussion was not possible; and the crowd did not wait to try.

Those nearest to the ends of the tents were quickly out of their seats and heading for the back of the car-park, as far away from trouble as possible. One or two tried to phone the emergency services, but found their mobiles had no signal.

There was a struggle to get out from those further inside, screams as many found their way out blocked by others.

One man, seated in the middle of the marquees, saw an alternative. With a struggle he managed to lift the heavy canvas which made up the back of the tent; lifted it far enough to crawl underneath; pushed through to safety beyond. He was immediately followed by several others. He stood holding up the canvas on the outside as more pushed through after him.

The whole panic was so unnecessary - so unexpected - that for a few moments no-one from *Splits and Schisms* knew what was happening or how to respond.

Laurie Lane, in the control van, could not hear the crowd noise over the sound of the rumbling and crashing of rocks coming from his equipment. Sharp-witted Sophie was the first to realise Laurie was the one man who had the power to bring the crisis to an end.

The door to the van had been located on the side away from the marquees - but Sophie knew where it was. She went round, pushed it open, clambered inside and grabbed Laurie by the arm. He hadn't expected to be interrupted and tried to shrug her off. 'What's the matter? Leave me alone.'

'Laurie, please, turn off the noise: they're all panicking! And, for pity's sake, kill those smoke effects. Someone out there thought it was a fire. They're all trying to escape.'

It was as well that Laurie was a practical man who could distinguish a prank call from a crisis. He had confidence in Sophie; she did not look like she was joking. Quickly he suppressed the sound effects; he could immediately hear for himself the shouts of alarm from the crowd outside.

Convinced, he moved over to the controls on the smoke generators and flicked them off. 'It'll take a few minutes for the smoke to die down, mind.'

Finally the special effects man seized a microphone. 'Ladies and gentlemen, please do not panic. I repeat: please do not panic. The smoke you have just seen is not the result of a fire; it's a special effect that is part of the drama. The smoke has now been switched off. Everything is under control.'

He drew a deep breath. Job Hockaday should have been doing the next announcement but the pulpit was hidden behind the smoke. Laurie couldn't see him so it was likely he couldn't see the crisis on this side. The effects man had his own microphone; it might as well be him.

'As you will see from your programmes, the next event this evening is the half-time interval. Fish and chips, beef burgers and hot drinks are available from the refreshment van which you'll find behind the main marquees. *Splits and Schisms* will resume with Act Two in about twenty minutes time.'

It took a while before order was restored. It was not until the smoke had cleared from the stage that panic started to subside: people could see for themselves there was no reason to escape. The man who had shouted 'Fire' tried to pretend it hadn't been him; and when that didn't work, to suggest it had all been a deliberate wind up. That didn't do much to diffuse criticism either.

Those who had retreated to the roadside started to edge back, many taking advantage of the refreshment van which had now opened for business. As the smell of fish and chips wafted down toward the marquees the remaining fear evaporated.

There was a good reason to get out of the marquees but it was no longer a reason to run away.

Mercifully, though there were a few bruises, no-one had been badly hurt. Dr Brian Southgate checked those around him but could see no one needing medical aid. It was a relief, he thought, that they had been reassured so quickly: a credit to someone behind the scenes.

Not every detail of the Quarry Disaster had been re-created but the audience did not know what they were missing; and for the time being no longer much cared.

Something, though, was still wrong. Quarryman Greg Wallis and Director Charles Rendle walked down from the hillside towards the rough ground below the stage. The bodies that had been victims of the Disaster still needed to be counted and removed.

According to the script this part should have been en-acted under the glare of a spotlight – a glare which slowly faded as the horror of the deaths struck home and the scene drew to a close.

In the confusion Laurie had forgotten about that light; the rescue party were searching in almost total darkness. That didn't matter too much; they had enacted this scene many times before. Several bodies were found, given a hand up and despatched to scurry under the stage and find warmth in the dressing rooms beyond.

They had found everyone they'd expected and were about to retreat to the warmth of the changing rooms. Then Greg Wallis noticed another leg sticking out from under the stage. He reached over, whispered: 'D'you want a hand, mate?'

There was no answer. Maybe the poor chap had fainted in the cold. Wallis turned back to Rendle. 'There's another one here. He's fainted or something.'

Together they each seized an arm to pull the man out from under the stage so they could see what was the matter. It wasn't the best of light but was better than the darkness under the stage. In the gloom they examined him more carefully.

'We need some help here, Paul,' said the man playing Dr Rendle. 'I can't really see in this light - but I think he might be dead.'

CHAPTER 17

As it happened, there was one off-duty policeman amongst the audience that evening. Sergeant Peter Travers was community policeman for the North Cornwall area from Bude down to Padstow; his base was the Police House in Delabole. Apart from a few years away at Police College he had lived his whole life in the area. A bright man, with family responsibilities towards his elderly mother in Port Isaac, he had no great desire to live or work anywhere else. He was here tonight primarily as a Delabole citizen, hoping to learn more about the history of his own community.

Peter Travers had thought he might have to take up an official role during the panic induced by the smoke. He had been easing his way out of one of the most inaccessible back seats, wondering how to contact the manager and whether to put himself back on duty, when the announcement had come that the smoke was a special effect, not a symptom of fire. Relieved, he had joined the queue for fish and chips, noting as he did so that his friend Dr Brian Southgate was standing in front of the stage, acting as medical orderly.

So it was a disappointment, ten minutes later, to be summoned once again, this time by the special effects man,

Laurie Lane. There was another problem. This one had apparently happened beneath the stage.

Fortunately Travers had nearly finished his fish and chips. Stuffing in the last mouthful, he squashed the polystyrene packet between his hands and popped the result into a well-placed dustbin; then followed Laurie across the car park. The policeman was not in uniform, but he was well-known in the area and the electrician had had no difficulty in recognising him.

As he followed he wondered what else might have happened. Experimental theatre was all very well but it still needed to stay within boundaries. As he reached the group standing under the stage he saw Brian Southgate had already been called; and was crouching down behind the others. What on earth was going on?

His friend was always a good man to have in a crisis. But the crisis must be serious if they were both needed.

Then he saw a glimpse of a body lying behind them. Southgate was obviously doing his best to care for him. It looked as if the other men were creating a shield to stop him (or her?) being visible to the wider public. Many of these were strolling about between marquee and stage, enjoying their fish and chips and waiting for Act Two.

Given the recent state of panic, the shield the men were providing was probably a sensible precaution.

'What's the problem?' he asked, as he reached the group.

'It's Joe Stacey,' said Southgate, without preamble, as he stood up. 'He's collapsed and unconscious. His eyes are

137

dilated and I can't feel a pulse; but that doesn't prove any-thing: he might have hypothermia. These guys found him under the stage, alongside the players supposed to have been killed in the Disaster scene.'

'Mobile phones don't work down in Trebarwith Strand,' the doctor went on, 'so I've sent Alice to ring for an ambu-lance from the Mill House, just up the road. The nearest ambulance station is in Camelford; it should be here in, what, ten minutes. They'll need to take him to the nearest Accident and Emergency - that's down in Truro, unfortu-nately.'

Travers took a moment to take it all in. He glanced around the group. There were a lot of questions needing answers.

'Is there anything we can do for Joe in the meantime?'

'If it is hypothermia, we need to protect him against the cold as much as possible. We've covered him over with several coats; made him as warm as we can. The trouble is, I don't know what else might be wrong – he could have cracked his head when he went over. It wouldn't be sensible for us to move him anywhere without a proper stretcher.'

All that sounded sensible, as far as it went. Travers hoped there would be no delay in responding to the call in Camel-ford.

'Am I right to assume we won't be going on with the drama?' he asked, not quite sure of his ground.

'Joe was the narrator. He was the one playing Job Hocka-day. We can't go on without him,' said the one person in the

138

little group he couldn't identify.

'And you are?'

'I'm Arno James. I'm the director of this historical event. I've been in the village since October, researching and writing the drama.'

'Pleased to meet you. Sorry I'm not in uniform – I was off duty, in the audience, enjoying the production - I'm Sergeant Peter Travers, the community policemen in these parts.' The policeman paused for thought.

'It's a narrow road down from Camelford. The ambulance could do without having to battle with loads of cars going the other way. Whatever happens, we don't want the audience driving off until the ambulance has got here and taken away the stricken man. But we do need to tell them something about what's going on. Otherwise they're likely to panic again when they see the ambulance.'

'Maybe we could link the event to the smoke alert?' This was Laurie Lane - another useful man in a crisis. 'Tell them someone has been taken ill, an ambulance has been called and the rest of the show will be delayed. We don't need to explicitly blame it on the smoke but it wouldn't harm if that's what they all thought. I could make the announcement if you liked?'

He looked across at both Travers and Arno, not sure who was now in charge.

Travers took control. 'Thank you. That sounds a good idea. OK with you?' He looked across to Arno, who nodded. The man looked to be in a state of shock – not surprising if

139

he'd lost a leading member of cast in mid-production. That sort of thing did not happen in the West End.

'You'd best make the announcement as soon as possible - before they start to settle down for Act Two,' said the policeman. 'Then, once the ambulance has gone, you'll need to make a second announcement, apologising and telling them the second half has had to be cancelled. And if you can think of a way to phrase it, encourage them not to hang about. The sooner they're dispersed the better. We will, though, need the cast to stay on for the time being.'

Twenty fraught minutes later the ambulance had arrived, driven through the car park, down the ramp to the park extension and as close as it could to the stage. The crew had made their way down the slope and liaised briefly with Dr Southgate and Sergeant Travers. Then they had eased the patient gently onto a stretcher, carried him up to the ambulance, stowed him carefully inside, closed the doors and, a couple of minutes later, hastened away.

Travers had spent the time until it came wandering among the crowd, a cheerful smile on his ruddy face, eyes everywhere, making sure there was no trouble brewing. He had watched out for Joe Stacey's wife, Morwenna, but had not seen her. Of course, she might not be there – might be planning to come for the second night.

It was dark below the stage. He was fairly sure the audience didn't know yet who was being taken away or exactly why the show had come to such a sudden pause. No doubt there was plenty of speculation. It was good that the hour's production they had seen had left them with plenty to talk about. Even an hour had been good value for money.

The policeman used the time to think, dragging his mind back on duty. What immediate steps did he need to take?

It wasn't clear that he needed to call up police reinforcements. They would take some time to arrive from Bodmin anyway. There was no sign of dissent from the crowd. If a van-load of police arrived, looking to practise crowd control, Travers would not be popular, either with his colleagues or the general public. It was better to go it alone. He needed to maintain his credibility for when it was really needed.

Could he account for what had happened: was there anything untoward? So far he had little to go on. Travers didn't know Joe Stacey well. The policeman had a wide patch to cover and had hardly ever been into the Stacey's photo-gallery, on the far side of Delabole. Could the collapse be related to the stress of performing in the drama? He didn't know how well Joe Stacey would have coped with that. He wasn't used to being an actor; the production must have been stressful for all the cast and worse for the most frequently seen player.

The policeman had never spoken to the director – Arno, was it? - but the occasional comments he'd overheard in the pub suggested he was a hard taskmaster – as he needed to be, no doubt, to turn a bunch of local amateurs into the professional-looking outfit they had become. But had that search for perfection – that desire to turn rough stones into

141

polished gems - brought Joe to a collapse? Had Arno pushed him too hard?

The loudspeakers crackled; Laurie spoke out again. After this second announcement, the crowd looked disappointed then started to thin out – no doubt many of them continuing their evening down at the Port William. That maybe explained the number of cars still in the car park – he knew parking on the narrow lane up to the pub was a nightmare.

Most were gone now. The policeman wandered amongst the stragglers, encouraging them on their way.

But there had been two unexpected events that night – first the panic from the smoke alarm and then the collapsed player. He couldn't help wondering what sort of incident was starting to develop.

CHAPTER 18

Once the ambulance had gone and the crowd were dispersing, and while the cast were gathering themselves in Annabel's house, Peter Travers took a few minutes to converse with his medical friend.

'I know you can't say anything officially, Brian, but what are his chances, d'you reckon? What could have been the matter with him? And have you the faintest idea what might have caused it?'

'Peter, it was too dark for me to give him a proper medical examination; and too cold. It wasn't the place to start taking off layers of his clothing and I'd only got a small selection of medical equipment. If we could have got him indoors and under a decent light I would have done a lot better; but there wasn't time to do so. From that point of view the ambulance came too soon. Medically speaking, given he'd been standing out in the cold, he could have been suffering from severe hypothermia - so it was right to get him into an ambulance and off to hospital as soon as we could.'

'You don't sound like you were convinced?'

'To be honest, I'm very sceptical. It's cold here and that wind is brutal if you're standing in the wrong place. The

143

turret thing he was speaking from wasn't well-protected and might really have copped it. But Joe was wearing a thick coat and – I checked – he had plenty of layers underneath. That should have kept him from the worst of the cold. I'd say the air temperature here is not much below zero; it's no colder tonight than it has been all week. And they've been rehearsing in costume, as they call it, for days.'

'But if it wasn't hypothermia?'

'Then I'm very much afraid, Peter, that he's already dead. I couldn't find his pulse. That might just have been the difficulty of the location we were in but I'm a pretty experienced doctor. It's more likely to be because there was no longer a pulse operating in his body.'

His stark words confirmed the policeman's underlying fears.

'If he hadn't got hypothermia, what are the alternative reasons for his collapse?'

'There were no obvious signs of blood – at least, on the parts of the head I could see. So the most likely cause would be something like a heart attack or a stroke; or maybe an aneurism.'

'But we'd heard him narrating all evening,' protested Travers. 'He didn't sound like a man who was about to go under. And there wasn't that long a gap between his last speech and his being found lying under the stage.'

'Well, something might have triggered a collapse.'

'How d'you mean?'

The doctor paused to arrange his thoughts. 'I had a look

round under that stage once the ambulance had gone. I couldn't see much – there's no lighting and I didn't have a torch, so it was pretty dark - but I could tell the whole thing is a mass of scaffolding. There are dozens of poles, pointing in all sorts of directions. I couldn't see if all the ends were covered properly. I don't know what Joe was doing in there but it's possible that if he was rushing through underneath the stage in the dark and tripped...'

'He could have cracked his head on the scaffolding in just the wrong place.'

'Yes. And in turn the fall might have precipitated something deadly, like a stroke or heart attack. I would say, at this stage, that the most likely thing is that Joe Stacey was the victim of a dreadful, one in a thousand, accident.'

The woman who owned the house at the top of Trebarwith Strand which provided dressing rooms, Annabel, had decided to be out for the evening. She'd seen and heard enough of the production during the final rehearsals. The keys had been handed over to Della Howell. As the place was in frequent use by the cast (for one thing it was the nearest toilet) it had been decided to leave the side door unlocked. So there was no difficulty in the policeman making his way inside, once he had finished being briefed by Dr Southgate.

When he went in, Peter Travers found the cast all standing or sitting in the main living room. At least someone had had the sense to make sure they'd all got warm drinks from

Annabel's kitchen, but there was not much talking going on. He had no doubt they all knew the fears of those who had found Stacey lying under the stage.

The policeman introduced himself, though he thought he would be recognised by most of those present, even without his uniform. Then he went on with the news – limited as it was.

'I guess you all saw the ambulance. They were dealing with Joe Stacey. He is now on his way to the Accident and Emergency Department in Truro. He had collapsed, was unconscious when found and was obviously critically ill.

'It's just possible that it had something to do with the cold but this stage all I can tell you is that the cause is un-known: we just don't know. I hope that will change once he's been examined at Truro Hospital; but I doubt that'll happen tonight.

'My next task is to go and find Joe's wife; tell her what's happened. She will doubtless want to be with Joe as soon as possible. If there's no-one else around I may need to run her over to Truro myself; she shouldn't drive herself if she's in shock. It's too late for her to get there tonight on public transport.

'There are a whole load of questions about what Joe Stacey was doing under the stage, when the collapse started and were there any forewarning signs. He may be able to tell us himself, of course, if all goes well at the hospital. But he may not. In that case I will need to talk to you all again.'

He looked across to the director. 'I'd be grateful, Arno, if

146

you could provide me with a full list of names and addresses for everyone in the production. I'll pick it up tomorrow.'

Travers had dozens of questions but they would have to wait. 'However we look at it, this is an immensely sad ending to what I for one thought was a memorable evening. It would be best, I think, for you not to get drawn into any discussion of what might have happened for the moment but to leave it all to me. The audience don't yet know who was taken away or what was wrong with them. It would be good if we could maintain that state of affairs for the rest of this evening.'

'I promise you I'll put out a statement as soon as I can - probably on the local police website. Right now I must go and talk to Morwenna Stacey.'

CHAPTER 19

At nine o'clock on Saturday morning Peter Travers was woken from deep slumber by the persistent sound of a telephone. His eyes blurred, he reached out and grabbed it. 'Hello, Delabole Police House. How can I help you?'

'Morning Sergeant. Inspector Lambourn here.'

It was his nominal boss, based in Bodmin. He sounded angry. The two had never been close colleagues; what did he want?

'I gather you had an emergency call to rush someone to the hospital at your local drama. Why haven't I been told this officially?'

How the hell did he know? Whatever was it to do with him?

Travers recalled that police standing orders declared that unusual deaths always needed to be reported upwards as soon as possible. It was just possible the man might be ringing to offer advice. That would be unusual.

The policeman reminded himself that his boss's speciality was avoiding trouble rather than dealing with it.

'Yes sir. A chap called Joe Stacey. I took his wife to Truro Hospital yesterday evening; that was after I'd been to see her and broken the news that her husband had been taken there. She was very distraught – sobbed all the way. When we got there we learned that he had been declared dead on arrival.

'We had to wait to see her husband's body – it was still waiting to be examined when we arrived – then she was left alone with him. It was a long time before she wanted to come back to Delabole. I didn't get back with her till half part three this morning. I apologise, sir, for not reporting the event earlier. I'm afraid I was still asleep.'

'I don't think you've time to sleep, Travers. Not with an unusual death to make sense of. What're your immediate plans?'

Travers was tempted to say 'go back to sleep' or 'have breakfast' but he thought these weren't the right answers – or at least, not the answers his boss was after.

'The dead man, Joe Stacey, was one of the key actors in a production called *Splits and Schisms*. He was found halfway through the performance, under the stage. I got the local doctor to examine him and we called an ambulance – which came inside ten minutes, pretty good to the middle of nowhere. The doctor feared the worst but thought it was just possible that Stacey was suffering from hypothermia – it was extremely cold down around the stage; Stacey had been standing, narrating, from an isolated turret thing, for an hour.'

'So was it hypothermia?'

'The doctor at the hospital didn't think so.'

'So what are the alternatives?'

149

'The doctor at the hospital wouldn't tell me: said we'd have to wait for the post-mortem. The doctor from Delabole thought the most likely explanation was that he'd been unlucky – tripped and caught his head on a pole while making his way under the stage - and fallen over. There's plenty of scaffolding to run into. And he thought the fall could have led on to something like a heart attack.'

Travers paused to let the point sink in. 'So there's no evidence that there's been any crime. I didn't want to call up more police resources or even the Regional Crime Squad from Exeter until I had a clearer picture.'

'I'm glad you didn't call in the Crime Squad. That goes on our budget. Plenty of time for that if there's any hard evidence it wasn't just an accidental death.'

Travers assumed his boss might also be giving the local crime figures the benefit of the doubt. It turned out his tirade was far from over.

'I suppose lying in bed was supposed to give you focus?'

'Yes – no – sir, the crucial information has to come from the hospital when they do the post-mortem. Even if the circumstances were unusual it would be a mistake for the police to take any action if the poor bloke had simply suffered a stroke.'

'But the sudden death of an apparently healthy man in full flow could have a more sinister cause.'

'I suppose it could, sir.'

'And you've checked, have you - there's no sign of a weapon?'

'I haven't yet, sir. I first had to talk to the widow.'

'Well, has the scene of the incident been closed off?'

'Actually, it's not that easy to close. It's not a theatre - or anything with a door I could lock. The drama was being performed on an open stage set on a hillside at the side of a car park. Not even the middle of a village.'

'So if there was a weapon, and it had been left nearby, the criminal's had plenty of time to make off with it?' The Inspector sighed.

'There was only me at the play, sir – and I was officially off duty. I did the best I could. I didn't want to make a fuss and worry the audience.'

'I don't suppose the prospect of a madman armed with a weapon worried them at all. Hardy lot, the folk of Delabole. Let's hope no more died on their way home.'

'I'd already had to cover a fire alert, sir - at the end of the Act One.'

'And no doubt a bomb scare was planned for Act Two. Good job the play didn't get that far, eh. You call this keeping the peace, Travers?'

'I can hardly attend every pantomime in North Cornwall, sir. Nothing like this has ever happened before. I had to juggle a number of competing priorities, one of which was clearing the crowd peacefully. It's not clear any crime has been committed. It's clear, though, that a woman has been widowed.'

'No crime? At the very least that stage sounds like a Health and Safety nightmare. Who gave permission to perform a drama on this rough terrain? Is it Council land? Did they approve? Really approve, I mean – in writing. A proper, signed letter – not just some default email. Specifically, did anyone check the whole stage to give it a risk assessment?'

It wasn't a video conference so Travers could only guess, but it sounded like the Inspector was going very red in the face.

'Someone needs to feel some pain over this, Travers; even if it was a natural death. When it's all over we need to make it clear that there's going to be much tighter control of these sorts of outdoor dramas in the future. If we're not careful this'll play havoc with the monthly crime figures.'

Travers put down his phone, wondering whether he could slide back under the duvet for an hour's more sleep. He recalled it used to be said that Margaret Thatcher only needed four hours sleep a night – but she only had to run the country, not to keep order in North Cornwall. He feared sleep was a lost cause.

How on earth had Lambourn heard about last night's incident? Normally his nit-picking boss only knew what Travers chose to tell him in his monthly report – and that was by no means all that was going on. The sergeant's policy was that 'ignorance is bliss' – and he wished his boss a blissful life.

The most likely explanation was that someone at last night's performance was a friend of a senior policeman -

someone higher up the chain of command than Lambourn - and they had been left upset enough by the evening that they wanted "something to be done".

Maybe they'd been frightened by the smoke alert? That had been a few moments of fiasco that didn't reflect well on the production. It was easy to imagine that someone trapped in the middle of the marquees – probably an older woman - might have had a panic attack.

That couldn't be all of it: Lambourn had also heard about the emergency ambulance. The suspicion that the collapse was serious could only have come from a member of the cast – one of that small group of people in Annabel's living room that he'd exhorted to keep their heads down.

It was puzzling - but he couldn't solve it without more information.

As he thought over the events of the night before, Travers could see he might have made a serious blunder in not calling for the Crime Squad - especially as Lambourn had now made that call more difficult. The crucial issue was the cause of death.

How long would it take for Truro to conduct a post mortem on Joe Stacey? He could at least make sure they realised the matter was urgent.

Fifteen minutes later the policeman came off the phone, thoroughly frustrated. It seemed that Truro Hospital – like every other part of the Health Service - was trying to reduce costs. One way to do so, his medical contact had explained, was to slow down all non-emergency activity where delay was not life-threatening.

A post mortem fell into that category - the person was already dead. The doctor had agreed they would start the analysis on Monday morning; would even let Joe Stacey jump the queue, ahead of other, more routine examinations. Moving the analysis earlier than Monday, though, was beyond their capability.

He wondered for a minute whether to ring back Lambourn. Could the Inspector pull rank with a hospital consultant and swing an immediate post mortem? Then he asked himself when was the last time Lambourn had gone outside his comfort zone and realised the idea was fanciful.

All he could do for this weekend was to fear the worst; and operate as if Stacey had been the victim of assault. Hit over the head, maybe - in malice or perhaps in anger?

CHAPTER 20

An hour later Sergeant Peter Travers – now in uniform, he didn't know what formal interviews he would need to conduct that day – set out to examine the Trebarwith Strand stage for himself.

Before he set out the policeman had posted a brief statement, stating that Joe Stacey had been declared dead at Truro Hospital, on the local police website. It was probably better that folk heard the news as soon as possible; and heard it officially. No doubt, after the appearance of the ambulance the previous evening, some would look there this morning. He assumed the village grapevine would pass the news on quickly from this point.

As he went the policeman was annoyed to realise that it must have poured with rain in the night. There were many water-filled potholes to be avoided on the narrow road down from Delabole. He didn't know if the rain had been local, while he was with Morwenna in Truro; or if it had happened during the deep sleep on his return.

Rain was a routine part of life in Cornwall and normally not worthy of attention. On this occasion he fervently hoped that the section underneath the stage was protected. He wouldn't like to account for a soaking crime scene – if that

155

was what it came to - to the Regional Crime Squad; or for that matter to Inspector Lambourn.

The car park had a forlorn look this morning. There were only one or two cars parked in it. These probably belonged to walkers exploring a chunk of the Coast Path, north or south of Trebarwith Strand - it was hardly the time of year to tempt anyone into the sea. Remembering Lambourn's comments, he was glad to see that, even if not locked, the stage itself was deserted.

Travers stood for a moment taking in the lie of the space around the production. Now, in the daylight, he could see the high-level stage which had acted as the lip of the Quarry at the start of the Disaster scene. He also noted the ladders up to the high level on either side of the main stage.

Off on the Trebarwith Strand side was the separate section from which Job Hockaday – whom he now knew to be Joe - had proclaimed his narrative. In later conversations he would discover that this section was usually referred to as the "pulpit". Travers couldn't be sure, without a sight of the script, when the last proclamation had come from the pulpit, but he thought it was the start of the Disaster scene.

That was quite a long scene, he recalled; it included the special effects simulating the quarry collapse. That gave ten minutes or so between Joe's last appearance and the discovery of his body under the stage – not long, but long enough.

Surely the risk of being overheard would put anyone off a vicious assault? Then the policeman reminded himself that this particular scene had been accompanied by a rising, horrendous sound of cliffs crashing and rocks falling down. It was the one time in the whole drama where anything could happen behind the scenes and no-one in the audience would hear anything.

As he thought around this, Travers remembered the clouds of smoke which had happened at the same time – the notorious effects which had almost sparked fire panic in the crowd. That would give visual cover for anything to happen under the stage. From his own experience the evening before, he knew that it was almost impossible for anyone in the audience to see anything.

All this meant that, if anything criminal had happened to Joe, it must have been a member of the cast who had been involved. For only someone who knew the production would recognise that this critical ten minutes was so suitable a time for such desperate activity.

Now was the time to check the space under the stage. Standing at the edge of the car park the policeman could see only two ways down: either from the grass which formed part of the extension car park and led on up to Treknow; or starting from Annabel's house and coming along the decking, past the pulpit and under the stage.

He chose to go via the grass. He saw, as he did so, that he was well below the level of the main car park. So anyone else could have crept along that way last night - and probably not be spotted.

When he got to the space below the stage he was bitterly

157

disappointed. For although the stage had kept out most of the rain from directly overhead, plenty had blown in from the unprotected sides. No doubt, being a Cornish storm, it had mixed wind with the rain. Now, as he stood inside, he could see that huge chunks of the scaffolding were soaking wet.

Travers spent twenty minutes examining the pipe work as carefully as he could. It didn't help that he hadn't been there when the body was found, so he didn't know exactly where it had been discovered. Nor did he know if it had been easy to find - or if the find was a fluke, not intended to happen. Though he searched hard, the policeman couldn't be sure he was looking in the right place.

He had to face facts. There was no sign of blood on any of the scaffolding poles. In other words, no tangible evidence at this point that Joe Stacey had bashed his head by falling into one of the poles. Which meant greater weight had to be given to the other possibility: namely that he had been hit over the head, at the critical point in the production, by someone else.

Travers needed to bounce ideas off someone; Dr Brian Southgate was the obvious person to call.

Travers and Southgate had been friends since secondary schooldays in Camelford. They had maintained that friendship even after the doctor had married – Alice sensibly recognising the benefits of a friend in whom her husband could have complete trust within a demanding career.

In addition, and more to the point in this case, Southgate knew as much as the policeman about the start of the incident the evening before.

A quick phone call led to the doctor meeting him for a light lunch at the Trewarmett Inn. The Inn had an advantage for private conversations: drinks could be consumed at the far end of the bar without risk of being overheard. Rumours would be unavoidable before long but for the moment secrecy was paramount.

Soon the doctor knew as much as Peter Travers about the declaration of death at the hospital, the damp state of the under-stage and the delay on Joe Stacey having a post-mortem.

'If you'd called the Regional Crime Squad straight away it might have been different,' opined the doctor. 'Trouble was, I'd called the regular ambulance long before we knew there was any cause for concern. It was so dark under that stage; I hadn't thought to bring a torch on my night out.'

'It's such an odd place for a crime – if that's what it was. Virtually in public with two or three hundred people watching – plus the sound effects.'

'As well as the smoke,' added the doctor. He'd had two stints of being medical orderly that night; the smoke was etched in his mind.

'One thing I did wonder about,' asked the policeman. 'You told me that if it wasn't hypothermia then, in your view, Stacey was already dead. If that was the case, had you any opinion on the time of death? You were there a few minutes

159

before me. Had it happened seconds before or slightly longer?'

'To be honest, I was more concerned to see if there was any chance of resuscitation; and even before that to make sure an ambulance was called. It was too dark for a proper examination.'

'But you must have had some idea?'

'Peter, I'm not a police doctor. I don't see many people who've just died. Stacey's body certainly felt cold. I couldn't be sure whether that was because he'd been dead for a while or because he'd been lying outdoors on a freezing January evening. It was bloody cold over there - almost like a wind tunnel under that stage.'

'I wasn't in there long enough to notice, Brian. I had to rush about, reassuring the great Cornish public in the car park.'

'Which you did well: don't underestimate yourself, my friend. There was an undercurrent of fear after that fire alert. That could easily have flared if you hadn't calmed them.'

A moment's pause.

'My plan for today, Brian, is to fear the worst – act as if it wasn't a natural death. Try and do as much background investigation as I can while it's fresh in everyone's mind.'

'Then when you hear on Monday afternoon that poor old Stacey had delayed concussion and keeled over – and that, now she thought about it, his wife remembered him cracking his head on the kitchen cupboard before he went out –

you've at least had practice for when you join the Crime Squad.

'As the first medical man on the scene I would bet it was an accident. But if you're still determined to be proactive, I reckon the obvious place to start is that director chap – Arno James. He's rented a cottage for the winter, you know, down in Treknow.'

CHAPTER 21

George and Sophie had returned late to Ivy Cottage on Friday evening, upset and shaken.

At first the two had not realised anything had happened after the fire alert. That had been dramatic enough. But they had been drawn in by Laurie Lane - 'You're both part of our team now,' he'd pronounced in a kindly manner, 'you'd better come along with me.'

George had started to gain a sense that something was badly wrong but neither she nor Sophie had any idea what that might be.

Following Laurie, they'd found all the members of the production gathered in Annabel's living room. There they had learned what had happened to Paul Wood and Martin Thorne. Then they'd been there when the policeman had entered to give them all his sombre and disturbing news.

George in particular had immediately felt immense sympathy for Morwenna Stacey. The policeman had sounded very pessimistic for Joe. It helped that the woman had been kind to her and Sophie in the Port William when the pair had been looking for a table for lunch. That had been only a week before.

It was less than a year since her own husband, Mark, had

been snatched from her in a Middle East plane accident. She had learned, the hard way, that every death is different because we are all such different characters, on our own paths through life. No two personal histories are ever the same. Whatever the particulars, she knew that Morwenna would go through deep grief if the worst happened to Joe.

And George knew, from her own experience over the last ten months, that losing a long-standing partner was an especially devastating form of loss.

The policeman had left them all in pieces rather than in peace.

After he had gone there had been desultory and subdued conversation. No-one knew quite what to say. Arno had started to make some comments on one or two aspects of the performance but only in a half-hearted way. It was obvious that at this moment no-one cared a hoot.

The whole thing was such a shock, compared with the celebration they had expected to share at the end of the evening. Arno didn't even think of bringing in the crate of wine and nibbles he'd stashed away in his car. Now was not the time for a party.

Given Sergeant Travers' request, they had decided, collectively, that it would not be right to join remnants of the audience at the Port William. That would surely invite questions to which, right now, they had no proper answers.

In the end Arno had suggested that, whatever happened, they should come back to Annabel's next day, late on Saturday afternoon. By then there might be some news from

Truro. That would give them a chance to share thoughts and feelings and to react to events together. Everyone remembered that there was supposed to be a second performance of *Splits and Schisms* on Saturday evening but no-one dared ask if that would still take place – or if they would want to take part. That was a judgement for an uncluttered mind, not one that any of them could make this evening.

There being nothing else anyone wanted to say, they had all set off for home.

As on previous nights, George had left her car at Ivy Cottage. She was not looking forward to walking back to Treknow up the dark footpath on her own.

Over the last ten months the analyst had grown gradually used to being on her own, making her own decisions and taking her own risks, with Mark no longer walking beside her. Mostly, nowadays, she could cope. But the sudden collapse of Joe Stacey, on a project she was a part of, had brought back a plethora of emotions. She was deeply sad, for herself as well as for Morwenna.

Fortunately Sophie had sensed that – or maybe her instinct was that tonight was not a night to seek a lift with Arno James. Wrapping up warm against the bitter cold, the two women had set off up the path together.

George had remembered to collect her video camera from its tripod on the side of the pulpit, as they passed on their way from Annabel's house. But when they got home she didn't want to look straight away to see if Joe had turned the camera on or off. Somehow that didn't seem to matter anymore.

When she did check, the following morning, she had a surprise.

CHAPTER 22

Peter Travers had been careful to note Arno James' contact details before he left Annabel's the evening before. He knew from past experience that visitors to the area were often harder to track down than locals.

It was now Saturday afternoon. He phoned to make sure the man was at home, drove the short distance from Trewarmett to Treknow and parked outside a small courtyard of cottages: Holly and somewhere anonymous (it had lost its name) – it looked as though the two had been built as a pair. He parked behind a red MG sports car and in front of a smart, yellow Mini Cooper; and guessed the director was the one owning the MG.

'Good afternoon, sir,' he began, when Arno opened the door of Holly Cottage and invited him in. There was no sign of anyone else in the house. He assumed the man lived here alone.

The policeman was pleased to accept the offer of a cup of tea, though judging from the empty bottles stacked outside the gate that wasn't the man's only tipple. Nonetheless the offer made for a cooperative beginning: and cooperation was going to be needed.

'I took Morwenna Stacey over to Truro last night,' Travers

began, once a tea tray had been placed on the coffee table between them. 'The Accident and Emergency doctor declared her husband dead soon after we got there. She was fearing the worst on the journey over, but nothing really prepares you for hard facts from an expert. Poor woman, she is obviously in deep shock. I'll go and visit her again when I have more news. I'm afraid I've been rather frustrated by the hospital. As far as ancillary services goes, they seem to regard weekends as an excuse for time off. It's a luxury I can't afford. I'm not nearly as far forward as I'd hoped.'

'So you've no information about the cause?' Arno seemed surprised, even disappointed.

'I still have no idea what really happened to Joe. It was all very peculiar.'

'That puts all of us in *Splits and Schisms* into a very difficult position. So what should we do about tonight's performance?'

'It hits me too, sir. I don't like it any more than you do. I've decided the most sensible thing to do for now is to learn as much as I can about the whole setup: the mechanics of the play, what was going on, who was where when and so on. In other words, to act as if his death were the result of crime - even though it's probably nothing of the sort.'

'Huh. You mean treat the arts world as guilty until proven innocent. The persistent view of the police force down the ages – here and abroad.'

'Sir, it won't help if you and I get ourselves at loggerheads. I have no wish to make this any more difficult than I need. I really enjoyed last night's production. I was there off duty, in my own time, just another member of the audience, learning so much more about the history of the village. It was great: a wonderful way of teaching history. Or at least it was until events intervened. I can tell you, sir, no-one would be happier than me if it turned out there was a medical explanation for what happened to dear old Joe.'

'You mean, you don't see this as an excuse for the police to bash the arts?'

'Not at all. I'm no sort of basher. I am, though, a public servant, charged with keeping the Queen's peace – paid by your taxes to do so. If the hospital finds that Joe's death didn't have a purely medical origin, then we'll need to do our best to find out what the cause was. Joe was your player – the lynch pin of the production, I would say - the embodiment of Job Hockaday. You'll be as keen as I am to know what really happened to him. The whole community will want to know.'

'You're really saying it's possible it wasn't just a natural death?'

'What I'm saying, sir, is that, at this stage, I have no idea. Medical science in Cornwall runs slower than I would like. The whole thing – the timing, the location, the occasion - was so bizarre.'

Travers paused. He sensed the director's hostility was starting to wane. Maybe he could win him over. 'So I'm aiming to do as much preliminary work as I can, as soon as I can, just in case the whole thing turns into a crime scene. By that I mean, for the moment, just me, sir – not dozens of detectives or hordes of reporters. It's in all our interests to keep the media at bay until we hear from the hospital. All I'm asking for is your full support and cooperation.'

Arno looked pensive. It was a unique situation – one day, maybe, he could turn it into a play. What the policeman was suggesting wasn't ideal – but it was probably the best deal he was going to get.

'OK, Sergeant Travers, we'll try and make that work. A sort of forensic "thought experiment" on both sides. So what do you want from me?'

'First of all, sir, I'd like to know what was supposed to be happening behind the scenes during the Quarry Disaster. What on earth was Joe doing there? Shouldn't he have been in his turret, preparing to make the next announcement?'

'That's what I find so puzzling, Sergeant. Job Hockaday wasn't meant to leave the pulpit at all – that was the name we'd come to call his turret, by the way. Job was the narrator throughout the play. He wasn't meant to be skulking about under the stage – he certainly wasn't there in any of the rehearsals.'

'Did he narrate during the scene itself?'

'No. Hardly in any of them. It got too complicated to switch quickly between stage and pulpit. For one thing the lighting man couldn't cope.'

'Might something have happened which made Joe change the plan? I don't know... say he'd been given an urgent

169

message for another member of cast that had to be delivered at once?'

'Once he'd introduced each scene, Job was left in darkness. No-one could see what he actually did. From the position his body was found I guess he must have nipped down from the pulpit and under the stage for some reason. There was probably ten minutes when he could have done so. I'm certain the movement wasn't in the script: remember, I wrote it.'

'Where were you during the drama, sir?'

'I was either in the dressing rooms, making sure the cast were ready to go on; or else behind the scenes, roaming about, making sure everything was as I'd planned. There was no point in me being at the front of house.'

'For the record, had anyone done a risk assessment on the stage?'

'You mean Cornwall Council? It was too far to come. No, I checked it myself. The guys who put it up had done a good job, as far as I could see.'

'Again,for the record, who were these guys?'

'Do I sense someone is being fingered as a scapegoat?'

'Not at all. I'm just trying to cover all bases. So go on, who were they?'

'A small company that does all the scaffolding work around these parts. I saw their van outside next door's cottage on Monday. They answer ultimately to Bill Howell, the husband of my sponsor, Della. She's funding the whole re-enactment.'

Della sounded like a powerful woman. Travers wondered for a second about the source of his early-morning phone call. 'Della wasn't in the group gathered in the lounge at Annabel's yesterday evening, by any chance?'

'Her daughter was. But no, she was busy squaring the high-ups from the Council that she'd persuaded to come and support us. I think she had a bit of a challenge. That smoke incident was completely unexpected.'

'Yes. I must say, from where I was sitting, there did seem to be a large amount of smoke.'

'That was the only big mistake we made on the production side. I take responsibility but the fault was down to Laurie Lane – our electrician. Somehow or other he reset the volume control on the generators from minimum to maximum. Result –as you saw – pandemonium. I haven't had a chance to ask him yet how that happened.'

Travers could see that an excess of smoke might have been deliberately contrived, if a serious crime was intended. He kept the thought to himself. It would be better to ask Laurie Lane about the details – were the smoke generators easy to find? How easy was it to reset their volume controls? How well were they labelled?

'I'm sure there'll be a lot more questions, sir. After I've talked to more of the cast and understand it all better. That's a good start, anyway. Have you any questions for me?'

'The most urgent one is about tonight's performance. Ought we to cancel it? Or go ahead as a memorial to Joe? As

171

a thoughtful outsider, what would you advise?'

'Joe seemed to me to have the largest part on the production – he had the most lines, anyway. How on earth could you do it without him?'

'Oddly, Joe's the only part that has a chance of being done by someone else without much hassle. You see, he had the whole script in front of him up in his pulpit. He said early on there was far too much to learn; and after I'd looked at it with him I had to agree. If he'd become ill, say, I would have taken over.

'I've heard the words in my head often enough when writing it, and listened to Joe spouting the narration. If I dressed up with the long white beard I suspect not many people could tell the difference.'

'Even so, sir, to answer your question, it seems to me tonight is far too soon. Most villagers would tell you the same. As I say, we don't know what happened to Joe. If it was certain he had had a heart attack; and if Morwenna was willing to let it run, then it might be on.

'From your viewpoint as author, I can see it's very disappointing. But I'd say, given all the uncertainty, it would show more respect simply to postpone. Putting it on, say, a week later might be an honourable compromise. After all, it's not as though anyone else is planning to use the site, is it?'

CHAPTER 23

An hour later Arno James drove down the hill to Trebarwith Strand for the meeting with the cast, feeling apprehensive. What emotions might he encounter? What stresses would emerge that he would need to manage? Were there any aspects of the crisis that he could resolve? In all his years of writing and producing dramas he had never had to deal with anything like this.

His cast had grown into a strong team over the last few months. He was immensely proud of their commitment and all that they had achieved together. But when all was said and done they were locals and he was an outsider. The death of Joe Stacey – completely out of the blue – was bound to affect them all deeply. He was affected too, but in a different way. He had lost a source and a writing associate whereas they had lost a friend.

The director was the first to arrive and quickly unlocked the door. He had managed to persuade Annabel to be out for the afternoon. He suspected that she had overdosed on the production during the last week of rehearsals – especially the sound effects, imitating the collapse of the local hillside. That wouldn't have done much for her nerves.

Fortunately, he gathered, she had plenty of friends she could visit in other parts of Cornwall.

He noted that Annabel had generously left the heating on to combat the bitter cold outside. They would need as much warmth as possible to cope with the bleak circumstances. He hastened to put the kettle on, ready for someone to make them all cups of tea.

One by one the company joined him. There was not much conversation; for the moment everyone was keeping their feelings to themselves. They had all heard, one way or another, that Joe Stacey had died. This was hardly a time for chit-chat or light-hearted banter.

Soon he saw that everyone had arrived – except for young Beth Howell. But it wouldn't set the right tone if he started to make a fuss. Probably she couldn't get away from her Saturday afternoon job in the village. It would be best to begin without her.

'Right, ladies and gentlemen, I think we'd better make a start.'

'Have you got some news for us?' This was Laurie Lane, his tone slightly truculent. It was an unsubtle reminder that these folk had known Joe Stacey much longer than he had.

'I saw Sergeant Travers less than an hour ago. He told me he took Morwenna Stacey over to Truro Hospital last night, where they got the news that Joe was dead. They had to wait ages for any diagnostic information from the medical staff. And the diagnosis was inconclusive. The hospital told him they'll be doing a post-mortem on Monday morning.

Until then all they could tell him - and all he could tell us - was that it was a sudden death. Travers was as aware as we are that this was hardly satisfactory.'

'Whatever does that mean?' asked Quentin Hocking.

'Medical mumbo-jumbo,' commented John Jasper.

'Poor, poor Morwenna,' said Martha Avery. 'She's the one the uncertainty hits most. It probably wouldn't matter what the illness was as long as she knows.'

'So does that mean Joe died an accidental death, some sort of medical emergency, but the doctors can't be sure exactly what?'

'Or does Travers' continued involvement mean that it might be far more sinister?'

'What do you mean, "more sinister"? It was sinister enough. One minute Joe was narrating away from the pulpit, a few minutes later he's collapsed under the stage.'

Arno sensed there was anger in the room – not with him, especially, or even with Travers, but because the whole event was so bizarre, so far outside anyone's experience or control. It just didn't make sense. These were down-to-earth people confronted by an extraordinary circumstance.

The director continued. 'If it was a medical emergency of some kind then Travers and I agreed it had happened re-markably suddenly – and, as far as we know, without any prior warning. There must have been something about the situation that gave rise to some uncertainty. Travers wouldn't tell me what it was. He told me he was starting to carry out preliminary enquiries in case the news from the hospital turned out to be too bad. When he explained what he was trying to do, I had to admit he had little choice.'

'Travers is covering his back,' assessed Laurie.

'He's got no option, has he? If something dreadful happened in the play while he was sitting in the audience, he'd be the laughing stock of the media. The Daily Mail would have him roasted. "PC Plod applauds Perished Player"; "Copper claps at Cast Collapse." And other such headlines.' This was Richard Penhaligon, landlord of the Port William - a semi-professional watcher of the habits of the tabloid press.

'It's not Travers that's got the problem. It's us.' Paul Wood, plumber, the man who'd been playing Greg Wallis, gave this sober assessment. 'After all, we were the ones around the spot when it happened – whatever "it" wuz.'

Arno recalled he had undertaken to give Travers all the help he could. 'In fact, Paul, you'd climbed down the ladder, past that end of the stage, before the sound effects even started. I don't suppose you saw anything?'

'How the hell could I "see anything"? There were no lights down there. It took all my efforts to make sure I didn't come off the ladder in the dark.'

'I was waiting for Paul further up the field,' said Martin Thorne, butcher. He'd been playing Dr Charles Rendle, the enlightened Board member. 'I could just see his silhouette coming down from the top stage. When he reached the bottom he came straight out towards me. He didn't stop anywhere.'

'You're in the clear then, Paul. You've got a witness to

support you.'

'Unless it was the pair of em, acting together.'

Arno wasn't sure who had made the last remark but he didn't think it was helpful. 'Gentlemen, this isn't Agatha Christie we're discussing. We're talking about the death of a real person – our steady as a rock Joe Stacey.'

There was moment of solemn silence.

Arno remembered his conversation with the policeman. 'It will help Joe's family if we can speed up the inquiry in any way or remove some of the fog. One of the puzzles is, what on earth was Joe doing out of his pulpit and under the stage? Has anyone got any ideas?'

For a moment there was silence.

'Suppose Joe felt ill,' suggested Paul. 'Say, he suspects he's having a heart attack. He knows he has to get out of the pulpit. But he doesn't want to disrupt the drama – he's put so much into it. Do you think he could be trying to reach a position under the stage where he knew he'd be found?'

'You mean, to join the rest of the Quarry victims?'

Quentin Hocking could see a snag.

'But if he was ill, wouldn't it be better to head for Annabel's?'

'He might not be thinking straight.'

'He might not want to be seen by the audience. He'd have more chance of staying out of sight if he was under the stage.'

There was silence for a few minutes as everyone pondered this scenario.

177

'The trouble was,' said Jim Melhuish, 'he didn't sound at all ill.'

Arno remembered the suggestion from Travers. 'Did anybody give him a message or anything?'

No-one admitted to having done so. Again some silence.

'There is one other possibility. Joe and I had a conversation after the dress rehearsal,' recalled Martin Thorne. 'Down in the Port William. We'd each had a couple of pints by then, mind. He said he was envious of me, having an acting part on the drama. I was a character that did something. Whereas all he did was to wear a long white beard and spout narrative. "I'm just the link-man" was how he put it. He might just have been tired, but he seemed a bit down about it.'

'Nonsense, he held the whole thing together.'

'Anyway, now you ask, I do recall saying to him, just a part of our conversation like, "The one place you could appear as a player would be at the end of the Disaster scene. If you got yourself across to the other side you could be one of the management party that came down the field and found all them dead bodies. Along with Paul and me."'

'What did he say to that?'

'Huh. He laughed; said Arno'd have a fit if we started amending the play between ourselves after the dress rehearsal. We'd been given plenty of times to experiment before that. He had a lot of respect for you, Arno, in the end.'

'Even so, it'd be worth us passing that on,' said the director sagely. 'It's not much of an idea but it's the best we've come up with. When all's said and done, there had to be some reason for him being there.'

'I've got one other snippet about Joe.'

Arno glanced to the side and saw George and Sophie, standing toward the back of the circle. 'Go on.'

George continued. 'I had a private arrangement with Joe about one of our cameras. You see, I wanted to be sure we could still get some footage of the drama, even in torrential rain.'

'You mean, your camera isn't waterproof?'

'It certainly isn't. Of course, we had plenty of film from different angles during the final rehearsals. It was a matter of finding a dry spot with a good view.'

'You could always have used one of the marquees.'

'I didn't want to pick up crowd noises. Or get in their line of sight. Then I saw that one of the cameras could be hidden in the side of the pulpit facing the stage. All Joe needed to do was to turn it on at the start of each Act – and off again at the end.'

'So you're saying you might have a video of Joe creeping down towards the stage at the end of Act One?' Arno looked pleased. 'That could be useful - it might give the police a better idea of timing.'

'Well, it might. Except that I had a look at the camera this morning. The memory is blank. There's no video footage of the evening at all. Joe obviously forgot to turn it on.'

'Now there's a riveting fact,' commented Jim Melhuish,

scepticism in his voice. The sense of anticlimax around the room was palpable.

'I did say it was only a snippet,' protested George. 'But it might tell us something. What it suggested to me was that Joe must have been very distracted about something to make him forget it. He promised me faithfully he'd help with our videoing. He was into photography professionally; wouldn't have wanted to let us down. So do any of you know what might have distracted him?'

Various vague suggestions were put forward, but no-one had any hard information.

'There was nothing he said to me made me think he was worried.' Variants were repeated from around the room.

'Morwenna Stacey 'ud be the one to ask, I reckon.'

'We can't ask her at this moment, can we?'

'Had you had any more rows with him, Arno?' asked Richard Penhaligon. 'Those were good bust-ups you two had in the early days.' He spoke as a connoisseur of spectacular rows.

'Yes, I have to agree there was some creative tension between us in the way I adapted his historic material,' replied Arno. 'But those were teething troubles. He was over-protective when we started. He needed to understand that I had to adapt his material to make it entertaining and dramatic. I had to edit out some bits and amplify others. There was some conflict between us but we were way past that now.'

It was clear that discussion of this topic was not going to

go any further.

'There was one other oddity about last night,' observed Arno. 'That was the smoke effects. They seemed much fiercer than they'd been during the rehearsals. What did you think, Laurie?'

'I'd been going to bring that up, Arno. I checked afterwards. Someone had deliberately fiddled with the volume settings on both boxes – reset them from min to max. It was the huge volume of smoke that gave us the fire scare, I reckon.'

'This is important. Did anyone here tamper with the smoke settings?' asked Arno.

No-one spoke.

'Did any of you tell any of your friends they even existed?

Again there was silence.

'That's very strange. Very strange indeed.'

Another moment of silence.

'What're we going to do about the second performance?' asked Laurie Lane, changing the topic.

'We can't possibly do it,' said Richard Penhaligon. 'It's much too soon after Joe died. At the moment we can't even tell everyone what happened.'

'I agree,' said Martin Thorne. 'It's very sad, after we've all worked so hard for months and months, but it wouldn't be fair on any of us.'

'There is one other possibility,' said Arno James. 'I rang Della Howell before I came down here and discussed it with her. She was clear that we needed to cancel tonight's per-

181

formance – even though, as she admitted, it's extremely short notice. No doubt the bush telegraph will help convey the message.

'She and I agreed, though, that it might be possible not to cancel it completely, but to delay the performance for a week; and go for next Saturday. How would you guys feel about that?'

There was a moment of silence as everyone considered.

'I for one 'ud be happy with that,' replied Laurie, 'provided the situation with Joe had been clarified. We could make it a tribute performance.'

'Yes,' agreed Richard, 'that'd be something very special.'

'Course, we'd need a replacement Job Hockaday. Would you fancy a role, Arno? You might have to brush up your Cornish accent. At least you wouldn't have to learn any lines.'

CHAPTER 24

As the cast of *Splits and Schisms* were gathering in Tre-barwith Strand, Sergeant Peter Travers was making his way to the one person on Arno's address list who, he had been told, would not be involved in their emergency meeting.

He was forcing himself to act on the possibility that something very unpleasant had been done to Joe Stacey - it hadn't just been a quick-acting illness. Where did that take him?

This could have been some personal issue for Joe, nothing to do with the play, which had happened to come to the boil in the middle of the performance; but that seemed very unlikely. For what could bring it to the boil at that moment? He could hardly have been caught up in an argument or quarrel. He might owe thousands to some bookmaker and have passed the last deadline to pay it back, but why on earth would something like that have to be settled halfway through a play?

Travers wanted to talk to the cast one by one and check their accounts of their movements around the stage. From what he had gleaned so far, it was stretching imagination past breaking point to think that an outsider would come

183

across Joe behind the scenes and deal with him while two hundred and fifty people were watching from the front.

"Come across" was the wrong phrase. It was one time that Joe's location was nailed down, predictable, known to anyone who could read a poster; though the policeman couldn't imagine he was that hard to find at other times. The name "J and M Stacey" was blazoned over his shop in Delabole.

It was, though, a very well chosen time. At the very least the murderer must have had some idea that there was about to be sound and smoke pouring forth around the stage.

It was hard to get away from the idea that, somehow or other, Joe's death (if it was murder) had been linked to the drama in which it occurred. Someone had being making a statement about the re-enactment itself, alongside their treatment of one of its players.

Was it was possible that the intended victim was the play itself – and Joe had just been its unlucky embodiment that appeared at the critical moment – the proverbial "man in the wrong place at the wrong time".

Where did that idea take his inquiry? One thing it meant was that he needed to understand as much as he could about the play: whose idea was it; how had Arno come to be involved; how had it been financed?

It was this last question which led him, now, to the home of Bill and Della Howell.

A random visitor, passing through Delabole, could be for-given for thinking that it was a working village with no big houses at all: small houses, many lacking a driveway. A lot of the village, certainly, was terraced, built to house workers at the Slate Quarry which lay half a mile behind the main road. But among these, a few larger houses had been built over the years - one of which was the end-point of this journey.

It was Bill Howell who came to the door when the po-liceman rang the stylish brass door bell. A large, well-built, prosperous-looking man with a weather-beaten face, who looked slightly troubled.

'Come in, Sergeant Travers, we've been expecting you all day. It's a terrible business. Della's waiting in the lounge.'

Travers had never had cause to visit this house before, but he knew from village gossip that he was in the upper echelons of Delabole life. It wasn't clear that the down-to-earth village had any movers and shakers, but if they had Bill and Della would have been welcome among their number. The policeman followed Bill down a wide hall with a polished grey slate floor, partially covered by smart rugs. The hall was embellished with photographs of earlier Howells. The whole thing gave a sense of a solid family home that had been here for generations.

Della Howell rose from her armchair to greet him. 'Good afternoon, Sergeant Travers. Would you like a cup of tea - or something stronger? Oh no, you're not allowed to drink on duty.'

'Tea will be fine, ma'm.'

185

Bill was despatched to mash and deliver. Whatever his role in the wider world – Travers had gathered he was some sort of high-class developer – he was certainly under authority within the home.

'We'll wait for Bill, if you don't mind. I've seen you around the place for many years. Were you born and bred in Delabole?'

'Camelford, to be exact. I've never wanted to be away from the area, resisted the lure of promotion to other parts - not that that came very often, you understand. My mother is in sheltered accommodation down in Port Isaac. I like to visit her most weekends – when I'm not on duty, that is.'

'So are you an only child?'

'No, I've got an older brother; he moved away - down to Penzance. He comes up when he can but he's a fisherman – so doesn't have a lot of spare time. Of course, when the weather's too bad for fishing it's not too good for coming back home either.'

The policeman feared he was starting to gabble. He was relieved to hear the sound of Bill coming back from the kitchen with a tray of tea. It would be a relief to put the interview back on track.

'No sugar, thank you.' The policeman took the delicate, flower-painted cup offered to him and sank back into his armchair. He turned to Della Howell.

'I understand from Arno James, whom I talked to earlier, that you are really the originator of this whole production – and the financial sponsor. Have I got that right?'

'More or less. I wouldn't put it as strongly as that. Basically, I was fed up with the village pantomimes that we'd had here every year since the year dot. I thought that as a village with a bit of backbone we could – should - be more ambitious. Then I got talking to our church warden one Sunday – that's Joe Stacey, you understand – and I learned that he was researching the history of the village. Not with any intention of publication, mind, it was purely for his own amusement.'

Bill, seated in an armchair on the other side, butted in. 'Joe had a strong interest in photography. It was the early photographs that captured him. From the middle of the nineteenth century. Black and white, of course, slightly fuzzy, but nonetheless strikingly authentic. They captured character in a way that oil paintings never would have – the Board members, anyway.'

'They would never have been able to afford paintings,' said Della. 'I doubt they'd have had the time to sit for the artist either. They were all so busy. Professional men, you know – doctors and lawyers – trying to control a slate quarry in their spare time. No wonder it never really took off.'

'That's not fair, Della,' replied her husband. 'It was the start of capitalism. All these guys had done was to buy shares in a speculative venture and become Directors. They put in a lot more time than most investors. Joe found out, you know, that at least one of the Directors visited here every month. Even getting here from Plymouth would be a struggle without cars or buses. Do you reckon they came on

187

horseback?'

If he hadn't been on a mission Travers would have found the conversation fascinating; but his concern was the present day. 'Anyway, there was a social history that could be dramatised. So how did you find Arno James?'

It was Della who replied. 'Actually, I knew him from school. He was always the leading light of the drama club, writing sketches and revues. In my last year I was his leading player. I was a glamorous actress in those days. That was long before I met Bill, of course.'

This was new information: it looked like it was new to Bill, too. Travers wondered if it had any significance for his inquiry then decided it would be best not to get side-tracked into long-ago memories.

'So you knew his capabilities. Had you kept in touch over the years?'

For the first time Della looked slightly uneasy. 'I followed his career in the press; and latterly on the internet. So when I had the idea of a historical re-enactment, his was the first name that came to mind; and I knew how to get hold of him. I invited him down for a weekend – it was that time you were off with your reunion at Bristol, Bill – and I sold the idea to him. That was how the whole thing began.'

'I think Arno saw possibilities of a social commentary,' added Bill. 'He was never sympathetic to a Board of Directors sitting away down in Plymouth.'

'What made the playwright equally mad was the lack of collective action up in the Quarry. They all played bosses and workers as though there was no other game in town. "Bunch of wimps" I heard him call them. That wasn't very fair. The workers here didn't have alternative employment they could bargain with. It was either work in the Quarry or starve.'

'By the end of the nineteenth century they could emigrate, Della. There were plenty of quarries in Pennsylvania or South Australia. These guys had the skills to make them highly profitable.'

This was all fascinating but Travers saw it was time to intervene. 'Is there any chance that Arno's play – *Splits and Schisms*, I mean - might have been so provocative in its social commentary – so critical of either the bosses or the workers - that it made someone want to sabotage it?'

A moment's pause while this idea was considered.

'Surely not,' commented Bill. 'Not in these days of subjective freedom. We may not like what we see, on television or whatever, but we are brought up to tolerate almost anything. No-one's going to be that upset by a play, however well done – even if some of the ideas challenge conventional opinion.'

'In fact it's the mark of a good play that it does challenge our ideas, isn't it?' added his wife.

'And in any case,' went on Bill, 'last night was the first performance. We didn't know what to expect. If the drama had been running for six months and had prominent reviews, then I suppose someone might have taken exception - but not the first time it was seen. Sorry, I don't think the idea's got legs.'

189

It was a clear reaction, anyway. Better than polite acquiescence. Travers checked his notebook for other questions.

'I understand there was due to be a second performance this evening?'

'That's been cancelled – or to be precise, postponed. I told Arno that over the phone an hour ago. If this whole dreadful business with Joe is resolved, there's just a chance it might go on next Saturday.'

'If it doesn't, will someone lose money? I mean, how expensive has the thing been to put on?'

'My business supplied all the marquees and staging,' replied Bill. 'That's quite a few pieces of kit so they would cost several thousand pounds to hire.'

'Though the drama's been set up as a charity,' added Della.

'- so I can declare it as a donation and offset the whole expense against tax. If I don't get any funds back it won't ruin me.'

'The other expenses are around twenty thousand pounds. There's a big electricity bill and the costs of hiring chairs and publicity. The actors are each given a small fee.'

'Pitifully small, I'd say, having to rehearse and perform outdoors in all weathers on winter evenings. I wouldn't do it for ten times the amount.'

'They agreed, Bill - the lure of the spotlights. Arno will get a more substantial sum – plus free accommodation for the winter. After all, it's his livelihood.'

Travers responded, 'You won't make – what – twenty five

thousand pounds from the audience – or anything like.'

The policeman did some mental arithmetic. 'If the overall attendance over two nights was, say, five hundred, each paying ten pounds for their tickets, that's only five thousand pounds. Do you have access to any subsidies?'

'I haven't publicised this, and I hope you'll keep it confidential, but Cornwall Council has offered us ten thousand pounds in support. It's from the pot they've set up to encourage new tourist attractions.'

Light dawned. 'Oh, you mean, if it's a success it might become an annual event?'

'That was the idea. It was intended to happen at Easter in the first place. Maybe daily performances over a week. Then Arno got an offer he couldn't refuse, to write a play about a colliery disaster in the north east. So *Splits and Schisms* had to be brought forward. That's why the actors are having to strut their stuff in freezing January.'

'If it doesn't complete a single performance, will you still get the subsidy?'

'Good question. It's all been so sudden I haven't had chance to ask yet. It must be doubtful.'

'So you two could be substantially out of pocket as a result of what happened to Joe. Is there anyone you can think of who might hate you enough to do such a thing?'

Bill replied first. 'I think of myself as a high-class developer; been at it for years. When you do that sort of thing you're in competition with other developers. There's bound to be antagonism and hostility here and there. On the whole we keep our battles professional – win some and lose some. I would be amazed if I'd upset someone enough they'd want to take revenge on Della's play. Even if they could work out how to do so.'

'I know I rub people up the wrong way,' added Della. 'I want to get things done; I'm rather impatient. Large parts of Cornwall are very traditional. There's probably a few that would be pleased to see me brought down a peg or two. Quite a lot would prefer to be left with their pantomimes forever; but it's impossible to think they'd be so upset they'd sabotage the play. Surely you couldn't think that?'

CHAPTER 25

Later that Saturday evening George and Sophie found themselves in the snug at the back of the Cornish Arms in Pendoggett as they awaited their meals. There was no-one else eating in that part of the pub.

The place had been suggested by Brian Southgate. After they had got back from the production meeting in Trebarwith Strand, George had rung the doctor and asked him to recommend somewhere to eat, well away from Delabole and its travails.

The Cornish Arms was a traditional pub, cosy rather than grand. Its oak beams and wall panels looked original, which suited them fine. The walls of the snug were decorated with prints showing hunting and sailing scenes from around Cornwall. It was at the centre of a village five miles from Delabole, on the road towards Polzeath.

Conversation on the way had been stilted, dominated by the challenge of finding the pub, which was new to them both. Sophie had turned on Radio One – it seemed to relax her, though it did the opposite for George.

Having arrived and placed their orders they could talk freely.

'If you remember, I suggested there might be something

odd going on here on our way down to Cornwall,' began Sophie. 'As I recall, you dismissed the possibility.'

'We don't know yet what happened to Joe: obviously even the police aren't sure. Arno was very cryptic, wasn't he? It must have been something fairly obvious for Brian to have spotted it. He's normally a man to let sleeping dogs lie, I would say. After all, murders can't be that common in Delabole.'

'OK, George, let's assume for a moment that this is a murder. On this occasion we were both there. We were at the scene – almost behind it.'

'Though neither of us saw anything.'

'We might have done - but not realised its significance. We don't know yet what we might have had a chance to see. Was it a dastardly trip, a narrow-bladed knife or a blow to the head? I presume eventually we'll be interviewed by that handsome-looking copper – that might give us a clue if we can winkle it out of him.'

'For goodness sake, Sophie, don't start taking a shine to Travers. I agree he was seasoned, savvy and smart, but right now he must be very busy. We'll both be low down on his list. If he's working through the company he won't get to us for days. We're hardly local, are we?'

'I dunno. We live next door to the director, easy walking distance from the stage.'

'Yes, but only for the last week.'

'And we are the only ones who've filmed any of it. Hey - are the cameras safe?'

'I hid them both in one of the kitchen cupboards before we came out. They're behind the porridge packet.'

'So, if we get a burglar, let's hope they're not in need of a meal. Ivy Cottage is not that secure, you know, George, if someone was determined to break in.'

'I've been thinking about that. Tomorrow morning we'll copy all the videos onto each of our laptops. Then we'll take the memory cards out and swap them for spare ones. Those cards are really small, you know. It won't be that hard to squirrel them away somewhere secure. Up in the loft, maybe?'

Their meals arrived at that moment and put an end to cloak and dagger deliberations.

Each had ordered fish. George had a plate of locally-landed sea bass and Sophie some baked hake. For a few moments there was silence as they arranged their food and started to tuck in.

'This is surreal, isn't it?' said George. 'Here we are, sitting in a fine country pub eating a scrumptious meal, discussing what happened as if it was a murder mystery play that we saw last night –'

'When it was someone we actually know that died – or was killed. Poor, reliable Joe. I'm so glad, by the way, that we met him and Morwenna together in the Port William last week.'

'Yes, they seemed a generous and loving couple. They were kind to us, anyway. Not someone to make enemies easily.'

'There are one or two members of the cast that you could imagine might rub people up the wrong way.'

'But annoying people, and annoying them enough to provoke a murder, are two very different things, Sophie. If there is a motive it must be more than the creative friction incurred in producing a play.'

'On that score, there's only one person I would say everyone must have fallen out with at some point in the rehearsals.'

'You mean Arno? He has been abrasive at times. He's tolerated us, just about - but he made sure we didn't interfere with the performance.'

'He didn't have much patience with poor old Laurie Lane, did he?' mused Sophie. 'Especially on those smoke machines.'

'It sounded as if he and Joe had had plenty of disagreements about how literally they should present known historical facts.'

'There was that skirmish over the cast all having a New Year dip.'

'What on earth are you talking about?'

'Richard Penhaligon whispered it to me the other night after the dress rehearsal, when we were in the Port William. I think you were in a different group. Apparently Arno had declared that a swim would help their bodies prepare for the cold of performing outdoors in January. I gather Joe was the one who managed to block it. That couldn't have endeared him to Arno.'

There was a pause as each sampled their fish, musing on motivation.

'How tall do you reckon Arno is, Sophie?'

'Medium height, I suppose. That's an odd question. Why d'you ask?'

'I just had a horrible thought. I'd say Joe was more or less medium height as well. They're both quite stocky in build. Both were wearing long, dark coats. It's not possible is it –'

Sophie gulped. 'You mean, we can think of lots of reasons why someone might want to do away with Arno - but none at all for Joe. We know Arno was lurking about behind the scenes during the performance. So what if, in the dark, someone mistook Joe for the director? And did away with the wrong man? It would be easy enough to do, wouldn't it?'

The possibility that the wrong person might have been killed in error halted their conversation for a while. Both women focused on their fish - they had been given generous portions. Both, though, were thinking hard.

'D'you think we should suggest the idea to Sergeant Travers?' asked George, sighing contentedly as she put her knife and fork together and pushed away her empty plate.

'It's not that wild an idea. He looked quite bright. He's probably thought of it himself.'

'Might not. He's not been at the rehearsals – or seen the men all dressed in similar long dark coats. He might never have seen Arno and Joe standing side by side. He doesn't know how Arno used to bully people.'

'Travers'll talk to us eventually, if he's working through the company. We can mention it then.'

'But if someone was trying to kill Arno and failed, they might try again.'

'That's true. We should at least mention the idea to Arno. Put him on his guard.'

The waitress turned up at that moment. 'Can I show you the dessert menu?'

'Oh, yes please,' said George.

She turned to Sophie, who, she sensed, was disapproving. 'With all this effort, physical and mental, we must be burning off the calories. This is quiet and warm - as good a place as any to talk.'

George ordered an Eton mess and Sophie a fruit salad: she had more concerns about maintaining her slim figure.

'Now we're sitting here talking about one possible murder, George, could I take you back, please, to Lily Turner's sudden death, in her bath in Ivy Cottage, last October. Was that purely old age? Or is there any reason – any reason at all – to suspect a connection between the two events?'

They had found no hard evidence that anything unnatural had happened to Lily, but George was no longer completely dismissive. If one well-disguised murder could happen around here, then why not two?

She pondered for a moment.

'There are a few similarities, aren't there? Both events happened within half a mile of each other and occurred within a few months. In both cases the victim was a long-standing local.'

'And in neither case, George, was the murder clear-cut. In fact, for Lily, no-one suspected anything at all.'

'M'm. There is one possible link, though. One thing that Lily and Joe had in common - one common interest that they shared.'

'Come on George, if you think you know don't keep it hidden.'

'All I was thinking was that both Lily and Joe had an interest in the past. Lily hadn't thrown away any of her old diaries - going right back to 1940. We also know she was reading a very old newspaper just before she died.'

'Yes. Alongside that we learned last week that Joe Stacey had been making a study of the history of Delabole.'

'That's what I mean. What's more, the overall context of the past few months is a historical re-enactment of the life of the Quarry. Do you think there's something in past events here – events maybe from the last century or even the century before - that someone doesn't want the world to rediscover?'

'It's an interesting idea. Though wanting to suppress a piece of history – say for fear of embarrassment - is a long way from being willing to commit murder to achieve that. The trouble is we've no clue at all as to what the trigger event might be.'

CHAPTER 26

As George and Sophie enjoyed their Saturday treat in Pendoggett, Peter Travers was settling down to a less enjoyable evening, interrogating his computer at his Police House in Delabole.

He could still hear the voice of Inspector Lambourn in his head, challenging his diligence and questioning his actions. If it turned out that Joe had been murdered, had the policeman done all he could to pursue the case? Would the Crime Squad have done anything much different? He didn't have much respect for Lambourn, but he had plenty of time for the senior detective he had met in the Crime Squad.

If anything had happened, those with a good knowledge of *Splits and Schisms* were the obvious suspects. He couldn't see how anyone in the audience could have slipped round the back and attacked the player. It would be an outlandish coincidence if a complete outsider had come to commit the crime, just as there was all the noise and smoke on stage.

He resolved that tomorrow, Sunday, he would go round the members of cast one by one and capture each of their accounts of the Friday evening. At present he didn't have a full picture of the mechanics. Presumably Arno would be able to give him a copy of the script to help this along.

He wasn't hopeful that the interviews themselves would reveal much. The cast list he'd been given showed that some members had several parts during the evening. That must have meant rushing about from one scene to another. It had been really dark under that stage. It was unlikely anyone would have seen anything.

One thing he could do this evening was to see if any of the cast had a criminal record. He sighed; it was a time-consuming process to check this on the police database - but it needed to be done. It was certainly one action the Crime Squad would take. Accessing the system remotely on his computer was always slightly flakey: he could easily lose the line. Once he had a connection there were a load of pass-words needed for each enquiry. These were changed monthly and weren't just names he could reconstruct – his mother's name and birthday, for example – but peculiar mixtures of characters and digits.

It took a few minutes to find the sheet of passwords he had brought back from his last monthly meeting in Bodmin – he recalled hiding it somewhere, but couldn't remember where. Finally he ran the list down; he'd hidden it under his spare-room mattress.

He took the cast list provided by Arno James and started work.

What was he supposed to do with "Arno", for a start? No-one called their child Arno. Maybe it was some sort of stage name the writer had adopted. Was he really an Arnold? He could see why someone might want to change from that.

201

Arnold Schwarzenegger had made it as an actor, but that was several decades ago; and he'd been known as Arnie.

He couldn't think of an alternative name that it might have come from, though, so entered "Arnold James"; and moved on to the next question. It was at that point the policeman realised he only had the man's temporary address in Treknow. He didn't have a permanent abode – assuming the man had one and didn't just wander the country as an itinerant playwright.

These were some of the things he must find out during the interview tomorrow. For now he decided to press on with the other names on his list.

It was slow work. Even when he'd entered the name and address (he didn't know any dates of birth, but fortunately that was optional) the computer system took nearly quarter of an hour to check all manner of files for any criminal activity by someone of that name. It even checked for traffic offences and speed infringements. This was a national database, he remembered – at least this was an improvement on the system of a decade ago, when each county kept its own separate records.

For completeness, when he started afresh, he began with Joe Stacey. If the victim had a criminal past, that would shine a completely different light on the whole incident. Gangland revenge of some kind? Knowing where illicit gains had been hidden? It all seemed pretty unlikely for Delabole.

Travers was relieved, though not surprised, to find a few minutes later that the man had lived a completely blameless life – or to be more accurate, had not been caught by the authorities doing anything wrong.

Now into the swing of it, Travers entered the names on his list in turn. Name after name were declared "innocent".

Then he entered the name of Martin Thorne – the local butcher in Delabole. According to the cast list he was playing Dr Edmund and later Dr Charles Rendle, two of the Directors of the Slate Company Board. There was no doubt about his address; Travers bought his meat from Thorne's Butchers in Delabole every fortnight.

It turned out there was something in this man's past. There were in fact several police cautions and a couple of appearances before magistrates in Wadebridge.

Progress! Hastily Travers printed off the details, made himself a mug of chocolate and sat down to examine them.

The offences were all low-level crime, fights outside one or other local pub. Almost certainly, therefore, they had been prompted by excessive drinking; and by some sort of argument that had got out of hand.

It wasn't recorded what the arguments had been about, if they had a common theme, or if there was a common victim. For example, had Joe Stacey ever been the recipient of Thorne's loss of control? Could the incident at *Splits and Schisms* simply be the latest manifestation in the series; but one that had gone horribly wrong?

Looking harder at his list, Travers could see it wasn't as bad as it had first seemed. True, there were half a dozen entries, but these had happened over fifteen years - with a significant pause between each. Almost as though something built up inside the butcher until it broke out in a fight.

This was certainly something to be pursued with an interview next day.

Travers dutifully went through the rest of the list he had been given, but with no further revelations.

By now he was tired. Why? It wasn't that late.

Then he remembered that, with the task of taking Morwenna Stacey to Truro, he hadn't got to bed until four am the night before - and then had been rung up by his boss at nine o'clock this morning.

A good night's sleep was needed to prepare for a busy Sunday. Travers headed for bed.

CHAPTER 27

George and Sophie had decided that they would give themselves a day off from cleaning and repainting Ivy Cottage; and concentrate their energies on the possibility that some event in the past, somehow or other, could be linked to the violent reaction being seen today.

'We'll go out for Sunday lunch again later,' said George. 'Although our kitchen is fine now. Tomorrow we'll buy fresh meat and start to cook ourselves proper meals. So how are we going to start our historical searching?'

'We know that Joe managed to find things out about Delabole. So there must be evidence around somewhere.'

'The trouble is, Sophie, Joe had spent ages pulling it all together. It was his passion, Morwenna said; almost an obsession. He lived here; we're only here for another week. We need a short-cut to the crucial events.'

'Y'know, we never gave Arno back his drama script. He's probably tearing his hair out looking for it. Why don't we begin with one of the incidents he dramatised in *Splits and Schisms*? - and assume that the author had got his facts more or less correct. Which one d'you reckon is the most explosive?'

'We've got to start with the Quarry Disaster,' said the analyst thoughtfully. 'On the basis of the drama, that was

205

the most far-reaching of all the things that happened to the Quarry in the nineteenth century.'

'In any case, it was the point at which the assault took place. That could link with it being a flash point for someone. So what did you do with the script?'

A few minutes later, each with a mug of coffee, they were seated either side of the wood burning stove. The script was in Sophie's hand.

'So what's our plan, Watson?' asked George.

'I reckon, Holmes, we need to get the actual events as clear as possible. Then to consider what else might have happened, before or after the rock fall, that could have long-term consequences.'

'Yes. We need to ask if it was just a dreadful accident – a freak of geology - or if anyone was really at fault? Who might have been embarrassed if the full story was ever told?'

George seized and studied the Disaster script carefully for a few moments. Then she handed back the file.

'Here, pretend it's a comprehension exercise. Ask me some questions to see how much I've taken in.'

Sophie glanced at the script for a moment. 'When were the first signs something was going to happen?'

'There was a crack – a sound from a seam which ran close to the top of the Quarry.'

'What sort of seam?'

'Quartz, I think?'

'That's right. Were these sorts of seam cracks well-known

in these parts?'

'If Arno's script is to be believed, they were. At least one of the quarrymen working on the terrace below – Cowling, was it? - thought it would be a good idea to get out of the way.'

'So the disaster didn't come completely out of the blue. There was at least a few minutes warning. In that case, why wasn't some sort of alert sounded? A general warning to the workforce?'

'M'm. I don't suppose they had a warning klaxon or anything in those days.' George jotted down a note for later discussion. 'In the drama, it appears Wallis was more interested in having the glory of reporting the crack to the Quarry Captain than in sounding the alarm.'

'The poor bloke paid heavily for that though, didn't he? His daughter, Fannie, was one of those killed.' Sophie glanced further down the script to Job's narrative at the start of Act Two.

'They didn't find her body for four years,' she went on. 'Four long years! Imagine the pain for all those years in the Wallis household. Not only to lose a daughter but not even to be able to find her and to bury her. Do you imagine his wife ever forgave him - do you reckon he ever worked in the Quarry again?'

'Are those questions I'm supposed to be able to answer from the script? Be fair, Sophie, I don't think it tells us.'

'No, but it brings home that the Wallis family might have suffered really long-term trauma. Maybe Fannie had a younger sister. If their descendants still live around De-labole, the drama could stir up bitter resentments.'

'Good point; but let's make sure we've got the whole picture, as given by the drama, before we extrapolate. Next question?'

There was a pause as Sophie studied the script.

'Here's one. What evidence is there that the Directors of the Slate Quarry knew much about the incident?'

For a moment George was stumped. Then it came to her. 'I know. There had been a visit by a Director that morning – Rendle, I think his name was. He hadn't spotted anything amiss. He was still arguing about the layout of the pit down below when the crash happened.'

'At least that meant he could be around to try and rescue the workers afterwards. What contribution, George, did the rest of the Board make to the Disaster?'

'That was another detail given later on, wasn't it? I'm better with numbers. It was a footnote: they gave something like sixty five pounds to the victims' families. Even though that'd be worth a lot more at today's prices, it doesn't seem very much. That works out at – what? - four pound per person killed.'

Sophie was looking at other footnotes as George spoke. 'There was a Disaster Fund set up, presumably funded from the area. That collected over six hundred pounds. Puts the Board's contribution into the shade.'

'So any – all – of the families of the victims might have an ongoing grudge against the management and owners of the time.'

'This happened well over a hundred years ago. Why on earth should it flare up today?'

George had far more industrial experience than Sophie. Her work included companies both striving and struggling. She mused for a moment.

'Do you remember the news we heard on the way down here – about that plane crash in New York? That shows how even a potential disaster can be mitigated by someone with good training and special skills.'

'You mean like the pilot, with all his past experience of flying fighter planes?'

'Yes. If Greg Wallis had been better trained it might all have been different. And were there other failures – or things that would be seen as failures if they happened today? For example, on risk assessment?'

'You mean, like insisting the men all wore helmets? I bet it never crossed anyone's minds.'

'More strategic things as well. Was the workplace over-crowded? Was it inspected? Did the management have safety drills? Why wasn't there a klaxon? Was there ever a plan to cope with a big rock fall?'

'George, we're looking at life in the nineteenth century. This is how things were. We do things better today, sure, but I doubt the Quarry was much worse than anywhere else at the time.'

'We could do some research about that on the internet. I'm a bit hazy; there were a series of Factory Acts in the nineteenth century, but did these apply to Mines and Slate Quarries? Should children have been allowed in the Quarry at all in 1869? That's something we could check on.'

'I've got one more question, but it's not one we can answer, I think, from the script. What happened afterwards?'

'Surely – with the number of dead in double figures - there must have been some form of inquiry? Were there recommendations that would have made the future any better? And were they followed? A report surely must have been published. If so, what did it say?'

CHAPTER 28

Whilst George and Sophie were wrestling to make deeper sense of the distant past, Peter Travers was focussed on the present day; or to be more precise, on the events which had happened the day before last.

Mercifully he hadn't been woken up today by a phone call from his line manager. He recalled that the man was an accomplished golfer – or rather, harboured the delusion that he might be one day, if he practised hard enough. The weather was fine – sunny, even. No doubt his boss was using his Sunday to hack away on the course in the dunes adjoining the River Camel near Rock. He would probably be there all day. Which was good; it meant Travers could go on with his enquiries without interference.

After breakfast he seized his annotated cast list and phoned up its members to make appointments to visit them over the day. Arno James was the only one he couldn't get hold of. Maybe he was sleeping late – or elsewhere?

Then the policeman settled down to give himself an underlying list of questions to be asked.

Richard Penhaligon was his first target – the man who played Robert Cowling. 'I'm happy to be interviewed,' he said, 'as long as it doesn't intrude on my work.'

'I am the owner of the Port William,' he explained. 'It's not just my address or job. Even at this time of year, with tourists non-existent, Sunday lunches are our most profitable offering. I can't afford to miss out.'

Soon the policeman had driven down to Trebarwith Strand, past the car park with its fateful stage and associated marquees, then up the pot-holed lane beyond the Inn, where patrons were supposed to park.

Travers had worked out that he didn't need to spend much time with this man giving a reason for his inquiries. Everyone on *Splits and Schisms* accepted something was wrong. When he had been guided into the landlord's den by Penhaligon he barged into his questions without further ado.

'Can you tell me, sir, how you came to be in the cast of *Splits and Schisms*?'

'It was my wife's idea. She came back one day last autumn from her meeting at the Women's Institute, really excited. She said they were going to do a drama about Delabole. They'd got a famous playwright lined up to write the script and they needed hunky men to play the key parts.'

'So you'd done some acting before?'

'Never. I refused point blank. Especially when I found it was going to be performed outdoors. That was even before we started planning the bloody thing for January.'

'So how come...?'

'My wife discovered the drama was going to be put on up the road here. Said I'd never live it down if it became known

212

I'd refused to take part. Whereas if I was involved... I could make sure the Port William was the place we all came back to after rehearsals. In other words it would be good for business. To be fair, once I was involved I generally enjoyed it.'

'What was the "famous playwright" like to work for?'

'Arno? I had no quarrel with his writing. It was his directing that was hard to take. The man was a bloody perfectionist – treated us as though we were West End professionals, not a bunch of amateurs acting way out of our comfort zones. Of course, it wasn't helped by being outdoors in January – it was pretty cold. Even so, by last week we were all keen to make it work. We could see that it was something very special – well, it would have been...' His voice trailed away.

Travers gave him a moment to recover; then continued his questions.

'Right sir, I want to understand as much as I can about last night – especially the mechanics of the play and the cast's movements. First of all, where did you all wait before it was your turn to come on stage?'

'We'd been given access to that house at the top of Trebarwith Strand – Annabel's - to use as our changing rooms. There was some scaffolding laid out, giving a decking ramp from Annabel's side door to the back of the stage area. Most of us sat indoors for as long as we could, to keep warm.

'We knew the scene when we needed to move out. Our

213

final positioning took place in the dark between scenes – usually whilst Job was giving the linking narrative. So when the spotlight came on, there we were, arguing - or in my case hacking away on the slate.'

'So could any of you have gone out from the changing rooms early and not been noticed?'

'If anyone had "not been noticed" I wouldn't have seen them, would I?' The man thought for a second. 'I suppose someone might. It wasn't as though any of us were talking much. We were all nervous – going over our opening lines. Especially as it was the first night.'

'You yourself didn't see anyone in an unusual place behind the stage on Friday evening?'

Penhaligon shook his head firmly. 'Can't say I did.'

'How about the director? Where was he?'

'Arno? He was roaming about, behind and underneath, making sure there were no problems emerging. I didn't see him myself; but then I was in a dense cloud of smoke by the end of the scene – it made my eyes run.'

Travers paused for a moment. He couldn't see how he could learn more about cast movement here.

'One other line of question, sir. Had you any reason to think Joe Stacey was worried - or under some sort of threat? Have you any idea about who – if anyone - might have wanted to do him harm?'

'Those are things I've talked over and over with Martha since Friday.'

'That's your wife?'

'Yes. We both know - knew – Joe and Morwenna Stacey as a couple pretty well. There was nothing Joe ever said which suggested he was the worrying kind. Their shop did regular business and he got on with people. I can't think that anyone would want to do him harm.'

Travers looked hard at him; waited for anything more. Was there a "but" following? It seemed, though, that Penhaligon had nothing to add.

'Right sir. Thank you very much. Needless to say, if you think of anything else, you know where to find me.'

He handed over his police contact card. 'Here are my details. I don't expect I'll be home much over the next few days. There are a lot of people I need to talk to. I'd be grateful for your discretion in who you talk to about this. I'm sure Morwenna Stacey would welcome that too; she's very distressed. It'll be a lot clearer when we hear from the hospital.'

It was half past eleven. Travers had one more interview scheduled before lunch, which was with Laurie Lane. The electrician lived in Tintagel and was awaiting him when he reached his house. Again the policeman didn't bother to justify his visit, though he was happy to accept the offer of a mug of coffee.

'Right sir. Today I'm assembling background on everyone directly involved in *Splits and Schisms*. I gather you were the lighting and effects man. Had you volunteered for that role or been pushed into it?'

215

'I've helped with the pantomime for years. So I guess Della Howell just assumed I'd be happy to help with *Splits and Schisms* when that came along instead. To be fair, I didn't put up much resistance. I didn't realise, when I started, how much harder it would be.'

'You mean, supporting an outdoor production?'

'I was thinking more of working for Arno James. Tyrant and bully; determined to have his own way. Although, I suppose, a genius in his own terms. There was a real clash, mind, between the professional theatre man and us local amateurs.'

'Maybe that was the only way a drama like this could be pulled off?'

'Probably. He could have been more tolerant, though. Writing and producing the drama was all he was doing here; the rest of us had jobs to keep on top of. Arno kept charging me with finding extra equipment – like those ruddy smoke machines - then managing to get the stuff to work.'

'Did others find him hard work as well?'

'Pretty well everyone, I'd say – apart from Beth Howell – Della's daughter. You'll remember her - the young girl who appeared in the Disaster scene and exited it climbing up the ladder through the smoke. She was Arno's pet. Could do no wrong – even when she was late for rehearsals. As she quite often was.'

'Tell me more about these smoke machines. Did they produce too much smoke last Friday?'

'Far too much. I looked afterwards. Someone had reset

the volume controls – moved them from min to max.'

For Travers this sounded like the first hard evidence of any active disruption to the drama. He leaned forward to clarify.

'Are you sure about that, sir? You couldn't have done it yourself, say, under the pressure of a live performance?'

'Travers, I'm a professional electrician. I'm used to gadgets. I know how I left those controls at the end of the dress rehearsal. Someone had fiddled with them by the time of the performance on Friday. I'm absolutely certain.'

'This is really important, sir. Would that be hard to do?'

'Well, the smoke machines weren't locked; and the controls were marked. So I suppose anyone who was minded for sabotage could have come along before the performance and reset them. I'd intended to check them but I had too much else to do.'

'Did you have any assistants? I don't see anyone listed here.' Travers had produced his cast list and was searching down the card.

'That was why I was so often in trouble with Arno. I couldn't do that many things at once - there were bound to be delays here and there. I only have one pair of hands.'

'So during the whole performance you were in the control van with all the switches? On your own?'

'Sophie was keeping me company beforehand. Then she went off to do her filming.'

Travers ogled. He must have misheard. 'Say that again, sir. The whole performance was being filmed?'

217

'There were two women, Sophie and George, each with video cameras. They had just moved in next door to Arno down in Treknow. I met them when I sorted their electrics a week ago.'

Travers was still dumbfounded so the electrician continued.

'I think their videoing was a pretext to come to the final rehearsals. They took plenty of video footage of the last few nights. Are their names not on your list? I can give you their number if you like.'

CHAPTER 29

George and Sophie had spent a couple of hours trawling the internet, once they had run out of ideas about the Quarry Disaster and why it could have left a long-term legacy.

They now knew rather more about the general history of the nineteenth century and how UK legislation had progressed in response to the industrial revolution and the growth of the British Empire. The concept of Health and Safety legislation and risk assessment was unknown. They had learned that the successive Factory Acts, whilst they gradually stopped the exploitation of children, did not apply to outdoor quarries until the end of the century.

'So although the whole setup was primitive by our standards, there was no law being broken in 1869,' observed Sophie. 'So no reason for anyone to get that upset about it.'

George was about to reply when her phone rang. 'Hello. Yes, I'm George – George Gilbert. I'm here with my friend Sophie Collins. We live in Treknow, next door to Arno James. Come and see us any time.'

There was a pause while the caller spoke.

George replied. 'We're about to go for lunch, actually. In Trewarmett. Would you like to join us? Right. Fifteen minutes. We'll see you there.'

She turned to her friend, a grin on her face. 'That was Sergeant Peter Travers. He'd only just learned that we've been filming the production. And he'd like to find out all that we know.'

There was no difficulty with recognition at the Trewarmett Inn, although it was busy; and the parties had never spoken face to face. The policeman's uniform rather gave him away.

Both women had taken a few minutes to change out of their working jeans and into something more striking. The policeman was quick to spot two unknown but attractive-looking females as they entered the crowded bar, looking round for him.

Soon all three were seated at a table at the far end of the restaurant, which the landlord had kept for them at Travers' request.

'I'm George Gilbert, new owner of Ivy Cottage; and this is my friend Sophie Collins,' began the analyst.

'You and I have talked before on the phone, I think?' responded Travers. 'Last September? That was crucial evidence. I've been looking forward to meeting you, to thank you in person. I didn't expect it would be in the context of another inquiry.'

Sophie was looking puzzled.

'I hadn't told Sophie about all that,' explained George. 'I didn't want to worry her.'

'I'll explain later,' she added to her friend.

The landlord was a long-standing friend of Travers. He soon brought them menus and they each ordered roast beef. George asked for three halves of cider – she'd found a week ago that the locally-brewed Rattlers was strong.

'Thank you for meeting me so speedily. To be honest, your names weren't on the printed cast list I'd been given by Arno - so you weren't on my schedule. I've got more of the cast to see this afternoon, but I'd deliberately kept my lunch hour free.'

'We thought you'd want to see us eventually,' responded Sophie, 'but we assumed that we'd be low priority. After all, we've only been here a week.'

'What made it more urgent,' explained the policeman, 'was when Laurie Lane told me you'd been taking video footage of the performance – and also the rehearsals. Added to which you're both newcomers, so likely to have an independent view of what's going on. I'm finding it hard to pick my way through all the actions and characters.'

'The videoing was mainly a device so we could get to see the production. All the tickets had been sold by the time we got here – that was only a week ago. Sophie is into photography professionally, you see.'

'So it was your idea to take the videos?'

'Yes,' said Sophie. 'No,' said George.

The two women spoke simultaneously but both answers couldn't be correct. The policeman smiled as he looked from one to the other.

'What happened was this,' said George. 'We met Arno

James for the first time a week ago – he's our neighbour. We'd no idea he was behind *Splits and Schisms*. When we found out, we asked about tickets. Sophie had mentioned she was a photographer; Arno saw that as a way for us to see it. I offered to provide him with a video and it went on from there.'

'You were taking footage on Friday evening?'

'We both were. Mine went wrong. You see, I'd hidden my camera inside that pulpit thing Joe spoke from, so I could get a steady view of the stage. Joe was supposed to turn it on when the performance began; but he didn't.'

'I got some footage of the crowds arriving,' added Sophie, 'then I stood off to the side, with my camera on a tripod, and tried to get key close-ups.'

Travers thought for a moment. 'So really you haven't got much footage at all that might help me.' He seemed disappointed.

'Friday wasn't the only night we filmed,' said George. 'We've got film from Monday, Tuesday and Thursday as well.'

'Wednesday was the technical rehearsal so we had a night off,' added her friend.

'On Tuesday evening I had my camera mounted on the scaffolding at the back of Ivy Cottage – we'd just had a wood burning stove fitted. It was pointing down the valley, on full zoom, focused on the drama. The sound wouldn't be any good, but it was an unusual angle of the Treknow end of the stage – and one which no-one knew about.'

That was more promising. 'It's just possible that one or other of those films might help me.' The policeman thought on. 'Consequently, it might be a risk needing to be removed for someone else. Are your cameras well locked up?'

George explained her procedure, which they'd implemented this morning. 'So the memory cards are hidden in the loft and we've each got a copy of the videos on our laptops. You could take the cards to the Police Station if you thought that was safer.'

'You're welcome to borrow my laptop to watch the film for yourself,' offered Sophie. 'There are hours and hours of it. What would you be looking for?'

'Right now I've no idea. It's a bit of a muddle, to be honest.'

All their meals arrived. For a few minutes there was silence as they shared the condiments and started to eat.

'One other question I thought you might help with,' said Travers, as he drew breath, deciding which vegetable to go for next, 'was anything you could tell me about the various characters in the drama. For example, did any of them seem particularly abrasive or difficult?'

'We've only been here a week. We don't know them all that well,' protested Sophie.

'We've one or two ideas. The one they loved to hate was Arno. He pushed everyone really hard. He was a professional amongst a bunch of amateurs. On the whole, though, they tried to follow him.'

'Of course, he had most to gain outside North Cornwall if

the drama was well-received. It was his livelihood. For the rest of the cast there would be plenty of local appreciation – whatever the acting standard - but it would soon die away.'

'It's a long shot - but did you happen to notice any oddities, during rehearsals or the performance?'

There was a pause as both considered.

'There was that minor oddity, a week ago yesterday, before we'd even met Arno – do you remember, Sophie?'

'Ugh?'

'There was that young girl - she came out of Arno's house about ten o'clock on Saturday morning. Just as we were setting off for Wadebridge. We didn't see her face, remember, because she was walking away from us. I was all for giving her a lift but you wouldn't let me. It was probably all perfectly innocent.'

The policeman jotted down a note. 'Anything else?'

'We had one idea yesterday evening, didn't we George, as we thought around the whole thing.'

'Go on,' said the policeman. He seemed to be taking them seriously.

'It occurred to us that it would all have made a lot more sense if Arno had been the one killed.'

'In the darkness, wearing his long coat and seen from behind, Arno would have looked much like Joe Stacey. So could it have been a case of mistaken identity?'

'There was some talk at the *Splits and Schisms* meeting yesterday afternoon. One of the men – I can't remember who - recounted a conversation with Joe the night before.

He suggested Joe might have unexpectedly decided to join the Quarry management group on the far side of the stage. Swapping sides would put him in just the wrong place at the wrong time.'

'It's a theory,' admitted the policeman. 'By no means impossible on what we know so far. So run past me again why you think someone might have wanted to kill Arno.'

'Two possible reasons,' said George. 'First of all, there was obviously some long-standing tension between Arno and various members of the cast – for example, he was pretty hard on poor old Laurie. Joe hadn't been too pleased at the way Arno had rewritten his historic material. That could have led to a deep grudge between them.'

'That could have been a reason for Joe killing Arno,' commented Travers, 'but it would hardly explain why Joe ended up dead.'

'Could it have led to a fight between them - in which Arno got the upper hand?' This was Sophie's contribution. Even as she spoke it sounded far-fetched. How often were fights to the death conducted in near silence?

'So what was the alternative reason?' It seemed Travers hadn't set much store by their first.

'We wondered if somehow the drama had stirred up old resentments or grievances in the village,' said George. 'One or other scene had a deeper meaning for someone in Delabole – something they would go to any lengths to suppress.'

'That sounds plausible when you say it quickly,' replied

225

the policeman. 'The trouble is trying to think of any event that happened so long ago that would have any real impact now. I mean, something twenty five years ago could have consequences today – the perpetrator could have been in prison in the meantime, for example.

'Or emigrated to Australia.'

'But *Splits and Schisms* is about the nineteenth century. That's several lifetimes ago - a very long time for a grudge to fester.'

CHAPTER 30

Glancing at his watch, Travers had announced that he would have to leave them; he was due for his next interview. He'd gulped the rest of his cider and was gone.

George had decided there was time, this week, for some chocolate fudge cake and it proved delicious (though Sophie smugly declined); after which the two women returned to Ivy Cottage. Despite the policeman's reservations – and maybe influenced by the ghost of Lily Taylor - Sophie was still adamant that something in the distant past must be behind current events and wanted to press on with their historical research.

'Let's take another scene and dissect it.'

Neither could see any reason to choose one scene in preference to another. The trouble – if there was trouble - could have happened anywhere.

'Why don't we work on the arrival of the railway in De-labole in 1893?' asked George. 'That's more recent than 1869. A thirty-year-old in that story who married late could have a grandson alive today. I have no idea what the link could be with anything in 2009, but we've more chance of finding it if there's a suspicious back-story.'

They started the process as they had before. This time

227

George made them a pot of tea. Meanwhile Sophie did her best to soak in the key events, as revealed in the script.

Dr Edward Jago, Chairman of the Old Delabole Slate Company Board of Directors, sits at the centre of a long table, facing the audience. Colleagues Dr Charles Rendle, Mr Hugo Higgins and two others sit alongside him.

Rendle: Gentlemen, we can no longer regard this Quarry as a cash cow, providing us with easy dividends year on year. The world is changing: and we must change with it.

Jago: Sadly the world is changing; and not for the better, I avow. What else can we do? It would be wonderful to mine diamonds or coal. The geology of North Cornwall, though, is God-given: the Quarry can produce only slate. The price we can sell is determined by the Welsh, with their massive quarries – twenty times as big as ours. All we can do here in Cornwall is to follow their lead.

Rendle: Sir, I disagree. Before the railways we could outperform every other quarry in the southwest. That gave us a strong regional market. In the 1880s that is no longer enough. Having no railway links to Delabole is a disaster. The Welsh have had tramways to their ports for most of this century.

Higgins: As you know, I am a newcomer to this Board. How is the slate moved away from Delabole?

Jago: The raw slate is split and sized at the Quarry. Then it is taken on horseback, a journey of four miles, to the hamlet of Port Gaverne.

Rendle: Where a bunch of women – women, mind – stack it on boats, to be taken to market around the southwest. I've seen them in action: it's grotesquely inefficient. The shoreline is only partially-sheltered; boats at Port Gaverne capsize regularly. I've commissioned a study - he waves a document *– which shows that we lose one eighth of the slates, so laboriously hewn and split, on their way to market.*

Higgins: One eighth! No wonder our profits are so pitiful.

Jago: It's a problem we've known about from the beginning. The Old Delabole Slate Company once tried to build a railway from Delabole right down to the port of Rock - but something went wrong.

Rendle: Another railway is being built as we speak - it has already reached Launceston: the North Cornwall Railway. I propose that we approach them to make the case for extending the line to Delabole.

Hockaday: Another Board meeting, two months later.

Rendle: I bring good news, gentlemen, from the North Cornwall Railway. I have now attended two Liaison Groups. They have surveyed the route to Camelford and purchased the land. The line should be there within three years.

Nods of enthusiasm from around the Board.
Rendle: Even better, gentlemen, their long-term goal is to reach the North Atlantic Coast at Padstow via Wadebridge – which route cannot but take them through Delabole.

More enthusiastic nods.

Higgins: Who said there was no such thing as a thrifty pasty?
Rendle: We have been invited to provide a spokesman, gentlemen, to sit on the Liaison Group and guide them on the best route around our Quarry.
Jago: 'Tis good, Dr Rendle: you have done well. The question for the route is: how close do we want their line to our Quarry? If it comes too close it will hinder our operations.
Rendle: Conversely, if it goes through the middle of Delabole, many houses will be demolished – most housing our workers. We have other production options. We could develop the far side of the Quarry, away from Delabole.
Jago: Wait, sir - we know the Quarry nearest the village is highly productive. That's why we bought that land. Be our liaison man with the Railway by all means, Dr Rendle, but I beg you: keep their line away from our Quarry.

Spotlight to Hockaday: So Dr Rendle joined the Railway Liaison Group and the line inched ever closer to Delabole. The dire state of the Slate Company's finances made it clear that links were needed – at almost any cost. The Railway offered two thousand pounds to the Quarry to settle the matter but this was rejected. After another battle with Dr Jago, Dr Rendle resigned from the Board; but he still maintained links with the Railway. Then he called an extraordinary meeting of shareholders.

Spotlight back to stage. The table has been moved to the side and the chairs removed.

A motley crowd of men in centre stage. Dr Rendle, stand-ing on the table, addresses them.

My fellow shareholders thank you for heeding the call to this extraordinary meeting. I've called it because I believe there are crucial decisions facing the Slate Company in connection with the North Cornwall Railway – decisions which the Board are not facing up to. Let me paint a broader canvas.

The Railway is now at Camelford; and has to choose where to go through Delabole. Do they take the line through the village, demolishing houses as they go? Or do they go round the edge, alongside the Quarry?

Dr Jago is adamant that the Railway should not be close to the Quarry. In my opinion this is a grave error. Whatever happens, the Quarry is already on the edge of Delabole: it cannot come much closer. Within the next few years the only direction it can expand is on the far side. Are you with me?

Muttering and gesturing from the crowd.

Crowd 1: Some of us have said for years that the far side would be safer to work.

Crowd 2: Yes, the strata are far less steep. It's no joy having to work on a near-vertical slope with others directly above us.

Dr Rendle (beaming): Since that is the case, we should not raise objections to the Railway being beside the Quarry. So what I propose is that we send a letter to the Directors, alerting them to our views.

Crowd 1: Dr Rendle, this is the Company Board. We can-

231

not force their decisions.

Dr Rendle: Even so, they will take note. I doubt the Chairman will be influenced but there are others on the Board who are more open to reason.

The spotlight fades once more.

Hockaday: The issue came once more to the Board. Dr Jago, Chairman, stuck to his position but this time he found himself isolated. A vote was forced; and he lost. North Cornwall Railway was told it could come as close as it liked to the edge of the Quarry. It was the best overall solution.

The first train arrived in Delabole on October 18th 1893. A day of great rejoicing - though not for all. Dr Jago resigned from the Slate Company Board, rejected and broken hearted. He cut off all links with the company.

As for Dr Rendle, he rejoined the Board and became its next Chairman. He had a lot more to give the Company; as we shall see in the next episode.

With tea in hand, George took the script from her friend and began the questioning.

'Was it an accident that the North Cornwall Railway came to Delabole - or was the Quarry a target destination?'

'The ultimate target of this Railway was Padstow. I don't know if passengers or freight was what they had in mind in Victorian times. I mean, there wasn't such a thing as a tourist industry then, was there? Let's look at the map.'

Sophie reached in her handbag for their tourist map of

Cornwall; the pair scrutinised it for a moment. 'Delabole was always going to be close to the route chosen. Probably it was Rendle's intervention that made it certain.'

'So why was the route controversial?'

'For a long time it wasn't. The problem came as they got close to Delabole. The argument was, would it be best to skirt the Quarry or to go right through the village?'

'What did the Directors think?'

'They were divided. The Chairman – I've forgotten his name – wanted to protect his Quarry. They'd always got the slate from the village side, he said. Rendle wanted to save the village.'

'You mean Rendle wasn't bothered about the Quarry's future?'

'He was looking further ahead. Eventually, he could see, they'd need to develop the side furthest from the village. It might even be easier geology – the gradient of the strata was less severe. He did his best but couldn't persuade the Chairman - could see he never would – so in the end he resigned.'

'Only to fight from another angle. What was his new line of attack?'

Sophie was stuck. 'I dunno. I couldn't really understand this bit.'

George had more understanding of business politics. 'Yes, it was quite subtle. Rendle called a meeting of shareholders and persuaded them to back the idea of the railway line beside the Quarry. Then collectively they wrote a letter to

233

the Board, pushing the idea.'

'Hang on, George. Why did a letter from the shareholders have more impact than Rendle would have had, banging on at the meeting?'

'Well, it didn't affect Dr Jago – he was the Chairman; but it did influence the others. So, when it came to the vote, Jago was defeated. Resigned as Chairman, quit the Board, sold his shares, left the company. That must have been a big event in Plymouth's financial circles.'

George posed her final questions. 'So could this have had long-term consequences? Can you spot anything under-hand going on?'

There was a pause. George poured them second mugs of tea.

'If Dr Jago had any descendants in these parts they might feel sore about the story. I mean, probably it was the best result – but it was hard on the old Chairman.'

'He'd been around for a long while – didn't he appear in a scene earlier on?'

'I think so. The trouble is, even if he had rough justice, it's a bit late to be taking revenge, isn't it? I'm starting to see what Travers was talking about – a hundred years is a very long time for a grievance to fester.'

There was silence. Sophie picked up the script and read it through once more.

'There's a bit you missed out, George. You didn't ask me about the Railway's bribe to allow the line to go near the Quarry. Two thousand pounds it says. What d'you reckon that is, in today's money?'

'We can probably find an estimate from the internet.' George seized her laptop.

'There's an article here; it suggests inflation has been about one hundred from the 1890s to 2000. So not that much, really – two hundred thousand pounds – maybe quarter of a million?'

'It would be interesting to know what happened to that money. I mean, if it was all above board, it should appear in the Old Slate Company's accounts. There was nothing intrinsically dishonest about money changing hands to settle the position of a piece of track. They didn't have Regulators in those days.'

'But don't you see, Sophie: Jago's bruised feelings couldn't possibly make any difference today. Money's different. If that money wasn't in the accounts, if it had just disappeared and appeared somewhere else, that might have a longer term impact.'

'Especially if the diligent Joe Stacey had found out where it ended up; and if there was any risk that the name of the winner might emerge from the drama.'

For the first time something tangible seemed to have emerged from their efforts.

'So our first move needs to be to get access to the Old Slate Company's accounts for 1893 – and the years on either side. How can we do that?'

'What did Morwenna say about Joe's sources? This one won't be an anecdote from an old timer in Delabole. Wasn't there some mention of Truro?'

'Let's see what the internet tells us.'

Once again George's fingers flew across the keyboard. 'I'm going to try "historical records + Truro"'

There was a pause as the request went across cyber-space. 'Here we are. The Cornwall Record Office. Old County Hall, Truro. Open nine till four thirty, Monday to Friday.'

George turned to her friend. 'You know, I think tomor-row might be a good day for us to go to Truro and look for some new furniture – and see what else we can find.'

CHAPTER 31

Meanwhile Sergeant Peter Travers, refreshed by his roast lunch, was continuing with his task of interviewing the cast and crew of *Splits and Schisms*.

There was one lesson at least from his lunchtime encounter. The list he'd been given by Arno – no doubt produced in a hurry - was incomplete. Were there were other ancillary members of the production to whom he should be talking?

He resolved to show the list to each of his remaining interviewees and see if they could spot any omissions.

When he'd rung them, most of his interviewees had said they were happy to talk at any time on Sunday afternoon. Was any one of them a priority? How would the Crime Squad arrange this? The trouble was, he didn't know enough about the whole event to be able to decide.

One thing that might just matter was a criminal record. On that basis his first interview after lunch should be with Martin Thorne. Travers set out back up the hill and, after the usual struggle parking, found himself in the living room over Thorne's butcher's shop in Delabole.

Travers repeated his questions about how the man had come to be on the cast; and the way rehearsals had progressed. Nothing much new emerged, although the irritation which Arno James had managed to provoke among his players recurred. The story of the narrowly-averted New Year's Day dip for the cast at Trebarwith Strand was repeated.

'Can I ask you a different kind of question?' Thorne nodded.

'As a routine part of an investigation like this I check the background of the people I'm interviewing.'

'Yes?' Thorne looked anxious now, a little aggressive.

'I discovered that over the last fifteen years you've had occasional brushes with the police. Usually for fights, taking place outside one or other local pub. Have you any comment?'

Thorne didn't speak for a moment, deciding how he should respond. Denial did not appear to be an option. How much explanation should he offer? What was Travers after, beneath the courteous tone?

'It didn't happen very often,' he began. 'Just when things got out of control. When I came up against someone who was too full of themselves - trying to be too bossy. Telling me exactly what I could do. Mostly I just contained myself and walked away, but sometimes, maybe when I'd had a pint too many, I flipped. That when I found myself in trouble.'

'I thought it must be something like that. Have you any idea what's behind it? Were you bullied at school or something? Beaten for scrumping a few apples? Or was there

238

some thug of a teacher who had made your life hell?'

'Oh, there's no mystery. If you really want to know, I can tell you. It'll take a few minutes though. It goes back many years.'

Travers remembered his recent conversation with George and Sophie. Was the past going to turn out to be important after all?

'Please continue, sir. Take as long as you want.'

'It's like this, sergeant. One of my ancestors was very badly treated by the management of the Delabole Slate Quarry.'

'That Quarry's pretty old, sir. Thirteenth century, I believe. How far back are we going?'

'The man in question was called Henry Penfound. He was my great, great grandfather. The line of descent was through his daughter, so that's why I've got a different surname.'

'And it bothers you, sir – even though this happened so long ago?'

'I've often tried to forgive and forget, Travers. It's not that easy. See, before the incident my ancestor – Penfound - was doing well for himself. He'd got a house in the village, a beautiful wife, a baby daughter – that's my great grandmother - and a job at the Quarry.' Thorne looked into space for a moment, wistful.

'Wages were low and there was a mediocre Welshman who'd been brought in to manage the Quarry. Robert Roberts – what a name. Maybe the vicar who christened him had a stutter? He knew he was struggling and that made him indecisive.'

Travers said nothing, listened hard, let him continue.

'This was the 1880s. Times were bad. Penfound went to see the manager and demanded a rise – for all the workers - or they'd be out on strike. Roberts was afraid. He sort of agreed. Then one of the Directors came on their monthly visit – hard as nails - and put a stop to the offer.'

'So your ancestor was simply sacked? Just for instigating a strike?'

'Eventually. There was an intervening step. A man called Cowling had heard Roberts' first response, thought the strike was over and started work. He was accosted by the workforce, led by Penfound. He quickly stopped; he'd never intended to be a strike-breaker. The trouble was, the whole episode had been seen by Roberts. He accused Penfound of industrial bullying.'

'But even in those days they had some form of justice, didn't they?'

'Oh yes. Penfound was hauled before a magistrate in Tintagel. He was followed by the workforce, who all denied anything untoward had happened. After a lot of argument the magistrate dismissed the case.'

'So why was he sacked?'

'The manager daren't back down. The Directors were behind him – "behind him" in the sense of ready to give him a push if he wilted. So Penfound was fired – despite having been found innocent.'

'It sounds very unfair - but it was a long time ago.'

'Our family have gone over the story so often it seems like yesterday. See, Penfound wasn't just fired. Oh, no. After that he was evicted from the house which he'd been renting from the Slate Company. Even when he found himself some other job, working on a farm nearby, the Directors had tried to take that job away as well. His whole life was ruined by that one incident.'

'That's very sad; but you shouldn't let it ruin your life as well.'

'I was just getting over it when I found myself in the cast for *Splits and Schisms*. I liked the sound of Arno's spiel, to be honest. He's a man who understands the working class; and the need for solidarity. I liked his message. As far as I could see, Arno was doing his best to show what the Directors of long ago were really like.'

'So what's the matter now?'

'Arno just cast the drama's parts at random — he didn't know any of us that well. I found that I'd been cast as a Quarry Director — as Dr Charles Rendle. So for the last three months I've been trying to play my bitter enemy. It's driven me crazy.'

Travers was about to ask if he'd been crazy enough to try and sabotage the whole drama; but whatever else he might be, he didn't think the man was stupid.

It was a question he might need to ask the butcher later on. But he needed to assemble a lot more evidence about the case before he did so.

CHAPTER 32

Travers sat back in his car, letting his body wind down. The interview with Thorne had taken more out of him than he'd expected. What other grievances lay beneath the calm exterior of this sturdy village?

Did he have any more data yet for fixing a logical interview order? He gave a hollow smile: he didn't even have a full grasp yet of the main events of the evening, let alone the build up over the preceding months or years.

The most crucial thing the Crime Squad would demand was interviews with everyone who was performing in the crucial scene – the Quarry Disaster, as he'd gathered they called it.

He tried to remind himself of how the scene had proceeded. It had begun with a couple of workers on the upper stage; then with two young girls down below, one of whom was visiting her father.

Next he consulted his programme for the performance and by matching surnames identified some key players. Fortunately the cast list was in "order of first appearance" so he could identify the girls and hence their fathers. These he translated to their twenty-first century players then jostled them into a pragmatic schedule. Once he'd done this he was glad to see "Cowling" (i.e. Penhaligon) had already been covered. It was clear, though, that he wouldn't get through the whole cast in one afternoon.

Jim and Jenny Melhuish ran the Post Office at Delabole; and Jim had been playing quarryman James Kellow on the top stage in the Disaster scene. Since Travers was already parked in the village, he was the obvious next port of call.

Policeman and postmaster in the same village had known each other for years; but both recognised that in the circumstances this was not just a friendly chat.

On the other hand, Melhuish had some inkling of the wider picture and of society's demands. He had thought hard about the tragic events of the live performance. His wife, too, had been a sharp-eyed observer of events. There was no harm, the policeman decided, in interviewing them together.

Mugs of tea were provided by Jenny and the conversation began.

'The trouble is, it's so completely bizarre,' began Travers. 'I haven't yet heard from the hospital. Whatever they tell me won't make much sense. No-one keels over, half way through a live performance, after looking so healthy and acting so well – unless there's a medical precondition that no-one knew about. But if it was the result of assault, what a crazy time and place to choose.'

'If it was a natural event, it might take some spotting,' observed the postmaster's wife. Travers remembered that she used to be a nurse. 'It'd be a great pity if we never found out. For all of us, but most of all for Morwenna Stacey.'

The thought that even a post-mortem might not settle the cause of death was a new idea to the policeman; and disturbing. He resolved to ask Dr Southgate about it later.

'What I want to establish today is the events in that critical scene. You were one of the first speakers, I think, Jim? Strutting about on that high stage?'

'That's right. Paul Wood and I were meant to be on the edge of the working face of the Quarry, looking down. Paul was playing Greg Wallis, a worry-guts who wanted to be the one to report the first signs of impending disaster to the authorities.'

'Did all that really happen in 1869 - or was it made up by Arno to enliven the scene – some sort of artistic license?'

'As far as I know, that's how it was. At least that's how Joe Stacey's account had described it, that he passed on to Arno.'

'I was just wondering, you see, if someone had been made very angry by some part of the drama being a distortion of what really happened.'

'Well, I'd read - or rather, heard - Joe's delvings over the years. Joe used to bring his work to the Methodist Community Lunch every so often. That's where he found most of his sources - he wanted to give them feedback. Arno's drama kept pretty close to his account, I'd say. In fact, Arno left out one or two of the more contentious bits.'

Melhuish paused to gather his thoughts. 'The only people who might have been offended were the old Board of Directors. Though the company was renewed several times during the last century. So nothing portrayed from the century before could possibly criticise anyone involved with the Quarry today.'

Was there a hole in this argument? 'If someone today was descended from a nineteenth century Director, though, might they feel their ancestor was being got at?'

'They might feel upset – annoyed, even - that something shameful was being brought into the open. But as I say, Arno didn't stray far from Joe's long-term findings. *Splits and Schisms* has nothing which would be a total surprise to the local community.'

Travers felt he'd taken this line of questioning as far as he could. 'OK, let's just stick to Friday evening. What were your movements, Jim, in the Disaster scene?'

'This was my first speaking part in the drama. Arno was very keen that no-one should suspect there was a high-level stage until that scene. So Paul Wood and I had to be up the ladder and sitting ready on the top deck, in the dark and the cold, most of the way through Act One.'

'I don't suppose you saw anything suspicious happening down below? You'd be unexpected witnesses.'

'Huh. Unless we had infra red cameras we were blind as bats. If the spots weren't on below we could see virtually nothing. We only saw the same as everyone else in the audience.'

'What happened to you and Paul as the scene progressed?'

'There was the first dialogue between us about the quartz seam. Then Paul climbed down the ladder and off to find the Quarry management team. The spotlight went off me and I sat down again.'

'Could you say for sure that Paul Wood didn't pause to do anything below the stage on his way to find management?'

'That's an odd sort of question.'

'Jim, if I don't ask it some arrogant detective from the Crime Squad will. I'm just trying to narrow down options.'

The postmaster saw that the policeman had no choice. He considered his answer. 'I saw Paul start down the ladder. Next I saw his outline in the field, meeting the management. I didn't have my stop watch out but it was only two or three minutes later. If he did pause it could only be for seconds.'

'And for completeness, how could I be sure you didn't trail down the ladder after Paul, do something under the stage, and climb back up again?'

'Well I didn't. I stayed put. I mean, I had to be ready to help Beth Howell when she climbed back up the ladder.'

The policeman's instinct was to believe him: was that enough?

But Jim hadn't finished. 'I reckon, you know, that although the ladder's off to the side, there would still be some light from the main stage where Beth and her dad were performing. I reckon I'd have been seen. Don't you?'

'I only saw the play once, Jim, I couldn't be sure. It's certainly something we could test out. A re-enactment of the re-enactment, as it were. What happened after Beth had climbed the other ladder?'

'What happened at the rehearsals was that I told her I'd go down to look for her dad and left her on the top deck. Then it was the interval.'

'The poor kid wasn't left to shiver up there for the rest of the drama, I hope?'

'No, she climbed down during the interval. Then slipped back to Annabel's house for a hot chocolate.'

'Was that the end of your acting?'

'I had another part in Act Two. I don't suppose that's relevant.'

'No, I don't think it is. Can I round off with a few more general questions, please. How would you rate the safety of the equipment around the stage? Were there any persistent failings?'

'I'd be happy to speak in defence of Arno's production. Sure, it was simple and not that comfortable. It was an outdoor production on a wild hillside; but I never felt any of it was unsafe. At one point we discussed whether either of us on the top deck needed a safety harness. Paul and I refused, point blank – we might have tripped over one another. We knew it was potentially dangerous so we just kept well away from the edge. The ladders themselves were very secure. We just had to be careful: which we were.'

The words would have sounded even better if one of the cast had not been found dead halfway through the production. Soon Travers had said his farewells and was on his way.

The policeman decided that while he was still in Delabole he would try and talk to Beth and Freya. A phone call told him that both were at Freya's house; and told him (or reminded him) that Freya was Paul Wood's daughter in real life as well as in the drama. Good. He could complete the interviews of all players in the crucial scene on a single visit.

Paul welcomed him in. He'd been the local plumber in Delabole for years and the policeman knew him well.

'I'm conducting some preliminary interviews to learn as much as I can about *Splits and Schisms*,' he began. He was happy to talk to all three together, in the plumber's living room. The girls sat side by side on the settee, looking unsettled; Paul was in an armchair, looking solemn. Travers had the second armchair, which he suspected was less comfortable. Or maybe he was just too tense after a whole day of interviews?

'Can I start with you girls? When did you leave the dressing room and come out to the stage?'

'We stayed inside as long as possible to keep warm,' said Freya.

'All the men were lucky,' added her friend. 'They could put on umpteen jumpers under their coats; we were just in lightweight dresses. We knew we'd be incredibly cold.'

'Arno was watching that part of the performance from the entrance to Annabel's. He knew we'd be cold; said he didn't want us outside too early. He told us when we needed to move.'

'We had to be out and under the stage before Joe started his next speech.'

'Then we had to climb up the low ladder, ready to come on stage, when our part of the scene began. That was when the cold really hit us.'

The policeman almost started to ask them how they would have coped with heavy rain, but realised it was not relevant. 'Please continue.'

Freya was the one who spoke, although the girls had been over these events so often in the last two days that it was a combined response.

'We acted our scene with Mr Penhaligon. Then I had to go down the far side, slide down and lie on the damp ground. At the same time the sound and smoke began.'

'In the meantime,' continued Beth, 'I had to help my "dad" to the side of the stage and then climb up to the top deck. That was through dense clouds of smoke – much worse than it had been at any rehearsals. My eyes were running with tears – I'd got them tightly shut and I couldn't see anything. I clung on tight and climbed a rung at a time. In the end Mr Melhuish helped me off at the top. I was shivering with cold and shaking with fear; I couldn't remember any more lines, let alone speak them. By then the whole place was on some sort of fire alert.'

'And what happened to you, Freya?'

'I lay down in my usual place in the cold bracken. A couple of men came out from under the stage and lay down beside me. Not too close, mind: Arno had been very strict about that. We all shivered for what seemed like ages and pretended to be dead. Then the Quarry management pair came and found us – and sent us back under the stage to the dressing rooms, to dry out and warm up.'

'So... you must have walked past Joe lying under the stage?'

Freya's eyes filled with tears. 'I never even saw him. It was so dark.'

There was a moment's silence. They had all known Joe, worked with him, loved him in different ways. This was a wretched business.

'OK, Paul. Can you just run through your movements during the performance, please?'

'These girls complain about the cold but at least they were inside till the scene started. Jim and I had to hide on the top deck all the way through Act One until the scene began; I reckon that wuz even colder. No, I couldn't see anything much down below. Unless the spots were on it wuz far too dark.'

'What happened when the scene began?'

'There wuz a bit of dialogue. That ended up with me having to climb down a ladder to go and alert the Quarry management - in the pitch dark. I'm a plumber; I'm used to ladders – I climb in and out of lofts every day. But I didn't much like that one.'

'During that descent, you passed the end of the main stage and the space below it. Did you see anything odd?'

'Travers, the only thing I wanted to do was to get off that

bloody ladder. It was all dark. I hurried off up the field to find my Quarry bosses. Never saw a thing.'

The policeman had no reason to disbelieve him. Somehow the presence of the girls made the whole interview emotional and tense. There might be other questions but this would do for now. Once more the policeman took his leave.

CHAPTER 33

George and Sophie had just finished a light supper, sitting in front of their warm wood-burning stove, when there was a knock at the door. It was Peter Travers.

'I'm just on my way back to Delabole – been interviewing all afternoon – and I remembered your videos. Is now a good time to collect them – in one form or another?'

'Hi. Come in. We've just eaten, but we can make you an omelette or something.'

After the wintry cold of the coastal villages, Ivy Cottage felt warm. The policeman quickly succumbed. 'That sounds delicious; and maybe you could give me a summary of which videos were taken on what days.'

The policeman was perfectly capable of cooking himself an omelette, but lived alone and was not averse to being pampered by a female household. Soon he had removed his jacket and boots and was slumped on the old settee in front of the stove. Sophie, meanwhile, was concocting another omelette in the kitchen.

'I know you can't tell us any details,' said George, 'but do you feel you're making progress?'

'I keep picking up new bits of information – probably stuff everyone else knew. For example, I've discovered that Joe

252

Stacey used to read out parts of his history of Delabole at the Methodist Community Lunches. So the drama could hardly have come as much of a shock to the locals.'

'I'd heard of the Community Lunches. I assumed they were for older people?'

'They are mainly, of course, but they make anyone who's less than fifty very welcome. I've been along once or twice. They reckon it keeps them in touch with the younger generation – stops them going senile. That's what they hope, anyway. Even you and Sophie could go. They're on Tuesdays.'

Sophie emerged from the kitchen with a tray containing a plateful of mushroom omelette and a second plate of buttered bread. 'Here, tuck in. We don't want our community policeman to starve.'

The speed with which Travers consumed the meal suggested he hadn't eaten anything during a long afternoon. For a few moments conversation was halted. While he was eating, Sophie went back to the kitchen to make a pot of tea.

This was very pleasant, but Peter Travers didn't want to outstay his welcome. 'Can we discuss the videos, please, and then I can get out of your way. I'm sure you've plenty of other things you want to get on with.'

'OK, we'll talk about the videos next. If you've a few minutes after that could we tell you our latest ideas on how Delabole's past could impact on the present? Add to your stockpile of theories.'

The policeman was acutely aware that he had no such stockpile, just confusion. He didn't want to brainstorm with two women he hardly knew – even though what little he did know must rule them out of local wrongdoing.

'What's the best way for me to take the videos?'

Sophie answered. 'How about if I lend you my laptop? I'm not using it much and I can borrow George's if I have to. We've saved all our films of the production onto each computer. You could have a first look at the videos on it. Pick out the bits that you might find useful. Then, of course, copy as much as you like onto your own computer.'

'That would be very helpful. Thank you. You'll need to tell me your password, of course. I promise I won't look at anything else; and I'll keep them confidential. I'll also need some help to distinguish the videos.'

'We've renamed them to make that easier,' replied George. 'They all start "slate_" then a day-name then G or S. We were getting confused ourselves. They're all fairly similar.'

'They only started when... last Monday?' hazarded the policeman.

'Crumbs. It seems as though we've been here for weeks but that's right. There's nothing on Wednesday. That was the technical rehearsal; lots of sound and light. George and I gave ourselves a night off.'

'There's just one video not taken from around the stage,' added George. 'That was on Tuesday. I took advantage of the scaffolding the stove people left around the cottage. I

254

attached my camera aloft, focussed on the near end of the stage.'

'It's a pity you didn't do that on Friday,' commented the policeman. 'That's the spot where something happened.'

'It's not a brilliant video, to be honest. The light's feeble at that distance. I found it nerve wracking, having to climb to the top of the scaffolding at half past eleven, when I got back from the rehearsal, to fetch it down again. But I had to; my camera isn't protected against rain. So I didn't do it again. Sorry.'

'Assuming Joe's death was a crime, there can't be many crimes which have been videoed, can there?'

'That's what I want to check, Sophie. It could be crucial. But I'm not going to make too much fuss until I've seen if it gives me something useful.'

'I need to be on my way,' he continued. 'So go on - let's have your latest theories about how the past could impact on the present.'

It was good to have a willing listener. The women took turns to explain their questions on the Quarry Disaster and on the arrival of the Railway.

'So how will you take these further?' The policeman worded the question so it was carefully neutral.

'We've decided our best hope is a day at the Cornwall Record Office in Truro. Chase the Old Slate Company's accounts and the reports from any inquiries into their disasters. We're going tomorrow.'

'It's not the only reason, mind. We also want to have a

look for new furniture. What's been left here is very old-fashioned – as you can see.'

'Best of luck, then. Do let me know if you find anything. Don't be heroic and keep it all to yourselves.'

The policeman started to ease himself out of the settee and reached for his jacket. 'I'd love to stay but I need to do some more research on criminal records. It's a great pity I haven't managed to find out Arno's proper name.'

'Oh, I have,' said Sophie, with a roguish smile. 'I bet you'll never guess.'

'Come on, then.'

'It's "Farnon".'

'Farnon?' Travers sounded incredulous.

'Yes. A dreadful name – almost as bad as Arno, but less artistic.'

'How the heck d'you know that?' asked George. She'd not dared to ask many questions of Sophie about her absence last week, but this was her chance to bring her doubts into the open.

'Well, one place where it's very hard to hide your proper name is with your bank. Usually your full name is shown on your chequebook. So if you order something and pay for it by cheque then the parcel tends to come labelled with your full name.'

'So you spotted Arno's newly-delivered post when you went to Holly Cottage - and picked out his full name?'

'George, I wouldn't dream of being so nosey. Last week, while you were up a ladder painting the chimney and I was about to have the porridge you'd kindly cooked me, the post came. I went to the door to collect it. One of the parcels had been misdirected. It was addressed to "Farnon James" at Holly Cottage. I saw it was from a theatrical supplier.'

'It might have been supplies of pseudo blood for that bloke in the Quarry Disaster scene,' suggested George, 'he seemed to get through plenty. His head was covered in blood in every rehearsal.'

'Whatever it was, I thought it was probably urgent: I mean, the live performance was only two days away. So I went around at once with the parcel and Arno invited me in. Asked me to join him in a full cooked breakfast – he was about to cook. He's not a bad chef. We chatted for ages about drama and painting and everything. I didn't realise till I came back that you had started decorating.'

There was silence. George was feeling guilty at the accusing thoughts she had directed at the missing Sophie as she painted away on her own. Travers sensed that there were words between them, waiting to be spoken.

'Anyway, one way or another, we've got his name now,' said the policeman. 'Thank you very much. Keep in touch, won't you.'

Half an hour later Peter Travers was sitting in front of his own computer and entering the name "Farnon James". He found the system was faster on Sunday evening – the system was under-loaded as most policemen were off duty. Maybe they were lucky enough to have a life outside crime?

It was, though, a worthwhile search. Arno James had gathered one or two reports over the years. Travers glanced down the list.

There was nothing to do with aggressive behaviour, and no trace of misbehaviour involving members of his casts, young or old, male or female.

There was, though, an irregularity reported five years ago in Colchester. He had been declared bankrupt at the end of a production, with a number of adverse side effects. It would certainly be worth another interview to take this further.

CHAPTER 34

Monday was cold and wet as George and Sophie set out for Truro. George had done her homework. She knew the Record Office's hours of opening and also the size of living-room furniture she was after. On colour and material she was prepared to take advice from Sophie.

Truro was thirty five miles from Delabole, mostly on main roads. Less than an hour later they were driving down the gentle hill and into the town. Sophie had not been to Cornwall's county town since her childhood. George had passed through a few times, en route to Falmouth or the Lizard, but had never had reason to stop and explore.

Fortunately the rain had eased during their journey and they could take a few minutes, as they parked the yellow Mini Cooper and got their bearings, to delight in the gentle and civilised atmosphere.

'There's not much sign of a tourist industry.'

'Not in winter, anyway. I guess most visitors to Cornwall like to stick to the coast. That's what we always did. Here's pleasant enough – and less busy than most county towns.'

'Hey, that looks like a cathedral.' Sophie had no religious affiliations but she lapped up well-designed structures. The stone-built cathedral was of a good size for Truro, substantial but not massive, nestling in the centre of the town.

'We haven't time to go there now. If it's still open when we've finished our furniture shopping and been to the Record Office then I'd love to have a proper look. Today it's low priority.'

They continued to walk briskly through the town centre. George spotted a van-hire outfit in a side street which claimed to lease vans on a daily basis. She made a note of the details. 'If we find the furniture we want, it might be cheaper - and faster - to fetch it ourselves later in the week. We won't be able to hire a van in Delabole.'

A few minutes later Sophie spotted the new Department Store. 'There's not much local competition, mind. And everything it sells has to be brought half the length of the country. So don't expect prices to be that low.'

'OK, but our first challenge is to see if they've got anything we really like. Which floor do you reckon we want for furniture?'

One benefit of Monday morning in January was that Truro was quiet; there were several shop assistants eager to direct them. The third floor was soon identified as their target. There was plenty of furniture and a big sign proclaimed "January Sale".

'That looks promising,' said Sophie optimistically.

'Let's look around separately for fifteen minutes. Then meet to compare notes.'

An intense twenty minutes later the women had reconvened. 'It'd be best to discuss this over coffee.'

'Good idea. We passed a Tasty Pastry on the floor below.'

'I confess I was looking only at colour and pattern,' said Sophie, after they'd taken a table by a window overlooking the High Street and a waitress had bustled over for their orders.

'That's your expertise. Go on.'

'Well I would classify most of it as respectable but dull. The sort of thing my parents would have bought – their generation but not ours.'

'Keep going.' George seemed to be amused.

'There were a couple of designs that would be great for a children's playroom – it might not last that long, though.'

'Yes?'

'Finally there was one fabulous design in turquoise and opal that I thought would suit Ivy Cottage like a glove. What did you think?'

'I concentrated on size. For a small cottage, Ivy Cottage has a fair-sized living room. It might feel small if the furniture was large. On the other hand, it shouldn't be sized for the altitudinally challenged. I'm not very tall but I might be visited by a tall man – or woman.'

'All very sensible. You might even make friends with a tall man from Delabole. Peter Travers is quite tall.'

'Anyway, that eliminated a few. Then I tried the rest. One or two were pretty uncomfortable. They were low-priced and you could see why.'

'So where did you end up?'

'I was deliberately ignoring colour. By far the most comfortable was a settee and a pair of chairs, down in the far corner of the showroom.'

'Which were what colour?'

'I would have called it a striking light blue and grey. That's not –'

'I think it is.'

'Fantastic. So whichever way you come at it we've agreed there's a single best option. Let's hope no-one else wants to buy it in the next fifteen minutes.'

An hour later the shopping part of the day's agenda had been completed. When they got back after their coffees, no-one else had shared their delight in the dazzlingly-coloured suite. Sophie suspected the colour and texture might be too striking for most Cornwall citizens; it would only really work if the whole house was styled in a modern way.

The furniture department manager may have reached the same conclusion. Anyway, for whatever reason, he offered George a further thirty percent off if she would accept the items of furniture already on show.

There was some haggling over delivery charge. Delabole was outside the firm's usual range. In the end a fee was agreed that George estimated would be less than the cost of hiring a van. Delivery day was set for the following Friday. 'This way will be a lot less work,' she told Sophie, as they made their way out. 'I can stay in and you can have a painting day, out on the cliffs.'

'Assuming, of course, it's a fine day.'

The two women had a light lunch of soup and rolls in Marks and Spencer, overlooking the market square. George had bought an A to Z of Truro and saw that the Old County Hall was at the top of the hill, with an adjacent car park. After lunch they went back to their car and drove up to the Cornwall Record Office. They would have made the journey on foot, they told themselves, if time was not so short.

The first challenge, once inside the single-storey building, was to register names and addresses. Sophie was about to write down her London home but George managed to stop her. 'If we need help it may improve our chances if we're seen as local. Put Ivy Cottage, Treknow. After all, that is where we're staying.'

George had hoped, naively, that the Record Office would be a large reference library, where the pair could delve into documents at leisure. This was not the case – could not be, when half the documents were microfiche versions of rare or old manuscripts.

The women went into a room with a number of tables, some with a device for reading microfiche and others with computers. On one side were bookshelves of folders. There was plenty of room - only half a dozen other researchers were present.

They had to find an item relevant to their search; and then request it at the inquiry desk. There would then be a wait while the item was brought – they were only fetched every half hour - after which they could browse to their heart's content. Where on earth should they start?

George opened a folder at random and skimmed the contents. The pages had a code in the top left corner. She frowned: what was the logic behind this?

It was Sophie who unravelled the puzzle; or rather, realised that the best response to ignorance was to ask for help. The lady behind the inquiry desk was free. Sophie explained her problem. It turned out that there was an upstream system, which was the index held on the computer.

'So you're researching the history of the Slate Quarry at Delabole,' the lady murmured. 'Let's have a look.' She entered various keywords and let the machine proceed. 'Ah yes, most of the Slate Quarry data has been grouped together. They're under the codes X533 to X537. You'll find all those in the folder over there.'

'I've cracked the system,' Sophie whispered as she passed George. 'It's called asking for help. The dimwit's alternative to working it out from first principles. We want that bookshelf over there.'

George felt an idiot. She put back the page she had been trying to decode, which referred to fishing permits out of Penzance in the 1920s, and followed her friend across the room.

'How about if you chase after details of the railway coming to Delabole, while I learn as much as I can about the Quarry Disaster?'

George knew Sophie was bright enough for the task; her only worry was that she could easily be distracted. 'Remember the question: did the bribe go missing? That was where we agreed to start.'

George seized a table nearby by putting her fleece on the chair. Then she started to examine the references. Wisely both women had brought notebooks. The first thing she was after was the Old Delabole Slate Company's Board minutes for the period around 1869.

How long would it take for her request to be processed? She was thankful when it was no more than a few minutes. After that life got harder.

The one microfiche George had been given condensed many raw documents. She had to concentrate to make sense of them. This could take months, not just an afternoon. She wondered how long Joe Stacey had spent here. After some time she spotted a pattern in the numbering. This enabled her to scan through the Board minutes for 1869 and 1870, omitting many other documents. She could see no mention of a public inquiry.

The analyst was about to conclude that no inquiry had been conducted – maybe nineteenth century capitalism was more primitive than they thought – when she spotted a new name in the minutes. A civil engineer had been recruited after the Disaster, with experience elsewhere in Cornwall. After two years he had produced a report. How could she find that?

George remembered Sophie's comments. The inquiry desk was there to help. Quickly she noted the report title and headed for assistance. Ten minutes later she had a second microfiche and was able to study the engineer's

265

findings. This was a solid piece of work; maybe nineteenth century Directors were not as sloppy as she had supposed.

At half past four the Record Office closed. George and Sophie gathered their belongings, handed in their micro-fiches and headed for the car. They had agreed not to waste time exchanging details of progress during the afternoon.

Once they were through Truro's modest rush-hour, sharing began.

'It's a pity they threw us out,' said George, 'Half an hour more would have made a big difference. I'd just come across a couple of entries for the Rev Jack Bucknall, but I didn't have time to find out what they were.'

'So much for staying focussed on the grand plan.'

'OK. Anyway, before that, I found one inquiry in the nineteenth century,' the analyst continued. 'It was impres-sive. After 1869 they had an independent civil engineer in to look at the whole Quarry operation. He made scathing comments on the way they let the contracts; observed it would be better for the quarry workers to cooperate than to compete. I don't know if the idea was ever implemented, but at least they were asking some key questions. How about you?'

Sophie took a few seconds to gather her thoughts. 'I may have been more successful – in the sense that we're looking for evidence that something went badly wrong – which means lack of evidence that it went right. I found all the accounts for the years 1891 to 1896. Luckily accounts were a lot simpler in those days. I couldn't find any mention of a contribution from the North Cornwall Railway – for two thousand pounds or anything else. It's as if the bribe never happened – or else was absorbed directly into somebody's pocket. It made me wonder, you know, if Dr Charles Rendle was really as pure as *Splits and Schisms* made him out.'

'Hm. Do you reckon that the bloke that was playing him – Martin Thorne, wasn't it – got wind of it – and decided for some reason to take revenge?'

CHAPTER 35

While George and Sophie had side-stepped Monday's rain by travelling to Truro, Sergeant Peter Travers was not so fortunate. As is so often the case, rain did not fall uniformly across Cornwall. This time most of it fell on the north coast.

Thinking about his investigation so far, the policeman was satisfied with his progress in interviewing the cast – though there were plenty more still to be seen. On the other hand the Crime Squad, if ever called – and especially the Scene of Crime Officers - would want to know the exact location of the body before they began their search of the immediate neighbourhood. "Under the Treknow end of the stage" would sound pretty inadequate.

There were just two men in the search party who knew where the body had first been found. That was the Quarry Management team, comprising Charles Rendle and Greg Wallis – known to him as Thorne and Wood. On Monday morning both men were planning to be at work; but neither could refuse an official request to attend the stage one more time.

'We're in your hands, Travers,' said Wood. 'What time do you want us?'

'Nine thirty? It shouldn't take more than half an hour.'

The rain had started almost immediately after the phone calls and was still pelting down as the three men, all in waterproofs, gathered under the stage. The close-laid planks of the stage above kept them reasonably dry, but each had been drenched in the short dash from the car park.

'What I need to know, if at all possible, is the exact spot you first found poor old Joe. I'll pretend to be the body if it'll help. It may be better if you don't confer for the moment. Martin, why don't you go first?'

Martin Thorne was still suffering inner turmoil but Travers' unemotional approach calmed him a little.

'The expected place for us to find bodies - the result of the Disaster – wasn't under the stage at all, but just outside. We were approaching, see, from the field that formed the overflow car-park - the start of the footpath to Treknow.'

'When did the smoke begin – I mean, on performance night?'

'The timing was exactly the same as at rehearsals. We were – what - twenty yards away when it started. It was just that on Friday night there was far more smoke than usual. Our eyes really stung. It made it very hard to see anything.'

'Did you not have torches?'

'Paul had suggested that earlier on, but Arno said we mustn't. The scene was supposed to be mid-afternoon in April. Even with the smoke, he said, it shouldn't be too hard to find two or three bodies in a well-defined area. All they needed was to be grasped and hauled up by one of us; then

269

they'd slide away under the stage and back to the dressing rooms.'

'OK. So I assume you found all the bodies you'd expected – including Paul's daughter, Freya. Then one of you spotted something else?'

'I did,' said Thorne. 'I wasn't sure, but it looked like another leg. Just in the shadow of the stage. I assumed that even at this late stage Arno was still fiddling around with the production and it was another body we were supposed to discover.'

'So where did you see it? Tell me where to lie.'

The butcher pointed to an area – just under the roof – and Travers, reluctantly, lay down. Although the bottom part was protected there was plenty of rain, gushing down the hillside and into the bracken. Underneath his waterproof jacket he started to feel cold and wet.

'Would you mind standing outside, where you found the other bodies, to confirm that?'

Thorne stepped outside into the rain, looked around and considered. 'No, it had to be further out of sight. Where you are now, everyone coming along the route under the stage would fall over you - but we know that no-one did. So you need to be further up into the hillside.'

Travers shuffled himself as directed. He felt even wetter. 'Like this?'

'I reckon.'

'Paul, can you join Martin outside and see if you agree?'

The plumber, who had been congratulating himself that

he was still fairly dry, grimaced and joined the butcher outside. As he did so the rain became even more torrential then turned to hail. Their coats were waterproof but not hail-proof. Even standing just a few feet away, it was hard to hear one another over the deluge.

'I'd say, if anything, the body wuz lying further back up the hillside.'

Travers tried to shuffle further up. The water was now seeping down his neck and infiltrating his whole body. 'I'm not sure I can push myself up any further. I must say, it's hard to see how someone could fall into this position by accident.'

He paused for thought. 'Mind, it's almost as hard to imagine how they could have been pushed up here, if they were already dead. It's not stable; I can feel myself sliding down.'

'That's probably the effect of the rain, see. Remember it wuz dry on Friday evening – hadn't rained for several days. Bodies would lie where they fell.'

'Have one more look, please. Could I have been further inside?'

'Lie inside as far as you like, Peter, as long as your leg sticks out. I mean, there had to be something visible that we could catch sight of.'

The whole thing was a farce, the policeman decided, as their combined attempt at replication came to a soggy end.

He managed to sound positive and grateful as his two sources retreated to their cars and drove away. Both in-

271

tended to go home and have hot baths before starting their working week. Travers decided he would have one more look for traces around the newly-settled resting space of the corpse before emulating their recovery mechanisms.

It was an unproductive search and he doubted SOCO would find much more. He even tried to move the scaffolding pipes but they were all secure.

As he thawed out in his bath and replayed the morning in his mind, the policeman felt certain that no-one could have fallen into that position by accident. Whatever the post mortem said, he was convinced in his own mind that it must have been murder.

Then he had a further thought. He had lain at the back of the stage underpass. He was sure there were plenty of ways a body could have been hidden under the stage, further into the hillside and maybe further from the end. That would have made it safe from discovery, at least for that evening. He remembered there was no light inside the tunnel at all.

What did that mean? The most plausible deduction was that someone had intended the body to be found at the point in the drama when it was.

Which meant that, whatever else had been going on in the murderer's mind, one of the targets for the evening was the production itself. They had intended to bring its first performance to an abrupt and dishonourable end.

Later, having recorded all the details he could remember about the dialogue under the stage, the policeman continued with his interview programme. He had found the names of the two men who played the dead quarrymen from Wood; fortunately both worked close to Delabole.

Neither had anything new to add. They had seen no signs of Joe Stacey's body, either on their way from the dressing room to setting themselves in position, or on their way back. 'Mind, we were very cold. I doubt we'd have noticed anything.'

There was, though, one disturbing new morsel. Travers learned both men had been in place, waiting under the stage, from almost the start of the scene. Which brought forward the latest time at which Joe Stacey could have been killed.

It left a very small interval indeed between Joe's introductory narrative at the start of the Disaster scene and his death, well before its end.

CHAPTER 36

'I've got a suggestion for something different we could do today,' said George, as the women tucked into their porridge next morning.

'Oh yes?'

'It's Tuesday. We could attend the Community Lunch in Delabole. We wouldn't look that out of place. Peter Travers told me it was for all ages, not just geriatrics.'

'Apart from putting down a marker for your own chair in forty years time, what good would that do?'

'I reckon we made good progress yesterday in the Record Office on past elements that might have been twisted over time. We haven't made any serious dent, though, in the story of the Rev Jack Bucknall.'

'That's true; and we've good reason to think that was the last story Lily Taylor was interested in. The trouble was, we never found out why.'

'Not if Bucknall was happily married, anyway. The young curate came in 1925 – not that long ago, really. There are bound to be people in the village that still remember him. If any of them were at the lunch it would be good to get their version of events.'

'I guess we've been neglecting the death of Lily Taylor. I

274

was worried about it before we even got here, remember. OK, George, I'm ready to join you. We'd better ring up someone, though, to get an official invite and to find out what time the thing starts.'

In the end Dr Brian Southgate gave them the data needed. The lunch always started at one o'clock, he said, but diners could arrive at any time from twelve thirty. There was never a need for an invitation. This was Cornwall and there would be plenty of food. He even gave them a couple of names of older folk to ask for, who would probably have something to say on Jack Bucknall – 'although it's not a subject that often comes up these days.'

They reached the Community Hall at 12:40, after spending the morning on the Ivy Cottage garden. After the storm the day before it was a cloggy mess and both were glad when they could stop. George entered the Hall first, Sophie a few steps behind. But there was no reason for her to feel embarrassed; both were warmly welcomed by the cheerful woman in the foyer.

'It's always great to have some new blood,' she gushed. 'Are you visitors to Delabole - or relatives of someone who comes here regularly?'

Sophie said she was George's friend and left it to her to explain their circumstances. There was a bowl for financial contributions for the meal and a suggested contribution of four pounds each. Sophie put in ten pounds for the pair – she had an income back in London and certainly wasn't

275

about to accept charity. Then she stepped through into the main hall.

The women had agreed that they would circulate separately. 'That should increase our chances of finding new information.'

There were a good sixty people in the room, two thirds of them women. The average age was probably sixty-five: most were older but some were no more than thirty – Sophie guessed these were daughters of the older folk, taking the chance of a meal which they hadn't had to cook for themselves. A warm hubbub of conversation enveloped the room; the newcomers found themselves completely ignored.

George was the first to make headway. She approached one of the oldest men, who was standing on his own, and asked if he could point her to Bert Dawe.

'Why, has he won the lottery or something?'

'No, it's nothing like that.'

'Pity. So you're a bookmaker's assistant. How much does he owe?' But George noted he said this with a twinkle in his eye.

'Hey, are you Bert Dawe? Someone said he was the really handsome one I should talk to if I wanted to learn about the Rev Jack Bucknall.'

'Oh – you saw me with Jack Bucknall as my specialism on Mastermind. It helped that I'd set all the questions, of course. Trouble was, I couldn't do a single general knowledge one in part two. Anyway, what d'you want to know?'

George introduced herself, wishing for once that she had a more conventional name. But Bert was too old to be put off by that.

'I'm here every week, George. I always enjoy meeting someone new. Especially a vivacious young lady. Would you like to share a table with me to ask your questions?'

The two sat down at a table near the corner; George got out her notebook.

'I've just moved down here. I've read one old newspaper account that I found in my new cottage. The Rev Jack Bucknall came in 1925, it said. You must have been very young then?'

'You're too kind, my dear. I was born in 1914. So Jack was here in my teenage years. After he'd gone I did my best to find out more about him. He was my hero, you see – and no-one's ever replaced him.' The old man's eyes seemed to water then he smiled ruefully. 'Even with our wonderful Health Service none of us lasts forever.'

'What sort of a man was he?'

'Well, can I ask, are you religious?'

George shook her head. 'Not very, I'm afraid. It never made much sense.'

'Now that was exactly the sort of person Jack appealed to. See, most vicars start with the theory and try and expand that out to the people – usually with limited success. Jack started with the world and its many problems – especially in the late 1920s - and tried to show how they were addressed by Jesus' teachings.'

'So he was a popular man?'

'Depends how you mean – or which ones you're counting. The first effect of Jack's preaching was to drive away all the church people that were here when he came. The religious old-timers, you might say. Then he attracted five times as many who'd never been near a church in their entire lives. It was a revolution – the most exciting time of my life, anyway.'

'Presumably most of his new followers were quarrymen?'

'That's all there was in Delabole in those days.'

'Did that antagonise the Quarry management?'

'You could say that. Even though they tried to work with him. As far as Jack was concerned, the workers here were all being exploited by the management. That was how it was. Unions were only just getting under way in North Cornwall. We were starting from a long way back, compared with the rest of the country.'

'So how did it all end – I mean, as far as Jack was concerned?'

'There were endless attempts to move him on. The established church people lobbied the Bishop of Truro, who'd first appointed him. The Bishop could see the problem, see both sides, but deep down I think he was on the side of Jack. The church could do with preachers that attracted crowds, not ones that drove them away. I mean, Jesus was hardly a moderate, was he?'

'You make it sound like a battle of extremists – here in Delabole?'

'It was. Jack was six foot tall, you see, hardly meek and mild. He regularly led marches through Delabole and he challenged Quarry management. He didn't make it easy for anyone. He would say Jesus never made it easy for the establishment either.'

'It's just ... Delabole hardly seems like the place you'd come to witness a civil war.'

'It was bizarre. Like something out of a time warp. A different sort of reality. It was several years before the sponsors for the curate's position, the group that funded it— a big church somewhere up north – received the letter.'

'What letter?'

'It claimed to be from the Quarry management and the leaders of the church – the two groups, of course, that Jack had alienated the most. It made some serious accusations. Of course, in those days, officialdom was always assumed to be correct. Jack complained bitterly, ferociously, to everyone who would listen, that none of it was true. But even he couldn't take on everyone.'

'What about all his supporters?'

'None of us were men of authority. We packed his church, week after week, but we were just working-class followers. By the time we realised there was a problem it was too late. Jack had packed his bags and was on his way.'

There were a few moments of silence. Bert had finished his tale and was carefully munching his shepherd's pie. George could think of many other questions but they weren't that critical to the overall account. She was an

279

analyst, not a journalist – her interest was in key facts, not necessarily the most lurid details.

She had no way of telling if Bert had managed to assemble the whole story. He would only have been a young man at the time. If the key letter was that secret, how had its contents become known? Here at least was one issue of justice from Delabole's past that someone, even today, might want to challenge.

While George was gathering the story of Jack Bucknall from Bert Dawe, Sophie had formed an equally interesting alliance with Ben Barham, on a table on the far side of the hall. Ben was a year younger than Bert, claimed no great knowledge of the militant curate, but did have a personal link with the Quarry Disaster.

The Community Lunch did not offer much choice on its menu, but was served by waitresses – one concession, maybe, to the older generation. Once both were launched into their generous portions of shepherd's pie, Sophie prompted her companion.

'So, you say, one of your relatives was killed in the Quarry Disaster?'

'Yes, my grandfather. He was working on the critical face when it all crashed down. He had no chance. None of them did.'

'How old was your grandmother at the time?'

'She was just eighteen. They'd only got married that Easter. Just long enough for her to be pregnant. My Mum was born in 1870.'

Sophie looked at Ben and did some mental arithmetic. 'She must have had you very late, then?'

'I was born in 1915, when she was forty five. She never said, but I think I was probably conceived just after my Dad signed up at the start of the Great War, before he disappeared to France. Never to return, unfortunately.'

This was a family that had seen more than its fair share of misfortune. 'Did you work at the Quarry?'

'I did. Although it was starting to change by the time I worked there. At least it was better than 1869.'

'So from what your grandmother said, do you have any understanding of what went wrong – what should have been preventable?'

'Everyone had their own views, of course, even in 1869. If that idiot Greg Wallis had been less keen to tell the Quarry Captain what he'd just found and more keen to warn the workforce to get out the way, it might not have been quite so calamitous. Overall, though, no-one could argue with the geology. Natural faults happen in slate quarries – however good or bad the management.'

There was silence as both ate their shepherd's pie. Ben seemed to have run out of steam. Sophie finished her own meal then tried to reignite him.

'My friend and I were in Truro yesterday, looking at some of the papers from the Quarry. She said there was an inquiry by an independent civil engineer, but it took two years to emerge.'

281

'Two years? That's not the official inquiry. The official one was undertaken by the local Coroner in Camelford and published within a week. It was a remarkably bland document. Said no-one was to blame; they could all carry on as before.' He sounded bitter.

'In essence that was right though, wasn't it?' Sophie found herself speaking up for the establishment. 'I mean, at the end of the day, it was an accident. Like all accidents, it might have turned out slightly different. Even the longer inquiry agreed that the overall cause was a quirk of nature. Quarries are dangerous places.'

CHAPTER 37

Peter Travers had been hoping that he'd heard the last of his boss's distant and ill-informed interventions in this case. With a sudden death half way through an open-air production, before an audience of hundreds, he had enough problems in making progress on the ground.

It was too much to wish for. At nine o'clock on Tuesday morning his phone rang once more; it was Lambourn, from Bodmin Police Station.

'You awake yet, Travers?'

'Sir, I've been assembling my interview notes from the last three days. We still haven't heard from Truro Hospital about the cause of death.'

Any hope that lack of data would dent his boss's interest or delay his intervention was misplaced.

'I'd like to have Arno James brought in for an interview later this morning. Say eleven o'clock. Can you bring him over?'

'What's your line of questioning going to be, sir?'

'I just want to make him feel uncomfortable, Travers. Even if Stacey died of a stroke and it was all a dreadful accident, there are still questions about James' "duty of care" and so on. I don't want him going away from Cornwall

283

thinking it doesn't matter if a few of his players get lost on the way. Make him a bit more careful next time.'

Lambourn was an idiot. Made it sound like Arno had misplaced a coin in his glove compartment. Travers wondered whether to argue then realised his boss's mind was already made up. At this point it was best to fit in as well as he could contrive. 'Right sir, I'll get round there straight away. If there's any problem I'll let you know.'

He put down his phone quickly, before Lambourn could make any more inane comments. Then put all his case notes into his briefcase, grabbed his jacket and headed for the door.

Two hours later Arno James sat on his own, in the least-friendly interview room in Bodmin Police Station, a glowering expression on his face, as he awaited the arrival of Inspector Lambourn.

Travers had done his best, on the journey from Treknow, to pretend to be the innocent chauffeur. The author had been seated in the back. Travers had made a few comments at the start: his senior officer wanted to go through the Health and Safety aspects of the *Splits and Schisms* production in detail. He suggested James should use the forty-minute journey to prepare himself for that area of inquiry. Then he'd kept quiet and concentrated on his driving.

Travers had had a few minutes to brief the Inspector on James's earlier interview on Saturday morning; also to alert him to the reported irregularity at Colchester. 'You'd better do that part,' Lambourn said, 'I haven't time to get my head round it now.' Travers wasn't sure whether to be pleased or alarmed that he had a formal part in the interview. He didn't like to think what Lambourn might want him to do if he got really desperate.

Now the two policemen entered the room and sat down opposite the author. Travers turned on the digital recorder.

'Interview at Bodmin Police Station on Tuesday Jan 27th, commencing 11:05. Present are Inspector Lambourn, Sergeant Travers and Mr Farnon James.' He had some pleasure in seeing the author flinch as he was ascribed his full name. Good: show him the police weren't totally incompetent.

'Now sir, I'm completely new to this inquiry,' began Lambourn. 'So forget anything you told Travers – if you can remember it, that is, I don't suppose he can – and focus on giving the whole story to me.'

'How far back d'you want me to go?'

'You're only here because of a death in mid-performance last Friday evening. We're still waiting on the hospital's verdict as to the cause. Let's assume for now it was a natural death. What I want you to do is convince me that nothing in the way you'd arranged the production could possibly have anything to do with that death.'

Arno took a deep breath. 'I see. Well, the stage was put up by a subsidiary of a firm called Howell. They've virtually cornered the market in scaffolding in North Cornwall. The stage had been put up the previous Friday. It came with all the usual guff – public liability insurance and so on - and a

285

safety guarantee. So if it did turn out that poor Joe had been a victim of failed scaffolding then at least there'd be some money for his widow.'

'I've had a good look at the scaffolding myself, sir,' added Travers. 'It's firm and secure. I couldn't find a single thing loose.'

'OK Travers, remember whose side you're supposed to be on. Now, Mr James, let's accept your comments on the scaffolding. What about the lighting? In particular, I gather there was no lighting under the stage. Had you done a risk assessment on that?'

'I'd thought about it, certainly - when we first set up the lights. I got Laurie Lane to put a set of dim lights under the stage that were on all the time.'

'So what happened to them?'

'The cast didn't like them. Said it spoilt their night vision for when they came back outside. As director I didn't like it either. It gave the whole stage a peculiar look. Without lights the audience simply looked at the stage. With the extra ones you couldn't tell which was the stage they were supposed to see; and what was something else, half-hidden below. So we took them out again.'

'You could have supplied torches.'

'I did supply bloody torches. I left half a dozen in the dressing rooms for the cast to use. Look, we're talking adults here. It wasn't a children's show – not a pantomime for kiddies. If the cast chose not to use them that was their choice.'

Lambourn paused. Travers thought he looked taken aback by this lucid defence. He wondered if he could stir the pot.

'There was an upper stage, a lot higher up. What was the risk assessment on that?'

Lambourn looked a bit more cheerful: surely that would get him? Arno dealt with it confidently (as Travers had known he would). He recounted the debate on safety ropes and the actors' refusal to use them.

'So what First Aid provision did you have during the performance?' asked Lambourn. He was more desperate now; this wasn't going as well as he'd hoped.

'The local GP, Dr Brian Southgate, was invited to come to both performances. We gave him a Red Cross armband – and a reserved seat on the front row. The doctor stood at the front during the fire panic – and was there, of course, when the body was found.'

'Ah yes, the fire panic, as you call it. Had you anticipated that?'

'No, we had not. I found out afterwards what caused it. Someone had reset the volume controls on the smoke machines. It was deliberate sabotage. I thought that chimed in better with the idea that the death wasn't natural at all.'

Lambourn reminded himself that James was an author and playwright. He didn't look like Agatha Christie but he'd probably written mystery plays in his time. If he wasn't careful here the man would be scripting his investigation.

'OK. Sergeant Travers has some questions for you too.'

The transition was abrupt. There was a pause while the

sergeant collected his thoughts.

'Sir, one thing we do in any investigation is to check the record of those involved. In your case the only thing I found was some discrepancy from a play you put on in Colchester about five years ago. Would you tell us your side of that, please.'

'Hell, I thought you'd picked up the time I was drunk in Glasgow.'

'Sir, many people are drunk in Glasgow. It doesn't make the records – at least not down in England.'

Arno almost smiled. 'The incident in Colchester was the last time I put on a drama without very carefully checking the terms of the contract. Some bastard stitched me up. Unless the play made an operating profit, it turned out, I was done for. Of course, it was experimental theatre – didn't even break even. As a result, I found I'd earned no fee at all. Worse still, I had personally to cover the losses. Six month's hard work for zilch.'

'So who wrote the contract for *Splits and Schisms*?'

'Della Howell – she's the patron – got a local solicitor from Camelford - Gifford. A family firm, they go back decades. I checked very carefully what he wrote in the contracts. He in turn checked my script wasn't libellous. Della isn't out to diddle me, anyway. She and I were at school together.'

This was new information to Lambourn. He wondered whether to pursue the possibility of pressure on James' part to win the *Splits and Schisms* contract – what photos might he have of the voluptuous Della in her youth? Then he recalled that his aim was to make Arno feel he'd been fingered by the law – not to give him the whisper of a case for wrongful arrest. It would be best to leave that idea alone.

'Right sir, that all seems satisfactory. I'm sorry we've had to drag you over here but we have to check every aspect.'

'Just one thing, Inspector. If this business is sorted in the next couple of days, is there any chance we would be allowed to put on the drama one more time? We could do it as a tribute to Joe Stacey. Obviously we'd only do it with his widow's permission. It might be a way to bring the episode to a proper finale.'

Lambourn had not expected to be asked questions. He glanced at Travers for a reply.

The junior policeman responded, 'Either we'll hear soon it was a one in a thousand accident – in which case I can see no reason at all why there shouldn't be a tribute performance. Or else it's a major crime, in which case the stage area is a crime scene. Even so, once the Scene of Crime Officers have finished examining the stage, I don't think the police would have any objections to it being used one more time. The people of Delabole would like that. After all, you've convinced us that the stage itself is pretty safe.'

CHAPTER 38

Peter Travers had talked more freely with Arno James on the journey back from Bodmin. This time his passenger had been offered, and taken, the front passenger seat. Nothing was admitted and Lambourn's name was never mentioned, but the author seemed to have more respect for the policeman – or, at least, a better understanding of the constraints he was forced to operate under.

Arno had spoken about the trials and tribulations of being a visiting author and the stresses of putting on an outdoor drama in a village which had hitherto only had kiddies' entertainment. It was clear the man hated pantomime with a vengeance. That hardly supplied a motive for murder: there was no reason to think Joe had been a pantomime acolyte either. Travers was left in no doubt that Arno had a passionate love of drama as a means of retelling tales of the past.

The policeman dropped off the author in Treknow and returned to his Police House in Delabole. His current task – one interrupted earlier by his boss - was to look over his interview notes and spot any questions which he had missed or inconsistencies he had exposed. As he learned more, the time-window within which Joe had died seemed to be reducing to a chink. Travers wondered for a second if there could be some sort of time-slip at work in the Trebarwith valley. Was that why mobile phones wouldn't work?

His phone rang. It was Truro Hospital. Travers flipped open his notebook to a new page as he waited for the key man to be put through. What was the verdict?

'Am I speaking to Constable Travers, dealing with the body of Joe Stacey, brought in late Friday evening?'

'It's Police Sergeant Peter Travers, actually, but yes?'

'Hello, Peter, this is Dr Alec Kidner. I'm senior pathologist here in Truro. We've been examining the cadaver of Joe Stacey over the last two days. There are still several aspects – blood and stomach analysis, for example - where we're awaiting results from the laboratories. So I don't have a final report yet, I'm afraid.'

The man couldn't just be ringing to tell him to hang on, could he? Travers wondered how to phrase his response: whatever he felt, he knew he had to be polite. As he pondered his caller continued.

'There's a note here saying the police wanted preliminary results as soon as possible. You'll need to use your discretion on whether any of these are passed on to the next of kin. I reckon it'll be a couple more days before we can give you a definitive answer.'

'OK. The widow can wait. So what are your preliminary findings?'

'The victim had received a heavy blow on the back of the head. And I'm equally sure it was deliberate - not just the

291

result of a fall. Hard enough to crack the skull, at any rate - but we can't say for certain that that was the cause of death. I need to be sure there was nothing untoward happening in the blood supply or heart or other organs. The crack on the head might have caused him to fall and in turn precipitated the fatal heart attack. That's why I'm waiting on the lab results. But I'd say it's ninety nine percent safe to deduce that the victim died, directly or indirectly, as a result of an assault.'

That was it: the news he'd been expecting, fearing, anticipating with his forest of interviews. Poor old Joe.

'Thank you, Dr Kidner. Can I ask a couple more questions, please? Have you any observations on the time of death; and have you any suggestions on the possible murder weapon?'

'I can't help much on time of death. He was probably dead before the ambulance crew reached him. He'd been lying out in the cold, hadn't he? That slows all the body functions – before and after death - makes it very hard to narrow down. In terms of weapon...'

Dr Kidner paused for a moment. Travers was happy to wait.

'It was something smooth, I'd say, Peter. The wound was fairly even. Something like a long pipe? Metal, probably, not wood. Another of the tests we're waiting for from the labs might give me more. Sorry. Is that any help?'

'It's a start. Thank you, Dr Kidner. Please ring me, night or day, as soon as you have any more information. In the meantime I'll get on and alert the Crime Squad.'

Travers put down the phone and made himself another mug of coffee as he pondered on what he had just heard; and whom he should now inform.

Lambourn had ordered him not to call in the Regional Crime Squad in Exeter until it was certain a crime had been committed. By excluding non-crime he was doing his best to massage reported crime figures downwards. 'We might as well make the uncertainty work in our favour.' No doubt he would expect any referral to go through him.

He recalled Lambourn had already hindered the call once and might delay it further: might insist, for example, on waiting until the pathologist could give a definitive report. Two or three more days before SOCO could examine the unguarded crime scene – probably days of wind and rain. The forecast had been for another storm in North Cornwall, starting midday tomorrow.

Travers had had one favourable encounter with a detective from Exeter – Detective Inspector Marcus Chadwick. The last time they'd met the man had been grotesquely overloaded. But if you wanted something doing, Travers knew, it was better to ask a workaholic than a layabout. He didn't need to refer the case. He would simply seek Chadwick's advice on when the Squad would like to be called in: and see if he took the bait.

He hoped Chadwick was still in post and not on leave. Fortunately, not many people took holiday in January –

unless they could afford to visit relatives in Australia or South Africa. He had seen no evidence that Chadwick was that wealthy. The phone numbers of the Regional Crime Squad were still on his notice board. After a glance he dialled Chadwick's direct line number.

"Direct line" was police force jargon, of course. It only got him as far as the man's secretary, Becky. Encouragingly, she remembered his name – or at least claimed to do so. 'You might be lucky, Sergeant Travers. He's been very busy but someone's just been appointed to share his case load. Hold on, I'll see if he can give you a few minutes straight away.'

There was a delay. Travers used the time to summarise the case in his mind. The more he thought about it the less simple it seemed: but it would be a mistake to start with the complexities.

'Afternoon, Travers, are you well?'

'Very well, sir, thank you. I'm just not quite certain whom I should report to with a local crime I've got here.'

'I'm happy to have a look at anything, Travers – at least, anything from a bright copper who thinks outside the box. I've got a few minutes before my next taxing administrative knockabout. Try me.'

'OK. It's about a death – not sure yet if it's manslaughter or murder - that took place halfway through a local drama that was being put on last Friday evening at Trebarwith Strand.'

'Travers, this sounds a hell of a sight more interesting than my allotted tasks here. Tell me more.'

'The victim – called Joe Stacey – was narrator in this drama. His body was found at the end of Act One, half-hidden under the stage. I've just had Truro Hospital Pathology on the phone. They're still doing tests but they've given me an interim report, which says he was almost certainly killed by a blow to the back of his head.'

This was the point at which Travers had expected to ask about when the Crime Squad should be alerted, but Chadwick had already grasped the case into wide open arms.

'I really can't get down to you until Thursday. I've had to set up a road show for the Chief Constable and her deputies, covering our work to tackle drug gangs in Exeter over the past year. That's an all-day event at a posh hotel on Dartmoor, ending with a banquet tomorrow evening. I can't get out of it. Murders have to take second place to jamborees, you know.' Chadwick sounded cynical – it was a different mindset to Lambourn, anyway.

'Is there any chance of you sending SOCO to have a look? It's been four days since the death – '

'Hell, you guys never give us a chance, do you? There's always evidence when a crime happens, Travers, always traces if you look in the right place - but it doesn't stay there for ever.'

'I wanted to call you, sir, but my boss in Bodmin insisted that we wait for the post mortem report so we were sure it was a crime.'

Although uniformed and plain-clothed policemen were

295

supposedly part of the same crime-prevention outfit there were often tensions between them. Inspector Chadwick had never met Inspector Lambourn but he had met his counterparts in Exeter - and could guess his philosophy.

'He sounds like a jobs-worth. So nothing's happened yet?'

'I've spent the last three days interviewing everyone involved in the drama –'

'Good, good, that's what I'd have done – or, rather, asked you to do. We might not have lost as much time as I feared. What's your next move?'

This was the sort of encouragement he needed. Travers was tempted to claim he would seize the reins in Bodmin and demote Lambourn to Special Constable but managed to restrain himself. Then he remembered the videos.

'I've manage to acquire some videos that were being taken of the production, sir. They're from various angles. I thought I'd spend the rest of the day watching them and see if they gave me anything new.'

'Excellent. This is what you and I do, Travers, help solve crime. Not put on bloody jamborees. I'll get in touch with the Scene of Crime people and get them down as soon as possible – might not be till tomorrow morning, unfortunately. They'll ring you to check the venue. I'll be down on Thursday morning for a full report and discussion. Don't bother with your man in Bodmin.'

Slate Expectations

CHAPTER 39

George and Sophie had been just setting out for their Community Lunch when they'd seen Arno being dropped off outside their house from a police car. The driver was Sergeant Peter Travers. He'd waved to them as he'd driven off but there was no time to talk.

'Poor chap, he looks a bit downcast,' said Sophie of Arno.

'We've no time to talk to him now, we'd best check on him after lunch.'

When they had dropped in at Holly Cottage, they had been called upstairs. There they found Arno, sitting in his bed and scribbling away in his notebook. He had another writing commission - a collapsed mine in the northeast of England, they gathered - that he was starting to get his mind around.

'Tell you what,' said George, 'we can see you're busy right now. We've plenty of odd jobs to do around Ivy Cottage. Would you like to come for a meal with us this evening? Be our first proper guest.'

Arno looked as pleased as punch that someone had invited him out – and with no strings attached. It probably helped that the inviters had been two attractive women. George wondered if he would have preferred it if there had

297

been just one.

'What time shall I come? Around seven? Great, I'll see you then. By the way, I'm not vegetarian. I eat anything. I'll bring a couple of bottles of wine.'

George thought two bottles sounded a lot for three people but said nothing. Probably his male artistic friends drank more than they did. He could always take the remainder home with him: he wasn't bringing it a long way.

'I wouldn't mind a stroll along the cliffs,' said Sophie, once they were back in Ivy Cottage. 'It's supposed to be fine for the afternoon. I'll take my camera and try and capture moody waves against dark clouds.'

'Would you mind very much if I didn't come? I'd be happy just to potter about here on my own. I'll put a casserole on for dinner in a couple of hours. But if you were going as far as Tintagel, maybe you could get us a dessert?'

Once she was on her own George enjoyed the feeling of prowling about her own cottage, fiddling with details as they caught her eye.

Lily had obviously not been much of a book reader. George planned to buy a large bookshelf and obtain a wide range of books, maps and guides. The best place for it would be underneath the far end living-room window which looked out onto the Treknow street. Then she got out her notebook and thought about which walls would benefit from another picture. Maybe she would need to let Polly choose one or two when the two of them came down in the Easter holidays?

That reminded her she needed to write her regular email to her daughter and append a few photos of the cottage. By Friday she would be able to send her a picture of the place with its new furniture. That would show her that her mother wasn't a complete fuddy-duddy.

Once her laptop was on there were other emails to be answered. It was astonishing how quickly time passed. She had just completed preparing the beef and wine casserole when Sophie returned. 'It's approaching dusk by five. I didn't want to be out on the cliffs in the dark.'

Sophie had managed to find a chocolate gateau in the Londis store and a fresh melon in May's Butchers. It might not be the most luxurious meal ever but they were at least trying.

Arno came on the dot at seven. He'd made an effort to dress for dinner – above his sandals, anyway. He was wearing light-grey chinos, a salmon-pink shirt and a dark green corduroy jacket. He had even trimmed his beard.

'My, you do scrub up well,' said Sophie as she let him in.

He held her hand lightly and looked her up and down. Tall and elegantly slim, her long blond hair newly washed, she was wearing a shimmering low-cut crimson dress, fishnet tights and sparkling shoes. A gold necklace and earrings completed the display.

'My dear Sophie, you look amazing.'

George was watching the pair of them from the kitchen doorway with a giggle. 'You two look like a teenage couple

299

on their first date.'

Arno turned to her and saw a small but slim woman in a stylish dark green dress. Brown eyes sparkled under dark curly hair. It was fortunate, George had thought, as she'd changed for dinner, that she had had no reason to wear her one special outfit before that evening: Arno hadn't seen it. Unlike Sophie, she had brought no choice of smart clothes on this trip.

'George, you look amazing too.'

'We can see you're an author, Arno. Once you've found a good line you keep repeating it.'

All three laughed. It was going to be a good evening.

'I may be a good author but I'm rotten at casting. The two prettiest women in the whole production and I've got you tucked away behind cameras.'

'Now we've all complimented one another on our appearance let's call a truce,' said George firmly. 'Arno, do come through into the lounge. You can see we've got our wood-burning stove alight.'

Arno went in and seemed to glow in the warmth. 'My cottage has never been half as warm as this. This is bliss.'

'It's pretty good. We have to keep feeding it. That's fine with several occupants. I can see why you wouldn't want to bother on your own.'

'That's why I write in bed, of course.'

George wanted to make sure her first guest appreciated her cottage. 'Effectively, the chimney's the centre of the cottage. It's between the lounge and the kitchen so it warms up both. Upstairs it runs between the main bedroom and the bathroom, so it helps there too. It's just the second bedroom that loses out. Sophie's used to hardship, though – she's an artist.'

Sophie smiled. 'It's worked out far better than I feared when we first got here – struggling to make the lights work in the dark and the cold. If I'd had a car of my own at that point, I'd have gone back home.'

Arno looked at George. 'You didn't muck up again?'

There was something here Sophie was missing. 'What do you mean?'

Dimly she recalled George's comment on that first evening about their neighbour being prickly. She'd never followed it through. Now she looked from one to the other. 'Had you two met before?'

Arno responded. 'All depends on what you mean by "met".' He looked at George to continue.

'I told you, Sophie, that I came down once to look at the cottage before I decided to buy. That was in October. Again I got here in the dark; but that time I hadn't thought to bring my torch. So I stumbled up the path to Ivy Cottage, fumbled for ages with the keys, walked in and fell flat on my face over the step in the hallway. With an almighty bang. Really hurt my right knee and my left ankle. I was in a lot of pain.'

'Meanwhile,' said Arno, 'I was sitting next door in Holly Cottage – in bed, not fully dressed. I'd heard a car draw up. I looked out. There was someone on next door's path; then I heard the door being prised open. I knew the last occupant had just died and the place was empty. '"It's a burglar", I thought. So I crept round to Ivy and through the front door. In complete silence.'

George took over. 'When I stopped cursing I crawled towards the doorway to pull myself up. My knee hurt like crazy. It was pitch dark. Then... in the doorway... I felt a pair of slippers. I couldn't see but I guessed they were Lily's - maybe they'd never been tidied away. Above them, as my hands explored, there was something else. Then, as my hands reached higher, I felt a pair of hairy bare legs. I screamed and screamed. I told you I didn't believe in ghosts, Sophie, but at the moment I could think of no other explanation.'

'In a sensible world I would have made introductions,' said Arno. 'It's easy to say with hindsight. But I could see difficulties. I was a visitor to the area, stripped to his underpants, inside his neighbour's cottage, with her holding my legs and screaming in fear. It doesn't often happen but I panicked. I ran back to Holly and locked the door. Prayed I'd left no trace. Hoped the local police didn't keep knee prints. Wondered how I'd fare in a knee identity parade in the dark. I just stayed in. I got some of my best writing of the winter done that week. By the time I dared to venture out, the visitor next door, whoever she was, had gone.'

Sophie's face had gone from one to another, trying to smother her amusement. Now she could no longer keep control. She howled with mirth. Dropped to her knees, buried her face in the cushion on the settee, shaking with laughter. Arno and George, too, could see the funny side more easily three months on than either had done at the time. They hugged one another, tears in their eyes.

'That's... that's the best ice breaker I've ever heard,' said Sophie.

'It sounds like the start of a good play,' added Arno.

Then they noticed George was laughing and crying at the same time. 'It's all right. Don't worry. It's just I haven't laughed like that at all from... from the time I heard that Mark had died, ten months ago. Oh how funny. I never understood why Arno was half naked, you see, till this evening. Or why he daren't introduce himself. Maybe I can be a whole person again after all. I can still laugh. Oh how wonderful. Thank you, Arno, thank you.'

The meal had been a great success. George suspected that though Arno mixed from time to time with movers and shakers in high society, he spent a much greater proportion of his time on his own. A home-cooked meal with neighbours, even a simple one, was as much a treat for him as dinner at an expensive restaurant.

He had regaled them at length with the story of his attendance in Bodmin Police Station that morning.

'I didn't think Peter Travers was the bullying type,' said George.

'It wasn't Travers' fault. He was simply the chauffeur, acting under orders. It was his half-witted boss. Trying to impose the iron tyranny of the establishment on the humble artist.'

George wasn't sure if she wanted to go further down this road – not this evening, anyway. They had already drunk a bottle of Cabernet Sauvignon and were well down the Merlot. It was too late for deep argument. Arno had drunk well beyond his share but George had lost her clarity of thought. How could she change the subject?

'By the way,' she said, 'we know that you were here the same time as me last October. Were you here earlier - did you actually meet Lily Taylor?'

'Lily? Wonderful old lady. She was one of my first sources. It was pure luck that I'd taken the cottage next door. It took her twenty four hours to figure out - goodness knows how - who I was and what I was doing. After that she was my unpaid assistant.'

'We knew she had an interest in local history,' said Sophie. 'We found an old newspaper she'd been reading in the greenhouse. 1925: the arrival of Jack Bucknall in Delabole. Why didn't you cover him in *Splits and Schisms*?'

'I wanted to focus on the life of the Quarry. Jack was an interesting character and if there'd been an Act Three – or time to run to 1940 - he would have been a major player. I decided I had enough material without him.'

'So Jack wasn't the one that Lily told you about?'

'Well, she did tell me, but I didn't do much with it. No, the person she told me about was Bessie Cowling.'

'Bessie Cowling? How on earth did Lily know her? I thought that after the Quarry Disaster that Bessie and her family emigrated – to Pennsylvania, wasn't it?'

'That's right. But for some reason Bessie came back to Cornwall in her later years. She was living in Tintagel in the 1930s.'

George gave a gasp. 'You don't mean – it's not possible – was Bessie the lady that Lily helped after she left school?'

'That's true. How the dickens did you know that?'

'I didn't; it was a guess. I found Lily's diaries up in the loft last week and I read the first one – it was for 1940. She describes how she'd gone to work for an old lady in Tintagel. She was very careful not to give the lady's name. The diary for the following year was missing. It was very odd. Every other year was there.'

'I can solve that problem at least,' said Arno. 'I was the one who had the diary for 1941. I'll make sure you get it back. That was a key source.'

There was a pause as this new information was registered.

'Wait a minute,' said Sophie. 'Have I got this? You're saying the 1941 diary, kept by Lily Taylor, gives some of the last thoughts of Bessie Cowling – that's the girl who was a hero of the Quarry Disaster of 1869. And it was kept here - in this very cottage? That's amazing.'

George was less concerned about the diary's provenance and more interested in its contents. 'So what was in the 1941 diary?'

'By that time Bessie was very old. All her family were in America. Here the war was all around her. She realised she

305

might not last much longer. She had a young carer in whom she had come to place great trust. So she shared all her observations and worries with Lily. Lily in turn entered these in her diary. Then in her turn passed the diary on to me, when she realised what I was trying to produce. "This is part of the history of the Quarry," she said.'

Arno looked frustrated. 'I wanted to make use of it. The trouble was I had made a promise to Lily: I would not betray Bessie in any way. In the end, after her sudden death, I found that promise limited what I was able to write.'

'That's your limit, Arno. On the other hand Lily left her diaries in her loft and her son sold the cottage and all its contents to me. Tomorrow, when you give me back the 1941 diary, I'll read it for myself. It would save time if you told me now what was in it that you thought was so revolutionary.'

Arno was used to arguing for freedom of expression and less used to arguing against it. He could see there was little difference between him telling the women what he had been told by Lily last October, and letting them read it for themselves the following morning.

After another glass of Merlot he succumbed.

'Bessie never forgave the Slate Quarry Management. Her best friend, Fannie Wallis, had been killed in the Disaster which she had survived. The loss left a permanent mark on her character. That was one reason the family moved away to the United States. As Bessie grew older, she thought more about the Disaster and kept asking herself if it could really all be blamed on Mother Nature.'

'Sophie and I spent Monday in the Record Office in Truro, looking at the Slate Quarry records. We were only there for one day, but I didn't come across anyone else who had questions along those lines.'

'No. Remember, Bessie was just nine years old when it happened. Even if there had been a serious inquiry, zealous for the truth, they wouldn't have taken that much notice of a nine-year-old girl. The thought she had was so awful that for most of her life she kept it to herself. It was only in her final years that she passed it on to young Lily.'

'So what was this observation or insight - or whatever you'd call it?'

'Well, Bessie saw for herself the gantry, the poppet head, starting to tip over and slide down the face. It was the beginning of the big rock slide. And she saw that all of its main guy ropes had come loose. She realised that wasn't right. The whole point of guy ropes was that they held fast when all around was shaking to pieces. They were there to anchor the poppet head.'

'Would no-one else have seen that?'

'All the men working beneath the poppet head were crushed under the subsequent avalanche. The men at the top were cowering as far from the edge as they could. There were huge clouds of dust blocking out the view for those further away. Bessie was the only one close enough to see the crucial event. The trouble was, she was nine years old.'

'I still don't see the significance.'

'Nor did Bessie for a long time. Then it came to her that

307

not only had she seen the guy ropes loose, but she'd seen the massive wooden pegs, that were supposed to hold the other ends in place on the ground, flying down as well.'

'You're going too fast for us Arno.'

George, though, was ahead of her, more used to the way industrial accidents unravelled.

'Can I guess, Arno? Did Bessie come to realise that the reason the pegs came out of the ground was that... that they weren't in solid ground at all?'

'You're on the right lines. Go on.'

'Someone had been lazy and hammered the key safety pegs directly into the weakened quartz seam. It was the easiest place to sink them but it was also the most danger-ous. How long had that poppet head been in place?'

Arno seemed unwilling to answer; averse to spelling out the truth.

'Come on, Arno. How long?'

'A week. That was what the Slate Director had come to inspect.'

'So just one week after four massive big posts are ham-mered into a weak seam – a seam which ran across the top of the Quarry - that whole weak seam crumbles. It splits in two. As it does so that side of the Quarry is loosened – it comes down in an avalanche, killing over a dozen people.'

George paused, letting her mind take in the whole revela-tion.

'Wow. No wonder the poor girl never ever forgave the Quarry management. The whole thing is horrific. I can see, though, why you hesitated to put it directly into your drama.'

CHAPTER 40

U p in Delabole Peter Travers was having a less engaging evening. He had not realised, until he looked in detail, just how many hours of video the women had filmed. He assumed that all the ones he had been given were related to *Splits and Schisms*. It was a mercy that George had been so systematic with the way the files were named - or he might have sunk without trace.

With a little effort – he wasn't much of a gadget geek - he managed to link Sophie's laptop to the big television in his living room so he could sit in comfort as he watched the videos play. He was stimulated by the new interest of the Regional Crime Squad. Could he possibly find something distinctive to report to Detective Inspector Chadwick?

At first he had watched the videos at random. They seemed to be interchangeable in the story they covered. Any one of them would give him the material contained in the drama – of course, he had never seen Act Two per-formed live - but was that really what he was after?

He soon saw this was hopeless: he needed structure in his search. The key thing – maybe the only thing – was the videos of the performance itself: and anything extra which they picked up of movement behind the scenes.

He could find only one video ascribed to Friday. Then he

recalled George saying something about a glitch with her camera. Never mind; what did the other one show?

It started with the audience arriving. They looked cheerful and expectant. If he had been looking into an act of terrorism this might have been useful material – could he spot the al Quaida representative with her head under a scarf? – but he wasn't. Only the absence of someone significant, who was supposed to be in the audience but wasn't (or maybe the converse) might turn out to be useful. But that was looking a long way ahead.

The video moved on to the performance. It was an assured piece of filming. There were plenty of close-ups of key utterances. The policeman assumed that Sophie must have had a good knowledge of the script; and had had her camera mounted on a tripod, ready to capture these.

The performed scenes were interleaved with commentary from the "pulpit". Job Hockaday, sporting his huge white beard, spoke eloquently. This was the last appearance of poor old Joe Stacey, the policeman reminded himself. He would flip back once the video concluded and check on how worried the man had seemed. Had he any inkling of what was to come?

For now he sat back, sipped his coffee, and let the video run.

An hour later the policeman was no further forward. He had watched the final scene of Act One – the Disaster – with great care. He had even rewound the last ten minutes to

311

watch it through again.

Just once or twice the camera angle had dipped below the level of the stage, but he could see nothing in the resulting blackness. Maybe the Crime Squad would have technicians that could make something out of nothing, but it was not obvious to him. He even watched the Disaster scene a third time but learned no more.

He recalled the idea of checking for signs of fear in Joe's performance. This time he rewound the video almost to the start and concentrated on shots of Job's commentary.

There were a few wobbles at the start but after that the man didn't seem frightened at all. He oozed confidence. The sound quality was not that good but the words were clear. No; there was no reason to think Joe Stacey had any premonition of his death.

Travers made himself another mug of coffee as he pondered his next move. He'd been lucky enough to acquire this stock of video. Not many detectives would be in a position to view the fatal event and its dress rehearsal in such detail. There must be something here that would help.

Then he remembered George's attempt at shooting the drama on full zoom from the Ivy Cottage roof. Might that give him something different? Had the fatal events of Friday been rehearsed earlier in the week?

He picked out the relevant video and started to run it. There was no useful sound track, no variation in camera angle and little action.

Impatiently, he fast-forwarded to the Disaster scene,

where he knew some action should be in view. At last something could be seen. First Greg Wallis climbed doggedly down his ladder. Then, without a single glance back to the stage, he headed off up the field to find his Quarry Captain.

A few moments afterwards, Wallis' daughter, Fannie, came to the edge of the stage, crouched down and lowered herself off it. She hung by her hands, then dropped a couple of feet onto the valley floor and arranged herself on her back. A few seconds later she was joined by the two general-purpose actors with non-speaking parts, who lay down beside her.

Finally, a few minutes later, the smoke began to billow. As it did so the Quarry management came into view. There were a few moments of confusion; then the pretend dead were roused and despatched under the stage.

It was all exactly as he had expected – and as his witnesses had testified.

The policeman was tempted to give up and turn to live television. He enjoyed watching crime, especially Lewis. The recent blossoming of the faithful underling, now promoted to Inspector, was close to his heart. He had seen from trailers that there was a new series starting in ten minutes.

He also knew Chadwick would want a full account of the videos' contents.

He decided that he would watch a dress rehearsal video through once then call it a night. What might he learn? It would be good to watch the whole of *Splits and Schisms* from beginning to end. Had Arno edited the drama between

313

the final rehearsal and the performance? Were there any additions - or subtractions - that might prove significant?

This time there was a choice of videos. He'd seen Sophie's offering – maybe he should give George a chance.

It seemed a good choice. Thursday was the evening George had set her camera entirely onto the pulpit. It was unvarnished Joe Stacey. George might lack Sophie's finesse, Travers thought, but she was still competent. Her tripod had allowed the whole video to be shot in close-up.

Then Travers noticed something odd. Joe's performance on Thursday was not exactly the same as on Friday. On Thursday he seemed to shout louder and quicker. Was that just camera position – or was George's camera picking up the sound better?

Travers kept watching but now he was watching with a purpose. There was something odd. After ten minutes he stopped the dress rehearsal video and switched over to the video covering the main performance, running it through to a point where Job spoke. Then he watched the same speech as he had just seen given the previous day.

It was hard to detect but now he was almost certain. Assuming that Joe Stacey was the actor playing Job Hocka-day on Thursday, his entire part had been played by some-one else during the live performance on Friday.

For half an hour the policeman sat with the idea going round in his mind; it was crackers, surely? Two hundred and fifty local people had seen Delabole Gallery owner Joe Stacey perform as Job Hockaday on Friday; and no-one – not even his wife - had queried the substitution.

On the other hand, it was a dark night; the audience were thirty or forty yards away. The pulpit was off to the side from the main stage. It wasn't an opera: the audience had not brought binoculars. The programme told them that Job Hockaday was played by Joe Stacey; they'd heard him talk about his role for months; so why should they disbelieve it?

It was the long white beard that made it possible. In truth, you couldn't be sure whose face lurked behind such a beard. Anyone of similar height and build to Joe, with a Cornish accent, could have got away with it. The sound of the voice was further confused by the background breeze and the valley acoustics.

What happened before the show began? The audience might not be able to tell the difference but surely the cast would. How did that all work?

The policeman did not want to alert anyone who might possibly be part of the crime - and now he was certain that it was a crime and not just a dreadful accident. Every one of his interviews had assumed that Joe had been in full view of the audience until just before his death: that was the basis of his time-line and the focus of all his questions.

Now, to his horror, he realised that the man could have been killed much earlier – before the drama even began. He berated himself. He'd not given any attention to earlier movements – had not asked about them - did not even know where any of the cast were supposed to be.

There was one source that he had reason to trust. Indeed, the basis of his new understanding of the whole sequence: the woman behind the key recording. It was late but he thought she would probably still be awake. The policeman reached for his phone.

CHAPTER 41

George Gilbert was surprised to have a call from Peter Travers that late in the evening.

'Hello Peter. No, I'm not in bed yet. We'd been entertaining Arno James. We needed to restore his spirits after your boss's assault this morning. He's just gone home.'

She listened again. What an odd question.

'No, there's no-one else here at the moment. Sophie went off with Arno to have a bath.' She was aware as she said it that her answer raised more questions than it answered. She blamed that on the Merlot - but she was not given the chance to explain. She listened again.

'OK, I'll leave a note for Sophie, go to my bedroom and shut the door. I must say you're sounding very mysterious.' This was turning into a jolly evening. She'd been hugged by one handsome man and rung up by another; to her embarrassment she hiccupped. 'Ring me again, please, in a couple of minutes.'

A few minutes later the two were able to talk more freely.

'What I'm about to tell you has to be kept absolutely secret. You can't tell anyone – not even your friend Sophie.'

'OK. I know how to keep secrets.'

'I've been looking at all your videos. The key thing I've found is that, in my opinion, the person who played Job Hockaday last Friday night wasn't the same as the man who played him the night before.'

There was silence. George did not doubt the policeman held that view but she didn't need to go along with it. It needed more thought - with less alcoholic interference.

'I need to think about that, Peter. It's been a long evening. Why are you ringing to tell me at this time of night?'

'Before I tell anyone, or take it any further, I need to know more about what happened before the drama started. All my interview questions have been dealing with the wrong time, you see. Was there some point when everyone gathered together for a final briefing?'

George tried to pull her thoughts together. 'There was something like that on the night of the performance. I don't know who was there. Sophie and I didn't need to be part of it. We were outside, filming the audience as they arrived.'

The policeman seemed disappointed; but he had another question. 'The other thing that occurred to me was: what happened about makeup? I couldn't see anyone mentioned on the programme: did no-one use any?'

'Sophie and I had nothing to do with that side of it. I can tell you who was supposed to be the makeup lady. It's the wife of our mutual friend, Dr Brian Southgate.'

'Alice?' The policeman sounded incredulous.

'How many wives has the man got? Brian and Alice invited us for a meal when we first arrived; it came up during conversation. Alice said it was the sort of commitment she could cope with because it didn't take any of her time until the dress rehearsal.'

'I'll ring her when we've finished talking.'

'Are you sure? She's a head teacher and it's half past eleven.'

'The Southgates are late birds. She's used to me. There was just one other thing I wanted to ask you. That is, could you come over here and look at these videos - see if you agree with me?'

'Now, Peter?' She giggled. 'If you want to invite a girl out for a first date I suggest you should start earlier in the evening.'

'I didn't mean tonight. Tomorrow morning – say half past nine?'

'Actually, that would be really helpful. Paul Wood is coming tomorrow to refit our bathroom and he wants us out of the cottage while he does it. There's only one toilet here, you see.'

Travers was tempted to suggest they could once again tramp round to Arno's but thought better of it. The less he knew of their ablutions the better. He gave George directions on how to find his Police House and rang off.

Alice Southgate was even more surprised to take a call from Peter Travers a few minutes later.

'Peter! Do you want Brian, he's –'

Travers explained that it was Alice rather than Brian that

319

he wanted to talk to.

'Me! I'm flattered. How can I help?'

The policeman explained.

'Yes, I was the only one doing makeup for *Splits and Schisms*. For those that wanted it, anyway. I was tucked away in that house at the top of Trebarwith Strand that they used for dressing rooms. From about six o'clock onwards. It takes a while to put the stuff on properly; I was kept very busy.'

'Did Joe Stacey present himself for your attentions?'

'D'you know, I was thinking about that afterwards. He was there for the dress rehearsal - but he wasn't one of those that appeared on performance night. Of course, Joe had that massive beard which covered his whole face. Once he'd got that on there was scarcely room for makeup anyway.'

So he hadn't yet found a reason why his theory couldn't work, thought the policeman as he put down the phone. Tomorrow would be a busy day.

CHAPTER 42

Sergeant Travers was out early on Wednesday morning. A call from Exeter at seven thirty had told him that a Scene of Crime team was coming to Trebarwith Strand car-park in an hour's time. The death of Joe Stacey was at last being taken seriously at Regional level.

As he waited for the team, Travers pondered what difference it might make to know Joe had been killed earlier than he'd thought. Wherever the man had been killed, the body had ended up hidden under the stage. An audience was in place throughout Act One, so it was almost certain the attack must have taken place somewhere under that stage. That was the only area he could think of which was near enough for a body to be dragged but which was also out of sight.

His conclusion was that the search area to be covered by SOCO had not changed.

In an odd way it helped that SOCO were coming to the event so late. He didn't need to bother them with his previous belief. He was in a position to say that the body had been killed somewhere under the stage and to demonstrate, lying down, his best estimate of where it had been found. Then he could leave the team to search the area to their heart's content. The trouble was, it had all happened several days ago. He didn't have much hope of anything useful being found.

'How long d'you reckon it'll take for your lads to cover this patch?' he asked the officer in charge.

'Two or three hours. Why don't you come down again at eleven?'

Travers was pleased to be given the time away. He recalled that he had George coming to see him around nine thirty.

Following Travers' instructions, George and Sophie arrived at the Police House one minute after the time scheduled. George got out; Sophie gave her a wave, let in the clutch and roared away.

'I'm sorry, I didn't intend to exclude your friend,' said the policeman, feeling slightly guilty, as he welcomed George in.

'Don't worry. She and I have had more ideas about how the past might impact on the present. Sophie's off to the Cornwall Record Office. We've agreed a list of topics that she can investigate. She'll be gone all day.'

'M'm, I don't suppose our discussion will take that long.'

'No, but Sophie can't be in Ivy Cottage while the plumber refits the bathroom any more than I can. We both need to make the most of not being at home.'

Travers prepared coffee and George took a seat in front of his television.

'I'd never have spotted this if I hadn't had your videos. It's not obvious. That huge beard makes it impossible to see the face clearly. It's thanks to your efforts we have got the opportunity to compare Job Hockaday giving the same speech – or I should say reading the same script - on two successive days. Watch this.'

Travers had made a note of the times where the best comparisons occurred. Ten minutes later George had seen the character playing Job speaking on Thursday and on Friday; and agreed it was two different actors.

'Definitely. It's all down to audience expectation. If you're not told at all – or you're told they're the same bloke - you don't notice. I'd say if you examine them carefully there's no doubt.'

She mused; then continued, 'That certainly explains why Joe never turned on my video on the Friday evening: he was never there. That must change the problem. For example, it must be murder, mustn't it? And presumably the man who was playing Job on Friday - and pretending to be Joe - was the murderer. So is there any trace of him left in the pulpit?'

It was blindingly obvious but the policeman had not thought to ask the SOCO team to check the pulpit. 'Good idea. Excuse me a minute.'

The policeman stood up, seized his mobile and contacted the leader of the SOCO team down in Trebarwith Strand. 'There's a separate turret to the left of the stage, looks a bit like a pulpit. Could you check that as well, please, for finger-prints or other traces.'

There was a question to which he replied. 'Yes, it's likely

that the murderer spent some time there. Three quarters of an hour, anyway.'

He listened to the reply then turned the phone off. 'They're already doing it. It's one of the few places down there that are well-protected from rain. They always look where there's the best chance of something still being present. They reckon there's more chance of finding something inside the pulpit than in those yards and yards of rough ground beneath the stage. Mind you, that must be where he was killed.'

'You mean, the body couldn't have been brought any further in secret with all the crowds hanging about outside. Unless he was killed much earlier indeed – but I guess the medical evidence gives you an earliest time of death?'

She was sharp, the policeman thought. 'I didn't push that as hard as I should. I assumed - everyone assumed – that the dead man was the man they'd heard narrating ten minutes earlier.'

'Have you asked Brian for the earliest time he thinks death could have occurred?'

Once again the policeman grimaced; then stood and seized his phone. There was some sort of telephone tag played within the surgery then he was put through.

'Brian, I can't tell you why I'm asking yet, but it's really important. If you'd come across Joe on Friday evening without having been at the play beforehand, when would you have given as the earliest possible time of death?'

George couldn't hear his reply. There was some interplay

then Travers turned off the phone.

'Well, Brian says he hadn't been dead for longer than an hour. How long was Act One?'

'You've got the video. How long was it?'

Peter Travers checked his notebook then did some arithmetic. 'The crowds were being filmed from six forty five. The drama started at seven thirty. Act One ended at eight seventeen. So an hour back from when the body was found, there were already crowds hanging about.'

'You're right. He must have been killed during the warm-up scrum, when everyone else was in the dressing rooms.'

There was still an hour before Travers was due back with the SOCO team. He had no inclination to dismiss George and she was happy to stay.

'If it happened beforehand then the intended victim must have been Joe. Though I've got absolutely nowhere on possible motive.'

'The cause must be something to do with events from the past. Sophie and I are still wondering about Lily Taylor – you know, that's the last owner of Ivy Cottage. We learned more about her links with the past last night from Arno. It seemed perfectly plausible, from what he said, that she'd found out something that could have got her killed.'

The policeman groaned. 'I've got enough on solving this crime without worrying about someone who died three or four months ago.'

'It could be the same murderer. Might well be, if the common motive is some event from the past that they're desperate to keep hidden.'

'George, there's no evidence at all that Lily was murdered. Died in the bath, didn't she? Good way to go when
your time's up.'

'The only thing is, Peter, I found a problem with the Ivy
Cottage plumbing. When Paul Wood came to look it over he
tried to fill the bath. After a few minutes there was a horrific
din. There was some weird pressure effect up in the loft -
the whole lot vibrated like mad. It was so bad it drove me
out of the house.'

The policeman had a growing respect for George. She
didn't just talk to keep a conversation alive. He thought
about her story and why she was telling it. 'You mean, if
running a bath caused that much noise, how could anyone
go to sleep in there?'

'That was my worry.'

'If it was murder, it's an odd way to kill someone.' The
policeman was thinking harder about this now.

'Unless the old lady was already in the bath. Then it'd be
an obvious way.'

'Why would her assailant be in the cottage while she was
having a bath?'

A pause as this question was considered.

'There was one other odd thing,' said George. 'I went up
in the loft with Laurie Lane, the electrician, to check it was
properly insulated. We found a load of old diaries that Lily
had kept since the 1940s. Laurie noticed the loft ladder had
been recently oiled - said it was odd. We couldn't really

believe that Lily would have been going up into the loft at her age. But suppose – just suppose – that our murderer was already in Ivy Cottage, up in the loft and going through these diaries, when Lily Taylor came home and ran a bath.'

'Maybe he knew that she had a regular date every Tuesday lunchtime – she was bound to be out. But what if she came home early that one time from the Community Lunch?'

'If the bloke was up in the loft, as she ran a bath and the loft tank noise started, he'd be deafened.'

'You mean - the noise would be right beside him: he'd have to get out.'

'So he's creeping down the landing,' went on George, 'and what if Lily Taylor saw him? Not just glimpsed a movement but recognised him, I mean. I think we're talking about someone she knew – someone local.'

The policeman thought hard. 'You mean, it might not have been a long-planned murder - just one forced by circumstances. All over in a couple of minutes. Imagine it, George. He's been spotted. He has no excuse for being there; decides he has to take pre-emptive action. He walks into the bathroom, reaches into the bathwater, grabs the old lady's legs and pulls hard. Before she knows what's happened, her head disappears under the water.'

'The din from the loft tank, which is still going on, drowns any noise she might make.'

'He hangs on to her legs, holds them in the air, holds on tight until she struggles no more. Hangs on one or two

327

minutes more to be certain. Once he's sure she's dead, he lets go, walks down the stairs, out the door and slides away. It's a perfect murder. Never even suspected by the local police force.'

There was silence as both of them replayed the scene in their minds.

'The trouble is,' said Travers, 'that was four months ago. Had he intended to kill her he'd have worn gloves. If it wasn't premeditated then he might have left fingerprints; but, even if he did, they'll be long gone.'

'I've spent the last fortnight cleaning and repainting the cottage. I've completed the perfect murder by wiping the whole place clean.'

There was silence as both reflected on what might have been.

'There's just one chance,' said Travers. 'It wasn't quite the "whole place" you cleaned, was it? How many times have you been up in the loft?'

'Just the once.'

'While you were up there, did you or Laurie touch the water pipes?'

'Course not. There was no problem. They weren't vibrating then.'

'If they had been?'

'I guess my first instinct would have been to grab them; try to stop them shaking and shimmering...'

George stopped talking; she could see where the policeman was heading. She could also see the showstopper.

328

'It's too late. Paul Woods is already in the cottage, putting in a new bath. He promised me he'd sort the sound from the loft whilst he was at it. He's probably been in the loft already and put his fingerprints everywhere.'

The policeman seized his phone once more. This time he handed it to George. 'Here, ring him now. See if you can delay him. We'll drive straight over.'

Paul Wood was a little surprised by the phone call from George. He'd made good preparations. Then with a struggle he'd brought the new white bath out of his van, into the cottage and up the stairs. That was hard work on your own.

He was having a short break over a mug of coffee, before he started work in the loft, when the phone rang.

'No, not been up there yet.' Another instruction came over the line. 'Wait till you get here? Sure.'

Ten minutes later George walked in. 'We'll have to wait five minutes more. Sergeant Travers has gone to pick up someone from the Scene of Crime team. We believe there's vital evidence up there.'

Paul Wood looked at George; looked at the loft hatch above her; then looked back once more at George.

She appeared sane, anyway. Perhaps it was him that had lost it?

He said nothing - though a huge question mark was almost visible, bulging incredulously out of his ears.

CHAPTER 43

It was Wednesday evening. Sophie Collins had returned safely from Truro with valuable information and documents, which she and George had assimilated over supper.

The plumber, Paul Wood, had finally installed the new bath – shining white – and fitted a new shower above it. There was a rail high over the bath ready for her to choose and fit shower curtains – perhaps they could do that tomorrow? The plumber had spent some time in the loft; had replaced the ball valve; and had declared – pledged - that they would have no more trouble with vibration noise when running a bath.

Before that the Scene of Crime officer had spent half an hour in the loft, dusting goodness knows where for fingerprints; and had come down with a smile on his face. 'Someone up there must have been thoroughly frightened. The cold pipe up to the loft water tank had been tightly seized by both hands. The finest set of fingerprints and palm prints I've ever captured.'

He had gone off to report his finding to Sergeant Travers, who was down with the rest of SOCO under the stage at Trebarwith Strand. George had not heard anything since.

Now the cottage owner was enjoying her first bath in Ivy

Cottage. Showers were fine if you were in a hurry – as she normally was, time was money for a business analyst – but a hot, deep, bubbly bath was the place for a leisurely soak. She was pleased but not surprised that the bath had filled in peaceful silence.

The conundrum was starting to shed its layers. There was, now, hard evidence relating to the mystery of Lily's death that would be a challenge to dismiss, collected from the loft above. It would be far from easy for anyone to explain why they'd been in someone else's attic. There was no clue yet, though, on the identity of the assailant.

It might be that the fingerprints were already recognised by the police – a well known local burglar, maybe, famous for raiding lofts. Though if that had been the case, Travers surely would have given her some hint that an arrest was being made?

Or perhaps not? She mustn't overrate herself. She had been some help to him but she wasn't yet an honorary member of the local police force.

This was luxury; George stretched out and lapped up the warmth. This was her home now whenever she wanted to come here. For one evening she would ignore the settling-in tasks still waiting for her in Ivy Cottage.

Could she do more? Given all the links from both deaths to the historical re-enactment, any motive had to be related to events from the past. She set herself to run through the various incidents which she and Sophie had been studying. They covered a long period – from the 1860s to the 1930s.

That was a long time - several generations. One of these incidents must still be biting hard on someone, worrying them beyond reason, even today.

The plumber had scarcely left before the appearance-conscious Sophie had cluttered the bathroom with her cosmetics. On the shelf behind her George saw bottles of foam bath, conditioner, shampoo and even one she didn't recognise. Looking closely, she saw a bottle of lubricant for contact lenses. She hadn't ever realised that Sophie wore lenses –maybe that was how her eyes always seemed to match her clothes?

Anyhow, they were useful props for her musings. George seized the large foam bath bottle and put it in front of her. This would represent the Quarry Disaster – surely the most significant of the past events.

Sophie had brought more detail back from Truro. What Ben Barham had told her at the Community Lunch was true: there had been an inquest by the local Coroner, published in the local paper a couple of weeks later. It had made no mention of fault or blame – was more of an obituary. Attention had been focussed on the lives extinguished and their long years of service to the Quarry. Sophie had even brought a hard copy of the newspaper report of the time back with her.

Reading through, the women had noticed that there was no mention, in the list, of young Fannie Wallis. Maybe the Quarry owners had wanted to suppress the notion that children were wandering the Quarry during working hours. It wouldn't be much consolation to the Wallis family. This was the nineteenth century: no point in hoping for twenty-first century levels of care. Whatever the personal anguish for individuals, it was hard to see that anything this far back could really upset someone today. Upset them enough to kill not just once but twice.

There was, though, no hard evidence yet that both deaths were from the same assailant. Logic must prevail: it would do her no good to get ahead of herself.

So was all the recent mayhem the consequence of another event from the past?

George turned, seized the bottle of hair conditioner and placed it alongside the foam bath. How about the shenanigans around the new Railway?

The events presented by *Splits and Schisms* seemed well-known, devious rather than dreadful: nineteenth century Board politics in the Old Slate Company. As presented by Arno, it was hard not to admire Dr Charles Rendle. He had shown considerable enterprise in outwitting the chairman and forcing a strategic plan on the company.

Sophie had done more work on this today. She had not come across any serious opposition to the plan, once the Railway had arrived and been bedded in between the village and the Quarry.

The only issue she and Sophie had been left with was the disappearance of the "bribe" from the Railway to the Quarry - though this was hard for the women to prove, over a century later. The relevant document – the receipt – might simply have been lost; or there could have been some reason for the funds not to be publicly recognised. Maybe there were tax-efficiency reasons for keeping quiet?

Again, avoiding embarrassment was not the same thing as an incentive to double murder. It was hard to imagine anyone being driven to kill by an old unpaid tax bill. Even with the legendary diligence of the Inland Revenue, it would not apply to someone alive today.

Was the crucial event something else altogether? Peter Travers had mentioned his discovery that Martin Thorne the butcher was descended from Henry Penfound, the man who started a strike and ended up being tried, fired and evicted.

George turned and retrieved a third bottle from behind her. This one was shampoo. The bottles were reducing in size. Maybe this reflected the chance they would be significant?

The story of the strike had featured in Act Two of *Splits and Schisms*. Its follow-up had not reflected well on Board management. Arno had clearly been incensed that the quarry workers were treated so badly.

What, though, was the alternative? The country was in recession in the last part of the nineteenth century; there was no way the Quarry could raise its prices and stay in business. It could hardly diversify: there wasn't much else to be done with slate – then or now. The Directors had taken a strong interest, visiting regularly; and when all was said and done, the Quarry was still in business a century later.

Henry Penfound might well have had a legal case for

wrongful dismissal; but Penfound was long dead. George knew enough about industrial law to know that being dead was a legal showstopper. In no circumstances would his case be reopened.

What did that leave? George turned once more and took the lens lubricant bottle – the smallest of all. The sad tale of the removal of Rev Jack Bucknall had not even made it into *Splits and Schisms*. It was the least likely of the past events they'd been considering to stir up murder today.

George applied some soap and added more hot water. This was delicious. Her preference for showers was looking under severe attack.

The Rev Jack Bucknall. The man had inspired many villagers and alienated many others. For Bert Dawe, the old man with whom she had had lunch yesterday, the curate could do no wrong; but for many others he had been trouble.

Even so, controversy was not a hanging offence. No-one had died. The curate had moved on and ministered successfully elsewhere. The only question which she had encountered today, from Sophie's research, was the means by which he had been dismissed: two official-looking and vicious letters to higher church authorities, from Quarry management and from local church leaders, which now started to raise her suspicions. Had these voiced false accusations?

She reminded herself that this was all eighty years ago. How on earth could this lead to murder – even double murder – today? It was fanciful, nonsense.

335

George turned to find another bottle. There were none left. There was no earthly reason, she told herself, why the number of bottles left in the bathroom by Sophie should match the possible causes of crime. It did, though, bring her train of thought to a close.

It would be time to get out soon. George stretched out one more time. Her eyes caught the cold pipe running up to the bathroom ceiling and she remembered the great din with a giggle. Paul Wood had tried to account for it, though she'd not taken much notice. But she was, after all, a mathematician. Could she recall or reconstruct his explanation?

Several factors were involved. Taps needed to be running into the bath for some time. This lowered the level of the water in the loft tank and dropped the angle of the ball valve arm. The pressure in the water system outside needed to be high enough to impact on the loft. There needed to be something wrong with the ball valve – so that, when the arm was pointing down, the vibrations started. Finally, the water pipe needed to be loose, so that the pressure vibrations transferred to the whole tank.

A whole series of causes before the trouble started. That was what the plumber had said. Good; she had remembered it after all.

The sequence reminded her of something else. Multiple causes, all needed to prompt a disaster. None of them serious enough to matter on their own, but collectively irresistible. Her eyes returned to the bottles before her.

Suppose it wasn't the case that any one of her "causes" was the killer motive? What if it was all of them, with some sort of cumulative effect?

Was there any type of person who could be involved in them all, for a start? Or - since no individual would live that long - any sort of organisation? It had to be someone from a particular sort of activity to cover them all – one with a very long life, a special mix of attributes, a distinctive set of skills. And it had to be one with a representative still at work today.

Was there any way that such a person might have clear motivation, knowledge and opportunity to take the dreadful actions which she had encountered inside her cottage - and on the stage in the car park below?

Maybe she had become obsessed with the past: were there other present-day clues that she had neglected? She thought back to the conversation with Arno the night before. Had he let something slip? Was there anything odd in that list she and Sophie had seen of Lily's contacts? Did she know of any long-established families - had she come across any names which had also occurred in the past?

George slipped down into the bath and added more hot water. She was going to be here for some time.

337

CHAPTER 44

Wednesday had been a good day for Sergeant Peter Travers. He would have plenty of news to give Detective Inspector Marcus Chadwick when he came down from Exeter later that Thursday morning.

He wanted to deal with as many loose ends as possible before the key man came. One was the question of public liability insurance: could it make a contribution to Morwenna Stacey? If so, how much?

After some inquiries he'd learned that the man who should know was the local solicitor from Camelford.

'We used Gifford to draw up all the contracts for *Splits and Schisms*,' he'd been told by Della Howell. 'He told me he'd sort out the insurance too.' Gifford had been reluctant to give him an interview, but the policeman had insisted on seeing him as soon as his office opened. He was outside waiting at nine as the receptionist unlocked the building's resplendent oak doors. She showed him at once into Gifford's office.

'Good morning sir. I'm sorry to have to bother you so early but I've got a lot on at present. It's all to do with the death in *Splits and Schisms*.'

Gifford seemed irritated by the policeman's presence. He

tried to look relaxed: he needed to stay calm. 'Ah yes, I heard about that – I wasn't there myself. Poor man; dreadful business. Tell me, are you making much progress?'

'Slowly, sir. There's a long way to go. We're still waiting on a definitive post mortem from the hospital in Truro on the cause of death. We'll let the public know, of course, when there's any news.'

It was clear Travers was not going to tell him anymore. He might be a lawyer, but he could take his turn at being told along with every other member of the public. 'So how do I come into this? What can I do for you?'

'Della Howell told me you were the person who drew up the contracts for the Splits and Schisms production?'

'Yes, I did, come to think of it. Last November, that'd be.'

'She said each contract included some public liability insurance?'

'Oh yes.' Gifford started to look relieved. He could cope with administrative minutiae – it was his speciality.

'So could you give me details, sir, of the public liability payment that might be available on Joe Stacey – that was the man who was killed, you understand.'

'Of course. I'm pretty sure they're all the same amount: a standard two million pounds.'

'Could you check that for me, sir, and give me a copy of the details? Joe Stacey's widow would find it some comfort, even if there's going to be a long time before any of it's paid.'

Gifford was looking for an excuse to delay. His anti-stress

pills meant he was not at his best early in the day. Then he realised the determined policeman would not be easily fobbed off.

Shrugging, he stood up, walked over to a dark green filing cabinet, opened the second drawer down, peered inside then pulled out a buff envelope.

'They're all in here, I think.'

The solicitor brought the envelope back to his desk and pulled out the sheets inside. One of Travers' skills, honed in his monthly meetings with his boss, was reading documents upside down. He could see that there was one sheet for each member of the cast, two for the author. The solicitor spotted Joe Stacey's name and took the sheet out.

'It's the insurance details I'm after, sir.'

'Oh yes. There's just one copy in here as they're all basically the same.' He peered at the back of the envelope and retrieved a clear plastic folder. 'It's all in here, I think.'

Travers was starting to get impatient. Chadwick was due shortly; he needed to be out of here. Goodness knows how long Gifford would take to get the multiple sheets photocopied.

'Why don't I take that, sir? I'll make a copy and show it to the widow. Drop it back here, say, tomorrow.' Reaching out, Travers grabbed the folder out of Gifford's hand and slid it into his briefcase.

Gifford looked like he was about to take offence. Then he noted these were insurance details: what difference would it make? He shrugged his shoulders. 'OK, that's fine; but please bring the original back here. Now, was there anything else?'

There wasn't. Soon Travers was in his car and on his way.

It was just after Peter Travers had got back in Delabole that his phone rang. It was George Gilbert.

'Oh, hello George. Hope this won't take long. My Crime Squad boss is due here in an hour; I need to be ready for him.'

'You should wash up more often. I've been trying to get through to you, Peter, since before nine. I know who you should be talking to – unless you've already arrested them, of course. I worked it out in the bath last night.'

'The wonders of a new bath, eh. OK George, I can give you ten minutes.'

'There's one organisation that was involved in all of the past episodes highlighted in *Splits and Schisms* and also with Jack Bucknall. A long-standing, local family firm. It would be completely destroyed – its reputation shredded - if all the stray bits of data and innuendo now hanging about were ever pulled together.'

'Because?'

'Because these show that this firm is repeatedly called in to muddy evidence, lose bribes, make sure sacked people stay sacked, even to make sure unruly priests are sent on their way. And probably dozens of other things as well. I reckon when you arrest the head of this firm, his fingerprints will match those taken from my attic.'

341

It was fortunate that Travers was up to speed on George's general direction of travel. Even so, this was a lot to take in.

'I'll give you a few more minutes if you like,' he offered. 'Crucially, can you give me a name?'

'I believe the person you want is Stephen Gifford. He's –'

'– a solicitor in Camelford. I've just been to see him about insurance taken out by *Splits and Schisms,* on behalf of Morwenna Stacey. She might have some recompense. What makes you think that he's our man?'

'The answer to that question has four parts, Peter. Are you listening?'

'My notebook is ready.'

'First of all, the Coroner that did a rapid inquest in 1869 was an earlier Gifford – but the same firm. The name was in the newspaper archive that Sophie brought back from Truro. There are serious doubts about the Quarry's behaviour and culpability. Lily Taylor heard about this from Bessie Cowling when she nursed her in her final year. Lily recorded Bessie's testimony in her diary, which she then hid in her loft. The inquest at the time either ignored them or hushed them up.'

'That makes sense. I suppose it would give a reason, too, for that person to be in Lily's loft. Go on.'

'Two. The Railway paid a big contribution – a bribe - to the Quarry to be allowed to run the track right beside the workings, rather than through the village. That money never made it to the Board's accounts. The local solicitor who handled the deal was another lawyer, also called Gifford. I believe Gifford's firm did all the legal work for the Quarry in

Delabole.'

'Sounds promising – though maybe hard to make stick. Next?'

'Three. Henry Penfound started a strike at the Quarry and ended up not only fired but also evicted; and then almost run off the land - in a highly illegal way. These letters are all held in the Record Office in Truro. The lawyer that wrote all the damning letters was –'

'Let me guess. Another Gifford? You're starting to convince me. But you said there were four strands. What was the fourth?'

'Four. The Rev Jack Bucknall was a divisive, militant curate here in the 1930s. He was removed via a letter to his sponsors, purporting to come from the Quarry management and the local church leadership. It accused him of something very untoward and non-clerical.

'We found two copies of the letter in the Truro Record Office; one under Delabole Slate and one in the archives of the Bishop of Truro. The only trouble was, when we looked at them very carefully, the two copies weren't quite the same. The Bishop was only told about bad behaviour affecting the Quarry and vice versa. They couldn't both be true – so probably neither of them was. And the firm that sent these letters was called... Gifford.'

There was a pause.

'Hey, Peter, are you still there?'

'I'm here. I was just thinking - about evidence rather than theory. When I was with Mr Gifford half an hour ago he gave me a plastic folder which I put straight in my brief case. I hadn't intended it to work out that way but –

'It means you might have his fingerprints. Can you compare them with those taken from my loft?'

'I can. But I can't do it one handed; I'll need to ring off. Don't go away, please.'

It was forty minutes before Peter Travers rang back George Gilbert.

'Sorry, George, it took longer than I expected. In the end I had to slide a black sheet of card inside the folder from Gifford, dust it with special powder then photograph every print revealed.'

'You got some prints, anyway. How did they compare?'

'To get the prints taken from your loft I had to use the internet to get to the SOCO files held in Exeter. That took a few minutes; but the end result was clear. Even by eye I could match half a dozen fingerprints from the two sources. Gifford was the man in your loft - so is almost certainly the man who drowned Lily Taylor in the bath.'

'I don't know what to say. What does a policeman normally yell at this point?'

'It hasn't happened to me very often. I haven't got the habit yet so I don't know. There is one thing more. While I was looking at the SOCO files I also checked on what they'd found in the pulpit down in Trebarwith Strand. There was just one print – on the lectern. It's not as clear to the naked eye, but I reckon it's from the same person. The evidence against Stephen Gifford is stacking up very nicely indeed.'

CHAPTER 45

Arno James had been given permission to stage *Splits and Schisms* for one last time on Saturday evening – a tribute performance for Joe Stacey. The permission had only come through from the police late on Thursday, but that was ample notice for the local grape vine to disseminate the information - and for the excitement to rise.

Tickets issued for the cancelled performance the previous Saturday would still be valid. Anyone unable to attend would be able to sell back their tickets to the Camelford Tourist Office, so one or two who had missed out would have a chance to see the drama after all.

Splits and Schisms had been intended as a one-off production but it was clear there was a big demand for a repeat performance later in the year. Arno James had managed to find a slot in his diary in September to direct it one more time. Those unable to come – and the audience whose previous viewing had come to an abrupt halt at the end of Act One – would have a chance to see it later.

There was relief among the cast that the later performance would be at a warmer time of year.

Arno asked George and Sophie if they would be on hand to video the Saturday night performance. The women had intended to return to London that morning but felt obliged to stay one more day to complete their task. They were part of the team now and could not just walk away.

On Friday George had stayed in at Ivy Cottage to take delivery of the furniture ordered earlier in the week. They didn't both need to be there, though; Sophie had taken the chance to explore more of the Coast Path.

It was a fine day, though cold; the forecast promised that this weather would last through to Sunday. Sophie had seen an opportunity for landscape painting. She had spotted a suitable subject on her last walk. Now she set out to capture it, weighed down with canvas, easel, oils and brushes.

'It'll be a slog with all that lot, climbing the cliffs up from Trebarwith Strand,' George had observed.

'I'm not intending to go down the hill at all. I can get to where I want by going on another path, straight over the top.'

George did not know where she was talking about. She resolved that one of the first things she had to buy was a large-scale map of the Tintagel area – in fact several, since she needed to cover the coast down as far as Port Isaac, Polzeath and Padstow and inland to Bodmin Moor. Once she was no longer encumbered with waiting for furniture, she would start to explore the area properly.

There was no word from the police. George assumed that Travers must be busy implementing the arrest and interview which they had conducted as thought experiments earlier in the week. She longed to know how it was all going.

347

The furniture came just after midday. The men even helped to take the old settee and chairs out to the skip – they had no choice, in fact, if they were to fit the new suite into the lounge. The old items had been very bulky.

Once the men had gone George was left to unwrap her treasures. This was a crucial moment: how would they look? She could see already that the size was more appropriate. The new furniture matched the size of the room much better than the old – made it seem larger. Gingerly she applied her large scissors to the plastic covering and eased it off – more material for the skip. Then she started to arrange the new furniture around the room.

It was fabulous. The light colours lit up the room and made it feel completely different. She had liked her new cottage before; but now she was in love with it. She would be back here as often as she could.

She gave a dance of glee. Life was different from what she would have predicted a year ago, but not as awful as she might have imagined six months back. There was no doubt she was "moving on" from her bereavement.

George was intrigued to know what Sophie was painting. When her friend returned, just after five, the analyst asked if she could see the subject as captured so far.

'It's not finished yet. I've got the canvas organised though: I know how it'll go. I took lots of photos, in any case. If I don't get over there tomorrow I'll finish it back in London.'

'You're being very secretive.'

'It's a present. You said you needed something big for that wall. It'll go beautifully with that suite. It's just I don't want you to see it till it's finished.'

George was gobsmacked. 'Sophie, you can't... I mean, you shouldn't... Look, you're a serious artist. Way better than my cottage deserves, anyway.'

'Listen, my friend. This has been a great fortnight. I haven't lived life so fully for years. This is my way of saying thank you. Don't muck it up.' She looked like she was about to cry.

 George gave her a hug. 'Thank you, Sophie, thank you. It's been good having you here – far better than I feared, to be honest. We've been good for one another. Can you at least give me a foretaste of what your picture is about?'

'If you walk along the cliff path from Trebarwith Strand towards Tintagel you find yourself looking down on the remains of an old quarry. There's a massive pillar of slate left standing, surrounded by cliffs holding remnants of slate workings. Behind it there's a glorious view across Port Isaac Bay and over to Pentire Head. It'll be something to look at, when you come and stay and it's raining.'

On Saturday morning the women decided they must at least see the Quarry which provided the background for *Splits and Schisms*. They drove to Delabole then down the side road and parked by the Quarry edge.

'It's absolutely massive,' said George as they stood by the fence on the Visitors' Lookout, 'I never realised it was anything like this big.'

'And deep,' added Sophie. A track spiralled gently down round the side until it reached the bottom. Far below an orange lorry, packed with slate blocks, was winding its way slowly up to the surface.

George pointed to the side nearest Delabole. 'You can see where the Disaster happened. Those narrow terraces are where they had to stand and hew the slate. It's much steeper on that side – practically vertical.'

'We could walk right round the top. It'll only take an hour.'

It was a pleasant, level walk. On their way back, beside the village, they realised they were walking on the old railway line. There were no rails or sleepers but the cinders were still in place - as was one of the platforms. 'You can see there's not much space between the Quarry and the village,' said Sophie. 'No wonder it caused such a row.'

That afternoon Peter Travers rang George. 'Are you both going to the final performance? Would you like some company?' Inevitably the policeman found himself invited to an early supper.

'I can't tell you anything officially,' he declared as he sat down to a meal of pork in cider, cooked by Sophie. 'But be encouraged: it was down to your efforts that we've got our man.'

George glanced at the inglenook behind her. 'Not just us. It was a bit like installing that stove. Some problems can only be solved by tackling them from several angles. Sophie and I gave you some ideas and videos; the Record Office provided historic documentation; your colleagues gathered traces and other evidence; and you put them all together. I hope your crime overlord was impressed.'

'I still don't understand,' confessed Sophie.

'The whole crime was all down to expectations,' said Travers. 'Gifford was Lily's solicitor; he'd come to this cottage several times last autumn to review her will – as George observed, that name on Lily's calendar was not a friend. He'd learned her habits, such as her regular Community Lunch on Tuesdays. So when he discovered Lily was assisting her next door neighbour, Arno, to probe historical events around the Quarry, he feared the worst.'

'But how did the lawyer know about the drama?'

'He'd agreed to check Arno's script of *Splits and Schisms* for libel. No doubt he made himself a copy as he did so. Gifford knew better than anyone there were skeletons left in the Slate Quarry – historically speaking, anyway. It was the demons of his slate expectations which drove him to action, first with Lily and then, a week ago, with Joe.'

'Has Arno been a witness for you over the last couple of days?' asked George. 'We noticed we hadn't seen him around.'

'He has – he's been a great help. He told us about Lily – and the din from her bath. He could hear it through the wall. In fact, he heard it on what was her final Tuesday afternoon of life. Of course, he didn't realise its significance at the time. But this was the same afternoon as his first encounter with Joe Stacey and his potted history of Delabole. Arno told us that Joe arrived at Holly Cottage just as Gifford was leaving Ivy next door. It was pure coincidence – but a fateful overlap.'

'You mean, it wasn't just knowledge of history that did for Joe?'

'No. Gifford knew he'd been spotted by Joe, as he left Ivy Cottage, and it gnawed away at him. For a couple of months he tried to convince himself he'd got away with it – there was no fuss about Lily Taylor's death, no suggestion of foul play, so no reason for Joe to talk to the police – but Gifford found his nerves were fraying - he couldn't handle the risk of exposure.

'Crucially, Arno recalled inviting the solicitor down to watch a late rehearsal to check for libel. The playwright didn't want to get caught out again. Seeing the whole rehearsal – especially the noise and smoke in the middle - gave Gifford the idea - and the chance to firm up his plans.'

'Do you know, there was someone I faintly recognised by the road when I was filming,' said George. 'I've only met him twice, both briefly; once was after Lily's funeral and the other time was to pick up the keys to Ivy Cottage.'

'In the end,' said Travers, 'we nailed him on hard evidence and induced him to confess. I spotted his face in the crowd at the first performance from Sophie's video: he'd claimed to me that he wasn't there at all. That was the point at which his story started to unravel. I think it was the cumu-

352

lative effect of the history linked to his firm – which of course he knew better than anyone – coupled with his fear of Joe's sighting that led him to act as he did. He wanted to do away with the probing hostile sources and at the same time do lasting damage to the drama. And he hoped that associating it with Joe's death would mean the locals would never want to act it out again.'

Sophie looked doubtfully from one to the other. 'I'm left thinking I muddled into a crime story but never found out the ending.'

The policeman could see the problem. 'For legal reasons I can't tell you anymore; but George isn't bound in the same way. You've a long journey back to talk in. After that, until the case comes to trial, you must be very careful to keep it to yourselves. Yes?'

The women agreed. George gave Peter a second helping and the conversation moved to less controversial topics.

Later all three walked down to Trebarwith Strand to fulfil their roles in the drama. The policeman would only have a role if there was a smoke alarm or a murder. He was hoping for a quiet evening.

Sophie took up the same position at the side as on that fatal first performance. All being well, this time she would also have to film Act Two.

George once more fastened her camera inside the pulpit, focussed on the stage. Arno (the latest Job Hockaday) had agreed to turn it on and off for each Act.

Then she took a seat beside the policeman. It felt good to

have him alongside her. It was the first time she had been out with a man since Mark died. It wasn't much of a date but it was a start.

She and Sophie would be off early next morning. Her daughter Polly was already back in London. She would be waiting when George got home, talking nonstop about her student exchange in Germany.

Though "home", now, was not so well defined. Treknow was her home too. And one she looked forward to knowing better in the years ahead.

AUTHOR'S NOTES

This story is fiction. No present day events really happened and no present-day characters really exist. The history of the Delabole Slate Quarry in North Cornwall, from which the story stems, is, though, close to that described.

Among many other events, there was a Quarry Disaster in 1869; a strike with serious repercussions for its leaders in 1888; a battle over the location of the railway in Delabole in 1892-3; and conflict over a militant curate in 1925-32. My principal source for these events is a wonderful history by Dr Catherine Lorigan: "Delabole: the history of the slate quarry and the making of the village community." I bought this after a conducted tour of the thriving, present-day Slate Quarry in 2013.

Any author who wants to set their story in a real place and relate it to historical events has to blend fact and fiction. One can write fiction using real place-names; set the events way back in time; or adjust real names. None of these tricks work in this case: these quarry heroes deserve our respect. My goal was to create a story linked to these real events. My professional career, after all, has been about analysing real incidents and distilling cause and effect.

So for clarity, I believe the Quarry Disaster was due solely

355

to geology; the Railway "bribe" was not stolen; the curate moved on under legitimate pressure; no inquests or letters were fiddled. In other words all the links given in this book between past and present are invented.

This book is intended only for the reader's entertainment – and to stir them to visit this delightful part of the world for themselves.

David Burnell
May 2014
Website: davidburnell.info

Read about George Gilbert's first encounter with crime in Cornwall in DOOM WATCH, as she is invited down by her uncle to help Padstow plan some modernisation.
A body is discovered behind the Engine House of the old quarry at Trewarmett. But identification proves tricky.
It takes the combined efforts of George and Peter Travers to make sense of a crime which seems, simultaneously, to be spontaneous and pre-planned.

"A well-written novel, cleverly structured, with a nicely-handled sub-plot..." Rebecca Tope, crime novelist

a tree fro

haiku

a book of haiku with some senryu,
an extensive foreword, and essays

by

David E. Navarro

cover photo and all interior art used in this book are original
manipulations, royalty free, and/or in the public domain

cover design by DE Navarro

NavWorks Press

Tucson, Arizona

NavWorks Press™
Tucson, Arizona 85710

Published in May of 2020.

Haiku is now the most widely recognized, published, and popular poetic form in the world. Accessible in its simple manner of presentation but sophisticated and profound in its impact and depth of meaning, haiku has transcended the limits of its cultural heritage to become one of the most globally celebrated and practiced poetic forms.

Haiku is a highly distilled brief form of poetry usually written by the Japanese in one line of 17 sound units divided into three parts of 5-7-5. In times past this was carried over into English as 17 syllables in three lines of 5-7-5. But recent increased understanding of the brevity of Japanese *on*, or sound units, compared to syllables, has encouraged new English haiku with 9 to 12 syllables in one, two or three lines.

In three short linguistic parts a good haiku presents a synthesized present moment of an event, image, or experience in which an inherent subtle force and dynamic activity, stated or not, encapsulates and conveys awareness, feeling, compassion, silence, temporality, awe, or some other profound intuition, that reveals a startling sense of wonder, mystery, or insight into the ordinary, and sometimes with a splash of surprise or humor. They paint a brief but vivid picture that leaves space for the reader to draw out meaning and complete in their own mind.

In the synthesized power of a few words, haiku conveys a universe of mystery and meaning and has served as an example of the power of direct and precise observation. Haiku is rooted in a tradition of close observation of life and nature made into succinct poetry that hints at subtle suggestions that are often infused with unspoken spiritual or philosophical underpinnings presented in the suchness of things—things as they are, often within the seasonal cycles of the life force of nature.

Always simple yet capable of great complexity, haiku are tightly compacted in a remarkably powerful way that distills the essence of a keenly perceived moment. They often contain a subtle dualism that connects the particular to the universal.

CONTENTS

Foreword

Context is incredibly helpful in clarifying particulars. I consider it important to share a little bit about my life and thought to put my haiku in context for the benefit of the reader and for a richer experience in making connections. Toward this end I have pulled together excerpts from other of my various writings and essays into this foreword. Please do not skim this foreword or you will miss a lot of details that will help you to enjoy the haiku in this volume as well as enriching your experience of haiku everywhere.

It seems like some past age in a far different world when, as a displaced homeless nineteen-year old living on his aunt's dining room floor, I ventured into a rickety old second-hand bookstore and found, *Zen Poems of China and Japan: The Crane's Bill*, by Lucien Stryk and Takashi Ikemoto, 1973. I read this little treasure with wide-eyed fascination experiencing its ideas, reflections, and poetry, and meditating on it between readings. After my first reading, I started over, but this time around I studied the *Introduction* in detail.

In the *Introduction*, Ikemoto challenges Western thinkers to pay attention to Zen poetry and to experience it for themselves, not just read about it. He suggests that to truly experience this poetry one must remove the Zen of it from the Zen of it to realize it is simply *poetry of being—dynamism that is life-activity beyond all that is relative*. Primed by the greater context of the entire book and *Introduction*, I re-read this poem on page 7:

Does one really have to fret
About enlightenment?
No matter what road I travel,
I'm going home.

> ~~ Shinsho

This poem led me to a deep realization beyond words that I can only describe as the peaceful recognition of being at home in the universe and at home in myself together both at once. I perceived that the unfolding of my life before me would be a journey that was to be enjoyed and experienced by making the most of each moment in the *here* and *now*; and that living each moment fully is how I would enjoy my own simple little life as an interactive part of humanity and an integral part of the bigger picture of the universe.

It gave me a certain kind of peace and an underlying optimism that was, at times, challenged and tested in life, but which did not subside, and which prepared me for when God called me out some years later to gain a spiritual perception and awareness of His Word, and to become a wandering minister who loves Zen, poetry, and helping people reconnect with God, nature, and a greater sense of self and purpose.

My own deep connections to nature and my transience in life have led me on a journey of self-discovery through myriad geographic, geologic, and natural terrains coupled with a great variety of diverse cultures and manners of life, which I have enjoyed thoroughly with great gratitude (see *life summary* in the notes below). I have always rejected materialism, the "rat race", keeping up with the Jonses, and falling in line with the accepted norms of society, choosing rather to live a more simple, natural, and pure life. For this reason I have come to view myself as not being wholly unlike the haiku poet-priests or poet-monks of Japan, just in a totally different context.

Over the years, reading, pondering, and writing haiku has helped me to sharpen my observational skills, increase awareness of the interconnectedness of everything, recognize the wake I leave as I pass, and embrace life in the here and now. It has affected the way I express myself in speech, poetry, and writing, and the way I think about life ethically, adding the dimension of collectivism to my worldview without abandoning individualism—a merging of East and West, if you will.

The Bible is an Eastern book, as taught by the great K.C. Pillai, Doctor of Divinity, a rare convert from Hinduism to Christianity, who taught the Eastern ways, manners, and idioms in the Bible to the Western world so that the strange scriptures that perplex the Western mind could be understood as light through an Eastern window. He opened my eyes to the reality that many of the same principles embraced in Zen thinking and haiku, such as single-minded focus in the present, the interconnectedness of everything, and living in the here and now, are taught in the Bible.

Unfortunately the Bible is viewed and used as a religious book shrouded in mystery rather than the practical spiritual guide to life and living that it is. The Word of God teaches us about the reality of life, spirituality, and the human condition. It teaches us about our minds, our hearts (the innermost mind), logic, will, and emotion, our free will choices, the cycle of life and nature, and how to control our thinking to redirect ourselves to a fuller life, physically, mentally, and spiritually.

This interwoven connection of God, nature, reality, and spirituality is an underlying driving force behind and within my haiku and is akin to *zoka*, *ma*, *tathata*, and *toriawase* as expressed through the functions of *kigo*, and *kireji*. These, to me, are the four core essentials and two core functional elements of classic haiku:

zoka – the natural reality of the continuum of creation —the creative, transformative force in nature within which transience and impermanence are aspects[1]; the seasonal reference, *kigo*, plays an important part in urging this sense of *zoka*[2] the transformative flow of nature through seasons.

ma – the unsaid space in a poem invoked by the *kire* or cut in haiku, which gives a reader a sense of time and space that is unfinished and must be completed in the mind or imagination of the reader, the activity of which leads to feeling and participatory experience.[3]

tathata – or commonly *sonomama* – suchness, things as they are[4]; reality as it is[5]; thusness, consciousness of reality[6]; the intrinsic state of being or ultimate reality of the nature of what a thing is in itself; this is the element seized upon by the imagist poets influenced by haiku.

toriawase – literally "take and put together", combining, arranging a match, by use of *kireji*, a cutting word[7]; said to divide and unite at the same time (we call this the juxtaposition in English); the *kire* (cut), leaves space for the unsaid (*ma*) and may engender an association, contrast, parallel, progression, similarity, dissimilarity, connection, disjunction, or some other possible interesting and often revelatory relationship; *toriawase* most strikingly can connect the particular to the universal.[8]

kigo – a season word or phrase that puts the haiku in context of its natural time of year[9]; haiku are ultimately nature poems in connection with humanity and the *kigo* unifies nature's season with man's activity implying the timeless involvement of human life with the flow of nature[10]; *kigo* in Japanese haiku trigger historical, cultural, and literary associations that have been gathered well over a thousand years and are codified into lists and seasonal books passed on to each generation[11]; we have no equivalent in English to actual *kigo*, thus, an English language haiku poet must skillfully use their own common seasonal and cultural associations instead[12]; some in Japan and in the West have modified this into use of keywords or just abandoned *kigo* altogether[13]; haiku has a long history of experimentation and adaptation, so I personally do not mind this variation myself, yet, I acknowledge that if a haiku poet wants to retain *kigo* sensitivity to connect nature and man in haiku, which is also important in invoking *zoka*, then *kigo* is vital; endeavor to use it naturally and with seamless ease, not in an artificial or disingenuous way; look not on *kigo* as a limitation, but rather as a master crafter's tool in bringing about an exquisite unification of humanity, life, and nature.

kireji – the cutting word in Japanese haiku which indicates the *kire*, cut or shift, and sets up the match or *toriawase*; again, there is literally no equivalent in English; think of it as a kind of verbal punctuation in the Japanese; since we have no equivalent, English haiku poets might use punctuation to indicate the cut, or interjections like "ah!" or "lo", or obvious syntax and line breaks; whatever the method, the cut should be clear enough to make a definite *toriawase* match (called juxtaposition in English).

Ask most practicing haiku poets how old haiku is or when haiku began, and you'll probably get the answer that it traces its history back to the Japanese poet, Matsuo Basho, who separated *hokku* from *renga* in seventeenth-century Japan.[14] Some might say that since Basho wrote *hokku* and the term *haiku* only came to be in late nineteenth-century Japan[15] that haiku originated then. These assertions do not consider and recognize the vast history of the heart and essence of haiku as it evolved from ancient forms to the present.

Although the term *haiku* only came to be in late nineteenth century Japan, the essence of the poetic form traces its origins back thousands of years to ancient Chinese poetry.[16] Chinese linked poetry was imported to Japan by a Japanese explorer who brought it back with him and it initiated a poetic tradition called *waka* that eventually evolved into and gave way to *renga*[17] which was initiated by a verse called *hokku* that Basho later separated from the *renga*, and which Masaoka Shiki later renamed *haiku*[18]. So you can see that it moved from China into Japan and that by multiple developments it was separated and refined into what we now call haiku.

But I am also speaking, by extension, of the original genetic coding or DNA of what later became haiku that coursed through early Chinese poetry. We can trace the DNA backward to the poetic work in China in the first millennium. The earliest master I have discovered who wrote poetry with the same sensibility we find in haiku today was Sensai who died in A.D.

671.[16] That gives us a history of at least 1350 years.

Here is a sample of the kind of Chinese poetry with haiku sensibility that I am talking about. This one is by the Chinese poet Hõ Un, A.D. 740-808:

how wondrous this,
how mysterious
I draw water, I carry fuel
    ~~ Hõ Un

This poem by Hõ Un, has some of the kind of heart and essence I aim to capture in the haiku that I write —a kind of personal wonder, mystery, and sensitivity to the human interaction of life and nature; per Ikemoto, a poetry of being, the dynamism of life-activity. It is admittedly outside the Western English language haiku box, but history shows that all the really memorable haiku poets were. Not that I am or will be, but the aspiration itself is worth it, as well as the satisfaction inherent in the journey. Where would we be without vision and a goal?

A comprehensive study of haiku, going back to its Chinese roots, reveals that haiku has always been evolutionary. Each took what they learned from the masters that came before them and then infused their own unique essence and quality into their work that was then passed on to the next.

I like to imagine myself to be a far removed and long lost student of these ancient masters through their works as translated into English. Obviously I am not literally, but I can imagine and envision it and aspire to learn from their work. This includes from ancient Chinese times through the four greats of haiku, Matsuo Basho, Yosa Buson, Kobayashi Issa, and Masaoka Shiki, their contemporaries and students, such as Natsume Soseki, and into modern times with poets such as Hosninaga Fumio.

My favorite Japanese haiku poet is, without a doubt, Issa, because he was so human and poured himself into his haiku poetry; and also because he was a Zen priest and Zen was an important aspect of his poetry. With its roots in Chinese spiritual poetry and its rise to greatness as *hokku* under the Zen monk, Basho, haiku naturally became a powerful medium for Zen expression.

Let it be clearly stated here that it is **not** required or necessary for haiku to be Zen. The vast majority of Japanese haiku simply have a rich, historical, literary, and cultural quality that in part reflects Zen thinking along with many other philosophies, ideas, and aspects of the Japanese cultural heritage. But it is worth noting that haiku is popular among Zen practitioners who are poets, including two of the four greats, Basho and Issa.

One aspect or element of Zen haiku that I am particularly fond of is *kensho* or little flashes of enlightenment, which are moments of profound or intense noticings of everyday life that reveal an exemplary truth or reality, a moment of realization that gives the reader an experience of their own little enlightenment that connects them to a greater sense of wonder and awe.[19] This internalized experience cannot be related in direct words by the haiku poet to a reader, it must be crafted within the four core essentials I spoke of earlier by the use of *kigo* and *kireji*. The haiku poet skillfully makes the space for the reader to engage in or complete an experience that is brilliantly hinted at.[20]

There are those who say that the individual poet should not, or even must not be present in his or her haiku. They claim that the poet should be invisible, removed from their haiku. Yet we saw from the Hõ Un example a personal poetry of being, and Issa was often very present in his haiku, and he isn't the only one. It is ironic that the very essence and nature of a good number of haiku and of haiku poets in the long tradition of Japanese haiku is a kind of expression of self-discovery and awareness and a sharing of one's experiences with another. But we are told by those who propound this myth to distance ourselves or keep ourselves out of the poem.

It seems that the Japanese haiku masters did not know this rule because they expressed themselves in personal and present ways in a good number of their poems, and some not infrequently. The doctors, scholars, and master poets who translated their work from Japanese knew that the semantics, context, and linguistics of certain haiku clearly indicated the personal presence of the poet, which is expressed in English by using personal pronouns. If we desire to write haiku in English in which we are personally present in the event, experience, or moment shared in the poem, we must state it by using personal pronouns. Not that the overall effect shouldn't be subtle, but it need not be absent.

Remember that these translators or teams of translators were experts in both Japanese and English cultures and languages, and in writing poetry, and they chose to add the personal pronouns in English to express the heart, intent, nature, and essence of the Japanese poem. Were they making this up or did the Japanese masters indeed write a good number of poems from a far more personal perspective than we have been led to believe?

There's a certain unique character and quality to the English *translations* of haiku that were originally written in Japanese by Japanese poets. This character and quality is wholly unlike haiku that are directly written in English and modeled after Japanese literary methods such as being parsed in 5-7-5 *on*, which are sound units akin to syllables in English, or those directly written in English according to newer guidelines derived from the truer linguistics of Japanese haiku, like gendai, or one line, and fewer than 17 syllables to better equate to the Japanese *on*, and more.

Translators of Japanese haiku have used a number of conventions and devices to endeavor to capture and convey the spirit and intent of the Japanese poem in English. Since the Japanese pictographic language, with its unique syntax, grammar, cultural, and codified conventions, is wholly unlike English, it is impossible to accurately and sensibly transliterate Japanese haiku directly into English. Therefore, translators have had to be fully knowledgeable of and immersed in the Japanese culture. They have had to understand haiku from a native perspective. They also had to have a mastery of the English language and culture, and have been poets themselves, understanding and embracing fully all the available conventions, tools, and devices of English language poetry in order to capture and convey the spirit and intent of the Japanese haiku in English.

Because of this, when Japanese haiku are translated into English there is usually no set syllable count whatsoever. The *content* and *haiku quality* becomes of supreme importance and prevails over any other consideration. Therefore, in whatever way and how ever the Japanese meanings fall out into English is how the haiku are crafted to best convey the essence. The haiku still presents the translated seasonal indication, if *kigo* is present in the Japanese; and it still presents some manner or form of a cut, whether by punctuation, interjection, syntax, shift of meaning, or other method. The resulting *translated* haiku is the best possible **approximation** in English of its original Japanese counterpart as interpreted through the savvy and skills of a translator-poet.

When reading these marvelously and exquisitely

translated haiku, a reader still experiences the essence and quality of haiku and is transported by them in a way that emulates the original heart and intent of the Japanese writer, even if not perfectly, and even though the minute linguistic and cultural particulars of the experience differ. Countless English haiku readers have come to admire, enjoy, and understand haiku through the work of the Japanese greats and their contemporaries into modern times, and to be greatly inspired and influenced by them through these *translated* haiku.

Many methods and guidelines about writing haiku in English have come to us from pioneers who first explained the Japanese haiku and how the Japanese write them. Many of these haiku pioneers gave guidance, sometimes inaccurate, on how to most closely follow the Japanese methods in writing English haiku. These methods and guidelines originally and most famously started out as three lines of 5-7-5 syllables with no rhyme and a kind of seasonal reference as well as a shift or cut to match or join or contrast the two distinct parts of the haiku. Some methods even erroneously included rhyme and the imposition of Zen quality as requirements.

Over time these inherited methods have evolved,

adapted, been experimented with, and have spawned multifarious offshoots of many different kinds and levels of haiku in English. Some scholars and researchers have gone back to more closely study the Japanese method, linguistics, and particulars and have brought new methods of emulation into English language haiku, such as fewer syllables, to better match the shorter Japanese sound units, writing in one line and a single breath, and using other methods of indicating the cut instead of punctuation or interjections.

But what about the possibility of a totally different approach to writing English language haiku—writing in the style of *translated* Japanese haiku. I have not yet seen this approach carried out in any clear or prescribed manner that I am aware of, nor have I seen it studiously applied in the way I envision and embrace it. I call this approach or style, the *Japanese haiku English translation style unrestrained*, of which the initials are *jhetsu*; so for short, I call it *jhetsu* haiku.

Practicing *jhetsu* haiku is simply to undertake writing haiku in the style of the English translations of Japanese haiku. Most of these translated haiku are in the famous three-line structure, though some few are two-line or one-line, and I have even seen the rare four-line as well.

This style is *unrestrained* by syllable counts, endeavors to use a seasonal indication or keyword as a matter of course (though not always absolutely necessary), and is free to use any method of indicating the cut or shift—punctuation, interjection, shift of meaning, syntax, grammar, whatever works for that haiku. The essence of haiku being brief and precise needs to be retained, as well as being an event or moment that aims to inspire in the reader a sense of awe, wonder, insight, or surprise, often called the aha! moment, but beyond just aha! all the way through the dynamic force of *zoka* to a reader's finishing of and immersion in the unsaid space or *ma* of the haiku itself.

I have been studying and practicing haiku since nineteen years old (almost 40 years) and in that time I have studied, learned, practiced, and published work in the traditional 5-7-5 method of writing haiku, and have experimented with many offshoots thereof, including fewer syllables, and have read and enjoyed the varying kinds and styles of haiku written by many contemporary English language haiku poets. Yet, in my haiku journey I have been most impressed by and influenced by the heart and essence of haiku that comes to us through the translations of poetry all the way back to Chinese poets of the first millennium, through the Japanese poets of the early second millennium, through the Japanese hokku and haiku masters since the sixteenth century, and their contemporaries through to modern times.

The style and essence of my haiku are a reflection of three main influences on the way I think about, compose, and craft haiku: 1) exquisitely translated Japanese haiku, which I call *jhetsu* haiku; 2) the Hõ Un / Issa style and quality of a personal poetry of being; and 3) Zen haiku and the art of *kensho*. So, as a reader you may see these characteristics in the haiku on the forthcoming pages. Yet, along with these kinds of haiku, you will also find everything from traditional 5-7-5 haiku to more modern renditions with fewer syllables, some gendai haiku, and even experimentation with the use of semantic disjunctions.

And then there are the list haiku. The Japanese are known to enjoy trios of favorite things, sometimes called trinities, where three things, three images, or three seasonal indications, involving multiple senses, are listed.[21] Thus, they are matched to each other in a manner. These are rarer in Japanese haiku, but they do exist and even among the four greats. Some of these are considered celebratory haiku—three things about a season listed to celebrate that season. Another kind is three seasons listed to express something about a year. So the reader may find a few of these list haiku included as well.

Also note that I believe that haiku should be dynamic. Something needs to happen in the haiku. Sometimes the dynamic or action in haiku is so subtle it is almost unnoticeable. And it is important to note that this dynamic or action does not always require a verb either. This is the essence of what Takashi Ikemoto noted in the Introduction to *Zen Poems of China and Japan* when he wrote *dynamism that is life-activity beyond all that is relative.*

Haiku that are nothing but a written description or report of a scene frozen in time in which nothing has happened or is happening will lack dynamic and be unable to effectually convey the life-nature force (*zoka*), the unsaid (*ma*), and the revelatory relationship of the match (*toriawase*).

This does not contradict those who maintain that valid haiku can present either a *static* or an *active* scene. When given static haiku by colleagues trying to show me that haiku can lack action, after I point out the clear unsaid dynamism between the parts of the haiku that had to have happened (action) to bring about the expressed present moment, they understand more fully what I mean by dynamism and action.

I could cite dozens of sources that discuss the importance of action in haiku showing how essential and vital it is.[22-25] These four should suffice for now. Haiku where nothing happens are boring, lifeless, dull, and anyone can write them by simply reporting what they see at any given moment in time. Genuine haiku dynamism goes way beyond just description.

Another aspect of classic haiku in Japan of which I would like the reader to be aware, is their fondness for the use of wordplay in their haiku, which includes double meanings, puns, alliterative sounds, front-rhymes, and onomatopoeia.[21] I am also fond of and well versed in these linguistic attributes and so they naturally seep into my haiku on occasion. What I mean by "naturally seep" is that I never preplan the use of, or force techniques into my poetry or haiku. That results in contrived and inauthentic poetry. A poet should become well versed in tools and skills and then let them naturally manifest and reveal themselves within the making of a poem, either freestyle or guided by a chosen form or pattern of expression.

Now, as a final word, I would like to discuss this matter of senryu versus haiku. I believe that many misconceptions about senryu arise out of some sincere but misdirected efforts to totally separate it from haiku. Some haiku purists, if you will, reject anything that hints at senryu as some kind of contamination to what haiku really is.[26] I can relate to that and appreciate it from the perspective of preserving the essential essence that makes for great, classic, nature-and-man connected haiku; but we also need to fairly recognize that senryu is a valid and unique adaptation of haiku in itself.

A study of its Japanese history reveals that senryu was born out of class warfare. Haiku was taught to and practiced by the elite and upper classes of Japanese society, so the common and lower classes began to write and embrace a variation of haiku that was exactly the same structurally but was a kind of anti-haiku in that rather than being reverent in conveying insight and appreciation of the beauty and simplicity of man and nature, it was irreverent in exposing the complex base vulgarity and profanity of man and society, especially in a satirical, witty, humorous way.

The contrast was initially stark but over time haiku poets absorbed elements of senryu and senryu poets absorbed elements of haiku so that today the distinction between them is sometimes blurred and even at times indistinguishable, especially when senryu use a *kigo*. You will find work published as senryu that looks and sounds like haiku, as much as you will find work published as haiku that looks and sounds like senryu.[26]

In my time and study I have come to certain conclusions about English language haiku and senryu, which are simply based on my best assessment of all the facts before me and my experience with each as commented on by reputable scholars and translators, who also often differ from each other in their opinions.

My organic experience with them has evolved to the point where I consider haiku to be a poem that reverently conveys the essence of an image, experience, or event about the simple beauty of life and nature and its intuitive connection to the nature of man; and I consider senryu to be a poem that satirically conveys the essence of an image, experience, or event about the complex nature of the human condition, which reveals man's foibles and idiosyncrasies in his interaction in society, and the world.

So while senryu is not haiku and haiku is not senryu, they are certainly travel companions that have rubbed off on each other. Therefore, you may find some senryu herein that you might deem to have haiku sensibility, and some haiku herein in which you sense the sharpness of senryu. Enjoy each poem for what it is and what it expresses and conveys—if it is haiku, read it as haiku and if it is senryu, read it as senryu.

Hopefully this Foreword has helped to put my haiku and haiku influences in context for the benefit of the reader and for a richer experience in making connections. Enjoy.

1. Baird, D. (2013) *As the Crow Flies*. Burbank, CA: The Little Buddha Press.

2. Wilson, R.D. (2011). Study of Japanese Aesthetics: Part II reinventing the wheel: the fly who thought he was a carabao. *Simply Haiku 9*(1).

3. Wilson, R.D. (2011). Study of Japanese Aesthetics: Part I the importance of ma. *Haiku Reality 8*(14).

4. Stibbe, A. (2007). Haiku and beyond: language, ecology, and reconnection with the natural world. *Anthrozoös, 20*(2), 101-112.

5. Wawrytko, S.A. (2014). Chapter Fifteen Aesthetic Principles of Epistemological Awakening: Juxtapositioning (bi 比 and xing 興) in Basho's Haiku Pedagogy. In *Inter-culturality and Philosophic Discourse*. New Castle upon Tyne, UK: Cambridge Scholars Publishing, 233.

6. Barnhill, D.L. (2016). A reply to Jim Kacian's "Realism is dead (and always was)". *Modern Haiku 47*(3), 47-51.

7. Greve, G. (2006). Kireji and toriawase. *Haiku Topics, Theory and Keywords*. [Online database]. https://haikutopics.blogspot.com/2006/06/kireji.html

8. Ross, B. (2007). The essence of haiku. *Modern Haiku, 38*(3), 51-62.

9. Arslan, F. (2017). *East in the West: Reflections of the Japanese Haiku on the Imagist Poetry of Ezra Pound and Amy Lowell* [Thesis paper]. Boğaziçi University.

10. Dolin, A.A. (2015). *The Fading Golden Age of Japanese Poetry: Tanka and Haiku of the Meiji-Taisho-Showa Period.* Akita, Japan: Akita International University Press.

11. Shirane, H. (2000). Beyond the haiku moment: Bashō, Buson, and modern haiku myths. *Modern Haiku, 21*(1), 48-63.

12. Capes, A. (n.d.) An Introduction to Advanced Haiku. *The Haiku Foundation Digital Library*. http://thehaikufoundation.org/omeka/items/show/796.

13. Wilson, R.D. (2011). Study of Japanese Aesthetics: Part III To

kigo or not to kigo. *Simply Haiku 9*(2).

14. Henderson, H. G. (1958) *An Introduction to Haiku*. Garden City, New York: Doubleday Anchor Books.

15. Trumbull, C. (2005). The American Haiku Movement. Part I: Haiku in English. *Modern Haiku, 36*(3), 33.

16. Stryk, L. & Ikemoto, T. (1973). Zen *Poems of China and Japan: The Crane's Bill.* New York: Grove Weidenfeld.

17. Miner, E. (1993). Renga. In *The New Princeton Encyclopedia of Poetry and Poetics*. Brogan, T. V., & Preminger, A. (Eds.). New York, New York: MJF Books, 1034-1035.

18. Sato, H. (1993). Haiku. In *The New Princeton Encyclopedia of Poetry and Poetics.* Brogan, T. V., & Preminger, A. (Eds.). New York, New York: MJF Books, 493-494.

19. Marsh, G. (2003). Haiku and Zen. *Simply Haiku 1*(2).

20. Rosenstock, G. (2009). *Haiku Enlightenment*. New Castle upon Tyne, UK: Cambridge Scholars Publishing, 100.

21. Bowers, F. (1996). The Classic Tradition of Haiku: An Anthology. Mineola, NY: Dover Publications, Inc.

22. Kacian, J. (2008, August 7). First Thoughts — A Haiku Primer. *f/k/a archives* [Harvard blog]. https://blogs.harvard.edu/ethicalesq/ first-thoughts-a-haiku-primer-by-jim-kacian/

23. Lucas, M. (2001). *Haiku in Britain: Theory, Practice, Context* [Doctoral thesis]. University of Wales.

24. Reichhold, J. (2001). *Lesson Six: Verbs in Haiku*. Bare Bones

School of Haiku. https://www.ahapoetry.com/Bare%20Bones/
BBless6.html

25. Welch, M.D. (2011). A moment in the sun: when is haiku?
Notes from the Gean 3(3).

26. Higginson, William J. (1985). *The Haiku Handbook*. New
York: Kodansha International, 229-233.

life summary:
— Lived in actual residences for a year or more in 26
different cities across 14 different U.S. states and in 4
different cities in England (United Kingdom). This includes
living in such geographies as a lakefront beach on Lake
Michigan (of the Great Lakes); deep natural woods with
canyons, rivers, swamps, and ponds; the brackish Southern
U.S. Gulfshore and salt marshes (Gulf of Mexico); the
mountainous evergreen forests of the Northwest with mighty
snow-capped peaks (Mt. Rainier); small thatched-roof
villages nestled between ancient oak forests (England); sub-
tropical beaches and the lagoons of barrier islands; a log cabin
over 8000 feet high in the middle of the pristine Colorado
Rockies; the sandy Chihuahuan Desert on the border of
Mexico; endless miles of rural farm fields with rolling
meadows and copses of trees; large fertile valleys stretching
to Pacific ocean beaches; and the Saguaro cacti forests of the
rich Sonoran Desert.

— Lived and worked in two of the three largest urban inner
cities in the U.S. (Chicago and Los Angeles) and in other

large cities and suburban areas, in rural towns, country villages, and small camps, in dwellings that ranged from being homeless, to a tent, to a simple cabin, a cottage, barracks rooms, apartments, simple homes, large homes, and even a large mansion.

— Lived among American populations, Asian populations, Hispanic populations, European populations, English populations, and African-American populations.

— Roamed the cities, towns, villages, fields, woods, rivers, canyons, mountains, forests, wilderness, and deserts of every locale where I have lived, always exploring and always more in tune with nature than with society.

— Lived in or traveled to 23 countries, and attended 9 higher educational institutions in pursuit of my degrees.

This summary illustrates my transient God-adventure life, which has led me on a journey of continued growth and self-discovery through a myriad of diverse places, locales, regions, geographies, geologic and natural terrains, cultures, populations, educational institutions, and kinds of residences where I have lived and traveled. This has afforded me the opportunity as a wandering minister serving in multiple communities and capacities to forge deep connections to God, life, nature, and humanity.

The Four Seasons of My Times

Winter was such a marvelous season—braving the snow, ice, cold, and blustery winds as I walked wherever I needed to go. It always seemed to be a rite of passage in its own way. I grew up in Chicago and Northern Indiana where wind chill factors easily dipped down to 80 degrees below zero in parts of January, and 30 to 40 degrees below zero at most other times in the month.

I loved the sense of accomplishment I got just walking a few miles through the bare woods and stubble fields. There was always a sense of regeneration and renewal coming out of the cold and back indoors as I peeled off the layers of winter clothing. I relished the act of clasping a hot beverage and sipping as I thawed; that smell of snow embedded in the scarf; thc crackling of a fire in the fireplace as I hung wet clothes on the mantle to dry.

I got to experience every nuance of winter from the steady floating snowfalls of billions of beautiful sparkling flakes, all different and amazing in their crystallized shapes, to walking through a foot or more of soft snow, to walking over or crunching through the icy frozen layer on top of compressed snow after days of heating and cooling and then a night of frozen winds. Yes, winter was always wild with its surprises, with blizzards that gave us 4 to 6 to even 8 feet of snow at various different times, with winds howling all night revealing 10 to 15 foot high sculptures of snow out the front door and at every corner around the outside of the house, and with the infrequent ice storms that coated everything in a brilliant sheen and crystallized the entire world.

It is no wonder then why years later I so easily took to my exciting adventures on the frozen and glacial slopes of Mt. Rainier, south of Tacoma, Washington. Such adventures as going snowshoeing beyond 10,000 feet high and looking up 4,000 more feet to its peak, hiking in its sunken trickling streams beneath an illuminated canopy of snow 8 feet overhead, building snow caves or burrows large enough to hold several people, where we could sleep at night, or spend half the day conversing with other adventurers. I remember seeing an actual real and threatening avalanche of tons of snow cascade down the steep sides of the mountain toward us, wondering if I'd be buried alive, ending some 500 feet up and away.

My adventures in ice and snow didn't end there. I got to enjoy the ice and snow of the Colorado Rockies, living at 8000 feet, climbing to the 11,180 foot summit of Manganese Peak in the dead of winter, watching mountain snow storms from above, and hiking through canyons with massive 20 to 40 foot icicles, 4 to 8 feet thick, hanging from cliff ledges ominously over our heads. Some of the smaller 10 foot icicles, no laughing matter themselves, occasionally broke off and I remember a near miss, dodging under a cove and getting pelted with pieces of shattering ice. Such are my fond memories of ice and snow and winter life, both on the Midwestern plains, and in the Western Rockies and Cascades.

Spring is so aptly named in English, because it does bring a spring to one's step, seeing and watching the vibrancy and rich verdant foliage return to the land, even as the chirping birds move in nesting and mating and all the fauna of the land are in their early reproductive phase. Soon the land is filled with animal young, even as the leaves turn from that lighter new green indicative of their springing growth to more mature and darker greens in preparation for the long summer.

When I think of spring, I see this light green foliage and hear the thousands of birds of many species, chirping away in delight with their new young in nests. I feel the squishy, soggy ground from the winter melt and later from the cleansing spring rains. I recall the comfort of relaxing in cool spring breezes, sucking the sweet young clover on seemingly perfect days of bright warming sunshine, not hot, just nicely warming. The sound of trickling and splashing water fills my ears, the frogs and fish, all come out from hiding and hibernating as the fragrance of beautiful flowers of every sort wafts in the air, their stems swaying in the breezes, the bright blooms blessing the eyes.

None of this is cliché to me, it's all so real, so vivid, so vibrant, so alive. I lived it. Each year similar but very different depending on the harshness of winter, on the amount of snowfall, on late freezes, the frequency of rain in spring, and the prevailing temperature. The populations of flora and fauna could take on a very different mix in proportions each year. Some years certain flowering trees arrived in full bloom early and certain insects were in abundance. In other years the trees might barely bloom but a certain wildflower spread everywhere and birds were in greater abundance. It always changed with the times and conditions and provided for a new and beautiful display each year.

Summer would follow with its long drawn out days of sweltering heat, humidity, pestilence, and severe thunderstorms. Foliage would grow darker green and taller, all the crops would be maturing, especially the corn growing knee-high by July and then over your head just like that in August. Wildflowers and flowering trees were a welcomed break from the otherwise constant blazing of the sun.

And boy, were summers fun with their barbecues, picnics, outings, sports games, races, and community events. Despite the pestilence, despite the heat, despite the humidity, I thrived in summer from early morning sunrises to the late gatherings watching the red and orange sky as the sun dipped away as late as 9 o'clock in the evening back when daylight savings time was different.

During summer we also went camping for weeks at a time in the deep woods of Michigan, Wisconsin, and Indiana—living in a tent in the woods and hiking every day, playing in ponds and lakes, fishing, practicing rifle skills, shotgun shooting, archery, canoeing on rivers, watching wildlife, learning Native American lore, and finishing each day around a campfire roasting things on sticks and talking. What was not to love?

Autumn, in some deep inner form or manner, as much as I loved every other season, was somehow my favorite. I say *in some deep inner form* because outwardly it is a season of finishing and falling apart and decaying. It starts out bright and colorful and ends up dim and drab. So why my favorite?

I say *finishing* because harvest time is the consummation of all the hard labor in the fields as the many fruits and vegetables finish and ripen; *finishing* because the leaves finish their work on the trees and turn many magnificent colors of golds, ambers, reds, maroons, oranges, purples, limes, and bright yellows; *finishing* because the plethora of natural foliage finishes by going to seed. Autumn is the finishing culmination of dazzling glory and rich abundance before everything turns brown, and gray, and bleak, and dies or falls apart and decays, or goes dormant for winter.

So after the finishing glory, the harvest festivals, the bright beauty of the fields and trees and fruits and vegetables, autumn enters that somber slide down in temperature as everything turns blanched, or brown, or gray. It dries out, stiffens, and crumbles. The days begin to wane in light, the birds migrate away, and clouds obscure the sun so that even the days become gray and wetter with fogs and drizzles. Rich earthy smells fill the air as leaves and organic matter begins to accumulate where water gathers; and as the water soaks away the matter is left to rot.

Eventually the scene is one of bare trees, dry and gray, bare bushes, dried out plants and stubble, and a wet debris-matted ground of bits and pieces of decaying organic matter. The gray days grow colder until the drizzle is freezing at night, breaking more things down, and making everything look dirty. It is a scene that is begging for the white-wash of winter snow—and when that first snow comes and all the land turns white, it is a glorious thing.

For me, the beauty of the glory of early autumn, the finishing and culmination of summer growth to feed man and nature, is a time of celebration with others for work well done, for a great summer, and looking forward to the next year. It launches me into a time of reflection, thankfulness for what I have, joy at reliving the highpoints of the spring and summer, and then it segues into a time of solitude.

Yes, that is what the downslide of autumn becomes for me, a time of solitude, creativity in art, prolificacy in writing, thought and solitary walks. Why? I don't know. The season just elicits it. And so it is my favorite. I start out in awe of the colors and dazzling displays of nature, I enjoy the socializing mirth of harvest celebrations, festivals, and feasts, and then I depart on a journey of solitude through the slumber of the land into winter.

The essence of four magnificent seasons, every year slightly different. Braving the magnificent *winters*, refreshed by some wild and stunning adventures of snow; relaxing and enjoying the renewal of *spring* life, vibrancy, fertility, and vitality; thriving in *summer* heat and long days filled with fun activities and time spent in nature; and being dazzled by the glory and abundance of *autumn* celebrating the harvest and embarking on a journey of solitude, art, and thought.

These are the four seasons of wondrous times to me— exactly in the order they should be.

HAIKU

Winter

deep tracks

gone this windswept morn

bird feet

last dance for leaves

in the howling wind

winter

pill bug

rolls itself into a ball:

first winter snow

this still morn

sculpted snowdrifts

viewed in silence

snowflakes

and no two ever alike

we watch together

silence

each step crunching

frozen snow

strange winter guest—

don't bother me fly

and you can stay

night snow sparkles

in the moon's reflection

the sun still shines

alone through town

many feet scramble...

blizzard white out

cold homeless man

a Santa cup for coins...

no tree this year

the thick silence

of heavy snowfall

white noise

a bare black birch

not even my own smell

in frozen air

only I remain

alone with me here

winter fog

bright white sun

icy fields steam away...

earth's facial

spring they shout

but their joy melts away

cold night snow

Spring

folks flee for cover

what? are they melting

cold spring rain

into wild spring

we break long winter

with a smile

frozen peak framed

in blooming red currents

secret of ice melt

another sunrise

wide-eyes skyward

what new thing?

swollen streams

yesterday's icicles

tomorrow's flowers

spring rain

snails climb on each other

housecleaning

tree buds

enclosed they await

the awakening

that rose granite stone

kicked home on my walk

rests under yarrows

a tree arrives

festival of blossoms

right on time

cool morning breeze

oh! to stay forever

under new green leaves

the young hare

watches me gaze on clouds

chewing

tree buds nap here

but downriver

the blossoms

Summer

evening talk

after the long sun

hot air blows

pink mammatus

underbelly of the sky

a calf's sunset drink

leave my fire, moth

tonight is not the night

for a last dance

blinded by sunshine

long gone the night

of moonshine

ejected bee drone

and flying male ant—

no life for you

burning trees

to put an end to

burning trees

a thorn bug clings

to a wild rose stem—

they won't find me

silent frog pond

a boy's rock dives

bloop!

quiet in thought

an avocado hits my head:

shrill parrots play

two moons in a tree

this dense starry night

wide-eyed owl

sweat and grime

coins for a cold brew

in a beggars can

a yellow sun

paints a deep purple sky

how wondrous this

whack!

a June bug stops

between my eyes

under desert stars

the summer queen blooms

one night of glory

the sun in the moon in my eyes at night

Autumn

the sun sets

on a northern hill today...

blazing red maple

see the wind

the crackling of leaves

blows by

so spectacular

so ordinary

orange drips down my chin

pitter-patter of rain

a multi-colored tree line

and pumpkins for pie

warm toilet water...

a struggling boll weevil

cupped and freed

at night

I drink the moonshine

and smile

wet cold apples

gift of October moon

this drizzling night

majestic gold

the tall bur oak's glory

spiked grasses bow

put a handle

on the crescent moon—

harvest time

all day shucking

her gaunt children wait:

thirty ears pay

succulent peaches

each day as I pass—

they saved me one tree

cold sun and wind

bring tears to my eyes

November chill

so what if beggars

drink strong autumn wine...

what else do they have?

once upon a time

under a crescent blood moon

twin outhouses

an empty bushel

under the cherry tree

red-lipped I snooze

Sojourner in the Earth

Trees, *woods*, *paths* hold and have always held a special fascination for me. I never missed the forest for the trees, and I never missed the trees for the forest either, but took both in together and apart. *Trees* are magnificent, mighty, beautiful living structures of growth life, the highest order of *flora* on the earth, and so much fun as a youth to climb up into, to sit, to read, to rest, to enjoy. I considered the trees I got to know around our property to be my friends. I still enjoy trees, sitting under them, in the shade, relaxing, thinking, writing, or reading. Many of them have unique aromatic smells they emit at different times of the day, some in early morning others at midday, and others in the evening or at night.

Being in the *woods* is always special, stopping to marvel at a unique tree, its shape, the way it grew, the different species, and wondering what past history made it into what it is today. There are so many varieties, gigantic redwoods, elms, oaks, firs, poplars, pines, birches, very full maples, and then there are the broad and spectacular willows, palms, the unique pinyons, ancient Joshua trees, and the saguaro cacti.

In the great deciduous forests of the Midwest,

Iroquois territory, there are long, spindly vines that grow around and through the *trees*. These dry out into inch thick strands that hang nearly to the ground. When I was younger, my companions and I would swing on these sturdy dried vines, sometimes out over swamps, or *ponds*, in canyon coves, sometimes out over the edge of a drop off or deep crevice. In summer we'd strip off our outer layers and swing out into the swamps and let go, plopping into the mucky waters. We'd get back to dry ground and do it over and over again.

There were always *paths* through the *woods* that seemed to have been there forever. We imagined the Native Americans who had taken these paths years before, and indeed we found arrow heads along them, a stone hammer head, and more than once, flint chips under a tree where some indigenous person had sat one or more times actually chipping away and making arrowheads. We wondered if these *paths* had been there since ancient times in America.

Not even knowing where we were going, we would often meet after sunrise with food, water, hunting knives, and hiking sticks and follow *paths* for hours on end, deeper and deeper into the *woods*. We always turned back with plenty of time to make it back home before sunset, a few times cutting it close at twilight. It is amazing that we never got lost.

Woods have always been a refuge and sanctuary for me. With the *trees*, *flora*, *fauna*, fish, birds, *insects*, and more, I can poke around all alone for hours on end, and it always empowers me and makes me feel better. I have always made it a point to make time to roam or to just sit in the *woods*, forests, or wilds wherever I lived.

Rocks, *rivers*, *streams*, *ponds*, and *lakes* are all similarly special places to me, most of them within or surrounded by *trees* and *woods*. They have always had and continue to have a strong pull in my life. When roaming a forest or sitting in the woods, I like to find an outcropping of *rock*, or a *river*, *stream*, swamp, *pond* or *lake* to sit by to watch and enjoy the unique features and *flora* and *fauna* of each.

Another magnificent natural feature that has its own intrigue and power is the *shore*, whether a *lake shore* or *ocean shore*, and I'm not talking about a small lake, but the kinds of *shores* you find on the Great Lakes. I have been to every one of the five Great Lakes, but the one I grew up around for many years was Lake Michigan. The *lake* beaches, *rocks*, coves, and **shores** are all fascinating. The Indiana Dunes are one of the best kept secrets on the planet, where there are large sand dunes on the southeastern *shore* of Lake Michigan, which feature plants and flowers that grow nowhere else on earth but in Africa. How they got to the dunes is a mystery.

Oceans and ocean *shores* are something I only sporadically encountered in my youth on various trips out to the Atlantic Ocean in the Cape Cod area of Massachusetts. But later I lived in central Florida on the eastern barrier island with the Indian River lagoon system on the west side and the Atlantic Ocean on the east. I lived right on the actual *shore* for several months and then moved to a place close enough to the *ocean* to hear the waves and occasionally, when windy, feel salt foam droplets from waves crashing into *rocks*. I also lived along the Gulf Shore in Mississippi experiencing salt marshes and brackish waters caused by the inflow of fresh water from the Mississippi River delta system. I explored them all and poked around in them all for many hours on end enjoying the solitude and the marvels of *flora* and *fauna*.

Mountains are another thing I had to wait until I was an adult to enjoy, but not too long. As a young man in my twenties I found myself living in the Cascades near Mt. Rainier, which, when I first saw it, was floating in the sky. I can see why the Native Americans of the region called it a god. It is the tallest peak in the Cascades at over 14,400 feet, and when the mists in the valleys are thick, which they often are, its base and all other *mountains* around it disappear and Mt. Rainier sits all by itself perched in the sky as if watching over the land. It literally looks like a singular massive floating *mountain* in the sky, at times.

Living in the Colorado Rockies at over 8000 feet was a remarkable *mountain* experience in itself. My first home was a small cabin shared with others, my second was a multi-level log cabin lodge (mansion) with an enclosed sky deck observatory, a three-story high living room, and a fully stocked library, way up in the *mountains*. An amazing and remarkable experience, where I studied the stars and the ancient significance of star names and their meanings—God teaching mankind before anything was ever written down.

Of course, living in *mountains* meant I got to experience earthquakes too, a unique event all its own, and remarkable in its way of reminding us how we are such small creatures to the massiveness of the earth and tectonic plates and geologic forces below and around us. Every time the earth shakes and moves me back and forth and I feel its rumbling, throbbing, pulsating shock waves through my feet and into my body—I truly experience a moment of recognition that I am a part of the whole earth.

Earthquakes remind me of the fragility of mankind and make me realize how thankful I am to be alive and to get to experience this planet before the next age.

The great *outdoors* with all its features, seasons, times, and conditions, is truly remarkable. And speaking of times and seasons, most of the haiku I have written about these ecologic, geologic, and natural features and terrains, and the flora, fauna, and insects, still carries the sensitivity of a seasonal indication. Just because I have not included them under the headings for the four seasons does not mean they lack them. I simply wanted to celebrate the power of each of these aspects of the great *outdoors* in a concentrated way.

Think about it. We get to enjoy and live in the most amazingly created, powerful, forceful, energetic three-dimensional, interactive work of art ever made—Nature. Don't hide from it. Don't let it get stolen from you. You don't need an app or a subscription. It's all yours and it is out there. Get out into it. Get out into the great **outdoors**.

To remain bound to man's works, man's buildings, man's monolithic cities and concrete structures, man's technology—as artistic and remarkable as they can sometimes be—still falls far short of the real greatness of the life-force, power, freedom, and fulfillment that is to be had by being interactively immersed in the real nature of life. It's all here for us to enjoy, preserved by the Almighty and made to teach us, educate us, challenge us, help us, nurture us, and move us along in our understanding of all things—physically, mentally, and spiritually.

That's why I endeavor to teach, and preach, and encourage all who will listen to step off the mad-dash rush of the world and disconnect from the endless mind feed, and reconnect to the universe. Get up and go out and interactively enjoy the magnificent details of nature with its plethora of treasures and gifts that Love, Light, and Spirit created for you in God's Green Earth, and just take a moment to **be here now**.

HAIKU

Trees
Woods
Paths

full moon date:

in a distant wooded copse

I sit with trees

lush carpets of moss

on wet stones near waterfalls

a tree frog's eyes

detour

the path I take is gone

new things ahead

silence

a yellow poplar's tulips

say it all

in a quiet forest a rotting log

of warring ants

the crow below me

craps from the treetop:

crossing the bridge

from bare naked

to buds and blooms and fruit

this tree losing leaves

alone in the woods

everything is gone—

see it all?

filled with feet

the empty path

of last night

a tree stands still

bored for hundreds of years

bark beetles

my dancing fire:

in the woods tonight

many glowing eyes

through the garden

a stone path meanders

yet it does not move

Rocks
Stones
Rivers

a rock among rocks

reposed in the riverbed

my hair flows

dry winter stones

colder in sunny spring

rushing ice melt

rippled reflections

hold still on the river

deep moving waters

the heron has claimed

the boulder you gave me...

courtyard garden

long blazing sun—

a parched stone riverbed

waits for a bath

cold wet stones

walking in a canyon stream

barefoot

still boulders

thrash and part waters

dam break

smooth stones float on the river

in a barge

walking the river

not with feet but eyes

what mountain power

Ponds
Lakes

sweltering sun

cool relief in the pond:

turtles on rocks

my boat is leaking

into the water—

it's me

at the pond

reading lilies and flies:

the frog too

looking down

at my face below the oar

in the sky behind me

a bent willow...

petals drop on the pond's

belly-up frog

unhooking the barb

left in the turtle's maw:

damn fisherman

placid lake

a kingfisher dives

into the moon

buzzing fly

frog on the lily pad...

silence

burning cattails

shoos the mosquitoes

firefly show

on my leg

a painted turtle...

no sun today

frog in the reeds

stares down dragonflies—

a blue heron's meal

a frog

on my back watching

the pond

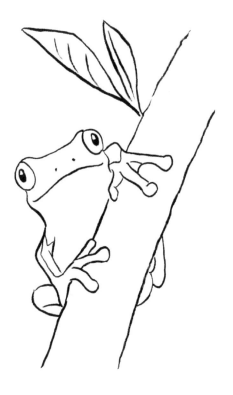

Flora

point man

a purple tulip

scopes out spring

welcome mat sprout

visitor in my doorway

breakthroughs

five fragrant days

in and out the door

a lone hyacinth

palms and ferns:

these fronds of mine wave

at the passerby

slow garden walk

vibrant fragrant roses

soon wilt

pavement crack—

oh! wayward seedling

find the light

a thousand suns

in the field of grass—

dandelions

an orange poppy

in the field of purple sage

lost child

snow-flower mountain

or mountain snow flowers—

what do I see?

delicate beauty

of Callery pear blossoms:

stench of rotting fish

carpet of purple

under the jacaranda

my dog's fragrant paws

tonight gardenias

absorb the sunlight

of a full moon

Fauna

a fish flies

up in the clouds—

eagle's talons

in the wash...

me and a coyote

face-to-face

on the flagpole

a prowling owl stares…

cat with wings

cemetery crow

in a bare black oak

dead silence

take heart baby bird—

I will stop the cat

from getting you

seagulls compete

for a bag of crumbs

summer Olympics

chattering squirrels

climb up for peanuts—

one holds my ear

I stub my toe—

a coyote somewhere

howls in the wind

dangerous path

I'd follow the parrot

but no wings

unavailable

old friends disappear

mateless gull

one toss up

is the pigeon's wing healed?

flapping for its roost

hermit crab

a snail's empty shell

estate sale

who? who? — the owls

me me me — the gulls

this bird has flown

lucky fellow

an aged turtle dies at sea

no one's soup

a mat of wet leaves

croaks

woodhouse toad

Insects

empty cocoon:

the form of a former self

is not here

no words to speak:

these ants march away

from empty tunnels

swallowing

there's a bug in my tea

I discover

eighty foot oak

ants scurry on top leaves—

out on a cliff hike

saving ants

from ant lion funnels...

must they eat?

thank you

for respecting me fly

sitting on my wall

fingertip sugar

behold—the drowned bee flies

back into spring

larger than life

ants carry thousands of times

their weight

snow-capped Mt. Rainier

framed in rhododendron

ignored by the bee

done gargling

I spit to miss the beetle

crawling in my sink

ant lion

the end draws near...

hourglass

the thorn bug

the walking stick

and me

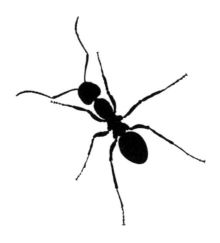

Mountains

white wolves watch:

into the mountain goes

a slow-stepping bear

a snow-capped peak

floats above white mists—

I shoo a gnat

the earth heaves

as boulders break and fall

sunset ripples

foggy drizzle

where is the mountain?

sipping tea

back and forth the trees

I dance but not for mirth

rumbling earth

it is not seen

falling from the mountain

yet grasses flatten

dark amber combs

the sweetness of a mountain

wildflowers

as we shake

parrots still play

no quakes in air

rain in the mountain

washes away debris

piles of rules

Oceans Shores

terns run

through melting castles

dodging waves

the ocean

beneath a silent fog

slaps the pier

war breaks out

over a tipped trash can—

Pacific gulls?

sky and ocean

such height and depth—

a dust speck in space

foaming waves crash

and crash and crash the shore:

daily market catch

what lunacy

this tranquil lunar sea

figment of dust

splash

into the bay of stars—

bobbing rowboat

the whole ocean

belongs to sand crabs

wave upon wave

barnacles

on the message

in a bottle

Outdoors

lost in my yard

the house suddenly gone

sandstorm

clothes on a line

fly in strong winds

trees clap

pulled from the lake

a drenched sock sizzles

in my fire

upside-down world

in each hanging dew drop…

all the same one

old pond

a frog floats

belly-up

just one summer night

the desert queen comes out...

are you Cereus?

to take again

the route once taken

old journal

through the woods

over and over this walk

each day different

sectioned bamboo stalks

bend and howl in wind tones

future flutes

Mindlessness

SENRYU

here with me

until the phone chimes

gone

two worlds

in your hand—as you stand

where will you be?

game apps

the earth could leave its orbit

what happened?

where are you

where will you go today?

ding—another message

through the mall

texting–posting–splash

into the fountain

black holes

suck up the universe—

cell phones

all day long

the phone, the phone

stampede

how can you be here

if you are always there?

phone mystery

walking

face riveted on his screen…

sound of screeching brakes

Be Here Now

HAIKU & SENRYU

this nest is not empty

I perch here—

alone

desert soldier

tears on a sand-caked face

for a lost child

word tiles shaken

dumped from a soft bag

enlightenment

this long journey...

a child still behind

wrinkled eyes

flowers in season

governments rise and fall

again and again

fire water dance

a consuming passion

one cup of tea

stayed waters…

hugging a grieving mother

by the dam

a blank mind

drooping eyes

and sour milk

in street clothes

he stands in the high court

an oyster's pearl

my own universe...

on the bedroom's black ceiling

painted glowing dots

you must write it—

no one can see tulips

unplanted

ramshackle home

covered in thick mosses:

nature's makeover

far from this world

because I'm here now:

green meadow

breathing the planet

sneezing out earth's dust…

myself included

facing mirrors—

in both directions

I go on forever

bright light

my shadow surrounded

bright light

a crow's shit falls

sends ants into a frenzy—

mind if I drop in

proving myself...

I grew up then returned

to childhood

peeling the lime to get to the pith

we talk

sensing myself before the journey

unwritten book

stepping on the welcome mat

as I leave

some prefer no roof but sky

a swallow's freedom

missing peace:

the puzzle will be solved

when we find it

is solitude

for the well born only?

homeless smile

picking a poem

which flower to cut

for the vase

a glass of water

not a glass of water

under water

denizens…

the homeless

wear the earth

in white space

a vacuum of words—

steaming tea

Afterword

Just to be clear, I am not opposed to or on some crusade against cell phones or technology. I own a smartphone and utilize it as a very efficient tool of modern day communication and information seeking. I can communicate to someone that I'm running late, or answer a critical question from wherever I am so a coworker can continue working.

When out and about on a hike or roaming around the planet, it is very convenient and wonderful to be able to look up, right there on the spot, a plant species or insect species I come across, and to read about it, so long as I have data reception. It has made the planet a living museum of sorts; instead of placards, I can find out all about things on my phone. I can find information for anything and everything I come across in life—when I choose to.

And that is the big key—when I choose to.

Unfortunately, rather than most people being the master of the tool in their hands, they have allowed it to enslave them, to rule their lives, to lead them around *mindlessly*. They hear a ding or chime and it kills them to stay engaged with you in the café sharing morning beverages because they can't stand NOT to look at it. They just have to. They have to know what that next social message is or if that new fun person posted a video, or if someone made a nasty reply to their last comment on a news board. Why?

The way these things have taken rule of our lives is what is not good. The device itself is neutral, just a thing, just a tool that can be used beneficially if not allowed to run our lives. Learn to live life without it for hours on end. Turn it off or silence it and ignore all incoming dings. Make it work for you in your real life on your time, don't be a slave to its constant random interruption of naturally unfolding life. That's *mindlessness*. Rather, be present where you are, not engaged somewhere else in some virtual reality that is irrelevant to what you are doing at this moment—except if that virtual conversation IS what you are doing at this moment.

So that is the other side of the same big key—engage in the digital world when you want to on your terms.

Set aside time to engage online and interact when you decide to, and then focus on your phone or your laptop or PC. Do it for whatever reasonable time frame you want, just don't let other people or other things disturb you or interrupt you while you are there. Be there.

Focus fully and engage fully in what you are doing, whether physically in life where you are, or digitally on a tech device. Be where you are. Avoid the distraction lifestyle of an endless feed of mass media information and social media interaction integrated into whatever you are doing whenever you are doing it no matter when or where it happens, and then trying to keep all the plates in the physical realm spinning along with all the plates in the digital world.

Recognize and admit to yourself when your phone is running you and then put your foot down. Don't allow the phone to become your go-to distraction for every single second of down time during the day. Instead, during down time, actually look at other people, nature, and the things around you. Talk to someone. Look around at the art, architecture, nature, the lights, the décor, the garden, the landscape. Enjoy the beauty of all these things. Appreciate the world.

I have seriously had some incredible fun with this. When I worked for a global bank on the 42nd floor of a high rise in the corporate metropolis of Century City, Los Angeles, California, on my sometimes long elevator rides down I would purposefully choose to engage someone in conversation before they plugged into the endless mind feed. I would see them reaching into their purses or pockets for their phone and before they could click it I'd say something like, "How was your commute into work today?" or "That's a very nice sweater, do you remember where you got it?"

It was incredible fun for me because I enjoyed seeing the shock in their eyes that someone they didn't even know dared to speak to them. Some of them cast nervous glances at the other elevator riders, who would look away as if to say, "It's your problem, you deal with him, I don't want to get involved." Some would fumble for words, almost as if conversing with a stranger was a lost art. Most would reluctantly engage, but by the time we exited the elevator they were actually enjoying the conversation and exchanging niceties.

My point is, don't be cajoled into *mindlessness*; don't let these little devices slowly and subtly become black holes that are sucking your universe away without you even knowing it. There is so much more in life to enjoy. Be mindful of where you are and what you are doing and fully engage in it and it will bring you a joy and peace you may never have experienced before, and an opportunity to reconnect with the Almighty through the great handiwork interwoven into the very fabric of the universe.

Hey, I got a great idea. Why not bring this book along with you, in your purse, or pocket, or attaché, or on your Kindle or eReader, and during the day when you have a moment or two of downtime, waiting time, or other break—re-read the book; if not the essays, at least re-read the haiku. There is good precedent and many agree that the nature of poetry and haiku requires repeated engagement for maximum pleasure and enjoyment. It's like music and songs, you don't just listen to them once and move on never returning to the song or musical number. As you listen to a song more and more you grow to like it more and more and it means more to you.

Haiku and poetry are just like this. So re-read and engage often with all the poetry you read and you will enjoy it so much more! It's supposed to be repeated again and again.

About the Author

David E. Navarro is a non-denominational Christian minister, author, poet, essayist, and scholar who lives in Tucson, Arizona with his wife and family—or as he says, "...a wandering minister who loves Zen, poetry, and helping people reconnect with God, nature, and a greater sense of self and purpose."

He was born in Newport, Rhode Island but grew up on the Southside of inner city Chicago, Illinois to age ten when his family moved to the rural setting of Crown Point, Indiana. There he learned to enjoy nature, free to roam in fields of swaying grass and wooded copses rich with ponds and swamps.

At fifteen he found himself in the suburban setting of Munster, Indiana where he remained until he went off to college at Purdue University, West Lafayette, Indiana to study literature and the arts.

He left college to enlist in the United States Air Force where he served for ten years and in three conflicts. His first tour of duty was at McChord AFB in Tacoma, Washington. He married and then with his wife moved to RAF Alconbury in the United Kingdom for his second tour where he was part of the

Air Raid on Tripoli.

He completed a degree in Communications and Leadership, then moved to Patrick AFB in Satellite Beach, Florida where he was part of the Invasion of Panama and the First Gulf War.

He separated with an honorable discharge and entered a Biblical Studies program where he completed a degree in Theology and served 35 years in the ministry as a Biblical research teacher and minister in various assignments all over the U.S.

During this time he worked as a corporate safety compliance officer and trainer, the CEO of a credit union, HR training specialist, financial institution compliance and tech writer, power utilities company corporate compliance analyst, clinical research associate, grade school/high school tutor, and online adult English writing and poetry instructor.

He writes about and teaches life and time management, quality of life, work-life balance, Biblical research and teaching principles, writing and communication, Zen, and mindfulness. He returned to school with Purdue University Global and completed a bachelor of science degree in Interdisciplinary

Studies, in which his emphasis was on the arts and humanities. His final thesis was a paper chronicling the far reaching ramifications and impact of haiku on the Western world. He plans to pursue a master's degree in the arts and humanities and maybe a doctorate later.

His first collection of poetry was published in 1980 in the *Purdue Exponent Literary Edition*, Winter Issue. Over the years, his poems, essays, and articles have been published in various magazines, literary journals, books, anthologies, and online. He plans to write, publish, and educate for the rest of his life.

Books and Publications

In the Praise of His Glory, 2020
Poems and Biblical notes

Archway to Beyond, 2019
An academic project book of haiku, haibun, poetry, and prose

Early Childhood Learning: An Instruction Focused Framework for Ongoing Assessment, 2019
Early learning educational guide

This Is the Way: Walk Ye in It, 2018
Biblical research studies and poems

Dropping Ants into Poems, 2017
Literary essays and poems

Sometimes Anyway, 2016
A compilation of poems by 39 poets

Dare to Soar, 2013
Life essays and poems

Between Life and Language, 2009
A compilation of poems by 107 poets

Planned Books

Rain in the Mountain, will critically handle some history, myths, and methods of writing English language haiku.

The Annals of Ghalensa, a sci-fi/fantasy series of novels.

Biblical Studies in Truth, a series of books with in-depth Biblical research and teaching.

Man's Search for Truth, a book about man's search for truth through science, philosophy, and religion.

And other non-fiction quality of life, life-balance, business, and time management works.

Please see his Author Page for a list of current books:

https://www.amazon.com/author/davidenavarro

earth's aroma
in one cup of tea...
pure land bliss

Preview of *Rain in the Mountain*

A preview of an important landmark work I have been researching and writing since 2017—soon to be released.

The book is called *Rain in the Mountain*, inspired by an Issa haiku about solitude, inspiration and deep thought —taking time to not allow the large overbearing presence of the mountain to dominate, but rather to listen "to the rain in the mountain" to clarify for ourselves the cleansing simplicity of what we may be missing in the large looming presence of the mountain.

Winter seclusion—
listening, that evening,
to the rain in the mountain.
      — Kobayashi Issa

The "mountain" of myths that has accumulated about writing haiku has imposed itself by many false mandates on the art and craft of haiku. By setting ourselves apart in some "winter seclusion" to listen to the soft and assuaging sound of rainfall, we can free ourselves from the imposing mountain of myths and wash away its debris to restore liberty in pursuing our haiku expression.

Chapter 1: Origins and Background — The ancient origins of haiku and tracing the essence of it through to modern times. The broad strokes of what haiku is and what the basic ideas in it are.

Chapter 2: Rain in the Mountain: A Selection of Haiku — A selection of 28 haiku by the four greats, Basho, Buson, Issa, and Shiki, and others, to illustrate the principles discussed in chapter 3 about writing and crafting haiku. These haiku were not selected with intention to prove the points in the book, rather they were selected because they are well recognized and acknowledged haiku or because of their appeal. These haiku, selected with no ulterior motive, keenly illustrate the points made in the book—credence that all haiku do.

Chapter 3: 14 Common Haiku Myths—Dispelled — The core chapter of the book, handling and dispelling some prevalent haiku myths. It also discusses some other important aspects of haiku and is designed to liberate the haiku poet from the plethora of often conflicting mandates and rules that some have tried to impose on us and to show by illustration and practical example why these myths are false.

Chapter 4: Gendai and Modern Experimentation in English Language Haiku — An informative and interesting discussion about gendai and modern haiku experimentation. As haiku poets it is good to know what is going on out there, what is trending, and what it brings to our art, whether we embrace it or not or choose to experiment with it or not.

Chapter 5: Some of the Core Essential Elements of Haiku — A discussion of some of the classic traditional elements of haiku, explained with their Japanese terms, but with very clear English explanations and English terms applied. Should we pursue these classic elements in our haiku? Knowing them will certainly help us to understand the classic haiku of the four greats and will inform our own haiku.

Chapter 6: Haiku versus Senryu — To simplify and clarify a confusing aspect of haiku with the ongoing battle between haiku and senryu. What do critics mean when they say your haiku is more like senryu—and is it? This chapter clarifies this and helps us to determine what we want our haiku to express.

Chapter 7: Zen Haiku and the Art of Kensho — It is important to be clear that Zen is NOT a requirement of haiku. Many haiku have very little to do with Zen. Yet, haiku is an exceptional medium to express Zen ideas, especially *kensho*, little enlightenments or noticings. This is different from *kensho* as used in Zen practice, but inspired by it. This chapter shows how this is akin to the "aha!" moment.

Chapter 8: A Unique Perspective: Jhetsu Haiku — A unique perspective on endeavoring to write haiku after the manner of the translated haiku of the masters. An unrestrained style that focuses on the core essential elements and essence of haiku being retained rather than trying to write using linguistic standards transferred over from the Japanese way. Another very liberating chapter.

Chapter 9: Poetry of Being: Pursuing Your Haiku Journey — Bringing it all together into the focus of your unique and particular haiku journey. A discussion of ideas about your endeavors, your goals, your purposes, your self-discovery, and your expression in your haiku. Being free and unfettered to pursue your haiku journey according to who you are will take you to unprecedented new areas and heights in your haiku and will help to shape your legacy as a haiku poet.